For Whom

To Die

A Beautiful Story
of a Terrible Time

By William Slusher

CMP Publishing Group, LLC
27657 Highway 97
Okanogan, WA 98840
www.cmppg.com

All inquiries, including distributor information, should be addressed to:

CMPPG, LLC
27657 Highway 97
Okanogan, WA 98840

For Whom to Die may be ordered from CMPPG, LLC at the above address and at **cmppg.com**

email: **info@cmppg.org**
website: **cmppg.com**

ISBN13: 978-0-9801554-3-3

LCCN: 2009926653

Author's Forward

There are always at least two sides to every story, and the truth is never either. It is always something nebulously between the perceptions that we must each determine for ourselves. Beware they who proclaim to know what is true. I am not among them.

For Whom To Die is fiction. It is entirely a product of the author's creative construction. Many readers may imagine they are or know characters in this story—there were so many of us—but nay, all are either invented, or, if real in name, history or public domain, are referred to in a wholly fictional context.

For Whom To Die is dedicated by its author to all honorably served and serving veterans of all wars, but particularly of the Vietnam War, be they American or Vietnamese, north or south, living or dead, whole or fragmented, sane or lost, and to all who loved them and love them still. You veterans of Iraq and Afghanistan, no day goes by that I do not think of you and attempt to relate what you are experiencing to my own time in harm's way for America and freedom. May you prevail and recover safely and soon.

Regrettably, it is not possible for an author to acknowledge everyone instrumental in the writing of his novel. In a sense, everyone the writer has ever known or learned of has contributed in their way to his work.

As alluded where used, very brief 'news broadcasts' in *For Whom To Die* are taken in part but not precisely from *Newsweek Magazine* articles of the day.

My warm thanks go to Edna Siniff and *Country Messenger Press* for its valiant effort to offer the reader an alternative to the narrow strictures of the traditional publishing monolith's limited menu selected through its very flawed process. Better to light a candle than to curse the darkness. A special thanks to fellow and recommended author Kimberly Freel who was tasked with editing *For Whom To Die* for the printers.

I once told a New York agent who demanded to politically censor my manuscript, under threat of rejection, that I had the world's finest woman, a good dog, a strong horse, and a pickup truck, so what the hell did I need with New York? That bull-headed witticism may have cost me a literary career, but I still have the world's finest woman, my wife Dr. Linda Shields, and I thank her with all my love that I still feel enormously blessed with the far better part of that bargain.

War, and sometimes warriors, can be easy for some folks to disparage, but such disparagement rings hollow, even pious, absent real, workable, alternative solutions to the great human conflicts that drive people to war. Before all wars commence, the best diplomats have long plied their trade and failed. Diplomats with insufficient military force behind them to put teeth in their diplomacy fail first and most often. Terrible though it is, the time occasionally comes when the talkers are done talking, and the doers must do. Thence cometh the warrior.

War will always be with us until our

survival, our values and beliefs, even they whom we love, are no longer so dear to us that we will defend them with force when all peaceful means are exhausted. The gentlest of mothers will fight when no alternative relief from a threat to her child is perceived. For better, or for worse, this is the human way.

I fear this will always be the reality, so let us avoid war at all cost short of life, freedom, loved ones, and honor, but when we must fight, let us be united, resolute and utterly ruthless, for therein lies the quickest return to peace for all, and the longest endurance of that peace.

—William Slusher, Riverside,
Washington—January 2009

Prologue

The soundest of minds are ruled by the heart, and without love even the greatest minds wither and die before the bodies that host them. Yet, absent hate, there is no human contrast to give love its greatness.

So, join me as I tell you of love and hate woven into a single story forged upon the hot crucible of war, where both love and hate reach a height and intensity not otherwise achievable.

This will be a story unlike any you have ever read. It will charm, frighten, thrill, amuse, embolden and move you, and these are wonderful things to experience, for indeed it is these emotions, these stirrings of our hearts that we seek in a story, even more than we seek learning.

Vietnam is only the center portion of the stage upon which my story of remarkable love plays out, of course. Love stories are eternal, and, if they're good, then their venue, wherever, is but the worn, smooth wood of the stage floor upon which the characters dance and laugh, sigh and cry, love and fight, live and die. My story has passion and love for women readers, heroism and the dark adventure of war for men, and yet I'll tell you of a heroic woman soldier and I'll tell you of deeply loving men.

I know all these people, you see, for I am the least of them.

Chapter One
Time Warp

"I'LL KILL YOU!" Pot is crying now; he's heaving and his voice is cracking. "I'LL KILL ALLA YOU MOTHERFUCKERS! I...CAIN'T...TAKE THIS SHIT...NO MORE!" The veins on Pot's forehead pulse like worms.

1968—perhaps the worst of those years of American and Vietnamese agony. West toward the setting sun in a thunderous Boeing 707.

For fourteen hours we fly in the smoky, compressed air of a plastic and aluminum cocoon which muffles the high whine of four jet engines and the rushing flow of a frigid Pacific upper atmosphere. We fly with over two-hundred other soldiers, most of whom are still teenagers, each pensively wrestling with the terrifying contemplations of young men speeding to war in an alien land.

Van is unique among the soldiers on this airplane to hell. His differentness is about to change some lives even more than the war.

On our 707, a chilling realization pervades that for many now breathing in these comfortable seats, the return trip will be made reclined in a sealed aluminum box about the size of a phone booth. A few will disappear and never come home at all. There is little conversation aboard this flight, and no laughter.

At a coastal US Air Force base called Cam Ranh

Bay, in the brief and futile Republic of South Vietnam, we deplane from the refrigerated aluminum time machine into a hot, tropical night which gives us to feel as though a blanket soaked in hot water has been thrown over us. Our skin prickles as our pores slam open from the humidity.

Descending the air-stair in the cloying heat, we note erratic flashes sparkling and flaring on the otherwise pitch-dark western horizon. We briefly take these flashes for lightning before realizing the storm we see in the distance is man-made; it is exploding artillery ordnance. A profoundly disturbing realization impacts, causing one's testicles to retract. If you have no testicles, imagine walking alone through the woods at night. Now you hear a stick crack...and something out there...breathing.

This is a war zone. There are not one but two enemy armies out there in the night, the Viet Cong and The North Vietnamese Army. Tens of thousands of heavily armed people scurrying like ants out there don't even know us, but they will kill us on sight. We are tempted to consider them aliens, but here it is we who are the aliens.

Van is an alien, even among us.

Somewhere out there in the jungle darkness near Cambodia is a woman named Sung Tranh who is to become a player in a room of crippled souls.

In two days, sweating to a merciless equatorial sun, we board a deafening Lockheed C-130, a droning, four-engined, turbo-prop transport. We sit en masse on our heavy, lumpy duffle bags as there are no seats. The C-130 flies north along the white sandy Indochinese coast, stopping for passengers at Nha Trang before continuing along the clear blue edge of the South China Sea to the city of Qui Nhon. There, on the scalding, pierced-steel runway, where everything wavers from the rising heat, we transfer to a giant, shrieking, thundering,

dull-green army helicopter with huge, flailing rotors
on both ends of its roof. Pungent, oily jet-fuel fumes
choke us. We brood about hearing-impairment and lung
damage until we consider that we are about to fly over
men and women with guns who will be squinting up at
us and pondering whether we are too high to shoot at.
Today.

The mammoth Chinook helicopter climbs almost
straight up and bears westward, away from the azure
South China Sea. Inland it flies, over flat watery rice
paddies, then higher still to cross emerald-green,
jungle-carpeted mountains that look from altitude
like wrinkled, dark-green velvet. The big helicopter
tosses about in the turbulent air of the Mang Yang Pass
before settling into smooth flight again as it crosses
above miles of grassy, rolling plains toward the Central
Highlands city of Pleiku.

We descend over a large helter-skelter city of
haphazardly clustered shacks and small, French colonial
buildings, down, past a small mountain, more a high
naked mound with communications antennas and dishes
on top, and aircraft wreckage strewn on its slopes.

The air blowing from the city to Pleiku airport
smells like dirty laundry. The hot wind is permeated
with a fine red dust that grits upon our teeth as we lean
against a scouring hurricane blown by the departing
helicopter.

Here we fling our duffle into the soldier's limousine,
a dusty, open-topped, camouflage-painted, ten-wheel
truck. It is driven by a bored, sullen, severely hung-
over, nineteen-year-old private who is deeply unhappy
with his miserable life and simultaneously terrified of
losing it. He drives accordingly.

The diesel engine roars and spews more throat-
clenching fumes as the truck bounces violently over a
narrow road roughly paved with an odd sort of tarred
dirt. It grinds through the crowded streets of Pleiku
past scores of tiny, colorfully advertised, open-front
shops selling everything from black-market c-rations, to

bright clothing, to live chickens, to multi-colored fruits and vegetables, to varying cut-grades of raw marijuana in plastic bags the size of basketballs. Tinny, nasal music on Vietnamese radio competes with the roar of the truck and the din of few cars but countless scooters, beeping horns, and the high frantic chatter of an Asian market.

We can actually feel the air pollution pecking our faces.

The streets teem with diminutive Vietnamese women on foot, most in some combination of loose, black-silk trousers and snug, colorful blouses, together with conical straw hats and plastic flip-flops. Women, and unattended children caring for still younger children, vastly out-number men. Most males present seem too young or too old for military service. Those few in between have the hard, hostile eyes of pimps, maimed combat veterans, homosexual prostitutes, or Viet Cong patriots waiting for the sun to set.

Some women carry chickens by their feet, or farm produce in big straw bags. Many more Vietnamese ride motor-scooters, bicycles and small, three-wheeled, Italian scooter-trucks. The only conventional vehicles are the trucks and jeeps of the South Vietnamese and American armies. A few soldiers of those armies walk the streets in pairs, all wearing green jungle fatigues and carrying black rifles. In places, erotically-dressed Vietnamese girls beckon come-on gestures to the occupants of the passing truck. The air is permeated with the damp, repugnant stench of sewage and unwashed humans mixed with the smoke of cooking meat.

"We'll all try not to make loud noises. Please, Pot. You don't need to kill us."

Soon the big truck clears the city and careens

rocking along a narrow, rolling road trailing a wake of red dust, its ship's horn blasting belligerently, forcing civilian vehicles, bicyclists and pedestrians to the edge.

Across a broad plain, we see in the distance a massive, sprawling, military city, easily two miles anywhere across it. The complex contains hundreds of acres of drab wooden buildings and a bustling army airfield. Everything is the color of mud. Sporadically, tall radio antennas sprout from bunkers like isolated hairs on a mange-ridden animal. The entire city is surrounded by a perimeter of more than a hundred sandbagged machine-gun bunkers aimed outward onto a broad killing field heavily mined and choked with coils of razor wire. Camp Enari, headquarters of the Fourth Infantry Division, Army of the United States of America.

The truck deposits us shaken but not broken at an enormous cluster of metal-roofed, one-story wooden structures. The Room is near.

We load into one last vehicle, a jeep, which bumps over the tarred-dirt roads of the base past endless rows of the long, narrow, unpainted wooden buildings. Each is, in theory at least, protected from artillery shelling by brownish outer walls of sandbags which extend from the ground to the bottom of a screened window which encircles each building beneath its over-hanging metal roof. In such a structure is The Room.

The jeep leaves us and we shoulder our duffle and walk through the hot, blowing dust, over boardwalks or gravel paths neatly bordered by sandbags. We stride past latrine buildings which contain the crude showers, sinks and toilets which the unplumbed barracks do not have.

We step around long, dusty mounds of still more sandbags which roof narrow underground chambers. When the rockets and mortar shells come in the night to spray white-hot shards of jagged, eviscerating metal, men will flee with wide eyes and clenched teeth down into the bosom of these bunkers.

We traverse a slightly elevated boardwalk to
building 4044, known as hooch-44. Hooch-44 is
visually indistinguishable from the hundreds of other
such Spartan barracks in the massive installation,
yet hooch-44 is quite special, for it is the interior of
hooch-44 that is The Room of crippled souls. It is
here that the battle will be fought, that the story will
transpire, and you will see it all.

Step through the narrow, L-shaped passage in the
sandbag blast-wall. I'll hold back the squeaking screen
door for you. Enter now and let me show you The
Room where it happens.

Walk through the door onto a dusty grey concrete
floor covered only partially in its center by a large rug,
more a mat actually, woven with a thick, brittle reed. It
was once colorful, but has now faded to vague hues of
umber and yellow in the year since it was traded from
a Montagnyard tribesman for a machine-gunned wild
hog.

Walk over the rug to the far wall and view a broad,
cork bulletin board hung between two banks of grey
metal wall lockers. On the board are mandatory army
memos and posters addressing everything from uniform
wear, bunker-access routes and authorized weapons,
to venereal disease, secrecy regulations and aviation
safety.

You need not read these items; no one else does. You
need only turn your back to this wall, then step back
into it. Yes. Be absorbed by this meaningless wall,
disappear into its insignificance, shelter in it. Hide. It
is only a vantage from which you will experience the
story.

From here you will suffer or enjoy all the emotions
born in the humid heat of The Room, and they will be
many. You will flinch from the flash of mortar shells
and wince at the concussion of the rockets. Your ears
will ring shrilly from the gunfire. You will see the tears
and blood, you will hear the laughter, confessions and
screams, you will smell the sweat and the perfume, and

7

you will taste the sour bile of fear. You will know all
this and more, but no one will be aware of you. You
have become a part of The Room of crippled souls.

Over your head is a false ceiling of camouflage-
colored parachute silk fastened to the tops of the
walls and rising to two peaks above fluorescent light
fixtures, much like the interior of a circus tent rises to
its two support poles. The walls are unfinished wood
extending upward from the floor six feet to a two-foot-
high, screened window that completely encircles The
Room. There is no glass in the window. Glass becomes
shrapnel when the rockets and mortars explode.
Regardless, it rarely gets cold enough here that anyone
would want to restrict the meager flow of hot, damp air
through the screening.

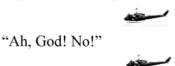

"Ah, God! No!"

The Room is the stage. So much will happen here.
Bear with me as I describe it. The stories begin soon.

From the wall to your left extend two, green-metal,
standard army bunks; one has its mattress bare and
folded over, its fence-like wire springing partially
exposed; the other is neatly made in a brown army
blanket, and has a small stenciled sign on its foot that
reads: CW2 Preston, Hale. The left wall is bare above
the empty bunk, yet rectangular silhouettes are visible
where photos once hung upon it, blocking the bleaching
sunlight.

Over Preston's bunk is hung a large, framed, M.C.
Escher print, an odd chain of ants composing a Mobius
Loop. Next to the print are tacked many pictures of a
striking, dark-haired young woman in her twenties.
In one shot she wears a college sweater with a large
V on it. In another photo, several happy young men
in the uniforms of army warrant officers stand arms-
on-shoulders, grinning and pointing proudly to silver

pilot's wings pinned above their breast pockets. They stand before a sign that proclaims: "Fort Rucker - Home Of US Army Aviation - Above The Best". Between those two bunks to your left is a crude desk made of boards scavenged from a shipping crate; on the desk is a worn, goose-neck office lamp, and on the floor before the desk is an equally abused metal chair.

Abuse is a feature of The Room in so many ways.

Across The Room from you stands a longer wall against which are the heads of three similar bunks to the right of an ancient, battered refrigerator. The old appliance is brush-painted dark blue, and has a reel-type tape player and a boom-box radio atop it. The refrigerator has "Old Faithful" stenciled across the upper, freezer door.

The left-most of the three bunks, by the refrigerator, is labeled: WO Dermott, Charles; on the wall above this bunk hangs a plaque embossed with a crucifix over a set of military flight wings engraved with the inscription: God Is My Co-pilot. Near it is a gold-framed portrait of Jesus Christ and a silver-framed picture of a pair of warmly smiling parents in their forties, standing before a large church. The father wears a clerical collar.

The middle bunk is unkempt, a mish-mash of soiled sheets and items of clothing. The name label says its occupant is WO Willows, Edward. Someone has line-item vetoed the name Edward with a felt marker and scrawled over it the name Pothead. On Pothead's little acre of wall space is a disorganized cluster of magazine photos of rock stars, a sign that says: "Make Love, Not War!," and one which reads: "Join The Army - Travel To Exotic Lands, Meet Interesting Native People - And Kill Them!" If one of these exhibits dominates, it is the one of a grotesquely made-up acid-rocker squinting menacingly through marijuana smoke from behind his extended middle finger.

The right-most of those three bunks before you has tacked above it several centerfold magazine layouts of young women, in various poses of nudity, and a poster proclaiming the theological premise that: "If God Didn't Mean For Man To Eat Pussy, He Wouldn't Have Made It Look So Much Like A Taco!" Above this display is a large portrait of a weathered, toothless, wino-like old man wearing an oversized army flight helmet. Beneath this picture is the caption: "Sleep Well Tonight - Your Army Is Awake!" The name tag on this bunk reads: WO Bleaker, Paul. Beneath the label is taped a scrawled addendum stating: "Home of the Spudster!"

On the wall between the bunks of Pothead and the Spudster hangs a large Playboy calendar with the days X'd off in red marker, prison-style.

"Sometimes I think, if there is a god, I'm in a lot of trouble, but...if there's no god...we're all in a lot of trouble."

There remains, of course, only the fourth wall, on your right by the door through which you entered. Here there is but one bunk labeled CW2 Hatchette, Jerome. Mr. Hatchette's bunk is isolated, apart from the others. It is neatly made and on the expanse of wall above it is hung a faded and bullet-holed Viet Cong battle flag, one corner of which is stiff with brown bloodstains. Also on this wall is a very large, framed and matted photograph of eleven Special Forces soldiers in their tiger-striped fatigues and green berets. They stand arms upon each others' shoulders or cradling weapons. They smile at the camera, but there is no humor in their eyes, only the borderline-psychotic look of men who have been killing other men for a long time. In the dust at the feet of the soldiers in the large photograph are a dozen recumbent young North Vietnamese Army soldiers in dirty, blood-soaked, tan uniforms and rubber-tire sandals. The men in the dust are returning to it; they stare vacantly through clouded eyes, and their mouths droop open.

An inscription written across the photograph reads: "To
Master Sergeant Jerome Hatchette, 'The Hatchet Man,'
from the men of Delta Team. Killing folks just ain't
gonna be as much fun without you, Sarge. Good luck in
flight school!"

One remaining item decorates the wall above The
Hatchet Man's bunk to your right. It is a cartoon
caricature of a C-model-Huey, gunship-helicopter,
diving and firing rockets, machine-guns and grenades
upon a ground target. Clearly visible through the
windshield of the ugly, weapon-draped aircraft are the
ecstatic faces of the helmeted pilots. At its bottom edge,
this cartoon is boldly captioned: "Happiness Is A Dead
Gook!"

There are few other items in The Room. Steel
helmets and flak jackets hang on wooden pegs, green
towels hang on nails. You can see fire extinguishers,
folding metal chairs, small ammo crates by the beds
supporting alarm clocks and magazines, footlockers
at the ends of the beds, boots and flip-flops beneath
the beds. The Room is neither a sumptuous nor lovely
place.

You survey The Room from your magic vantage
in the wall of the lockers and bulletin board. You see
it all without being seen. Once you have reconciled
your eyes to the contents of The Room, your remaining
senses suddenly come alive. There is the oily smell of
turbine exhaust fumes on the warm, moist breeze. The
Room vibrates with the hallmark sound of the Vietnam
war, the fluttering thunder of big helicopters departing a
nearby airfield.

In a moment the rotor noise fades and all you hear
is a faint scratching in the dust and the rattle of an
empty beer can rolling on the bare concrete. Then you
see it, you see the rat furtively scurrying along the wall
beneath the bunks across from you. It stops abruptly
and sniffs the air with its whiskered, twitching nose. It
looks about nervously; it looks for you, but it cannot
see you.

   The rat jerks its head toward a sound from outside
The Room —you hear it too—footsteps thumping on
creaking boardwalk planks. The rat squeaks and flees
out of sight just as the footsteps draw near. The screen-
door spring twangs as it is stretched.
   The story begins.

Chapter Two
The News That Was

Good evening American soldiers, sailors
and airmen! This is Armed Forces Radio, and
I am Specialist Fourth-Class Barbara Stafford
bringing you this edition of Events In Review.
As you regular listeners know, Events In
Review is brought to you with the assistance
and best wishes of the folks at *Newsweek
Magazine* who want you, the American
fighting man, to be informed!

The big story, of course, is the election this
month of the thirty-seventh president of the
United States, Richard Milhous Nixon. As
President-elect Nixon's campaign came down
to the wire the handwriting was on the wall.
His crowds were big and adoring, nationwide.
A *Gallup* poll showed Nixon leading with
43% against Hubert Humphrey's 28%, and
George Wallace's trailing 21%. Still another
poll showed Mr. Nixon ahead in likability and
charisma.

In victory, Mr. Nixon has shown traits of
character that foretell something of the Nixon
presidency to come. He has established himself
as a skilled political tactician. He proved
himself a shrewd analyst of the predominant
trends in the land, and a master of the latest
political weaponry: television, stagecraft and
computers. *Newsweek* describes President-
elect Nixon as the quintessential politician of
these troubled times: more competent than

inspiring, more flexible than philosophical. These are respectable credentials vital to survival in the White House. Mr. Nixon's close friend, H.R. "Bob" Haldeman, says the president-elect has a deep inner security which will distinguish him among presidents. Still, no presidential candidate has talked so much to the American voter yet revealed less about himself. The window to the inner man remains closed.

Moving now to other news: In the months since the Reverend Martin Luther King fell to an assassin's bullet in Memphis, Tennessee, most American cities have regained a semblance of normalcy. Not so in Wilmington, Delaware, however, where the National Guard still patrols, armed and helmeted. Wilmington is the only U.S. city still regularly patrolled by military force. The city's black leaders see the Guard presence as an attempt by whites in power to suppress Wilmington's 40% Negro population. City fathers counter that the Guard patrols are necessary to protect Wilmington's law-abiding citizenry from heavily armed, underground black-militant groups.

Meanwhile, on the opposite end of the United States, in Everett, Washington, the Boeing Company is scheduled to roll out for public inspection its first 747 jumbo jet. At 185 feet in length, the new 747 is 65 feet longer than the entire first flight of the Wright Brothers at Kitty Hawk in 1903. This giant of the sky will weigh in at 350 tons and will carry as many as 490 passengers nearly 600 miles per hour. The Boeing Company has already received 158 orders for the new 747 at twenty million dollars each. The 747's unprecedented luxury of two-story passenger decks and roast beef carved at seat-side may be only a year away for American air travelers.

Even more incredible in the realm of flight, at Cape Kennedy, is the towering white Saturn rocket. Soon, the great Saturn rocket will lift three American astronauts into earth orbit. This Apollo flight is the first in a series which will carry Americans to the vicinity of the moon by this Christmas and onto the lunar surface itself before Christmas of 1969. The American technological spirit is beckoned by the symbolic appeal of the moon and is spurred on by the nagging suspicion that the Russians, long competitors in space, may reach the moon first.

Elsewhere on the home front, McGeorge Bundy, advisor to Lyndon Johnson on foreign affairs and staunch supporter of President Johnson's commitment of half-a-million U.S. troops to the Vietnam war effort, seems to be undergoing a change of heart. In a recent statement, Mr. Bundy said: "It is plainly unacceptable that we should continue with annual costs of thirty billion dollars and an annual rate of sacrifice of over ten thousand American lives. It is equally wrong to accept the bitterness and polarization of our people. There is special pain in the growing alienation of a generation which is the best we've ever had. The contest in South Vietnam is a contest for the allegiance of the South Vietnamese people. No foreign force can win that battle." Mr. Bundy emphasized, however, that it was not his intent to second-guess the President.

In other news today on Events In Review, the social world was stunned to learn of the marriage of former First Lady Jacqueline Bouvier Kennedy to Greek multi-millionaire Aristotle Onassis. Reaction to the announcement was one of universal shock.

The Roman Catholic Church was especially upset due to Onassis's status as a divorced man and his celebrated ten-year affair with opera star Maria Callas. A Paris newspaper referred to the marriage as 'the latest Kennedy tragedy.'

Former President and five-star general Dwight David Eisenhower recently celebrated his seventy-eighth birthday. Appearing with the old soldier at his Walter Reed Army Hospital window was his ever faithful wife, Mamie.

It may come as no surprise to you guys that there's a war on. This week President Johnson ordered a halt to all bombing north of the 17th parallel in a gesture aimed at bringing North Vietnam closer to a negotiated peace at the conference table in Paris. "I have been assured by top military sources," President Johnson said, "that the cessation of the bombing of North Vietnam will in no way add to the danger faced by Americans fighting in South Vietnam."

Speaking of top military sources, the Commander of U.S. Forces in South Vietnam, General Creighton Abrams, famed World War II tank officer, is presenting a contrast with his predecessor, General William Westmoreland. Forsaking Westmoreland's search and destroy methods which are thought to have accounted for a hundred-thousand enemy deaths in last February's Tet offensive alone, General Abrams is known to favor small-unit reconnaissance patrols and the substitution of armor for manpower. Another Abrams innovation is the expanded close support of the high-flying B-52 bombers. A single large-scale B-52 bombing raid, called an "Arc-Light Strike" in military jargon, delivers more explosive tonnage than was dropped on all of

Germany in all of World War II.

And that's it for this edition of *Events In Review*, brought to you with the assistance of *Newsweek Magazine* so you, the American fighting man, can remain informed. This is Specialist Fourth-Class Barbara Stafford saying, keep checking those days off the old calendar, guys, and here's to your speedy and safe return to the world. Good night!

Chapter Three
The Room

Hale Preston is tall and young-man lean. He struggles through the screen door into The Room of crippled souls dressed in faded, solid-green jungle fatigues and dusty boots. He carries a green nylon flight-helmet bag in one hand and his black M-16 rifle in the other. Over his shoulder is slung a heavy, ceramic chest-armor plate contained in a green nylon and velcro vest. The screen door bangs shut behind him as he wearily crosses the rug to the bunks at your left. He drops the flight equipment bag and vest, leans the rifle in the corner by the refrigerator, and strips his sweat-stained shirt from a tanned and almost hairless chest. Dog tags dangle from a chain about his neck.

Hale squints through sun-cooked eyes aged before their time. His is the wary, hostile, super-max-prison gaze of someone who's been defending his life against motivated killers.

Hale sighs deeply, yanks open the refrigerator door and extracts a rusty steel can of Pabst Blue Ribbon which requires a triangular opener as it was canned shortly after World War II. He draws long on the beer, grimaces at its icy bite and emits a satisfied "Aaaah!" He reaches to the radio atop the refrigerator and switches it on, then he collapses onto the bunk before the refrigerator. Hale closes his eyes, and holds the cold, wet beer can to his temple.

Hale Preston is the sort of male beautiful that provokes pretty young girls to slip him little tears of paper with their phone numbers written thereon in a trembling hand. His shining black hair, his

brilliant, white-toothed, natural smile and his chiseled
musculature have brought him the occasional attention
of homosexual men, some young and strikingly
handsome like himself and some old, though all, he
thinks, repulsive. He worries, because he is rarely
approached by 'queers,' that there is something about
him which suggests that he too is homosexual, which
he emphatically is not. He is at an age, twenty-one, that
this confuses and troubles him.

The radio throbs with one of the hottest songs of the
day by one of the many new British rock groups now in
vogue:

"...I cain't git nooo...sat-tis-FAC-shun! An' I try, an'
I try, an' I try, an' I try! But I cain't git nooo...sat-tis-
FAC-shun!"

Hale Preston's left foot moves slightly to the beat.
The song booms to an end and a young, 'groovy' DJ
yells: "Yeah! Mick Jagger and the Rolling Stones, and
Satisfaction! Now there's a song that is going places
guys, or my name isn't Specialist, Fourth-Class, Barry,
'Hip-man' Hines, and this isn't another rockin' evening
in the Nam on Armed Forces Radio. Many thanks to
beautiful Specialist Fourth-Class Barbara Stafford for
today's edition of Events In Review, but now it's boogie
time! Time for more of the latest, the greatest, the
rockinest tunes of today! Stay tuned for this message
and then we'll be back with this week's most requested
hit, Ike and Tina Turner, and Rolling On The River!"

Hale pulls on the beer again, aspirating it in his
mouth and letting it trickle slowly down his throat.
Sweat drips from his chin. He removes his dusty
boots and drops them to the floor, then he returns to
the refrigerator, turns the radio down to a murmur and
pushes off from the appliance. The refrigerator rocks
and from behind it the rat scurries along the baseboard.

"God damn it!" Hale hisses. He frantically snatches
up one of his boots and hurls it at the fleeing rat. It hits
the wall six inches above the rodent. Hale seizes the
other boot by its toe and slams the heel at the rat but he

19

misses again. He scampers around the bunk to the right
of the refrigerator and raises the boot to swing again,
but the rodent has disappeared in a hidden crevice
leading to capacious rat colonies in the outer blast wall.
Hale remains poised, sock feet apart, boot upraised,
in case the rat reappears. He breathes hard, and seems
much angrier than the situation calls for. A glistening
stream of sweat trickles down his back between
taughtly-muscled shoulder blades.

Behind Hale, the screen door squeaks open again
and he twists about to see who enters. The boot is still
held over his head.

In the doorway stands another young man in his
early twenties, also in jungle fatigues, shouldering one
duffle bag and dragging another. His shirt is blackened
with sweat stains, but his boots are still shiny with
newness. He is Hale's height and lean build, but he is
pleasant and gentle in appearance. He has sandy blond
hair above a high forehead, prominent cheekbones,
and a narrow roman nose between strikingly blue eyes.
Genetically, the newcomer is Dr. Mengele's prime
Aryan breeding stock. He bears a soft smile and a
curious look.

Hale suddenly realizes the spectacle he presents; he
slings the boot to the floor beneath his bunk. "Sorry.
The rat that ate Cincinnati just ran through here and I
was trying to get him. Come on in."

The newcomer looks vaguely like someone Hale has
seen but cannot name.

"From the conspicuous absence of corpus delicti, I
gather you were unsuccessful," the stranger says, still
bearing the gentle smile. He enunciates flawlessly, yet
his voice is soft, warm and unpretentious.

Hale snatches up the stranger's duffle. He looks
for the embroidered name tape above the newcomer's
uniform pocket but there is none; Hale dismisses this
as it is common for new arrivals just issued jungle
fatigues.

"Yeah," Hale says, smiling and offering his hand.

"No body count. Guess my military career's a wash. I'm Hale Preston. You must be the new guy the major said we'd be getting."

"I am if this is pilot-quarters forty-four." He takes Hale's hand in a firm grip. "I'm Van."

"Well, welcome to hooch-44, Van. Put your gear over here; that's your bunk there by mine, and the locker nearest it is yours also." Hale drags a duffle to the vacant bunk, throws the folded mattress flat on the springs and deposits the bag on the bunk. "We'll get name placards made up for you soon."

"No rush on that, thank you," Van says, crossing the rug and throwing his shouldered duffle down by the other. The bedsprings creak.

Van wipes his face on his sleeve and runs his tongue over his teeth. "I finished the in-country briefings in Cam Ranh Bay yesterday, and I arrived in Pleiku this evening. My word. I have never known such heat and dust."

"The soldiers of Genghis Khan had the same complaint when they were marauding here," Hale says, going to the old refrigerator. He extracts two more cans of Pabst and spears them both. "That's the Central Highlands for you, but don't worry about the dust. The monsoons will come soon and turn it into more mud than hippo heaven. Get used to it; these palatial accommodations will be your home away from home for the next long year..." Hale averts his gaze, and sucks through his teeth, "...if you're lucky." He hands Van a beer. "There you go—beer older than we are—nothing but the best for the...gallant sky warriors of the U.S. Army. I understand you're assigned to the medevac flight platoon, you'll be a flying ambulance driver."

"Fortunately, yes. Thanks for the beer."

"Fortunately, my ass. You medevac guys get shot at just like those of us flying the slicks and the hogs—you just can't shoot back, in accordance with the Geneva Convention, which, as we all know, is scrupulously adhered to by everyone here in the Land of Lunacy.

God forbid we forget our manners while we're trying
to kill each other. By the way, I didn't catch your last
name—Van who?"

Van eyes the parachute-silk ceiling nervously.
"Well..."

To his visible relief, Van is interrupted by raucous
laughter from outside, and the approaching footsteps
of other flyers. The screen door crashes open and three
boisterous young pilots spill into The Room grinning
widely, fixed on a story being told by the shorter,
chubbier member of the group. The latter pilot drops
his flight gear and green ball-cap to the floor, lifts his
plump red face to the ceiling and extends his thick
grimy arms. "I shit you not!" He swears. "I saw it with
my own eyes!"

The other two new arrivals struggle to pass him, still
laughing. One is very tall, red-haired and freckled, and
bears the name-tape Dermott. He goes by Charlie. The
other has a hooked Arab nose and a protruding Adams
apple; in another story he might be called Ichabod, but
in this story he is Pothead Willows. Charlie Dermott
looks like a fresh-scrubbed Mormon missionary.
Pothead looks vaguely unbalanced. He is.

Pothead heaps his flight gear onto his rat-nest
of a bunk, drops to his knees, nervously fingers a
combination lock and throws open the lid to his
footlocker.

Charlie eyes Van briefly, then he says, "Hale! Hale,
you gotta listen to this! Tell it again, Spud!"

"Play it again, Sam," Hale mutters, amused at the
theatrics of Spud Bleaker.

"Okay! Okay! Get this, Hale! I'm walking back
to my ship out at LZ Bluebeard when I see some TV
fucker interviewin' this grunt, some dumb nigger. The
TV guy says, 'Soldier, tell us in your own words what
you saw.' Well the nigger, see, he's tryin' to profile
like John fuckin' Wayne for all the brothers back in the
fuckin' ghetto, right? So he looks the TV guy in the eye
like he's Sergeant Fury or somethin', right?"

Spud's eyes become widely bulged and he mimics with exaggeration. "And the nigger says,'Slowly Ah turned around, you know, and I seen my man Jackson, you know, only you couldn't tell it was my man Jackson, you know, because his head was blowed clean off, you know?'" Spud loses it briefly and bellows with laughter with Pothead and Charlie, before returning to his tale. "Well, the nigger says to the TV guy, with a face as serious as a body-bag, he says, 'And right away, Ah knowed something was wrong!'"

Pothead, Charlie and Spud howl and slap their knees.

"He sees his buddy's had his head vaporized, and 'right away' he 'knows somethin's wrong'," Spud screams again. "Is he Dick fuckin' Tracy or what?" Spud plops heavily onto his bunk, tears mixing in the dusty sweat of his meaty cheeks.

"Outa sight, man," Pothead cackles, dragging a bottle of Jack Daniels and several pill containers from his footlocker. "Outa-fuckin' sight."

Charlie Dermott shakes his head, sniffs and wipes his nose. "That is a great story, Spud," he says. "But I declare it would tell so much better if you didn't use that word."

"Oh shit," Spud sighs. "Stand by for another sermon from Pope Charlie." He giggles again. "What word, Charlie?"

"You know, Spud."

"You mean, 'fuck'?"

"Well, that too, but I was referring to the fact that the Lord means for us to regard our fellow man with respect and dignity, and—"

"Oh Jesus Harley Davidson Christ, Charlie! Are you tryin' to tell me I cain't say 'nigger'?"

"And you shouldn't refer to the Savior that way! It's God's will that—"

"An' I suppose next you'll be tellin' me I cain't say 'gook' neither?"

"It's true, Spud, what can I say? God doesn't mean for us to use disparaging epithets on either our Negro

23

brothers or our Asian brothers. See—"

"Well, I don't know about you, Pope Charlie,"
Pothead Willows pulls hard on the bottle of Jack,
winces, swallows and exhales with satisfaction. "But
I ain't got no nigger brothers. And I sure as hell ain't
got no gook brothers." Pothead eyes Charlie with a
contempt not missed by the observant Van whose eyes
are narrowed slightly and flick quickly from person to
person.

"The Bible says—"

"Now lemme see if I got this straight, Charlie," Spud
says rising to his feet.

Hale elbows Van and nods at Spud with amusement.

"Ever since we was kids we been saying America
was 'one nation, under God,'" Spud continues,"so I
guess that even though ole God don't want us to call
gooks gooks, he don't seem to mind if we come over
here and kill a coupla million of the little fucks, is that
about it?"

"War is not God's fault, Spud!" Charlie protests.
"It's—"

"Oh yeah, I forgot, we're all natural born fuck-ups
and so God had to nail his kid to a tree to rescue us and
ever since then all the fuck-ups are our fault and all
the neato shit is ole God's doin'. I'm with you brother.
Hallelujah!"

Pothead tosses back two unidentified
pharmaceuticals and flushes them down with another
stiff slug of the whiskey. Although he is considerably
more absorbed in the gospel according to Jack Daniels,
he nonetheless observes, "Outa sight, man. Shit, I ain't
even a queer, but if I thought God would fly my young
ass back to the world right now I'd fall on my knees
and suck his dick."

"Hey!" Charlie exclaims in equal parts astonishment
and outrage. He stands over Pot, glaring. "Knock that
off! I don't have to listen to that kind of blasphemy!"

Pot rises, his lips pursed tightly. He sways, but is
wide-eyed, ready to engage. He hisses low and deadly.

"Ffffuck you, preacher-boy."

Hale correctly judges that this a good time to intervene. He sighs. "Well, I hate to interrupt this meaningful spiritual seminar, but let me introduce you to our new roomy. Gentlemen - more or less - this is our new medevac pilot, Van, uh...?"

"Van!" Van repeats, seizing the moment, extending his hand to Spud who has hurried to meet him.

"Hey!" Spud says warmly, "Paul Bleaker; everybody calls me Spud. Welcome to The Nam!"

Charlie, still recovering from Pot's vulgarity, shakes it off, smiles and shakes Van's hand. "Charlie Dermott; Macon, Georgia. Nice to meet you."

Pot ignores all but the bottle he holds with both hands as he sits morosely on his bunk. The chemicals have come ashore and established a beachhead in Pot's brain.

"Mr. Charm, here," Hale says, indicating Pot, "is Warrant Officer Eddie Willows, known throughout the land as Pothead."

"Fuck you and the mule you rode in on, Preston," Pot mutters, remaining on his bunk, ignoring Van.

"I'll pass, thanks; but you might check with the mule. Van, what did you say your last name was? I need to have name placards made up for your bunk and locker, or they'll jam us on inspection."

Van exhibits a resigned expression. "I had hoped to avoid mentioning my last name for a while, but I can see I was dreaming."

"Shit," Spud says returning to his bunk. "I once knew a guy in basic named Harris Butts. How'd you like to go through army basic being called Private Harry Butt by every drill sergeant?"

"Heck, that's nothing," Charlie says. "My dad had a seminary school roommate named Franklin Norman Stein. How'd you like to be Pastor Frank N. Stein?"

"I might prefer it actually," Van says, smiling wanly.

"Name can't be that bad," Charlie offers. "What is it?"

"Savatch," Van Savatch replies.

The Room freezes.

"Oh shit," Spud whispers. Even Pot's fogged head snaps up.

"Yep," Charlie says with quiet conviction. "It's that bad."

"Okay," Van says. "So I'm Robert Vanning Savatch, Junior. So, yeah, Major General Robert Savatch, Senior, the division commander, is my father."

Hale sighs. "Nooo kidding."

Van is plainly distressed. "Look, guys. I was afraid you'd react this way. Please, it makes no difference to me; it shouldn't to you either."

Hale is touching his forehead with his fingertips. "Something just doesn't compute here, Van. With General Savatch's pull you could have been a captain in charge of, oh say, water skiing at the Cam Ranh Bay Officer's Club. How did you wind up flying an unarmed medical rescue helicopter way out here in the shooting war?"

Van is troubled. "To tell you the truth, I'm not exactly my father's image of a career soldier. In fact, I'm not a soldier at all. See I...well...I don't believe in war. I just—"

"Ha!" Charlie cries loudly, causing Pot to flinch and glare furiously at him. "Boy, are you in the wrong place!"

"Believe in it?" Spud interrupts, "Hell, none of us believes in it!"

"I do," Hale says, leaning on Old Faithful. "I believe that war is inevitable, like hurricanes. It's the unalterable nature of mankind. The choice isn't whether to go to war periodically; never has been. It's always been to fight and prevail when war can't be avoided, or to hide out while somebody else does your share of the fighting for you. Plato said it: 'Only the dead—'"

"'Have known the end of war,' yes." Van smiles sadly and looks at the floor. "I certainly hope there's another choice there somewhere, Hale. I almost took

conscientious objector status when I was at Berkeley,
but there were too many guys doing that for all the
wrong reasons. I didn't want to be part of that group
every war produces that tries to perfume its cowardice
or self-obsession with righteous, pseudo-intellectual,
peace-at-any-cost rationales; and it would have
embarrassed my father unfairly. Besides, communism
is oppressive, and its expansion into South Vietnam is
wrong. But I truly don't believe in war. So, I felt the
only way I could do my duty to my country, placate my
father, and yet avoid killing anyone was to become a
medevac pilot. That way I'd just transport the wounded
and not be involved in any direct killing. So, I enlisted,
requested medevac pilot training, and I got it."

A drunken, derisive cackle rips from Pothead, who
wipes his nose on his sleeve. "Unbelievable. We got
a hippie general's kid for a hoochmate! Wait 'til The
Hatchet Man hears about this. Un-fuckin'-believable."

"The grammar you just used suggests the general is
a hippie, you cretin," Hale says, exchanging cold stares
with Pot. Pot flips Hale the bird.

Charlie Dermott also watches Pot. "Pay no mind
to Pothead, Van. If he isn't defiling the body the good
Lord gave him with alcohol, he's befuddling his spirit
with drugs."

Pot sneers. "At the moment, preacher-prick, I am
both defiling and befuddling!" He shakes the pill bottle
at Charlie while sucking hard on the Jack bottle again.
Charlie shakes his head.

Van asks, "Who's...The Hatchet Man?"

"Don't you worry, newby," Pot snorts. "You'll find
out soon enough."

Spud answers, pointing at the bunk in the corner
to your right beneath the big photo of Special Forces
soldiers and NVA bodies, "He's talking about Chief
Warrant Officer Jerome Hatchette. Hatch is an old
guy; God, he must be nearly forty. Him and Pot are
hog pilots; gunships are called hogs over here. Me and
Charlie and Hale, we fly slicks, that's what we call

the plain ole Hueys that move the bullets, beans and bodies."

"Yeah," Hale adds, "But for God's sake don't call him Jerome —he gets all psychotic if you do—call him Hatch or Hatchette or anything but Jerome. He's a lifer who fought in Korea. He did an extended tour here in '66 in the Special Forces as a master sergeant. He was some kind of classified green-beret snake-eater living in the tri-border mountains with the Montagnyard tribes. Then he went to flight school and came back for another tour in...this geographical armpit. He lives and loves the war. He's a psychopathic lunatic, is what he is."

"Yeah ..." Pot slurs, "And he's fuckin' crazy, too."

"So let him alone about his name; actually, it'd probably be best if you stay as clear of Hatchette as possible. He's not exactly Miss Congeniality."

Van sighs and smiles with only half his mouth. "I can see I've got a lot to learn," he says softly.

Hale eyes Van with a grim look. "Actually, Van, there are several important things you need to know right away. The situation here is not good. The—"

"Yeah," Pot interjects before drawing on the Jack yet again. "No round-eyed pussy."

"Ah, but plenty of rats," Charlie adds, pulling sore feet from dusty boots.

Irritated, Hale eyes Pot. "Pussy doesn't have eyes, shit-for-brains."

"Man, I'm sure relieved to hear that," Spud mutters.

Hale again. "Anyway, Van, Charlie's right, the rat problem here is bad and it's getting worse, but what really concerns me is the flight situation."

"Eighty-percent!" Spud suddenly yells as though it were a college cheer. Pot jumps, sucks a sudden breath and whirls to glare at Spud, who fails to notice.

"The colonel commanding this aviation brigade—"

"Matlock!" Pot slurs. "Colonel 'nervous Purvis' Matlock!"

"—is determined to make general if it kills us all,"

says Hale. "He's pressuring everybody for the blessed eighty percent."

"Eighty percent of what?" Van asks.

Charlie breaks in, shoving his boots beneath his bunk. "He means eighty percent of the ships in the fleet flyable at any one time. Most helicopter units here are barely able to maintain sixty percent. With the problems of maintenance, scarce parts, and operational damage—"

"Not to mention the accident rate," Spud says, squinting out the high, long, screened window at a pinkly setting sun.

"—no combat helicopter unit in The Nam flight-readies eighty percent. It can't be done, but Colonel Matlock hasn't figured that out yet."

Hale speaks again. "Van, maintenance is simply not equipped to maintain eighty percent of the fleet flyable at once, but the pressure from brigade is ferocious. To comply, maintenance is forced to put ships on the flight line with poor, if any, scheduled service. The aircraft perform poorly and are dangerous to fly."

"It creates a vicious cycle," Spud says, his plump brow creased. "Division Operations sees that more of our ships are supposedly flight-ready so they assign us more and more missions. More missions mean more hours flown and the more the ships need the service they aren't getting. Flight crews are flown ragged. Pilots get jumpy and nervous—"

"You got that right!" says Pot, now visibly agitated.

"—and the poorly maintained aircraft combine with stressed-out flight crews to become a...crash just looking for a place to burn. This is no way to run an airline, I'll tell you."

Hale yanks open the ancient refrigerator, arcs a beer each to Spud and Charlie, and extracts another for himself. "Spud's right," he says, "It's a time of glassy stares, forgotten details and slowed reactions. Anywhere in the flying business, that's bad news. In the combat flying business, it's fucking suicide."

Hale points with the beer can at the unmade bunk with Van's duffle bags and flight gear heaped on it. "That used to be Arnie Wycovski's bunk 'til he and his crew failed to see a stump in an LZ on a night landing and balled up their ship."

"How bad?" Van asks.

"B.B.R.," Spud says. "It don't get much worse. Burned be—"

"Beyond recognition," Van whispers.

Hale kicks one of his boots which slides across the dusty floor and stops near Van. "Why do you think brigade requires us to lace one of our dog tags into our boots? Hell, feet were all they found left of Arnie. The accident board hasn't issued a determination of cause yet. It happened under fire so they'll probably sweep it under the rug and call it combat loss, but everybody knows Arnie and his crew had flown a hundred-nineteen logged hours in the previous seven days—you figure it out."

"Ain't it funny how them log books just disappeared?" Spud says with an edge.

Though he has tried hard to forget it, Charlie remembers all too well the night Arnie Wycovski died in a flaming crash. The bending aluminum and shattering rotor blades sounded like a dying dinosaur crying out in agony. In another helicopter nearby, Charlie felt the heat of the roiling jet-fuel fire warm his face, he smelled that hideous bar-b-que odor on the wind, and he stared horror-struck at the silhouette of something moving, waving stumps of arm, as it was consumed in the conflagration. Charlie remembers. It was the night he was forced to become God, and he learned how badly he didn't want the job. Charlie shakes his head of the disturbing vision. Yet another replaces it.

"Give you an example!" Charlie says, springing up from his bunk, startling Pot who flinches and stares poisonously at Charlie. "Just yesterday I was flying a low-level reconnaissance mission for division intel."

Charlie yawns, lets it out slowly, and rubs his eyes. "I topped this rise at about three feet above the jungle and a hundred knots, and here's this old dead tree sticking up above the others. I had flown eighteen hours the previous day and I got three-and-a-half hours sleep that night. I was about to flake out right in the cockpit. I saw the dead tree coming and I remember thinking, it'll get outta my way—all the rest of 'em have—and I just watched it coming...and...BA-WHAAM!! Knocked the top right out of the tree and busted the pilot-side chin-bubble!"

Pot, who at the moment of Charlie's loud noise effect is nursing from the inverted bottle of Jack, suddenly chokes, sputters and spills whiskey down his neck. He leaps to his feet coughing, and whirls on Charlie who has his back to Pot and remains immersed in his recollection.

"God-d-damn it, Ch-Charlie!" Pot spits savagely, eyes bulging. "Will you c-cut that shit out!" He breathes heavily through flared nostrils. He sits down on his creaking bunk, seizes the bottle with both hands to steady it and sucks from it again.

Charlie is still reminiscing. "No real damage. But you know I never had a mid-air with a tree before. I was trying to figure if it might be a sign from the Lord."

"Oh yeah!" Pot rages, increasingly drunk, nervous and exercised. He stands to face Charlie again, now panting. "It's a sign alright! He's trying to tell you not to fly through trees, you stupid dick! That ain't no bush-hog you're flying!" Pot glares at a somewhat hurt Charlie and then flops back onto his bunk. "Man! Sky-fucking-King out there mowing the goddamn woods with a Huey. Outta sight, motherfucker."

Van now speaks gently as though to calm Pot. "Ah...well. I can see I've got more to learn than I thought...uh...Pot. I appreciate you guys filling me in."

Pot sneers contemptuously at Van. "Fuck you, newby."

Spud drinks from his beer and belches richly. He

stares out at the darkening dusk. "I'm afraid that ain't the half of it, Van. We're drawing an awful lot of ground fire lately. G-2 thinks Uncle Ho's moving the Ninth NVA Regiment into Two-Corps. Those little fuckers are crack North Vietnamese Army Regulars, Soviet-trained pros with modern equipment; they ain't a bunch of barefoot rice farmers with rusty muskets."

"Not to mention the rats," Charlie adds, grimly.

"And the r-rockets." Pot croaks, as though about to cry.

With an urgent tone to his voice, Hale says, "Van, you may have noticed when you came in before dark that the engineers are tearing down the sandbag blast walls around these hooches because the old burlap sandbags are rotting away. They're going to build new blast walls using plastic sandbags."

"Ain't that the U-S of Army for you?" Spud says incredulously. "They order new blast walls to protect us better, and in the process they leave us for days with no fuckin' blast walls at all."

"Yeah." Charlie says, "And don't think the NVA doesn't know it too. They got spies among the little... um...foreign hooch-maids who come on the post every day to clean the hooches and do laundry. They're gonna hit us any night now, while the blast walls are under construction, you watch."

"Sheeyit," Spud laughs, "Ole Deacon Charlie's got a hard-on for that cute little Sung Tranh, one a the hooch-maids—"

"I most certainly do not!" Charlie doth protest a little too much.

"—and 'cause she ain't no round-eyed, bible belt, Baptist white girl, he thinks his dick is crazy, so he calls the hoochies 'foreign' in their own country. Me, I think Charlie's worried that a little Buddhist gook might not be what ole Reverend and Mrs. Dermott have in mind for a daughter-in-law."

"That's ridiculous!" Charlie huffs. "You don't know what you're talking about!"

"Little slant baby might be a bit awkward at the baptism, huh?" Spud winks at Hale and Van.

"That's not funny, Spud!" Charlie shouts, standing to tower over Spud. He does not see Pot Willows jump at his loud use of the word funny. Pot fixes Charlie with a look of drunken fury.

"Charlie, what did you mean by 'hit us'?" Van questions, watching Pot. Once again Van becomes the pacifier.

"Shell us," Hale replies instead, "With heavy mortars or those awful 240mm, anti-personnel rockets. You have a lot to learn, Van, and it'll come in time. But there are two things you need to know right now before we all sack out. There were huge colonies of rats living in the blast walls. While the engineers have the blast walls down, the rats have moved in with us. Check for them everywhere; your bed, your clothes, your boots, your food, everything. Even the toilet seats in the latrine shack. The rats are everywhere."

"Delightful," Van mutters.

Spud says, "And if you're bitten, the flight surgeon will ground you for three weeks to take the rabies series, and brigade will scream at the major 'cause of reduced pilot availability, and then the major will make life hard on all of us."

Pothead is now quite drunk. "And don' for...get the fuggin' rockets," he groans oddly.

"And that's the second thing," Hale continues. "While we're without blast walls, the danger from rocket and mortar attacks is especially bad. You won't have any trouble telling when we're under attack. It's usually after midnight when they think they can get the best kill ratio of sleeping pilots crowded into flimsy hooches. Our bunker is toward the road two hooches; you passed it coming in."

"I remember."

Spud stands and makes eye-contact. "Listen to me, Van. Artillery will shred these hooches like they were made of paper, trust me. And you don't want to know what a guy looks like who's taken a hit of shrapnel. Makes a chainsaw accident look neat. If we're hit, just grab your vest, your grunt helmet and your weapon, and didimau for the bunker without passing go or collecting two-hundred dollars."

"And dee-what?" Van asks.

"Di-di-mau!" Pot suddenly says, with effort. "Fuckin' new guys. Iss Vetnameese. Means...haul ass, motherfucker."

"Oh. Well. You can certainly count on that."

Charlie extracts a shoe box from atop Old Faithful. "Cookies anyone?" He says, smiling and offering the box to Van. He removes the box top. "My mom made 'em. They're chocolate-chi—"

"Watch it!" Hale shouts.

Pot whirls, bug-eyed.

To his horror, Van sees a slick, black-haired, yellow-toothed rat's head appear from beneath the waxed paper in Charlie's cookie box. The creature springs from the waxed paper onto Charlie's arm. Squalling hysterically, Charlie drops the box and leaps about, whipping the arm violently to dislodge the tenaciously clinging rodent. Everyone else in The Room ducks or dodges, not wishing to be in the trajectory of an eight-inch, aggravated rat when Charlie finally launches it. "Aaaaaah! " Charlie shrieks, whirling and whipping the arm. "Aaaaaaaaaaaah!"

Pot is electrified in spite of his intoxication. His teeth are bared and his eyes bulge. He chokes and spits whiskey, then lurches up and stumbles over Spud's bunk, crashing to the floor between the bunks, breaking the liquor bottle and turning over an ammo-crate bed-stand. An alarm clock clatters to the floor and begins to jingle loudly. In spastic panic, Pot claws his way to his feet and leaps upon his bunk where he sways, feet spread, trying hard to salvage some balance from his soggy brain. He is wide-eyed and gasping. His hands begin to bleed from glass cuts.

Not unlike a voodoo witch doctor, Charlie howls and

hops and cuts a sweeping figure-eight with his assaulted arm, sending the rat arcing into Old Faithful. It bounces and hits the ground running. Charlie loses his balance from the exertion of his final swing and himself crashes into Old Faithful before sliding to the floor. Frantically, he rotates his arm, searching for rat bites.

"Oh Jesus," Charlie gasps when he looks up.

The fallen, cheap alarm clock jingles maniacally.

Pothead, very near a breakdown and still standing precariously on his bunk, has jammed his cocked .45 automatic pistol at Charlie's face; the gun-hand trembles noticeably, and Pot's respiration is heavy and rapid.

The Room is suddenly very quiet, but for the strained breathing of Pot and Charlie and the tedious jingle of the cheap alarm clock.

"Oh Lord," Charlie says.

"CHARLIE!" Pot snarls savagely, heaving for breath between phrases. He shifts his weight from foot to foot, swaying on the sagging mattress. He swallows. "Goddamn it, Charlie! I...warned you about that... YELLING! I cain't take it no more! I CAIN'T TAKE THEM LOUD...NOISES NO MORE, CHARLIE!" Pot now screams, gasping, about to cry, spittle wetting his lips, "I WARNED YOU, GODDAMN IT!"

All eyes are riveted on Pot, directly before you. Veins stand out on the trembling, sweat-glistened hand that grips the pistol, shining in the bluish glare of the ceiling lights.

Spud, to your right, looks for cover but is afraid to move. Van stares in shock. Hale, scared but angry, is the first to recover.

"Put that fucking thing away, Pothead! You're going to get somebody killed with this stupid bu—"

"YOU BET YOUR ASS I AM, PRESTON!" Pot howls hoarsely, waving the weapon in Hale's direction. "Maybe you, motherfucker! I cain't take them loud noises no more! No more! No more!"

Hale's face twitches as he looks up the bore of the

quaking pistol.

"Come on, Pot!" Spud pleads. "It was just a rat, man! You can't—"

"SHUT UP!" Pot roars at Spud, pointing the gun at him now. Spud lifts his arms and waves his hands before his face, and his eyes blink rapidly. "YOU SHUT UP, MAN!" Pot croaks, still gasping.

"Okay!" Spud says quickly, "Okay."

"I'LL KILL YOU!" Pot is crying now; he's heaving and his voice is cracking. "I'LL KILL ALLA YOU MOTHERFUCKERS! I...CAIN'T...TAKE THIS SHIT...NO MORE! NO MORE!" The veins on Pot's forehead pulse like undulating worms.

The persistent jangle of the alarm clock penetrates sounds of heavy breathing.

Van now eases his way around Hale. Cautiously, gently, he speaks. "Please...Pot," he says.

Pot whips the weapon around and sights it at Van. He sways on the sagging bunk. "SHUT UP, NEWBY! I'LL KILL YOU TOO!"

"That thing is cocked!" Hale hisses, hotly. A drop of sweat drips from the tip of his nose.

The alarm clock jangles.

Van does not flinch or blink; he casually extends his left hand, palm up, to Pot.

Pot stares, wide-eyed, breathing hard through clenched teeth. Again, he shifts from foot to foot.

"Please Pot," Van repeats softly and slowly, barely audible over the jangling clock. "We didn't mean to upset you. The noise hurts, doesn't it?" Van studies Pot carefully. With his right hand, Van motions subtly to Spud to silence the clock. Watching Pot nervously, Spud eases to the little alarm clock and shuts off it's tinny alarm tone.

The ensuing silence fairly roars.

"I know...the loud noises hurt," Van continues softly. "Charlie didn't mean to be loud. He just forgot. But he won't forget again, Pot. We'll all try not to make loud noises. Please, Pot. You...you don't need to kill us.

36

We'll be quiet. Please, put your gun away, Pot. Let's talk about it."

Pot's mouth twitches as if trying to smile. There is confusion in his eyes. His nose runs. Slowly he lowers the muzzle of his pistol away from Van's face. "I cain't take this fucking place no more," he whispers, tightly.

"I know," Van says, understanding in his eyes. "I know, Pot. Please, put your gun away and you can tell me about it. You don't need to kill us."

Pot seems to be relieved of an immense load. His gun-hand drops and dangles by his knee. "Talk," Pot almost whimpers.

Spud straightens. Hale takes a deep breath. Charlie closes his eyes and bows his head.

The Room suddenly jumps at a the growl of a deep voice, like a grizzly in a cave, coming from just outside the screen door. "Talk, my achin' soldier's ass!"

The door is thrown back against the outer wall of the hooch with a bang that makes everyone jump. Pot jerks as though shocked; that expression of desperate panic galvanizes his face again; he weaves about on the bunk and stabs the weapon at the doorway with a shaking arm.

Ducking his head slightly, a very large and hard-faced man steps into The Room. He is six-five and two-hundred-seventy pounds. He too wears faded, light-green jungle fatigues, but on him they look like the armor panels on a tank. He removes his green ballcap slowly, surveying carefully through pitiless wolf-eyes. His scalp is shaven and his neck lines descend vertically from beneath his ears to intercept high sloping lines of shoulder muscle angling out and down to the tops of thick arms that strain the rolled-up sleeves of his fatigue-shirt. He has the pitted, scar-marked, bronze face of a Huron war chief.

"Hatchette..." Spud whispers.

"SHUT UP!" Pot cries with venom, still pointing the pistol at the big man. "YOU SHUT UP, HATCHETTE, OR I'LL KILL YOU, MAN!" Pot's voice breaks falsetto on the word kill.

The giant hisses sharply through his nose, as though suddenly amused. He deposits his flight bag and a rifle on his bunk, and walks in no hurry toward Pot's quavering, cocked handgun with an amused but arctic look in his eyes. Spud moves out of his way with dispatch.

"Pothead..." says Chief Warrant Officer Jerome-don't-call-him-that Hatchette, never taking his wolf gaze from Pot's own bulging eyes.

Pot still stands on the bunk thrusting his cocked pistol like the Sword of Gideon. Hatchette positions himself before the quivering weapon so the muzzle is one-half inch from the bridge of his nose, but his eyes look calmly past the maw of the gun at Pothead Willows. Pot's upper lip is drawn back exposing his gum and gritted teeth; he seems to be struggling to breathe.

The gun barrel shakes.

Hatchette speaks softly at first, but his deep, resonant tone is quite audible in The Room. "You little shit. You don't have the balls to kill a man face to face... up-close and bloody. I know it and you know it. But by God I do...and by God I will...in about two seconds... if you don't get that...fucking sidearm out of my face. RIGHT...FUCKING...NOW, TROOP!" The gravelly roar flies in Pot's face.

With Hatchette's first bellowed syllable, Pothead withers, trembling all over. He emits a high wail, throws the weapon to his bunk as though it has suddenly stung him, and he sinks to his knees upon the bunk, weeping wretchedly.

Hatchette looks on in disgust. He picks up the .45 and expels the magazine onto the floor. He racks the slide, ejecting the live round from the barrel. The shiny brass cartridge rolls harmlessly across the dirty concrete. Hatchette, as he has been trained to do in total darkness, deftly field-strips the weapon by feel, all the while gazing calmly around The Room.

Pot weeps wretchedly.

Charlie whispers, "Thank you, Jesus..."

Hale sighs, eyes shut. "Christ, Hatchette. I never thought I'd be glad to see you."

Spud sinks to his bunk, head in hands. "Man. I am too short for this crazy shit. Pot, you stupid dickhead."

Hatchette chuckles mirthlessly. "What a strack bunch of troopers you brats are. Leave you alone for a minute and you go Hollywood on one another." Hatchette flings the disassembled pistol parts at the sniveling Pothead who cries out and covers his head with his arms. The parts clatter about the floor.

Hatchette suddenly steps at Pot who still kneels on his bunk. He seizes Pot by his militarily-too-long hair and yanks his head up to face him. Pot cries out, reaches with open hands to grasp Hatchette's wrist, but freezes when he makes eye contact. His stiffly extended hands quiver.

Van looks on with concern and a certain not-in-Kansas-anymore bewilderment.

"Listen to me, you pissant excuse for a soldier," Hatchette says to Pot in a low, pleasant tone that would still make a pit bull flee yelping. "If you ever...ever... point another weapon at me, you better use it, because if you don't...are you listening to me, troop? If you don't, I will compound-fracture your upper right arm, I will break out the lower half of your humerus, I will jam the jagged end up your nose, and I will rip out your fuckin' face. That is not a threat, troop, it is a promise I have made three times in my life and kept twice."

Pothead is beyond terror. He heaves with racking sobs. Hatchette releases Pot with contempt. Pot collapses weeping. Hatchette moves to his bunk, peeling his sweat-stained shirt from an enormous, muscular back with three odd scars. The other young men in The Room look on in stunned, exhausted silence.

Van strives to break the pall. "Um...there was a rat," he says.

Hatchette's massive head rotates like a turret, and his wolf eyes fix Van. "Who the fuck are you, troop?"

Van strides toward Hatchette with a smile, his hand extended. "I'm Van, uh, Van Savatch. A pleasure to meet you, sir."

Hatchette ignores Van's outstretched hand. "Who?"

"Savatch," Pothead sniffs, his sobs residing. "He's the fucking general's kid, Hatch."

New contempt wrinkles Hatchette's scarred face. "I know who he is. I got a buddy who's a first-sergeant up at division headquarters, told me all about this punk."

Van's gaze drops and he lowers his hand.

Hale is incensed. "Well goddamn, Hatchette, you really know how to make a guy feel welcome don't you, you asshole?"

Hatchette shifts his steel gaze to Hale Preston for a moment, but Hale does not look away.

Hatchette turns back to Van. "Troop, I hear you got a thing about not wanting to kill gooks. I hear you was gonna go conscientious objector, but your old man threatened to cut off your funds for medical school."

Van replies gently, with no defiance or anger. "That's not exactly how it happened..."

"In fact, I hear General Savatch told you he wadn't gonna send you to medical school unless you done right by your family and your country. You told him you wadn't gonna kill no gooks for him or nobody else. Then y'all...com-pro-mised...on you being a medevac pilot for four years, and then he would send you to medical school; that's how I heard it."

"That's close enough," Van says, without rancor.

"Yeah?" Hatchette snaps belligerently, "Yeah? Well you listen to me, troop. I been in this man's army a long damn time, and I seen plenty of you pacifist pussies get your little love beads blowed off. You just stay the hell out of my way. I'm here to kill gooks, and I don't want no marrywana-suckin', tie-dyed, peacenik flower-child cramping my style. You got that, troop?"

Van raises his gaze to Hatchette and smiles very

slightly. "I... I don't want to be a problem to anybody," he says.

"Oh," Hatchette sneers, stepping toward Van, leaning close and staring. "So you don't want to be a problem to anybody, huh? Well that's good, troop, that's real good, 'cause I heard something else about you that could make you a real big problem. I heard you...well, you mighta joined a army fulla men for some other reason than keepin' your old man's money for medical school."

Van stares back, his heart thumping. He is fixed by Hatchette's boiling malevolence.

Hatchette continues. "Yeah. I heard you might be... oh, let's be delicate about it...I heard you might be a asshole-jammin', cock-suckin' faggot!" Hatchette's expression bears the compassion of an alligator.

"Hey, Hatchette!" Hale says angrily.

Pot stares at the ceiling above his bunk through catatonic eyes.

Spud looks at Van with a new wariness.

Charlie stares in shock.

Van's breathing has increased and sweat beads on his upper lip.

The Hatchet Man is unfazed. He tilts his head like a tyrannosaurus-rex examining its next meal. "Well, what about it, Savatch? You join up for the barracks showers? You a rump-ranger, boy? Hanh? You a fudge-packer?" Hatchette's nose wrinkles, and his lips curl back from his teeth. The meanness in his voice sizzles. "Are you a fuckin' dick lickin' queer, Savatch?"

Chapter Four

May 1967

Berkeley, California

In April, 1938, during his plebe year at West Point, Cadet Robert Savatch was devastated by the drowning of his mother in a sailboat accident. In 1945, on Eisenhower's orders that no German historian ever be able to deny the Holocaust, Captain 'Savage Rob' Savatch's infantry company herded hundreds of German civilians through newly liberated Buchenwald, past the hideous mounds of reeking, skeletal Jewish cadavers.

Early in 1953, Lt. Colonel Savatch's best friend since childhood, Major Pete Scally, was critically injured by a North Korean bullet. Also shot, Rob Savatch was holding Major Scally's hand in the ambulance when the vehicle ran over a tank mine. Scally, the ambulance driver and the medic were vivisected. Rob Savatch was hurled thirty yards into thick brush, unable to move. To contain his agony, while listening to the voices of Chinese soldiers probing the wreckage in darkness, he bit an incision in his lower lip. Conversely, at dawn, he struggled unsuccessfully for enough strength to call out to the American search patrol which had finally arrived. Were it not for the tracking dog, he would certainly have been left to die. In his fourth month of hospitalization, Colonel Robert Savatch received his eagles.

In 1965, when his command/control helicopter was shot down, Brigadier General Savatch became the highest ranking American army officer to that date awarded a purple heart for injuries sustained in the 'police action' being conducted against communist insurgents in the obscure Republic of South Vietnam.

Yet, none of these horrific experiences had even slightly prepared Major General Robert V. Savatch, Sr., for the catastrophic shock he was to encounter at Berkeley, California, on a Saturday morning in May of 1967.

As the Air Force Falcon business jet descended into San Francisco on that gorgeous spring day, General Savatch was elated. He had known for months that his new post as commanding officer of the Fourth Infantry Division, at war in the central highlands of South Vietnam, would prohibit his attendance at his son Van's graduation from the University of California in June. It was a circumstance that greatly disappointed the entire Savatch family, even if it was a facet of military life that all were long used to.

So it was with delight that General Savatch received surprise orders to spend a week of May briefing the Joint Chiefs at the Pentagon. If he could not watch young Van receive his pre-med/chemistry diploma in June, at least he had manipulated a fine May weekend in transit to visit him. It wasn't the same thing, but Rob and Van would make the most of it. They were used to that, too.

Rob Savatch's orders had come with only twenty-four hours notice, and he'd only been able to tip off his wife in Washington. Van's phone had been busy or unanswered, so the general's visit would be a surprise, but it would be one Rob was certain his close, only-son Van would be delighted with.

It had been nearly a year since they'd jogged together enjoying their shared sense of humor and the sheer...a word caught briefly. Undoubtedly, love was what the father felt for his son, but he was uncomfortable with the word. Comradeship, the general thought. Yes, they'd enjoyed the comradeship of mutually devoted father and son. This timely if short

43

visit would help offset Van's clear disappointment that his father could not attend his graduation. The general had the keys to a paid-for but undelivered new Mustang convertible in his briefcase to help show Van how proud he was.

Rob had treasured his boy since reading the birth announcement telegram while serving in post-war Germany. It had taken extraordinary effort over the years to compensate for the absences of a professional soldier on the fatherhood of a son, but Rob was proud of the results. All the struggle to find time to write and call and send eight-millimeter home movies, all the sacrifices made to spend as much quality time as humanly possible with Van when Rob was stationed with his family, had paid off.

Van had grown up to be an engaging, accomplished young man so unusually handsome he constantly drew the attentions, discreet and otherwise, of ladies young and not so young. A cognizant, thinking man, the general had worked very hard to avoid the gulfs that military mindsets and long absences often cause between soldier and son. He had striven from year-one to be more than a father, to be a friend with whom his son could feel comfortable, to whom Van would always go promptly with whatever was on his mind. It had taken admirable effort on the general's part, but it had worked. Robert Savatch, senior and junior, were exceptionally close.

Rob had only been mildly disappointed during his son's last year at Fork Union Military Academy when Van had decided he preferred a California pre-med curriculum to West Point. With his academic and his track-and-field records, Van could have secured an appointment to any of the service academies even without a decorated, active-duty, general officer for a father.

Van had consulted his father in depth about his college future as he had in all things. His planning and goals were laudable, and Rob had carefully taught Van to be his own man. Besides, in due time Van could do his duty to his country as an army doctor for at least an honorable four years. Inwardly, Rob had hoped that Van would opt for a military career, but a physician for a son wasn't the worse thing a father could brag about.

Briefly, General Savatch considered changing out of his uniform before leaving the San Francisco airport for Van's apartment near the Berkeley campus. Among so many of today's college kids, there was a disgraceful disdain for the proud profession of military service, a moral sickness which totally baffled and deeply offended the dedicated American warrior. There were even stories about 'hippies' spitting on soldiers in uniform, though General Savatch had never heard of a confirmed instance.

Typically decisive, the general quickly dismissed the notion of changing into 'civvies'. Any spoiled-brat longhair so confused as to spit on a combat veteran of three wars could take their best shot and enjoy the consequences; Major General Rob Savatch was damned if he would let anyone intimidate him into disguising the profession of which he was so profoundly proud.

Van lived in a comfortable second-floor apartment of a Spanish-style quadruplex located in an affluent, tree-shrouded, neighborhood where 'serious' students resided. Rob Savatch parked the rental Plymouth in the street and walked up the open-air, central stairway.

An exquisite violin concerto played loudly on the stereo in Van's apartment. The general couldn't place it—something baroque, Handel maybe—whoever it was, it was damned loud. Well, that was kids in every generation, right? At least it wasn't that awful British rock racket that was the current fad.

Because of the music volume from the other side of the door, Rob wasn't surprised when his knock went unanswered. He knocked once again, louder, but the door didn't open and all he heard from within was the

cascading orchestral accompaniment to the violinist.
The general tried the door, which opened easily. "Bob?"
He called, but inside the living room, the stereo was
even louder. The windows quivered with the vibration
of the thundering brasses in the recorded orchestra.

Never long on patience, Rob Savatch strode down
the hall to the bedroom door which was cracked open
three inches. He was reaching to push it open when he
froze.

On the double bed, covered only from the hips-down
by a sheet, Van Savatch was moving atop a nude young
lady who lay face down, her face concealed by her hair.
She had a smooth back and beautiful, shoulder-length,
blonde tresses.

It didn't take a PhD. in anthropology for General
Savatch to determine what he was inadvertently
witnessing. Son of a gun! He thought with a mixture of
shock and fatherly admiration, that rascal has a girl up
here! Well, that was kids in every generation too, wasn't
it?

The general was about to tear his eyes away, beat
a hasty retreat to the door before the music quit, and
knock real loud this time, when the passionate couple
disengaged. Van rolled onto his back laughing and
pulling the sheet away with him. The smiling girl
propped on her elbow and leaned to kiss Van lovingly.
But not before a clear view of 'her' flat chest, scrotum
and penis hit Major General Robert Savatch, Sr., harder
than any bullet ever had.

Even disciplined, measured men like Rob Savatch
had snapping points, synapse explosions that suddenly
focused into rage. The general would have held his
composure better if he'd just witnessed a murder. In a
very striking sense, he had.

"My God!" The general said involuntarily and with
force.

Van and a young man named Ramsey Willamere
both recoiled in shock and grabbed for the sheet.

General Savatch shoved the door open, breathing

in hard gasps through his nose. The door swung back toward him and he kicked it so hard it crashed back against the wall.

"Dad!" Van gasped, "Good God, what—"

"Oh no," Ramsey Willamere whispered, glancing at Van.

The general did what his instincts commanded when he perceived a threat, he charged. With a look of cold savagery, he crossed the bedroom in three strides and seized Ramsey by the lovely hair that had fooled him so readily. "Get out!" The general shouted, he dragged Ramsey by the hair, nude and stumbling, toward the door. "Get out! Get out, you...you...you filthy little... animal! Get out of this house, this instant!"

Rob Savatch flung Ramsey about like a dog with a kill in its jaws.

"Dad, don't! Stop it! Dad! Dad! No!" Van called, stuffing his feet into jeans.

"Please!" Ramsey cried, grasping the general's wrist in a frantic effort to keep his scalp.

"Get out, goddamn you, you degenerate little faggot! Get out of this house!" General Savatch dragged Ramsey Willamere down the hall and across the living room where he whipped open the front door. The door slammed back against the wall, and the stereo needle leaped across the record with a screech ending in ominous silence. "Get out!" The general roared again, seeming even louder in the sudden absence of the music. He heaved Ramsey out onto the stair landing where the young man fell to his knees and clutched his burning head.

"Dad, stop it!" Van yelled, running down the hall clad only in jeans, carrying Ramsey's clothes and shoes. "Stop it!"

General Savatch didn't hear. "You get the hell out of here!" He bellowed at Ramsey. "You ever come near my son again, and I'll kill you!" He slammed the door viciously.

"Dad, for God's sake, stop it!" Van repeated,

hurrying past the general and opening the door. Rob
Savatch heaved for breath and fought to regain his
composure.

Van pitched the clothing through the door to
Ramsey. "Ramsey, are you hurt?"

"No, Van, I don't think so," Ramsey replied in a
strained voice. "What about you? Will you be alright?
I—"

"Yes! I'll be alright! Don't worry! I'm so sorry! I
didn't know—Go home! I'll call you later! I'll—"

General Savatch kicked the door shut. A framed
picture nearby fell from the wall and shattered its glass.
"Like hell you will!" He shouted. "You listen to me
good, mister! You will never, ever, see or talk to that...
that perverted little vermin ever again! Do you hear
me?"

Van raised a hand to his forehead, breathing hard,
struggling to think. "Dad, please calm down. Ramsey's
not...perverted, for God's sake."

"He is a disgusting animal!"

"He graduated a private high school with honors at
fifteen. He took a degree from Julliard at nineteen! He's
a serious violinist from a good Denver family, Dad. You
don't know what you're talking about!"

"I don't believe this!" General Savatch seethed,
pacing about the living room, hands on hips. "Jeee-sus,
Van how could you? My God. Treatment! That's it.
Therapy. We'll get you psychiatrists, we'll—"

Van sighed and rubbed his eyes. "Ah Dad. It...
homo...sexuality isn't a disease, Dad. You don't get
cured from—"

Rob Savatch whirled about and stabbed an arm and
finger at Van. "You are not a homosexual! Do you hear
me? You are not a homosexual!"

Van's gaze was sad but unbowed. "Yes, I am, Dad.
I'm sorry you had to learn it this way, but you—"

"No! No! Goddamn it, no!" The general shouted,
jumping toward Van and raising a hand as though to
strike him. "No son of mine is a goddamn homo queer!

Do you hear me, boy? You are not a homosexual!"

Van's face quivered from the impulse to flinch or duck, but he stood with his hands down, looking his father squarely in the eyes. He spoke softly. "Yes...I am...Dad. I am so sorry it hurts you, but I am."

Chapter Five
The Room

"Speak up, boy!" Hatchette snarls. "You one a' them little dee-generate fairies? You a fuckin' butt bomber? Hanh?"

Van seems to be struggling for control. An agonizing silence passes in The Room, and then he speaks. "Of course not. No. Absolutely not."

The Hatchet Man stares for interminable seconds, like a condor trying to determine if its prey is at last dead.

"Well, I'm real glad to hear that, troop," Hatchette rumbles, sweat glistening on his scarred, bald skull. "'Cause if there is one thing on this earth I hate worse than a live gook...it's a goddamn sicko, faggot queer." Hatchette extends a huge forefinger and taps Van stoutly in the chest. "And it's a good thing you ain't a homo, 'cause if you were...well...if you were, General Savatch's kid or not, you might take a hike out to the piss tube some night and...never come back, you know?"

Van's glance snaps down at the finger in his chest, then it re-engages Hatchette's bloodless stare.

Hatchette continues. "Maybe you noticed this ain't the University of California Berkeley campus over here, troop. Over here a whole lot of killin' goes on, and folks just don't pay quite the same attention to a dead queer like they might back in the world. In The Nam, troop, everybody carries a gun. Hell, over here, smart-lip lieutenants, even colonels who try to stack body bags to climb the rank ladder, can turn up with bayonets in their backs, or grenades wired to their toilet tanks. One missing queer or two wouldn't rate more than an entry on the daily report." Hatchette taps Van in the breastbone still again. "So. It's a real good thing you ain't a queer, troop. It's a real good thing."

The Room is silent as a tomb.

Hale Preston steps up and locks eyes with Hatchette. "Don't take the Hatchet Man too seriously, Van," he says. "He hasn't been the same since his mother died when her broom crashed."

Spud and Charlie laugh loudly in relief from the tension, but are silenced instantly by a glance from Hatchette.

Hatchette's big head on it's thick brown neck turrets to engage Hale. "Preston," Hatchette says, "My mother was a loveless, trailer-park whore. I didn't even go to her funeral, but some day your mouth is going to throw a pass your smart ass can't catch."

"Besides," Hale says, meeting The Hatchet Man's gaze unconcerned, "Hatchette's getting short; he ships back to the world next month."

Hatchette turns to his bunk and throws his wadded fatigue shirt into an ammo crate in the corner. "That's all you know, Preston. I'm having too much fun killin' gooks, and I ain't about to miss the party in January. Truth is, I'm puttin' in for another tour. I'm sticking around, troops; get used to it."

"That's just precious, Hatch," Spud says. "Somehow I just cain't picture you in the world, anyway. But I can damn sure picture my fat ass back there. Yesterday."

"What party?" Van asks absently, still shaken, as he returns to his unmade bunk.

"Tet." Hatchette snaps. Again his huge head gimbals about and trains its gaze on Van. "It's a gook religious holiday in January, flower-baby. Sort of like Christmas and Thanksgiving and New Year's and Fourth of July all balled into one. Last January the little fucks surprised us. They got high on Buddha and Uncle Ho and opium and attacked us all over the damn Nam. It took us a couple hours to get our heads out of our asses, but when we did, we killed gooks by the thousands. We killed 'em until we had to replace overheated machine-gun barrels, and our arms ached from throwing grenades. I was R-O-N'ing with the Team at Dak Trung Special Forces Camp over in the tri-border area 'cause my hog took a round in the oil cooler that day. Even grounded, we still wasted so many NVA Regulars we could walk across a six-acre field of fire without touching earth for all the bodies. We had to have a bulldozer sling-loaded in to cut hundred-yard trenches for graves. Fucking asshole press made out like the US Army was defeated, but the gooks didn't hold a single acre they took that night, and they paid off a hundred to one in deaths. Hell, I was on the ground and I still killed at least thirty gooks myself. Lost count at twenty-seven. Things were happening too fast and it was hard to see in the dark. Killed two with a bayonet after they broke the perimeter, and I choked one little shit to death with commo wire. Next January I'll be ready, bet your ass. If the weather don't fuck us up, I'll be flying a gunship helicopter that fires eight-thousand rounds a minute—I will steady fill Hanoi up with orphans."

Everyone is staring in chilled discomfort at Hatchette who does not notice.

"Man," Hale says in genuine awe, "You are stark, raving mad."

Hatchette sneers in amusement. He turns to stare at The Room. "What would you hippie punks know about madness? You pussies can't kill rats, let alone people. Shit. You ever seen what ole Luke the gook does to captured American pilots? Maybe you'll get to find out." Hatchette smirks, collects his shave bag and towel, and walks out into the night.

The screen-door spring twangs.

A pall hangs over The Room.

"Well," Charlie says, "On that charming note, I'm hitting the sack. I gotta roll out at oh-four-hundred for a division intel flight."

"Me too," Spud says. "Soon as I brush my teeth and

take a dump. That fucking Hatchette is crazier than a baboon on acid. He scares the shit out of me." Spud grabs his kit bag and goes out the door.

A drunken snore emanates from Pot's bunk. He has passed out on top of it, fully clothed, a clutter of collected pistol parts laying about him.

Hale is still staring after Hatchette in amazement. He moves to his bunk and prepares for bed. "Better sack in, Van. You won't see much sleep for the next year."

"I still have orientations and check rides tomorrow," Van says. "I won't be flying missions for a few days. With the jet lag and all, I'm not very sleepy. Mind if I write a letter by the desk lamp? Will that keep you awake?"

Hale smiles. "Listen, when you fly fifteen-hour days on five hours of sleep a night for months, nothing but the rockets and mortars keeps you awake. Help yourself." Hale strips to his green boxer shorts and peels back his bedding to inspect it for rats. Satisfied that he is bunking alone, he slides beneath a sheet. "See you tomorrow sometime."

Charlie Dermott also checks his bunk and reclines. "G'night, guys," he mumbles. Charlie Dermott is very confused. He instinctively likes Van, but the Bible clearly tells us homosexuality is an abomination. He prefers to think Hatchette is wrong. The Hatchet Man is very scary, and besides, Van looks...normal...he doesn't swish or mince about so he must not...you know...really be...one of them. Homos. Still, Charlie worries and he will not sleep soon.

Van begins to unpack his duffles and stow the uniforms and equipment in his wall and foot lockers. He extracts a framed photograph of a physically blessed, young, blonde woman in a knitted string bikini posing insouciantly against the mast of a small sailboat. "Stay safe, Van— hurry home soon—I love you, Susan!" A bold, handwritten inscription reads. He hangs the photo prominently on a wall nail above the desk.

As Van labors with his gear, Spud returns from the

latrine and spies the photo of Susan. He leans close to examine it. "Aw-right!" he remarks. "Man, she is one sweet pu—, uh, chick! Hell, I knew Hatchette was fulla shit all the time, Van. He's meaner than a badger with a kidney stone." Spud busies himself preparing for bed. He sheds his fatigue shirt, revealing a plump white belly, strips to his regulation green army shorts, and checks his bed for uninvited guests. Then, he kisses his finger tips and pats a wall pinup of a nude girl on her sumptuous fanny. "Man, I'm glad I ain't a fag either. I love pussy too much, and anyway, a queer would get killed around here in a New York minute. Yes sir. Real guys hate fags." Spud slides into his bed and is almost instantly asleep.

Van makes up his bed. Hatchette returns, freshly shaven and shirtless, his bald head and hulking muscles shining with sweat. He eyes Van for a moment, then he slaps the overhead light switch off leaving The Room only dimly lighted by the old desk lamp where Van sits. Van pulls his eyes from Hatchette's massive, developed, fatless body. Hatchette is menace enough already.

Van places a pad of stationery on the rough ammo-crate desk, pulls the battered lamp near, and begins a letter.

There are both goods and bads to your vantage, dwelling as you do unseen in the wall between the trios of lockers. You can smell the stink of stomach acid mixed with whiskey wafting from Pot's snoring, wasted body. You can see the slow, rhythmic rising of the sheets that cover Hale and Spud. You can see, even in the dim light, the wide-open eyes of Charlie, who is now thinking of cute, petite Sung Tranh, and is discreetly stroking the erection he is having.

You hear the distant rotor beat of the flare-patrol helicopter orbiting the perimeter of the sprawling Camp Enari compound. You hear distant machine-gun bursts and through the high, wrap-around, screened window, you see red tracer shots arc out into the black night sky as the oncoming guard-shift tests its weapons in perimeter bunkers. You hear the springs of Hatchette's bunk creak with strain under his immense weight. You also hear a small alarm clock you had not previously noticed, ticking on top of Old Faithful, the refrigerator. You become aware of thousands of crickets in the darkness.

And you see what Van writes.

Dear Susan,

I promised I'd write soon, but I've been in transit practically nonstop since I left you and Ramsey at the airport. Thank you for the lovely photograph - it may already have saved my life, standing in as it does for you in the role of surrogate girlfriend. Remember to perfume your letters to me. I need armor to keep the North Vietnamese army from killing me, and I need a convincing hetero-hoax to keep the American army from killing me. It's going to be a fun war, I can tell.

Somehow, one of the older men I'm rooming with, a huge and incredibly aggressive guy, has found out a twisted version of my agreement with Dad. Worse, he has also heard a vague rumor about Ramsey and me. Although it is not enough yet to move him to violence, he has nonetheless made it very clear to me that the life of a "queer" in "this man's army" is not a good insurance risk.

Please keep this to yourself - Ramsey will absolutely collapse if he knows - he is already ill with concern for me. He was so devastated when I told him I had changed my mind about the run to Canada, or even applying for C.O. status. He thinks I was insane to cover up our relationship to get into the army when scores of hets are pretending to be gay to escape the draft. My departure left Ramsey a wreck. I'm glad I can depend on you to look after him. I'm additionally glad that I have you to talk to - I can see that

*I'm going to need someone I can trust, to whom
I can speak the truth. I trust Ramsey, of course,
but though he is so strong in so many ways, his
incredible love for me renders him dangerously
weak in others. I will have to withhold so much
from Ramsey or he will be miserable with worry.
It will be a long year for all three of us.*

*Please stick tight to Ramsey through
his audition with the National Symphony
Orchestra—I fret terribly that I cannot be with
him at this key time in his career, and that I have
compounded the stress by departing for a war
zone, worse, for the Vietnam war that Ramsey
feels so vehemently is wrong. We all know the
reasons why I came here, but that doesn't make
me feel less guilty where Ramsey is concerned.*

*Tell Andy I send him my best and I expect him
to love you night and day in the manner you so
richly deserve. Good luck to you both in second-
year med school—I hope to be following you
there someday soon. Save all your notes!*

*I'll write again and send you and Andy some
photos when I can.*

Love always,
Van

After addressing and sealing this letter Van begins
another.

Dear Ramsey,
*Finally, I'm settled enough for a brief moment
to write. I miss you already of course and that is
only slightly offset by the wonderful yet ominous
beauty of this incredible land. I have had little
chance to see much of it yet, but what I have
seen has been quite striking. The crystal waters
of the South China Sea at Cam Ranh Bay gave
way to the muddy rice paddies of the coastal
plain. Moving inland, we rose over mountains to*

*the rolling Central Highlands, which eventually
join the phenomenally rugged and steep,
jungle-choked mountains near the borders with
Cambodia and Laos.*

*The mountains go west for as far as one can
see from the air. It is like an unbroken expanse
of lush, deeply-wrinkled, forest-green carpet. It
is enough to make me ever more glad I opted to
become a pilot - I can only imagine what it must
be like for infantrymen humping an eighty-pound
pack in that thick, vertical jungle where the
number one-hundred can at once describe both
the temperature and the humidity.*

*I can't express how much I regret not being
with you as you audition for a chair with the
National Symphony. You are a truly gifted
violinist, Ramsey, my dear love. Have faith in
your talent, for it will see you through. Do not
worry for m—*

Van senses something so alien it instantly fills him
with alarm, though he cannot define it. Then he hears it.
A loud hiss, like escaping steam, growing louder even
in the fraction of a second Van has heard it. His pen
freezes at the end of a short, jagged line on the page.
His eyes lift and his mouth opens.

For a nanosecond, The Room is brightly illuminated
by a brilliant white flash from well outside the
screened windows. Sooner than immediately, the flash
is followed by the most painful noise Van has ever
experienced. It is a blast that stabs the ears and collides
with the sternum like a hard-thrown baseball. The
concrete floor flinches, dust springs from it, and there is
a clatter of falling objects. There follows a crescendo of
dirt and rock raining loudly down upon the sheet-metal
roof of The Room. Outside, men are shouting. Farther
away, another man screams with the shrill, panicked
agony of an injured dog. Footsteps stampede on the
boardwalks outside. Van is immobilized with shock.

"Incoming!" Hale Preston yells, kicking his way out of bed. "Incoming!"

"Shit!" Spud says, almost as if he is about to cry. "We're gettin' hit!"

"Oh dear Jesus!" Charlie Dermott whispers yanking on his boots. "I knew it. I knew it. Oh dear sweet Jesus."

"Run!" Hale screams at Van who is knocked to his senses by the impact of a heavy flak jacket someone has thrown at him. "Get to the bunker, fast!"

The lamp goes out as power to the compound is cut to inhibit target assessment. It is a fearsome, threatening darkness. The eerie howl of a siren rises to a high, steady shriek. In the darkness, Van struggles to don the flak jacket when he hears a nearby wail.

"Aaaaaaaaaaaaahhhh!" Pothead Willows is awake.

There comes another tremendous, fast-closing hiss.

"Down! Downnnn!" Hale shouts. There is a clatter of bodies and equipment hugging the floor.

An arc-light flash illuminates The Room and Van is transfixed by the freeze-frame photo it makes of a standing, open-mouthed, horror-locked Pot, screaming. "Yaaaaaaaaah!"

This blast is closer. The floor recoils, the air is cloudy with dust, the concussion takes away the breath. The noise is like compressed thunder.

"Ruunnn!" Hale, Spud and Charlie sing in unison. The screen door flies back at their exit.

Van gropes in the dark, struggling desperately to contain his fear. His heart pounds so that it restricts his ability to breathe, and makes him feel physically weak, as though sick.

From outside in the darkness, Van hears frantically scrambling footbeats on the boardwalks. Farther away he hears a man's voice screaming, "Medic! Medic! Med—" Abrubtly, in cadence with the arrival of still another white flash and disabling boom, the voice is cut off.

Van moves toward where he saw the door in

the last flash but he runs into a blindly groping and hyperventilating Pothead Willows. Van seizes him by the shirt and propels him ahead out the door. As they exit, Pot breaks free and runs in panicky, stumbling strides headlong for the bunker.

From the dark corner nearest your right, in brief breaks in the commotion, you hear an odd, gutteral whimpering in the darkness.

Outside hootch-44, Van's voice is heard. "Hey! Wait a minute! Where's Hatchette? Anybody seen Hatchette?"

Spud's voice is farther away and is punctuated by the struggle of an overweight man trying to run very fast. "Fuh-fuck Hatchette, man! Run!"

The screen door is thrown back again and Van enters on the rush, sucking hard, deep breaths in an attempt to calm his racing heart, and think. Something is on fire outside and the growing flames offer a ghostly, flickering, orange light broken by darting shadows.

Comes another rocket. Van dives to the floor. In the flash he sees Hatchette's bulk, cowering in the corner at the end of his bunk. The floor flinches and earth and rock spray against the sandbag outer walls of the hooch but do not yet penetrate. When his ears recover from the blast, Van crawls to Hatchette. The big man is on his knees, pressed hard into the corner, covering his head with his arms, and he is gasping audibly.

"Hatchette!" Van croaks against his terror, anxiously pulling on Hatchette's thick, hairy arm. "Come on! The rounds are getting closer; they're getting the range! Come on!" Van pulls at Hatchette.

"Nooo!" Hatchette howls, effortlessly flinging Van backward onto the old Montagnyard rug. "I cain't! I cain't go out there! I cain't!"

Van scurries back to him. "Hatchette, you've got to go! You can not stay here; a close round will tear this place apart!"

A fourth round detonates. The hooch trembles.

"Aaah!" Hatchette cries. Each rapid, guttural

exhalation screams his verging panic. "Ah! Ah! Ah! Ah!"

Van leans over Hatchette and puts his mouth near Hatchette's ear. "Hatch. Listen to me, Hatch. We've got to go. We've got to go now. Come with me. Come with me."

The sixth round. The noise burns like a whiplash and shrapnel chunks tear out the screens and thunk against the walls.

"Aaaaah! Ah! Ah! I cain't do it! I ... cain't go out there! I can't fight them! I can fight any man, but I can't fight artillery!"

"You can't stay here, Hatch!" Van hisses urgently. "You must come with me. Come with me now, Hatch."

Suddenly, a huge hand slaps hard onto Van's arm in the dark corner. The grip is crushing. "Don't leave me! Don't you leave me out there!"

Van grimaces at the pain of Hatchette's clutch. "I won't, Hatch," he says into Hatchette's ear. "I won't leave you. But we cannot stay here! Come on. We are going as soon as the next round hits. Here, here's your vest and your helmet. Get ready."

Hatchette is clawing for a grip on himself. "Don't leave me! Don't you leave me out there!" He turns and clutches Van to him.

Van struggles free but holds a tight grip on Hatchette's big hand. The eighth rocket arrives. Hatchette wails; Van pushes him down to the floor and covers him as much as he can. "Hunh!" he grunts from the concussive explosion. Jagged plank splinters blow about The Room as sizzling shards of shrapnel tear completely through the hooch. Ears ring shrilly. Noises seem far away.

"Now!" Van says. "Let's go now!"

Hatchette heaves himself up, still crushing Van's hand. "Don't leave me! I cain't fight artillery! Don't -"

"I won't, Hatch," Van answers as they squeeze through the door and exit the blastwall passage. "Hurry. I'm with you."

60

"Ah. Ah. Ah. Ah. Dah...don't leave me. Don't..."

Their voices and their footsteps fade rapidly.

The ninth round lands on the opposite side of the hooch. The corner where Hatchette sought refuge is torn away. Burning chunks of lumber rain down where his bunk used to be. The corrugated metal roof is rent back like a pull-top can lid. Hatchette's and Spud's bunks are blown into twisted tubing and flaming mattress shreds which land forty yards away.

Blazing buildings cast an orange glow on the blasted end of The Room. The air is soaked in the thick smell of jet-fuel smoke from burning helicopters on the distant flight line.

Thirty-three rockets impact throughout the pilot's quarters compound before the brutal blasts end. The death song of the siren fades.

Chapter Six
1944

Hatchette

Walking in the cold darkness with his head down, Jerome Hatchette thought there were some really shitty things about being twelve years old in McMinnville, an eastern Tennessee town which most locals pronounced "Mac-man-vul". It was 1944, the war was almost over, the grownups said, and scores of local men who fascinated Jerome were coming home from the service. He admired their uniforms and the cocksure way some of them carried themselves, but he was scared by the crippled ones and puzzled at the oddly quiet ones, and there were several. The men were resuming their jobs, on the farms mostly, but some had hired into the growing nursery industry that had taken hold in Warren County's productive climate and soil. A couple of the men had enrolled in college. Everybody said the GI Bill was a good thing, though Jerome wasn't quite sure why.

Jerome was sure, however, that being the chubby, only-child of a fat, mean cocktail waitress living in a shabby trailer-park down by the river had a number of regrettable drawbacks. One was that he was too close to school for the bus route to carry him yet he was far enough away to get soaked on rainy afternoons and frozen on dark winter mornings, even in the old Navy pea jacket the welfare lady had given him.

Jerome hated when the welfare lady came because Samantha Hatchette would insist Jerome back her up on all the lies about not having a job or a husband. It was true that neither Jerome nor his mother had any idea who or where his father was, but Samantha was gainfully employed at the Main Street Bar and Lounge, in addition to her age-old self-employment.

Jerome could never figure out why they called the loud, stinking pool joint a lounge, but it was damn sure a bar, and Samantha Hatchette damn sure worked there. On the frequent evenings when she "forgot" his lunch money for the next day, Jerome would go to the rear door of the Main Street Bar and Lounge and knock. The door would open to a cloud of blue smoke, a jukebox thundering country music, and a grimy cook in a dirty T-shirt with a cigarette stuck in his face. "Sam!" The cook would call, without speaking to Jerome. "It's yer fuckin' kid again!"

Samantha would weave her way to the door with that bleary look in her painted eyes, her too-tight and too-short skirt showing way too much of her chunky thighs, and her voluminous bosom spilling out of a low-cut blouse. She'd suck on her lipstick-stained cigarette and peer at the fat, ugly anchor that hung around her neck. "Goddamn," Jerome had heard her tell a customer once as she walked back inside, "A girl fucks up one time and bam! She's stuck with some little shit, eating her out of house and home, always wanting money for this, money for that."

"Come here, honey!" Somebody had called, "By God, I'll eat you out an' I won't ast fer a damn dime!" The whole place had roared, including his mother, but Jerome couldn't see anything funny about it.

Walking back to the river in the dark, Jerome didn't think he asked Momma for much. Besides, if he tried to wake her when he left for school in the mornings, she would scream about a headache and throw things at him. He would leave the dirty old trailer, hearing her call him all the names that made it crystal clear Jerome Hatchette wasn't loved by anybody, particularly his own mother. Some mornings he knew not to even knock on her door because a car would be parked outside and the grunting and groaning carried through the flimsy trailer walls.

Then there were the infamous Puckett brothers, sixteen, seventeen and nineteen. Marvin, the oldest and meanest, and Glenn Puckett had dropped out of school in their tenth grades; Ronny Puckett was sure to follow any day. They seemed to be everywhere in Marvin's old Hudson. They always had money and they always had girls and it was a painful mystery to Jerome why they'd be interested in making his young life any more hell than it already was. But somehow the Puckett brothers had adopted pudgy young 'Jee-rome!' Hatchette as their personal project.

It began with Ronny Puckett punching Jerome up regularly before a schoolyard of kids and taking his hard-gained lunch money. The beatings hurt and the kids jeered when Ronny called Samantha Hatchette a whore, but worse, no lunch money meant no lunch, and Jerome was a growing boy. He got no breakfast at all, and what supper he had was canned soup or bread slices or warmed-over hotdogs he fixed himself, if there was anything in the trailer to fix. Many a night, Jerome's only meal of the day was three rolls of Ritz Crackers or a bowl of dry, frosted-sugar-pops. This diet resulted in Jerome being constantly hungry and fat at the same time. There was rarely milk, and often it was too sour to stomach. There was always plenty of cheap beer in the smelly refrigerator, but Jerome hated the taste and found it didn't mix well with frosted-sugar-pops.

In the summer of Jerome's fourteenth year, the Puckett brothers, now all three dropouts and career thieves, noted Jerome riding the old used Sears bicycle the welfare lady had given him. "Hey, Jeee-rooome!" They called, slowing their car to pace Jerome's nervous pedaling up Chancery Street. "Hey fatboy!" Ronny called, his arm and face out the passenger window. "You better stop that piece a shit! We want to talk to you!" Jerome kept pedaling.

"Hey, you little fuck!" Marvin's deeper voice roared from behind the wheel. He glared at Jerome furiously

between glances at the road. Jerome was pedaling
as fast as his beefy legs would move the rattling old
bicycle. He was across Main now, and it was a steep
coast to the river, half a mile away. Jerome considered
that merely making it to the ratty old trailer probably
wouldn't save him from the Pucketts, but he didn't
know where else to go.

Jerome was doing about twenty-five miles-per-
hour, which felt like the speed of light on the bike,
when Marvin Puckett lost what little patience he had
and steered the Hudson coupe onto the sidewalk,
sideswiping the speeding bicycle. Jerome was still
cartwheeling when he was snagged to a ripping halt by
a rusty barbed-wire fence. He lay hung in the fence,
bleeding, for ten minutes before a Tennessee Highway
Patrolman happened along. Jerome arrived at the
Warren County Clinic looking like the loser in an axe
fight.

Samantha Hatchette was furious. Goddamn if she
was gonna stay home all day looking after a kid with
sixty-eight stitches in his face and arms! He was a ugly
little fat shit to start with; now look at him! Hell, she
wadn't no goddamn nursemaid! This was it! She'd had
it with Jerome and all the trouble he caused. God knows
she'd tried to be a good mother, but the little shit was
always causing some kinda problem, and now this!
Hospital bills! Ambulance bills! Doctor bills! Enough
was enough, by God.

This was it. Jerome could go live with Samantha's
sister, Lucille Womack, in Van Buren County. Hell,
that little bitch had four kids and a clod-kicking farmer
husband. One more mouth to feed wouldn't make no
difference and besides, Jerome was getting bigger;
when he got the stitches pulled he could work out
his keep. Samantha would lie to the welfare lady as
long as she could get away with it, then she'd just do
without the child-dependent money somehow. Least she
wouldn't have to feed Jerome, who lately had begun to
eat like a logging crew.

65

Three very significant things happened to Jerome
Hatchette over the next four-and-a-half years. One was
that Lucille Womack fed Jerome all the fresh, well-
prepared, farm food he could eat, which was a lot.
Another was that Homer Womack worked Jerome hard,
if fairly, along with his own sons and daughter. And
the third was that Mother Nature paid young Jerome
a visit and left him a trainload of hormones. By his
seventeenth birthday, Jerome was six-feet, four-inches
tall, weighed 245 fat-free pounds and was still growing.
He could lift a tractor engine, throw hay bales from the
ground to the loft of Homer Womack's barn for hours,
and pull a young bull right off its feet for castration.
Last but not least, he could finally out-box Homer
Womack, who in his day had been the Seventh Fleet
Golden Gloves middleweight champion for six years. It
was also useful that Homer had been an industrial-grade
Atlanta street fighter before he'd gone into the Navy.

The Womack kids had reacted predictably to the
ragged, dot-lined, pink scars on Jerome's face when
he had come to live with them, but over the years the
pinkness gave way to less-ghastly white lines. Most
everyone in the remote mountain community got used
to it; anyway, would you tell a grizzly bear you didn't
like his face?

The Van Buren County High School football and
basketball coach begged the enormous Jerome to show
some interest in sports, but Jerome had farm work to
do after school. Besides, he got plenty of sport out of
boxing Homer and his sons, sometimes at once.

On the Saturday after he turned seventeen, Jerome
asked Homer if he could borrow the old farm truck.
Homer looked up at Jerome and squinted. "So it's
time?" he asked.

Jerome nodded. "Yes sir."

"You sure you got to?"

"Yes sir. I done thought a lot about what you said
about the world being full of fools and all, but it's a
debt I owe and I feel I oughta pay it, you know?"

Homer Womack studied the huge boy. "Yeah. I reckon I had to pay a few of my own."

Jerome took the truck keys and turned.

"Hey." Homer said. Jerome faced him again.

"Remember. Big ain't always enough. Outside the ring, they ain't no rules, boy. On the street, they ain't no fair fights, just the ones you beat or git beat. The only thing you rule out is losin'. Savvy?"

It was predictable enough that the Puckett brothers would be boozing it up at the Main Street Bar and Lounge in McMinnville on a cold December Saturday night. A pathetic little decorated Christmas tree in the front window bay couldn't compete with the flashing neon beer signs, the clouds of blue smoke, and the booming country music. There weren't many devout Christians in the Main Street Bar and Lounge to lament the little tree anyway.

Samantha Hatchette had been refueling Marvin, Glenn and Ronnie Puckett and six of their deer-hunting buddies for two hours. Samantha thought they were disgusting, all dressed in hunting clothes and boots, smelling like deer spoor and telling the same goddamn stories over and over about their stupid fucking deer kills. But they kept tucking bills between her tits and as long as they did she'd bring 'em their beer and pretzels and smokes and let 'em pat her on the ass. The stupid fucks.

Samantha just hoped they didn't get drunk enough to start no trouble with the nigger in the corner booth. Hell, niggers was everwhere these days. Like that goddamn recruiting sergeant in the corner. It's like 'cause he fought in goddamn Saipan or someplace and got that chest full a ribbons he can walk into any place a white man can. Shit, they act like they was real people or somethin', goddamn.

Still, the nigger sergeant only came in on the Saturday night of the one weekend a month he visited the McMinnville post office to do his recruiting thing. Initially, the boys had bitched to crusty old Leon

Cantrell, the "lounge" owner, about lettin' niggers in the place. Leon, a U.S. Marine veteran of Belleau Wood, promptly told the boys that no niggers but the sarge ever tried to come in the place, and besides, the sarge had fought for his country in dubya-dubya-two, which was a damn sight more than the Puckett boys had. Moreover, the nigger minded his own business, drank quietly and tipped well, and by God when the boys bought the goddamned bar they could kick him out. In the meantime, Leon had concluded, if they didn't like his choice of customers they could line up and kiss his bony ass. This innovative customer relations ploy pretty much put a cap on the matter.

Samantha had to admit the nigger was nicer to her than them shithead Puckett boys and their crowd with their stink, their stupid pussy talk and their free-roaming hands. Samantha had been afraid the nigger would cause a fight when he first started coming in. But because he didn't come often, and he wore the paratrooper's uniform of his nation's army, and sat to himself when he did come in, the boys mumbled and snickered but left him alone. Samantha also knew enough about men to understand the respectful but searing look of one who didn't scare easily. Some niggers could fight, she knew. This, as much as anything, was probably why even "Big Marv" Puckett might make the occasional snide remark when well accompanied, but otherwise he let the nigger sergeant drink in peace.

Speaking of big, Samantha noticed the white man just entering, mostly because he was the size of a house, but, especially in the sleazy lighting, she didn't recognize him. Probably just another hunter in for the opening of deer season. Then she dropped the tray of beer bottles she'd been carrying and shrieked, getting the attention of everyone in the place. "Oh my God! Jerome!"

Marv Puckett was also a man who didn't scare easily, but neither was he a fool. When he turned from the pool table to see the Hatchette kid for the first time since running him into a barbed-wire fence four years earlier, right away he sensed an alarming potential for rudeness.

"Ho-lee shit," Glenn Puckett whispered.

"Shut up," Marvin snapped, fingering the pool stick in his hands. "Get behind him, quick. When I get his attention, bust him with your stick, and I mean bust him hard an' keep bustin' til I tell you to stop. Ronny git your ass out to the car and bring my gun. Move!"

No rules, Homer Womack had said, and Jerome Hatchette had listened.

Ronny Puckett almost made it to the door before a heavy oaken poker chair, whirled from twelve feet away, decked him like a charging bull, and the party was on.

Samantha screamed and ran for the phone.

Glenn Puckett quickly computed the estimated strength rating required to hurl a thirty-pound oak armchair like it was an empty milk-carton, and he decided that if Big Marv wanted the mutated version of the Hatchette kid busted, he could bust him himself. He said "Jeeesus Christ!" and ran for the front door with less than no concern for the recumbent and motionless Ronny. To Glenn's considerable dismay, the big, scar-faced kid was much faster than he looked. Glenn screamed like Samantha Hatchette just before he descended from an altitude of about eight feet and slammed face-down onto the bar, sustaining a flattened nose, a shattered jaw and several lacerations from crushed beer bottles.

Marvin Puckett was impressed. He bolted for the kitchen door but was perturbed to find it blocked by a nigger sergeant with a pleasant smile on his face.

"Git outa my way, nigger!" Marvin swore, and he swung hard without breaking stride.

Staff-Sergeant Alfonse Beaumont broke Marvin's stride. He dodged the punch, spun Marvin about and shoved him careening back toward the center of the room.

Jerome Hatchette delivered a monumental challenge to dental science with the fist that caught Marvin Puckett on the rebound. Marvin went down like a lassoed rodeo calf when the slack twangs out of the rope. Both Marvin and Glenn would come to know the delights of sucking baby food through wired teeth for many months.

With several adolescent years of rage squirting out of every seam, Jerome pounded Marvin to puree. Then he drew and opened a large folding knife and raised it over Marvin who now lay moaning on the floor. It was Jerome's intent to fix Marvin so he too could experience the unique thrill of seeing girls wince when they looked at his face.

When he knelt and drew the knife back for the first slash it exploded from his hand, and he twisted to see the army sergeant holding a two-fisted grip on a pool stick. "Anh-aaanh!" The sergeant said. "Tha's enough, boy! You cut him or kill him an' the laws'll come for you!" Staff Sergeant Beaumont's eyes were white piano keys set deep in a black face. The eyes searched the room, but saw no one terribly interested in challenging the monster kid who'd put all three Puckett brothers in la-la land, let alone the mean nigger soldier who'd just hit him with a stick!

"Ole Sarn't Al, he got some plans for you big white ass, boy, an' jail will fuck 'em all up. Tha's enough. Come on now, le's git you outa here fo' the Man show up. Come on, son. Now!"

Jerome went. Two weeks later, Samantha Hatchette was thrilled to sign an underage waiver for Jerome to enlist in the United States Army. Jerome never saw his mother again.

Even at eighteen, Corporal Jerome Hatchette knew a snafu when he saw one, and he was seeing one. Supported by scathing Chinese artillery, the North

Koreans were crawling up the devastated slope like a
million ants with guns. Ammunition was dwindling
fast, Hatchette's fellow paratroopers were being blasted
to hell by the shells, and that was only the good news.
The reinforcements promised by brigade had failed to
arrive, and the hot, jagged shrapnel that had bisected
the radioman had passed through the radio enroute.

Hatchette fired another clip, trying hard to aim
as he had been trained, but the Chinese artillery was
devastating. The noise was indescribably painful,
like ice-picks jabbed into the ears, like being inside a
covered steel garbage-can furiously beaten outside with
ball bats. Each round would be preceded by the split-
second sound of an arriving jet, and then the detonation
noise would impact like a train and roar away like one.
The blast waves from the shells swept over him like hot
wind, causing his body to feel as though it were ripped
through a hole several inches smaller in diameter than
the body itself. The giant, scalding shards of twisted
shell-casing blew away dirt, bunkers and men like a
shotgun blast hitting a watermelon.

The bolt on Hatchette's M-1 Garand rifle locked
open on the last round and ejected the spent clip with a
ping barely audible over the crescendo of explosions.
He frantically dug in the pockets of his fatigue jacket,
located a loaded clip and stuffed it into the weapon,
being careful not to let the heavily sprung bolt slam
shut on his thumb. He'd only felt three more clips in the
pocket.

Hatchette was struck by a funny thought. Here he
was taking care not to mash his thumb in a rifle bolt
while scores of heavy artillery rounds were blasting his
world apart and hundreds of grim little men with rifles
and quilted uniforms were coming to shoot him. The
fact that he saw anything as funny at the moment gave
Corporal Hatchette cause to question his sanity, and that
was most frightening of all.

He could not fight artillery. At least Hatchette
could see, assault and kill the determined, chunky

little soldiers clawing their way up the smoky hillside jagged with splintered tree fragments. He could fight the soldiers, and Jerome Hatchette was not afraid of a fight. But the relentless, pervasively-painful artillery bombardment was a faceless hell raining from the sky. You couldn't shoot it, stab it or beat it with your fists. You couldn't even run from it because it was everywhere.

Each shell ripping in was, for Jerome, a death sentence followed by a momentary reprieve, only to be immediately followed by a renewed death sentence. And it was so cruelly random. Artillery cared not a damn for your skill, your strength or your bravery, only your luck. The true horror was repeatedly facing the question of whether this one was the one that would kill or maim you. Terror, foom, relief. Terror, choom, relief. Terror, boom, relief. Terror ... God, the noise. The earth jerked and generated a dust-fog three feet deep. Sod and rock and tree stumps poured down.

"Airborne!" The boys had fiercely yelled when the shooting began at dawn. Later they shouted angry commands; still later they screamed "Incoming! Incoming!" And most recently the only human sounds discernable in the death-thunder had been wails of agony and the moans of the dying. Now they too were silent.

A round hit so close it hurled Hatchette and several cubic yards of dirt and rock twenty feet. The concussion voided his lungs of air. Somehow he held onto his rifle, but there was nothing left to shoot out of it.

When Corporal Jerome Hatchette stood swaying on trembling legs, and slid his bayonet onto the stud at the tip of his rifle, he had ceased to notice or care that all he could hear with his bleeding ears was a shrill ringing. Dimly he could discern a score of the scowling little men with rifles closing on him, and he was barely aware of a North Korean officer snarling urgent commands. Later, he would realize the officer had ordered the mammoth American be taken alive for interrogation.

Later still, he would learn he was the only survivor of
Hill-3325.

It took the concerted efforts of eight hardy PDRK
soldiers to subdue Jerome. In the process, Jerome
succeeded in seizing two by their throats, one in each
hand. As the soldiers were under strict orders not to kill
the crazed, giant American paratrooper, several minutes
were necessary to bludgeon him into unconsciousness.
By then, both the bug-eyed men in his grips were
deader than Hiroshima flowers.

Jerome had been briefed that he should give only his
name, rank and serial number when interrogated. It was
a matter of honor, allegiance to his fellow soldiers, and
military law punishable by court martial. The Geneva
Convention forbade torture.

Regrettably, the North Koreans thoroughly
understood Homer Womack's admonition on the day
Jerome asked for the truck. The only thing you rule
out is losing. They were defending their homeland
from huge, smelly foreigners. The Koreans had seen
Japanese occupation forces press hundreds of Korean
mothers and sisters into service as troop whores—no,
even whores got paid—and the PDRK soldiers were
motivated.

Most torture was administered with excruciating
pain and diabolical mental anguish, but only as
necessary to gain vital information from resistant
prisoners about the enemy and his plans. For the most
part, it was rendered impersonally; it was a necessity
of war, and in war, especially war in your own land,
you did whatever you had to to prevail. Still, as in all
races and all armies, there were a few North Koreans
who tortured for fun. The huge, brave, incredibly
strong American paratrooper fascinated these men, and
challenged their talents.

Beating the big American soldier proved futile.
The most entertaining methods of platoon-level North

Korean interrogation, involving telephone-generator
shock and brass artillery-shell casings heated by
campfires, were not successful. Even the usually
reliable saturated-towel-over-the-face techniques
proved no match for the crazy American. Interrogators
became convinced the insane giant would drown
before giving up information, and if he died they would
probably be shot for incompetence. All they extracted
from him were endless, glassy-eyed stares of hate. It
was discouraging. Experts were needed.

Major Soo Jung Bai and his aide, Lieutenant Kwon,
were ordered down from division.

Along with the delicate Lieutenant Kwon who
traveled everywhere with him, Major Soo brought a
reputation for unfailingly successful interrogation.
He was known to be a genius at finding the breaking
points in all men without killing valuable intelligence
resources before they were spent.

Major Soo and Lieutenant Kwon listened patiently
to the reports of the oafish amateurs who had miserably
failed to get as much as the big American's name,
and the two officers smiled at each other. They knew
there were two basic realms of torture: That based
on physical agony, and that based on mental anguish.
Clearly these peasants were failing to see that brutality
was the wrong technique for this colossal savage.

As Major Soo studied the interesting scar-faced
American, he was concerned with the signs he saw. The
giant boy merely gazed back at Soo, never wavering,
always looking directly into his eyes with calm, if deep,
contempt. Obviously the American was too strong
to have even passed through the begging/pleading
stage. Yet neither did he bluster or threaten or brag
or dare, or do any of the theatrics with which scared
men, even brave scared men, defended themselves. He
merely observed his captors with cold, unemotional
malevolence. This was the mark of a man who,
probably because of a difficult home-life as a child,
was not afraid of pain or death. Soo had seen such

men before, rarely, and they were very difficult. Still, Soo reflected, every man and woman, all of them, had a breaking point. Successful interrogation was about finding it. His was a mind game, not a matter of mere muscle or instruments.

Major Soo was lost in these contemplations when the Americans opened up with another of their damnable heavy artillery barrages. Soo knew that, this deep in an underground command bunker, nothing less than a lucky direct hit was likely to threaten him, but the noise was deafening and the bunker filled with dust from the shuddering earth. Though it frightened Lieutenant Kwon, it was only annoying to Soo until he glanced again at the shackled American in the corner.

The heretofore defiant American paratrooper was now curled in a fetal ball, covering his ears, shivering and moaning. Fluency in English was a requisite of Soo's specialty, and he understood the broken man's whimpers. The noise. He could not fight the noise, the man repeated over and over. He could not fight the noise.

Soo smiled. Eureka, as Aristotle had said.

Immediately Soo ordered the bound American dragged up the tunnel to the surface, much to the consternation of the infantry commander and his men who had seen what American 155mm howitzers could do, but Major Soo was insistent and he ranked. Soo ordered the American dragged into the open, above ground. Insanity! Captain Hyoun shouted over the din. The American's are coming in battalion strength! They're prepping the area with heavy artillery! Assault would follow! It was almost time to pull back!

Indeed, the artillery rounds were crashing in ever closer; Soo knew the Americans were getting the range. Astonishingly, though, the soldiers watched Soo lie near the huddled, trembling American, pull his arms away from his head, and whisper into the huge enemy soldier's ear.

Captain Hyoun recoiled from the blast of another

close round, and he saw two large trees topple a
hundred meters away. He watched the lunatic Major
continue to whisper in the quaking American's ear, then
Soo turned to Hyoun and shouted to have the prisoner
dragged back into the bunker. The American was
talking.

Underground, in the blast-dusted bunker, Captain
Hyoun repeated the urgent need for withdrawal to
Major Soo while Soo questioned Corporal Jerome
Hatchette and made notes of his answers. Lieutenant
Kwon cowered in a corner, much to Hyoun's disgust.

Major Soo ordered Captain Hyoun's men to tie the
American face-down over a table, securing his wrists
and ankles to widely separated tent stakes driven
in the hard earthen floor of the bunker. Hyoun had
no idea what the Major planned but he knew Soo's
reputation as a master of interrogation horror. When
Hyoun's men had bound the American according to
Soo's instructions, Soo ordered the Captain to begin his
pull-out. Soo advised that he and Kwon would follow
shortly, after killing the American. Hyoun could only
speculate on how Soo planned for the American to die,
but he had a retreat to organize, so he left promptly,
vacating the bunker to Soo, Kwon and the awkwardly-
bound Yankee-dog corporal.

As soon as the infantrymen fled, Soo withdrew his
bayonet and inserted the blade downward beneath the
belt at the small of Jerome's back, and he cut Jerome's
fatigue trousers and shorts to the crotch, exposing the
unusually large parts of the American about which he
had fantasized throughout the interrogation.

Harshly, Soo commanded the terrified Lieutenant
Kwon to hold his equipment belt while Soo dropped his
own pants and centered himself between the American's
enormous hairy thighs. Kwon looked on, his fear
turning to perverse fascination.

Jerome Hatchette's first sexual experience was
certainly not poignant, but it was not especially painful,
physically. Jerome had undergone a rectal examination

during his military physical, and while the rape hurt worse, it was nothing compared to the hot shell casings held to his nipples earlier. But Jerome felt an overwhelming and unnerving sense of shame, though he was unable to reason why. Though he could not have articulated it, what pained Jerome most was the statement of human insignificance the arrogant North Korean officer was making about him. Jerome became enraged that anyone could so demean another human being as to use him involuntarily and painfully for no more noble or vital a cause then base pleasure.

Major Soo was having difficulty completing his base pleasure. The nearing American artillery blasts were breaking his mood, in spite of his erotic concentration. Frustrated, he withdrew and turned to his reliable stand-by. Obedient as always, Lieutenant Kwon dropped to his knees and began to fulfill his principal purpose in the life of Major Soo Jung Bai.

Absorbed in his rising ecstacy, Soo neglected to notice the tent stakes securing the American being whipped back and forth in ever-loosening holes.

Kwon's eyes were open, so he saw it first. He pulled back and screamed.

Soo had known little fear in his life, but what he saw upon turning galvanized him into a pillar of salt.

It had been a real bad day for Corporal Jerome Hatchette and he was in a fussy mood. He seized Major Soo by the upper arm and yanked him so hard the humerus broke just beneath the shoulder and the jagged upper end protruded through the flesh. Jerome seized the bone tip, wrenched it down and tore it out from the elbow, leaving Soo to briefly consider a little pain and horror of his own.

Kwon recovered and scrambled to pull Soo's pistol from the equipment belt, but his young life was already history. The monster American kicked the pistol from his grip and fatally brain-damaged him with a single punch by a fist nearly as wide as Kwon's head.

Soo recovered enough to know what was happening.

He gaped at his limp, flopping arm, then at the jagged-tipped, bloody bone in the hideous American's fist. Queerly, Soo thought of the Christian biblical legend about their god removing a rib from the first man to make the first woman. It was not much comfort.

Jerome intended to drive the broken arm bone up under the Korean officer's chin, but his aim was a little off from the day's aggravations, and the splintered bone ripped beneath the Korean's upper lip and lodged behind his nose. Hatchette's frustrated jerk pulled most of Soo's nose and upper lip from the front of his skull.

Major Soo Jung Bai died never knowing that the information he had at last extracted from Jerome was false to the word, and was fabricated to have led whoever heeded it straight into American mine fields.

When American troops overran the position and invaded the bunker, they found a North Korean Lieutenant dead in the corner from obvious blunt trauma. But they were puzzled by the Major with his pants around his ankles, his face ripped out, and with a seven-inch section of what was evidently his own arm-bone protruding from his chest. Jesus, war was hell, but this was getting a little carried away.

Earlier they had discovered a brutalized, dazed, American paratroop corporal wandering through the shell craters, mumbling about not being able to fight the noise. Big, scar-faced guy. Real big. Maybe he had something to do with this.

Chapter Seven
The Room

Dear Ramsey,

The weeks go by so slowly in this tense and hostile land. Lunacy is the order of the day.

Christmas is upon us. It is "the season of love", Chaplain Perry tells an audience of grunts fresh in from a mission to burn Viet Cong villagers out of their homes, crops and livestock. Armed Forces Radio is playing Joy To The World between announcements of the latest body counts. I flew four bodies into graves registration at the army hospital in Pleiku last night, and some guy dressed in a Santa suit came out of the hospital and said, "Ho, ho, ho! Merry Christmas!" Then he tossed some candy-canes onto the blood-slick floor of the aircraft. He was still ho-ho'ing when he walked back into the hospital. I tell you true, Ramsey, this place gives a whole new meaning to the term insanity.

The reminders of Christmas cause me to miss you all the more. The carols evoke vivid memories of last Christmas when we were at Vail with Steven and Carl and Susan and Andy, before we all split to go home for the holidays. We stood in the crisp, cold air on the balcony of our cabin after dark and watched the skiers descend the slopes, carrying colored lanterns while Silent Night played. There was so much warmth that night, so much love. How brutally it contrasts with this place and this time. I'm here fighting, in the broader sense, in the name of freedom, yet

*I'm not free to hang your pictures on my wall
lest someone kill me for loving you. If they were
censoring letters like they did in World War II, I
couldn't even write that I love you or they'd throw
me out of the Army, if I lived long enough. Why?
Who is hurt by our love? How does anyone gain
by hating us?*

*There I go again, expecting life to make sense.
How wretchedly silly of me.*

*It is evening. The sun is setting beyond the
Ia Drang mountains way to the west, toward
Cambodia. The crimson sunset is beautiful,
but, mercifully, the darkness left in its stead
obscures the ugly scars gouged in the thick
jungle mountainsides by "Arc-Light Strikes", the
incredibly violent and destructive B-52 bombing
raids on the NVA base camps known to be dug
into those mountains.*

*Our awful problem with the rats has only
gotten worse, if that was possible. Colonel
Matlock has at last gotten onto the issue since
enough of the pilots in the aviation brigade are
out on sick leave taking the rabies series that
reduced mission availability is beginning to make
him look bad. He has announced an award of a
three-day-pass to Cam Ranh Bay for the officer
who invents the best rat trap. It's a morale thing,
see. Supposedly, they are going to have the
Chemical Corps come in soon to really fix our
rat problem. That should be some fix; the hideous
creatures are everywhere.*

*I garnered a day off today only because my
ship is down for maintenance. I thought I'd
be here months before they gave me my own
aircraft and crew, but I'm an "AC", an aircraft
commander, already. I like the independence,
but the responsibility for commanding a hugely-
expensive machine with a crew of four in a war
zone is scary sometimes. No, it's scary all the*

*time. Anyway, having a day off seems almost
decadent after back-to-back, seven-day weeks of
twelve and fifteen-hour flying days. It's great!*

*Ramsey, I cannot express how thrilled I am
that you made the National Symphony! I wanted
to shout it from the rooftops when I got your
letter and I would have, except someone would no
doubt have thrown me off the rooftops for doing
so. How proud of you I am! I can't wait to get
home and see you perform.*

*It's dinner-time soon, and I want to dash off
a note to Susan before I eat, so I'll close for
now. Congratulations again, my love. I miss you
terribly. Merry Christmas!*

> *I love you, always,*
> *your Van*

Dear Susan,

*Thank you immensely for the wonderfully sexy
photos for my wall—they have had the desired
effect many times over—all the guys are jealous,
which is hysterical, given what they don't know.
Please tell Andy I thank him dearly for taking
such fabulous pictures and for allowing me to use
you so effectively as my "girl back home".*

*I'm off today while they put a new tail-rotor
gearbox in my aircraft, which is the only reason
I have this long-overdue opportunity to write.
Yesterday was a typical day, if there is such a
thing in this crazy place. We were in the air before
dawn and did not return to base until after dark.
We logged eleven hours picking up medevacs—we
call them "dust-offs"—from the bush, and moving
patients to and from various hospitals. When we
landed it took us a half-hour to debrief, and it
took the crew twice as long to clean the mud and
the blood from the aircraft, service it and secure*

81

it for the night.

Strange. When I first got here and listened to the screams of the wounded as we flew them in, it made my skin crawl; I felt their agony. Yet, now those same screams are music to my ears, for I have learned that the ones with the strength to scream will almost always live. It is they who lay back there silently, with vacant stares, that I now worry for.

They have made me an aircraft commander already, weeks before I expected it. Not for Ramsey's ears of course, but it seems the attrition rate for helicopter pilots is growing faster than expected. Certainly our lifestyle, with dry rooms to sleep in and regular hot food to eat, is preferable to the that of the valiant, long-suffering grunts in the field, but it is not without its hazards. I was shot down a few days ago. We had just lifted off from a firebase, with two wounded grunts aboard, when we took several hits from AK-47's (the Soviet or Chinese manufactured, automatic assault rifles that the NVA are equipped with; Andy, your southern, gun-raised lover, will know what they are—ask him). One of the rounds came through the aluminum cockpit floor and splattered against the ceramic-armored bottom of my seat. I took some lead fragments in the backs of my legs but, considering where the bullet was headed, I'll settle for a few painful stings in my calves. Another round hit us in the N1-turbine section of our engine and it exploded. Luckily, there was an elephant-grass meadow within range and we autorotated (what passes for gliding, in a helicopter) successfully. We had not flown far enough from those who shot us down, however, and soon my co-pilot, crew chief, gunner and I were taking heavy fire from a tree line bordering the field. Downed helicopters are highly prized for the weapons and code books

*we carry. Further, the enemy reserves a special
hatred for helicopter crews for reasons that will
soon become apparent. Happily for us, a gunship
flown by two of my roommates, Pot and Hatch,
was responding to our mayday call, and they
were positively thrilled with the opportunity to
annihilate our attackers for us. It was a target
the gunship pilot mentality dreams of. Just as the
NVA were in the open, charging us from the tree
line, the gunships came from low over the hill and
hosed the enemy soldiers with thousands of slugs
from their six-barreled, rotating machine guns,
air-to-ground rockets and grenade launchers.
Eight decimated enemy bodies were recovered
and there was evidence that more were dragged
away. It was grim, but better them than us. (An
uncharacteristically glib response to the deaths
of a dozen or more human beings? I worry the
same thing —I'm disturbed to find that war does
some strange and frightening things to the mind.)
An Air Cavalry "reaction platoon" was air-
lifted in to pursue the surviving attackers, and
we were taken out by the ships that brought them
in. Two of those aircraft were piloted by more of
my "hoochmates" I've told you about in earlier
letters, Hale and Spud. Then one of the huge, CH-
54, "Flying Crane", heavy-lift helicopters sling-
loaded our crippled aircraft back to base.*

*The guys will be in soon before we go
to dinner, and I have to prepare some little
Christmas presents I bought for them, so I must
go. Merry Christmas, my dear friend, and the
same to Andy. Thanks again for the pictures!*

Love,
Van

Chapter Eight
The Room

Hooch-22, Camp Enari, Pleiku, Republic of South Vietnam, is in no danger of a white Christmas. The nights are somewhat more comfortable, but the days remain hot and humid. Rain has poured like Niagara Falls on the metal roof for several days, leaving the ground outside a slippery, muddy morass, but at the moment the rain has ceased. The air smells damp and feels clammy to you, and it bears a faint, fetid odor like a laundry hamper left unattended too long.

A tiny, scraggly, but richly decorated artificial Christmas tree atop Old Faithful, the refrigerator, makes a valiant if futile effort at instilling The Room with suitable yuletide spirit; it is aided slightly by a string of colored lights, sent by The Reverend and Mrs. Lester Dermott, which hang across the ceiling. Not perhaps so contributive to the holiday scene are Pot's bird-throwing acid rocker, Spud's gynecologically explicit posters and Hatch's macabre photo memento from his former Special Forces buddies, its glass cracked from the last rocket damage. The Room smells of fresh-cut lumber from recent shelling-damage repairs.

Van is hastily wrapping the last of several shoe-box sized Christmas presents. As he has done with the previous four, he carefully folds the colorful wrapping and tucks it neatly, securing it with tape. He then ties it in ribbon which he fashions into an elaborate bow. It is tedious work, but Van enjoys it, and he anxiously anticipates giving the presents to their intended. He stows the wrapped gifts in his wall locker to your left, and as he closes the door, he hears footsteps clumping on the wet boardwalk outside.

The door spring twangs and tall Charlie Dermott enters, carrying flight bag and rifle. "Hi, Van," Charlie says glumly.

"Merry Christmas, Charlie," Van replies. "Is something wrong?"

Charlie deposits his equipment, sits on his bunk and sighs. "Van, can I ask you a question? I mean, I gotta talk to somebody and, well, you're...well, you're maybe the only guy who will listen and not make fun of me, you know?"

"Sure, Charlie. I'll be happy to help if I can."

"Well, it's...I mean it's sort of about..."

Van smiles. "Let me see if I can save you some effort, Charlie. Does this have anything to do with Sung Tranh?"

"How did you know?" Charlie replies with alarm.

"Because I know a little about love, and I've seen how you look at her when she comes to do our beds, boots and laundry."

"Oh love, phooey, I don't love her!"

"OK. You're the only one who knows for sure. But it sure looks like it. And she's clearly struck with you."

"You think so?" Charlie brightens markedly, then catches himself. "I mean, like I care, right?"

"Come on, Charlie. If you don't care, why are we having this discussion?"

"Okay," Charlie reluctantly confesses, as though just confronted with evidence of his having committed a bank robbery. "Maybe I like her, a little."

Van walks around to make eye contact. "Charlie, what's the big problem? She's as cute as a puppy, she seems quite intelligent and she speaks English better than any of the other hooch maids. She's obviously interested in you; she works on your bunk area longer, polishes your boots better, and she folds your laundry when the rest of us get ours dumped on our bunks. And she stays around long after the other girls have left post, just so she can get you to notice her. What's not to like?"

"Well, I don't know, Van, it's just...well...she's...aw shoot...it's kinda hard to talk about, you know."

"Ummm. I can sure see that, Charlie. Let's go at it this way. If Sung's name was Carolyn, and she was, oh say, a Protestant American girl, would you be stammering around like this?"

Charlie looks up. "But she's not, Van! She's a...she's..."

"A 'gook'?"

"I didn't say that! It's just that she's not...aw Van, I feel awful about this! She's...real different. Spud says she's just another piece of 'gook' ass but that's bullcrap. I've talked to her, man; her English is real good. I figured she'd be just another dumb, smelly, little betel-nut-chewing Vietnamese peasant like all the others I've seen over here but...Sung's different, Van, she's clean and smart and she's got some education. Her father was a restaurant owner in Saigon 'til he was killed a couple of years ago. She speaks French, too!"

"Well. Sounds like you two have been talking quite a bit together."

"We have, Van. And she's real neat and interesting and...you know...sweet."

"So Charlie, what is the big dilemma? I don't understand."

"Well, she's...not like anybody I ever knew!"

"You mean you wish she was white and Christian instead of oriental and Buddhist."

Charlie is silent for several seconds. "Van, it's confusing! I mean, I've always been taught that we're all God's creatures and none of us are better than anyone else, but I've also been taught that they who aren't Christian are lost. Worse, I hate to admit it, but Spud was right a few weeks ago—my folks would have a stroke if I got...you know...involved...with a girl of another race. Criminy, I don't know what to do. I don't know why I'm telling you this, Van. I don't suppose you ever...fell in love...with somebody your folks wouldn't like."

The right corner of Van's mouth smiles, but the rest of his face is sad. "Maybe I have."

"Really? You mean before Susan? What was she like? Oh God, she wasn't a...a black girl was she?"

"Well, Charlie, let's just say the situation gave my parents a more colorful stroke than yours would ever have over Sung Tranh."

"No kidding? What'd you do? I mean did you...you know, like do what your heart told you, or did you leave her?"

Van stares at the pictures of sexy Susan hanging on his wall, but it is not her he sees. "Charlie, I struggled with it terribly for a very long time -"

"I know what you mean, man! This has been eating me up for a week now!"

"—and ultimately, I decided that if you don't think enough of your heart to follow it then your heart is no good to you or anyone else."

"So you followed your heart?"

"Yes I did. The cost...can be very...steep sometimes, Charlie. Very steep. But in the end, what does it matter? The only alternative is to abandon your heart, and where are you then? Are you any happier that way? And is it right?"

Charlie considers this. "No. I guess—no, I know— you aren't any better off that way, and no, it isn't right. If my father taught me anything he taught me to stand by what I believe is right." Charlie looks up at Van with a new respect. "Thanks, Van. I guess I knew all that. I just needed somebody to explain it to me."

"I'm not saying you should love recklessly, Charlie. I'm saying follow your heart with caution, but follow it."

"I understand. Thanks, man. Wow. I feel a hundred pounds lighter. I feel...like untangled, you know?"

"I'm glad." Van's Christmas spirit improves. It is pleasantly alien to talk about love instead of body counts, crash fires, the torture of captured pilots, and the guy at breakfast who will never be here for dinner.

Loud voices approaching from the direction of the flight line now distract Van and Charlie. Both know well the voices of Pothead Willows and The Hatchet Man.

"Aw, get off my case, Hatch!" Pot whines as they draw nearer. "I need the shit, man, it relaxes me!"

The door is whipped open and Pot is forcibly propelled into The Room by the hulking Hatchette, who is clearly furious. Pot stumbles and crashes to his knees, his flight bag rolls and his rifle clatters. Hatchette slings his flight gear and rifle onto his bunk; he whirls on Pot, who is helped to his feet by Van.

"Relax, my ass! You about got us all relaxed!"

"Well, I thought the grunt said three-hundred meters west of the creek, Hatch!"

"You didn't think shit!" Hatchette rages. "You were so fucking spaced out you couldn't find your own ass with both hands and a five-cell flashlight! The grunt said three-hundred meters east of the creek, you fuckin' tiddlywink! Thanks to you we rolled in on our own troops!"

"Oh no," Van says. "Was anybody hur -"

"Nobody got hurt, goddamn it!" Pot shouts at Hatchette.

"Only because I caught your dumb-ass blunder, and pulled us off the target dive before you fired! We almost greased our own people! Again!"

"Aaah, fuck you, Hatchette," Pot mumbles beneath his breath. He drops to his knees and opens his foot locker, retrieving from it his whiskey and pills. He pours an indeterminate number of pills into his palm, swoops them into his mouth, and flushes them down with Tennessee whiskey.

"Yeah, nobody got hurt!" Hatchette raves. "No gooks got hurt either unless they died laughing at us! By the time we recovered for another pass, they disappeared."

Still on his knees by his footlocker, Pot gulps hard

from his fifth of JD, squints and exhales. "Well, fuck it. I'm still alive; that's all I know." He tips the bottle up again.

Hatchette covers the distance between his bunk and Pot in two strides and he slaps the bottle from Pot's grip. It careens across The Room, bounces off Old Faithful, and lands spinning in the floor, spewing it's bronze liquid in a revolving stream. Hatchette's hand collides with Pot's chest, forcing a loud grunt from Pot. Hatchette hauls Pot off the floor by his shirt. He dangles from Hatchette's huge arm like a rag doll, his nose inches from Hatchette's.

"You listen to me good, you little Angela Davis/ Abbie Hoffman/Joan Baez/Tom Hayden group fuck," Hatchette seethes. "Next time you show up in my cockpit under the influence of any of that shit you suck on all the time, you won't have to worry about the fucking gooks, 'cause I'll kill you myself! You hear me, troop? When you fly with me, I want your head clear!"

Pot is no genius but he knows when to smart-lip and when to shut up and nod; he opts for the latter.

"Listen to me, boy," Hatchette says, now in an urgent whisper, his bloodshot eyes wide in his huge skull. "I have seen what the gooks do to captured pilots and believe me, you'd rather I killed you. There is no room for fuckin' around out there!" Hatchette shoves Pot reeling   backward onto his bunk. There is an awkward silence in The Room.

"Uh, Merry Christmas!" Van says.

Hatchette's big, bald head swivels around to Van and tilts like that of a puzzled dog. "What?" he says.

Pot slinks to the fallen whiskey bottle and retrieves it. There is a little puddle of his courage remaining in it. He sits on his bunk and drains the bottle.

"Merry Christmas, Hatch," Van repeats.
"Tomorrow's Christmas!"

"Yeah, come on Hatch," Charlie says. "Cheer up, man, it's Christmas Eve."

Hatchette sneers at Van and returns to his bunk.

89

"Shit, Savatch. Pothead can't kill gooks 'cause he's stoned, and you can't kill gooks at all. What the fuck is this man's army coming to?" Hatchette flings his hat into the corner near his bunk.

Pot rummages in his footlocker and comes out with a new bottle of Jack which he hurriedly uncaps.

"Man," Hatchette reminisces fondly. "Early last year—before I got assigned with you buncha clowns—I flew guns with the First Air Cavalry. We had body-count contests. Every Saturday night we bought drinks for the gunship crew that killed the most gooks for the week. The crew that killed the fewest got thrown in Dragon Lake. Me and ole Bernie Clark got sixty-one confirmed bodies one week, and we never did get wet. We got steak dinners at the Colonel's table if we zapped a gook officer. Man. Those were the good ole days."

Pot nurses from his new bottle. "I hear you killed a few Americans one those good ole days, Ace; what'd you win for that?"

Hatchette homes on Pot who looks up with renewed alarm. "Listen you little pussy," Hatchette says, "I don't have to take that shit from gutless wonders like you! When you control that much firepower under those conditions, mistakes are going to happen! You almost made one today!"

"Ah, tell it to the widows," Pot mumbles.

"How much GI life insurance you carryin', troop?" Hatchette threatens, stepping toward Pot.

Van unobtrusively moves between Hatchette and Pot. "Hey, come on you guys. Lighten up. It's Christmas Eve. The other guys will be in from the flight line soon and we'll all go to chow. It'll be turkey and dressing tonight!"

"Always the fuckin' peacemaker, ain't you, Savatch?" Hatchette growls, leaning close to Van. "Don't try to make peace with me, troop. I still ain't sure about you, but I'm checkin' my sources, and don't you forget what I told you about queers, when you first swished in here." He returns to his bunk and begins to stow his gear, as commotion is heard at the door.

Hale and Spud enter, fast and excited, tossing their flight gear by their bunks. Spud is red-faced and wears a grin that threatens to sever his head.

"Eat your hearts out, you guys!" Spud is bursting to say, waving his arms in the air. "Guess who we flew today?"

"You won't believe it," Hale says, shaking his head in wonder. "You will not believe it."

"Jane Fonda?" Van answers with tongue firmly in cheek.

"Fuck 'Hanoi Jane', man!" Spud snarls. "I wouldn't fly that treasonous bitch to a hospital if she was bleeding to death in front of her kids!"

"Do I take that as a no?" Van asks.

"Merry Christmas," Pot mumbles.

"Come on, guys!" Hale prompts. "It was much better than Jane Fonda!"

"Alright!" Charlie finally explodes in exasperation. "Who the hell, I mean who was it?"

"Joey Heatherton and Racquel Welch!" Spud fairly screams.

"No shit?" Pot finds sudden interest in the discussion.

"You're kidding!" Van says.

"No, he's right!" Hale answers. "I could not believe it! We went into flight operations this morning expecting to fly the same old tons of c-rats and ammo, or get assigned to some big troop-lift like always, and there it was: 'Assist Fourth Division Headquarters Flight Platoon with area transport of Bob Hope Christmas Show personnel'. I'm thinking, sure, the starched-shirt-and-ascot boys who fly the generals all the time will get the VIP's, and working pilots like us will get stuck with the camera men and wardrobe guys."

Spud interrupts, "But Racquel and Joey musta heard that the world-famous Spud-stud, Ace Bleaker, was available and insisted on our crew for such a once-in-alifetime opportunity! Lucky for you I was your co-pilot today, Preston!"

"I owe it all to you, dud-stud."

"What'd they look like?" Charlie asks. "What were they wearing? Did you get any pictures?"

"They wore nothing, and they sat on my face for the whole damn fli—"

"Sure, Spud," Pot sneers. "And Janis Joplin's flight leader for the fuckin' Blue Angels."

"They wore jungle fatigues like everybody else," Hale says, "but you can bet your ass those fatigues didn't look like they do on everybody else. We flew 'em around to the firebases, 'to raise morale in the field', like the major said."

"Wow!" Charlie says with awe. "What a mission!"

"They raised a lot more than morale in the field, I can tell you that," Spud mutters.

"Don't worry," Hale says. "We took rolls of pictures."

"Make lots of copies," Van remarks wryly.

"We'll tell you the whole tale over chow," Hale says, "but first the major told me to make sure everyone has their entries ready for the colonel's great rat-kill contest. The colonel is supposed to come around tomorrow and judge the winner. Got yours, Hatch?"

"Hatchette rolls his eyes. "Fuck the colonel's contest. I came here to kill gooks, not rats. Any rat crosses my path, and I'll trap him with this." Hatchette rips his long, Smith & Wesson, .44 magnum revolver from its waist holster, pointing it at the ceiling.

"Innovative. Pot, you got yours ready?"

Pot is feeling his liquid mercy already, having poured it into an empty stomach. "I got some poison, man -"

Spud hoots. "Poison! Bullshit. These are gook rats, man; they pepper their food with rat poison!"

"Who said anything about rat po-poison, pig-dick? I got some real poison, man, I got the best poison there is, one-hundred-percent pure Chinese heroin! I got it

cheap from one a my enlisted buddies who bought it off
a dink pusher in Pleiku. I'm gonna mix it with some a
that German chocolate cake Van's girlfriend sent him.
Man, those ugly little bastards love that cake. I'll mix
it about sixty-forty. The fucking rats will go out with
smiles on their faces, but they'll never be back."

"Jesus," Hale sighs. "Dr. Jekyll had nothing on you,
Pot. That's just what we need, a bunch of stoned rats
running around here. Best you keep that heroin talk out
of the colonel's earshot, or the prize you win will be ten
years in Leavenworth."

Hatchette booms in, "You better goddamn sure
see to it all that powder goes into the cake and all the
cake goes into rats, you fuckin' dope-head! And you!"
Hatchette aims a thick finger at Van. "I ain't sure
whether you really got a girlfriend or not. You better
hope I don't find out you got some faggoty boyfriend,
flower child. Some evil things happen to homos in the
army."

Van looks at the floor silently.

Hale Preston is not silent; he leaps up from his
bunk. "Hatchette, you closet Nazi! If you paid half
the goddamn attention to your flying as you do Van's
alleged sex life, maybe you wouldn't have shot up a
platoon of American Marines early this year!"

"Fuck you, Preston! You don't know what the hell
you're talking about!"

"I know you were transferred here for other reasons
than your charming personality, by God. The way I
hear it, they had to ship your fascist ass clear out of III-
Corps to keep the Jarheads from wasting you for your
little fatal fuck-up!"

Hatchette advances on Hale who does not retreat.
"Goddamn it, Preston, I've about had it up to here with
you!"

Van moves quickly between Hatchette and Hale.
"Please Hatch! It's Christmas! Can't we all just cool off
and enjoy it?"

"You better carry your peacenik ass out of my way,

93

sweet-pea, or I will beat the t-holy shit outa you too!"

"Uh! Uh!" Charlie suddenly stutters. "I - I got
a great idea for killing the rats! Ya'll want to hear
it?" Everybody in The Room gawks at Charlie in
astonishment.

It works. The prevailing mood is cracked. Hatchette
pauses. Hale sighs, eyes Hatchette one last time, then
turns to Charlie. "Sure, Charlie, what's your idea?"
Hatchette pulls his gaze from Hale and turns back to his
bunk.

"This!" Charlie says, pulling something wrapped in
burlap from his flight bag. "I figured the best way to
find out about killing rats was to talk to some experts on
killing people. So I took up the problem with some of
the grunts in the field today. They gave me this thing."
He fumbles in the sandbag. "Said set it up in The Room
and fire it off when the rats come out." Charlie extracts
from the bag a curved, green object about the size of a
designer telephone. "They said this would do the rats
for sure!"

"Jesus Harley Davidson Christ!" Spud exclaims.
"That's a claymore mine, you dummy!"

Charlie looks insulted.

"Give me that thing!" Hale says, gingerly taking
the deadly anti-personnel mine from Charlie. "This
would 'do' the rats OK, Charlie, it'd also do everybody
else within thirty feet. The idea is to kill the rats,
independent of killing ourselves, Charlie. This thing is
a powerful shape-charge that explodes into thousands
of steel darts. It's designed to clean an alley through
charging infantry." Hale puts the device on top of Old
Faithful. "We'll give it to the armor sergeant in the
morning."

"Somewhere out there," Van says, grimly, shaking
his head, "is a grunt with a very dark sense of humor.
What's your anti-rat idea, Hale?"

Hale takes a drawing from his locker and passes it
around to everyone except Hatchette, who continues to
sulk in his private corner. "I figure a variation on the

latrine cans we crap into. We put a small gangplank fixed to a spring on the edge of the sawed-off oil drum half-full of kerosene, and put some of that famous German chocolate cake out on the end of the plank. Rat walks the plank to get at the cake; when he overbalances the plank it tilts, dumps him in the kerosene, and springs right back up for the next victim. Drag the barrel out the next morning and burn the floaters. What do you think?"

"Hey!" Spud says with respect.

Charlie agrees. "There's a winner for sure!"

"How about you, Van?" Hale asks.

"Oh, I just thought I'd buy one of those neat little wooden live traps the Montagnyards make to catch rabbits, trap the rats and carry them out in the bush on a flight and turn them loose. Not winner material, I'm sure, but it'll get rid of them."

Hatchette allows a derisive laugh. "I don't believe it," he says with disgust. "I do not fuckin' believe it. This chicken-hearted pussy ain't even got the balls to kill a goddamn rat!"

Pot giggles to ingratiate himself with Hatchette.

"Well, what the hell," Hale replies, "if it helps get rid of the damn things, who cares? All this talk of rats is making me hungry. Let's get some turkey and dressing!" Everyone stands.

"Now you're talking!" Spud says.

"Wait!" Van cries. "Wait just a minute, please."

Hatchette is still in a foul mood. "What the fuck do you want now, Savatch?" He snaps, hands on hips.

Van is not to be discouraged. "Hey! Tomorrow's Christmas, guys—we'll all be out on missions tomorrow—so I want to give you your Christmas presents now!" He hurries to his locker and extracts the gaily wrapped gifts; a bright look decorates his face.

"Presents?" Spud exclaims. "Well awright!"

"Hey, Van," Hale says, "you shouldn't have."

Van moves among his roommates, handing out the gifts. "Oh, don't get your hopes up guys, it isn't much.

Just a few small things to say Merry Christmas. I'm afraid there wasn't much at the PX to choose from that I could afford."

"Thanks, Bob," Charlie says, accepting his present. "I'm ashamed to admit it, but we've all been so concerned with ourselves we've forgotten what Christmas means. Thanks, man."

Van beams. "Merry Christmas, Charlie. Hale, here's yours; merry Christmas; Spud, merry Christmas; Pot, this one's for you; merry Christmas."

Pothead stares in shock at the present in his hand. "Hey Van, thanks, man," he slurs. "Muh-merry Christmas, dude."

Van smiles. "Hatch," he says pleasantly, extending one last gift to the scowling Hatchette, "This one's for you! Merry Christmas, Hatch."

The Hatchet Man frowns down at the present in Van's outstretched hand for several very long seconds while The Room watches in tense silence. Hatchette's wolf eyes rise from the gift and drill into Van who does not blink, but instead looks warmly at Hatchette with a genuine smile. Slowly Hatchette's mammoth arm rises from his hip and hovers over the gift as though to swat it down. Then his hand descends and snatches the gift from Van's hand. Hatchette turns away to his bunk without a word.

There is a rustle of ripping wrapping as everyone but Hatchette tears into their present. Hatchette slowly pulls his open.

"Hey!" Charlie says. "Look at this! Some fruit, some playing cards and a...?" Charlie is puzzled at a small, hollow, bright-red, soft-rubber toy animal.

Spud cries, "Hot damn! Some fruit and a subscription to Playboy! And this, uh, this..." Spud has never seen such a bizarre, yellow rubber creature about six-inches long.

"Thanks, Van," Hale says. "I've been wanting to read this book, but what on Earth is this thing?" Hale examines his green, rubber critter. It is made in Taiwan, and it looks like a preposterous approximation of a puppy with a dragon's head.

"Holy shit!" Pot says, gawking at his purple rubber critter, identical to the others, but for its color.

It is The Hatchet Man's turn to be astonished. "What in the hell is this goddamn thing?" He says, scowling fiercely at his orange rubber critter.

"They're dog toys, guys!" Van explains. "You know, like you buy for a dog to play with. I know it's a silly kind of thing, but the sergeant at the PX said he got in a whole shipment of dog toys by mistake. They just seemed to be a great symbol of army craziness, you know? Some typist in the Pentagon makes a one-digit error and five-thousand rubber dog toys show up in a war zone PX. That just seemed like a metaphor for this whole Vietnam experience. Anyway, like I said, there wasn't much to choose from at the PX, and I just thought you guys would get a charge out of the rubber critters."

Suddenly there is a piercing, two-tone squeal. EEH-EEE!

"Hey, man!" Spud says with a grin. "Mine squeaks!" He squeezes the rubber toy, and it squeaks loudly again. Spud laughs.

Charlie squeezes his dog toy which emits a squeal of its own. "Ha! Mine too! Thanks, Van!"

Van is thrilled. "It's nothing guys. I'm glad you like them."

Hale is squeaking his own toy and shaking his head with a sheepish smile. "Well, I'll be damned. This thing is a hoot!"

Pothead holds his critter at eye level and gives it three quick squeezes, each of which emit a shrill squeak. He stares stone-faced at the creature for a moment, then he explodes in a fit of hysterical laughter, which has the effect of moving everyone to squeaking their critters and laughing richly.

Everyone except The Hatchet Man.

"This is about the dumbest goddamn thing I ever

heard of!" Hatchette roars, standing. "Giving grown men a stupid fuckin' rubber toy!"

"Hey, Scrooge!" Hale challenges again. "It's Christmas! If you can't say something nice, just shut up!"

Hatchette hurls his rubber critter to the floor before The Room. It squeaks as though injured when it bounces on the concrete. "You know the worst thing about this? The worst thing about this is you morons get a thrill out of it! No goddamn wonder we're losing this war! Well, you fuckin' clowns play with your stupid, kiddie toys; I'm going over to the MACV compound and eat dinner with some real soldiers! Hatchette gives everyone a scathing look of disdain, and then he stalks to the door, forgetting his cap which lies on the floor in the corner.

"Hatchette!" Hale yells. Hatchette jams to a stop and spins about. "Suck on this, Hatch." Hale says calmly. He lifts his rubber critter, points its butt at Hatchette, squeaks it three times and cracks up in laughter.

Hatchette displays an expression of fury and he takes a step in Hale's direction but then, as if on cue, Charlie, Spud and Pot also aim their critters at Hatchette, and a cacophony of furious, high-pitched squeaking ensues. Hatchette hauls up short at the chorus of squealing dog-chews and looks about in incensed confusion, much like a bear surrounded by wolves. "Fuck you!" he shouts, cleverly. The squeaking instantly doubles in volume, mixed now with laughter. Van looks on in wonder. Hatchette does the only thing he can do. He whips about and blasts through the door into the night.

Hale, Pot, Charlie and Spud are convulsed in laughter for nearly a minute. As their hilarity begins to taper off, Spud points his critter at the swinging screen door and squeaks it again. All four young men collapse in renewed hysterics, and now even Van can't keep from laughing at the spectacle. Spud cries and points at the door. Pot falls onto his bunk, howling. Charlie slaps his knee and struggles to get enough breath between

bursts of laughter. Hale chokes trying to get himself
under control; barely so, he puffs his shoulders and
grunts, "Fuck you!", and The Room derails in helpless
laughter still again.

"Ah ha, oh God. I never laughed so hard in my life,"
Hale wheezes. "Never mind Scrooge Hatchette, Van,
you sure brightened up our Christmas!"

"Hear, hear!" Charlie cheers, wiping tears from his
eyes.

Pot stands up, weaving, and eyes his critter. "I'm
namin' mine Arlo," he announces, as serious as a bullet.

"Arlo!" Spud screams, and the laughter explodes
again, except from Pot, who looks genuinely puzzled,
magnifying still further the howling of his hoochmates.

Hale throws an arm around Van's shoulder and they
head for the door, all still laughing. Charlie claps Van
on the back, and Spud helps Pot navigate through the
doorway. Outside, as their footfalls fade toward the
officers' mess, you hear happy voices singing, "Jingle
bells, jingle bells, jingle alll the waaaay! Oh what fun
it is to ride, in a one-horse open sleeiiigh, hey!" This is
followed by a distant symphony of shrill squeaking and
out-of-control laughter.

The Room is quiet for a moment, but then you
hear heavy, fast footsteps pounding closer. The door
is pulled back and Hatchette storms in, stalks to his
corner, snatches up his hat and turns to leave. He jams
the hat onto his bald pate as he heads for the door, but
he freezes when he spots his orange rubber critter on
the rug. He scowls at the dog toy, then he walks over
and swoops it up in his colossal hand. As he examines
the little creature, which is molded like a comical
puppy with a dragon's face, Hatchette is unaware that
his fierce expression is fading. Involuntarily, a snort
of amusement escapes him and the right corner of his
mouth struggles upward in the beginning of a smile. He
squeezes the critter. EEH-EEE! EEH-EEE! it squeaks,
and a short but genuine laugh escapes Hatchette.
Quickly, he glares around to ensure he is alone. He

squeaks the toy once again and this time a decidedly hearty laugh erupts from him. Then he squeezes it several times in rapid succession, EEH-EEE! EEH-EEE! EEH-EEE! EEH-EEE! the little rubber critter squeaks. The Hatchet Man guffaws richly, shakes his scarred head, and stuffs his critter into his fatigue shirt pocket.

"Dumb fuckin' toy," he mumbles, exiting. His footsteps fade toward the MACV Special Forces compound. Before they are gone, you hear a faint but distinct squeaking, followed by a deep baritone chuckle.

Chapter Nine
Winter 1967

Spud

"Bleaker!" The tac officer bellowed, his polished black helmet liner and combat boots gleaming, his fatigues pressed and creased like green paperboard. He consulted the clipboard in his hand and roared again. "Listen up, pee-pul! Bleaker! Candidate Bleaker, Paul, one-each! Sound off like you got a pair, goddamn it!"

Spud Bleaker was suddenly ripped from his masturbatory daydream back into the formation of Aviation Warrant Officer Candidates standing at attention in a parking lot before a long wooden building. The large, neat assemblage of 'WOCs' in fatigues, boots and colored ballcaps denoting their flight training classes had just been marched to the supply warehouse. All were freshly graduated from two months of basic infantry training at other army posts all over the country, and had recently reported to Fort Wolters, Texas, for five months of primary flight training in helicopters.

Spud flinched, knowing the price for inattention. "Sir, yes sir!" He answered loudly, hoping his terror didn't show.

The tall, rigid tac officer whirled angrily. "Where? Where, goddamn it? Which one of you pansy-assed, hippie-yippie, peacenik flower-children is Candidate Bleaker? Sound off!"

"Sir!" Spud screamed as manfully as he could muster. "Private Bleaker—ah—right here, sir!"

The tac officer descended on Spud, who had the

alphabetically-first surname in his class, and, being not
only beefy but short, was in the front row of his training
flight formation. The tac officer jammed his nose to
within an inch of Spud's. "What did you say, you
yellow puddle of self-propelled blubber?" He shouted.

"Sir! Private Blea—"

"Private?" the tac officer screamed, deafening Spud.
"Tell me I didn't really hear you say private!"

"Sir! I—"

"Shut up, Candidate!" The tac officer spun on his
heel and marched before the formation. "Listen up
carefully, you herd of tie-dyed turtles! You are not in
basic infantry training anymore! You are in the primary
training phase of the United States Army Warrant
Officer Rotary Wing Aviator Course, at least until such
time as I can run your ground-bound asses outa here
and back to your mommies! The United States Army,
in its unfathomable wisdom, has seen fit to promote
you moles to Specialist, Fifth-Class, which is six
fucking classes more than you deserve! So! You are not
privates! You are Warrant Officer Candidates until I can
throw you out, which I intend to do soonest because
none of you pathetic, pacifist pussies is worthy of
wearing the bars of a warrant officer, let alone the proud
wings of a United States Army Aviator! Until I bust
you back to the ground-pounding infantry where you
belong, and make you a private again, you will refer to
yourselves as Candidate! Do you hear me, pee-pul?"

Fifty motivated voices roared "Sir! Yes sir!"

The Tac Officer scrambled back before Spud.
"What's your name, you wingless worm?"

"Sir!" Spud shouted, "Pri-ssspffft! Candidate
Bleaker, sir!"

"Carry your fat ass in that door, Candidate Bleaker,
and draw your flight gear! It'll be a waste of time
because you're going to be the first of these heavier-
than-air retards I wash out of the elite brotherhood of
Army aviation, but carry your ass anyway! What're you
waitin' for? The war to end? Move, fat boy!"

"Sir, yes sir!" Spud said, and he bolted for the warehouse door.

Ten minutes later, back in his place in the formation, waiting for his classmates to draw their flight gear, Spud felt pretty damn good, in spite of having been whipping boy of the moment for the tac officer. They had told Spud in basic that he'd never last there either, but by God here he was, beginning ten months of helicopter flight training, and not on his way to Vietnam as a private in the infantry. Even more to Spud's delight, he now carried a double-armful of brand-new, out-of-the-box, mothball-smelling, shiny, unscratched, plastic-wrapped, sexy flight gear! Pilot shit! Hot damn! Among the new toys were two, one-piece, zip-up flight suits and one of those neato Chuck Yeager pilot helmets with the giant sun visor that slides down out of a shield.

Oh Jesus, Spud thought, I'm gonna be one walkin' talkin' pussy-magnet, now. He could not wait to swagger into an officer's club in that flight suit and have to fight the honeys off with a chair! This was it! This was the culmination of all that Audie-Murphy soldier shit in basic. This was why Spud Bleaker had joined the army. Spud knew he would place the helmet in the rear package tray of the old '56 Pontiac he'd bought from his mother after basic. Then, when he went on leave, all the world would know he was that sexiest of all professional men, a military pilot! Women would jump-stride his face, he was confident. Spud was fairly dying to get back to the barracks and try this shit on!

At last Spud, reflected. He would finally redeem the humiliating spectacle of his life in general, and the nightmare of his last day as a civilian in particular.

Spud Bleaker was obsessed with becoming a pilot, not at all because he yearned to "slip the surly bonds of earth, spin deliriously through endless halls of cloud, reach out his hand and touch the face of God." Spud discovered his ambition to fly at precisely the same time he discovered that girls weren't so yucky after all. Spud's need for speed grew strictly from his conviction

that silver wings, leather jackets, aviator sunshades
and flying stories would get him laid on a broad scale.
Spud knew he was short and dumpy in a world where
girls went for the tall lean types, and it was clear he
needed an edge to offset his curse. At fourteen, he had
vowed to become a pilot, and it was this determination,
irrespective of its motives, that had gotten the
unscholarly Spud through high-school and a year of
college so far; after all, a college degree was required to
get into military flight training.

Sort of.

Late in the year of our Lord 1966, coincidentally the
nineteenth year of Spud Bleaker, Spud found himself
the windfall break he was long overdue: Vietnam.
Initially, Spud had never heard of the place—it was a
town in China he thought —but it didn't matter. What
mattered was the US Army reacted to its involvement in
the southeast asian "police action" by shifting hugely to
a new form of strategy called the Airmobile Doctrine.
Spud was no more a military strategist than he was a
Vegas show dancer, but he knew what the Airmobile
Doctrine meant for him. The Airmobile Doctrine was
based on helicopters, hundreds of them, and somebody
had to fly them. The U.S. Army of the era was about to
become the service that possessed more aircraft than the
U.S. Air Force; it needed a lot of pilots in a hurry and it
was not so choosy about college degrees.

As Congress limited the number of commissioned
officers the army was allowed to have, but placed no
limit on the number of non-commanding "warrant"
officers, the generals saw their opportunity and went for
it. In the mid sixties, the army aggressively recruited
hundreds of high-school graduates and college students
for its new Warrant Officer Rotary Wing Aviator
Course.

For Spud this was a development along the order
that the Second Coming might have been for an

evangelist. It meant Spud could become a pilot now. That he would fly helicopters and not fighter jets was immaterial; Spud hated the tall slender Hollywood assholes that flew fighters anyway, because everybody knew they got so much pussy they needed to be inoculated against feline leukemia.

Spud didn't give a fat damn about the morality of America's Vietnam involvement and he couldn't fathom why so many of his fellow students at the University of Wisconsin were so worked up about it. Spud didn't even give much concern to the grim logistical fact that one reason the army needed so many pilots was that a gruesome lot of them got killed "over there". All that was of any significance was that the silver wings of a military pilot, and the legendary sex-life of same, could be his now instead of a millennia later when, and if, he graduated. While his classmates were excoriating 'LBJ's immoral war', and were desperately fabricating excuses to avoid the draft by extending college as long as possible, Spud Bleaker promptly sought out the nearest army recruiter.

Spud's obesity almost crashed his dream, but he crept by his flight physicals with barely a two-pound margin. In the spring, to his ecstatic delight, Spud received his acceptance to the flight program and was ordered to report for induction in the morning. His dream had come true—soon he would be a pilot whose only worry would be how to take enough time out from fucking to eat—and he intended to spend his last night in Wisconsin as a civilian celebrating.

Studying himself carefully in the bedroom mirror of an untidy, off-campus, Madison apartment he shared with Frankie Spellman, Spud reflected that this would be the last night for his shoulder-length hair with the Sonny Bono bangs. Spud's friends said Bono looked silly, and because he couldn't sing he'd never be anything after Cher went on her own, which was inevitable. But Spud figured any guy who got to put his letter in Cher's envelope on a regular basis probably knew something about hair his buddies didn't.

As fate would have it, Frankie Spellman burst through the door of their apartment with a timely if classic dilemma. Frankie had four tickets to a rock concert in Milwaukee, he exclaimed, it was some here-today-gone-tomorrow group called The Grateful Dead, but who cared as long as it got him into Tricia Molovari's pants? Spud drew a breath to ask what this had to do with him when Frankie breathlessly explained that Tricia wouldn't go unless her roommate, Dreamy Wilcox—

"Dreamy!?" Spud exclaimed.

—went too, so Frankie had gotten Jeff Neely to agree to blind-date Dreamy, but Jeff was in the hospital with acute alcohol poisoning from the Delta Chi party last night. So—

"Wait a minute," Spud said, "How come you asked Jeff first? And what's this "Dreamy" look like? Mama Cass?"

"Naw man," Frankie replied frantically, looking at his watch and tossing his head to throw the hair out of his eyes, "Dreamy's, well, Dreamy's—"

"You've never seen this Dreamy chick, have you Frankie?"

"Well, no, but Tricia says she's got a great personality and—"

"That's it. Forget it. This is my last night as a civilian, man, I ain't buying drinks for some frigid Holstein heifer all night just so you can slide the ole spam javelin to Tricia Molovari. Forget —"

"Aw come on, Spud," Frankie pleaded with genuine worry. "We're going on a chartered Trailways bus, man! I got a cooler of beer and enough grass to put Mexico City on the moon, man! It'll be a blast! The Dead're cool, man!"

"Hey, do I look like a dairy farmer to you, man?"

"Come on, Spud! Tricia says Dreamy's cute and—"

"Bullshit. Tricia said Dreamy's got 'a nice personality'. That means she's ugly as a syphilitic warthog. I ain't—"

"Spud!" Frankie pleaded, looking like someone just
ran over his puppy. "Man, Tricia won't go if Dreamy
doesn't go! Come on man, the damned bus is leaving
in a hour! I've bought the tickets and I'll buy the drinks
and food, man! Besides, what the hell else you got
to do tonight, your last night before doing that stupid
fucking...helicopter John Wayne bullshit? Christ, man,
I still can't believe you're gonna go be a mercenary
baby-killer in Johnson's illegal war! A bloodthirsty—"

"Awright, for Christ's sakes! I'll go if it'll shut your
draft-dodging, coffee-house bullshit up!"

Wearing his coolest bell-bottomed jeans, white
patent-leather, elevator shoes with matching belt, and a
psychedelic shirt with five-inch collar tips, the fledgling
mercenary baby-killer helped Frankie carry the cooler
to the student union.

Tricia Molovari had a nose like a russian wolfhound,
Spud thought, but the rest of her was passable. He
couldn't see his blind date anywhere, and he just
hoped this "Dreamy" bitch wouldn't scare the balls
off a bronze gargoyle. Standing by the smelly, idling,
big diesel bus, Frankie slipped his arm around Tricia
and explained that he had decided Dreamy rated a
more mature man than Jeff Neely, and he'd asked Paul
Bleaker to join them instead. Paul was a Tri-Delt man
and—"

"Spud." Spud said dryly, peering around. "My
name's Spud. And I quit that dumb boy's club. Where's
this...Dreamy person?"

"Frankeeee!" Tricia said, turning her head to remove
her ear from Frankie's tongue. "Dreamy's gone to the
lady's room, uh, Paul. She'll—"

"Spud."

"—be back in—oh, there she is now!"

Spud glanced over his shoulder, and he accepted the
Lord as his savior on the spot, no questions asked. Spud
thought Dreamy Wilcox was so sexy she could raise a
boner on a jellyfish in a force-ten gale.

Dreamy, like Spud, was a little plump, but she seemed to grasp the Wall Street secret that most of marketing was in the packaging. She wore the requisite headband around her forehead. Long, frizzy black hair framed a pleasant face with a knowing gleam in her eyes that put Spud on red-alert. A glorious pair swung entrancingly, clearly without much textile restraint, beneath a short, snug, tie-dyed t-shirt of many colors. Her Rubenesque hips oscillated in a red mini-skirt that descended barely a scant couple of inches below The Promised Land, and her legs curved nicely into high-heeled, black-vinyl knee boots. Yes, Virginia, Spud said to himself with conviction, there is a Santa Claus.

At first it looked like Spud's night. Initially, while the big Trailways diesel bus rocked and rolled for Milwaukee, the students sang along with Dylan's Blowin' In The Wind, and Joan Baez's Where Have All the Flowers Gone. As the trip progressed, a pungent marijuana smoke cloud grew thicker, and the various bottles and cans were passed around. The radio got switched to a channel blaring The Who, Jimi Hendrix, The Doors, Jefferson Airplane and other groups way outside the folk music genre. The more of Frankie Spellman's beer they drank, the more Dreamy giggled and lay her blessed breasts on Spud's arm on the seat armrest. In direct proportion, Spud Bleaker became more convinced that he would surely get to fire the ole heat-seeking meat missile into Dreamy Wilcox on his last night before joining the military to become a pilot.

Spud passed on the occasional toke that was offered him, as he didn't wish to explain any blood-analysis peculiarities to the army, now that they owned him for the next four years. Spud knew the looks on the faces of some of the kids on the bus meant they were tripping on acid, and Spud suspected the army would prefer its pilot selectees not to have LSD in their blood either.

Not so concerned, Dreamy Wilcox said, "Hey man, never pass a chance to get high!" She drew heartily and held on every pass of the joint. At one point, Spud

108

jumped when Dreamy slapped a hand down on his thigh and let it lay there, rubbing gently. Electrified, Spud's very own inflatable wonder-weenie began tunneling out to greet Dreamy's hand.

Given Dreamy's fragrant cleavage, her thigh bumping his with every roll of the bus, and Dreamy's election not to remove her hand upon the arrival of Spud's organic temperature probe, Spud could hardly stand up to exit the bus in Milwaukee. He and Dreamy swayed arm-in-arm behind Frankie and Tricia outside the auditorium past all the vendor trailers which offered bead-necklaces, head-shop toys, psychedelic posters, tie-dyed t-shirts, bleach-dyed jeans, and drug paraphernalia.

Dreamy Wilcox giggled. "Spud! That's such a cute name!" She leaned heavily on Spud and pressed her lips to his ear, which nearly blew every rivet in him, and she whispered, "Kinda goes with your cute butt!" Spud jumped as Dreamy slapped his fanny for emphasis.

Oh yeah, Spud thought, my ship has come in. The ole cervical service sabre is going to see some action tonight.

During the concert, however, Spud's ship sprang a leak. He thought this bunch of Grateful Dead clowns weren't bad, but they'd never last. Whatever, more alarming concerns were now gurgling ominously beneath Spud's broad, white, patent-leather belt. All the beer Spud had downloaded for the two hours enroute to Milwaukee had gone through him like grease through a goose. On the way the hops, grain and alcohol had not been kind to Spud's empty stomach and historically weak bowel, the latter of which now sent an emergency action directive to Spud's cloudy brain: Bathroom now, Junior, and this is not a drill.

Distressed, Spud made hasty excuses to Dreamy and began a laborious clamber over the knees and feet of a score of cheering, clapping, whistling Dead-heads in his row of seats. As Spud climbed the steep aisle past row PP, his gut sounded general quarters and rang the

collision alarm. Spud clenched like a hay baler and
pushed past the dancers thrashing in the aisles.

He made it to the third mezzanine level and saw the
red neon MEN sign only thirty feet away, as beautiful at
the moment as the Pearly Gates. But as Spud attempted
to squeeze past a hefty black girl boogeying violently
in the passageway she let out a yell and hipped him
hard against the concrete wall. The oppressed gases and
liquids demanding freedom in Spud's nether regions
abandoned ship.

In a stall in the weed-smoke clouded bathroom, Spud
was on the edge of panic. He'd soiled himself seriously,
and while he'd washed the ole happy harpoon and
associated anatomy, and flushed his jocky shorts down
the commode, there was precious little he could do to
decontaminate his jeans. He'd even managed to stain
the tail of his shirt. Spud did the best he could with
paper towels and faucet water, but as he slid the damp
jeans and shirt back on, he knew he smelled like a Rio
slum. Glumly, Spud struggled back to his seat, terrified
that this newest disaster in his life would keep the ole
sword of giddiness from its appointed rounds tonight.

"What's that smell!?" Dreamy promptly shouted
over the din as Spud sat down. Spud punched Frankie
hard in the arm, "Hey, knock off the farts, Frankie!"

"What?" Frankie replied, baffled and rubbing his
arm.

Mercifully, the concert soon ended and, as they
made their way back to the bus, Spud announced that
he'd decided to buy a pair of the bleach-dyed jeans and
a t-shirt on sale in the vendor area.

"What?" Frankie repeated. "Man, they charge you
two balls and an eye for that shit! You can buy jeans
at the Savage Surfer in Madison for three bucks a pair
less!"

Spud didn't hear him. At the clothing vendor's
trailer, he elbowed his way through the drunken,
stoned crowd clamoring for merchandise, and bought a
colorful t-shirt and a pair of the jeans. "Any pair!" Spud

shouted to the stringy-haired space-cadet in the trailer, "long as they're thirty-eight-short!"

"Shit, maaaan," the cadet reported with a slur, "only got thirty-eight regu—"

"I'll take 'em, quick!"

Spud snatched the brown paper bag with the jeans and shirt from the salesman's hand and set it on the ground at his feet beside another belonging to the girl next to him while he clawed a ten from his billfold. Then he split the crowd and ran for the bus, dismayed to feel the bubbling of Montezuma's legions on the move again. Spud arrived at the bus walking like he had a tight skirt on.

"Damn!" Frankie said at the bus door, pausing to examine his soles. "Somebody step in somethin'?"

Spud groaned when he saw a girl hurry into the little bathroom in the rear of the bus. He sat down in the seat next to Dreamy as gently as he could. As the bus groaned up onto I-94, Dreamy Wilcox gazed at Spud with a pouty if slightly glazed look, and made an announcement straight from Heaven. "Gee, Spuddy-buddy, Trish has thrown me out for the night so she and Frankie can...you know. And...now I don't have any place to stay tonight!" Dreamy raised her eyebrows and waited for Spud to make the most obvious invitation in the history of romance.

Yes, Lord! Spud exulted silently. The ole bone ranger rides tonight! Hi-yo-Sil—!"

"Sheeeuuuew!" Dreamy said recoiling and wrinkling her nose. "What is that smell!?"

Spud heard the bathroom door bang and, looking over his shoulder several rows past Frankie and Tricia, he saw to his quantum relief that the bathroom was finally vacant.

"Chili!" Spud said, grabbing the bag under his seat and lurching to his feet. "Frankie ate ten gallons of Crystal chili for lunch! I'll be back in a minute!" Spud seized the bag with the new jeans and shirt and wove his way along the narrow aisle of the dark, swaying

111

bus between pairs of cuddled students, some of whom groped and kissed and some of whom were asleep or stoned from various substances of questionable legality.

In the back row seat by the narrow bathroom door sat a lone Dead-head with a headband, long hair, bell bottoms and a WWII army fatigue shirt. As the guy appeared to have been on Gamma-Five at the concert, Spud was mildly surprised to see him look out the back window, then turn to wave at someone in the front of the bus. Spud couldn't have cared less, as he wedged himself into the microscopic bathroom just in time.

"Jesus Harley Davidson Chriiiiissssssst!" Spud hissed in relief, sitting on the tiny stainless-steel commode. He ripped off his shirt and tugged his soiled bell-bottoms off over his white patent-leather platform shoes, a struggle in the phone-booth sized restroom. His heart was pounding so violently and his guts were bubbling so bad he wondered if he'd live to launch the ole pocket rocket at Dreamy Wilcox tonight. Anxious to get back to Dreamy before she lost the mood, Spud attempted to stuff his dirty jeans and shirt into the bathroom waste bin, but the opening, like the commode, was too small. Looking around, he noted a hatch with the sign PUSH OUT FOR VENTILATION. Buck naked but for his shoes, Spud rose and braced himself against the sway of the bus. The noise of the engine just beneath the floor was deafening. Spud opened the little hinged-metal hatch and pushed the stained and smelly jeans and shirt overboard. He hoped the stinking garments didn't cause some car behind to wreck, but he had much bigger dragons of his own to slay. The ole passion pecker was on a mission.

But, when Spud shook out the contents of the brown paper bag and gaped at them in horror, he would cheerfully have swapped them for a loaded .45 to blow his brains out with. There, on the minuscule stainless steel counter by the soup-bowl-sized sink, lay a yellow-vinyl mini-skirt embossed with peace signs and flowers, and two bead necklaces. And nothing else.

Spud had somehow picked up the wrong bag at the vendor's booth. There was no god, after all.

It took ten miserable minutes for Spud to determine that there was absolutely no effective way to kill yourself unarmed and with no chemical enhancement in a Trailways bus bathroom. He would have to go on living which was much worse than hell at the moment. He switched out the bathroom light and cracked open the door to peer down the aisle. The Dead-head from the back seat was dizzily weaving down the aisle toward the front of the dark, quiet bus, but everyone else seemed asleep or enmeshed in each other's tonsils. Spud couldn't see Dreamy, who was in a window seat, but he could see Frankie's elbow protruding from the row behind her.

Frantic, Spud tried his old emergency stand-by— what would John Wayne do in a situation like this?— but it never got off the ground. Try as he might, Spud could not possibly imagine John Wayne ever winding up stark naked, having thrown his clothes overboard from a Trailways bus bathroom between Milwaukee and Madison, with a hot-to-trot Dreamy Wilcox only twenty-feet but an eternity away.

In the rocking, roaring, diesel-smelly little cubicle, a faint glimmer of a partial answer began to form in Spud's anguished mind. Frankie Spellman always wore voluminous boxer-type underwear. He was the joke of their apartment building because of it. If Spud could get to Frankie and get him to come to the bathroom and lend him the shorts, at least he'd have something to cover the ole slinky salami. Maybe Frankie even wore an undershirt which he'd lend Spud. Maybe Spud could save it with Dreamy after all.

The yellow-vinyl mini-skirt was nowhere near big enough to fit Spud, of course. Understandably motivated, however, he managed to squirm and tug until, with the side zipper gaped open, the taught skirt finally rose just high enough. Though his white belly poured over the top and his hairy thighs squirted out

113

from beneath, the flowery mini-skirt with the peace signs barely covered the ole one-eyed trouser-lizard. With the white patent-leather platform shoes, it made for an ensemble to remember.

In the dark and with a little luck, Spud thought desperately, he might get past all the sleeping or pre-occupied passengers to Frankie, get his attention, and beat it back to the bathroom unnoticed.

Again Spud switched out the light and peered through the opened door. The bus was still dark and silent except for the subdued roar of the diesel. Nothing was moving except the Dead-head who was now conversing with another psychedelic refugee up front near the driver.

Spud took a deep breath, shoved the door back, and began frantically hobbling down the aisle in the hyper-stretched, yellow-vinyl mini-skirt. He took great care not to bump anyone or otherwise attract attention. Frankie was only ten feet away squirming with Tricia Molovari, when Spud noticed through the front bus windows that ahead in the highway were numerous flashing red lights. The diesel engine spun off to idle as the driver began to slow the big bus.

JEE-sus Harley Davidson Christ! Spud thought, nearly choking. There's been a goddamned accident ahead and the bus is stopping! Everybody would start waking up and looking around any second. Spud mini-stepped at warp speed for Frankie Spellman's seat.

I'm gonna make it! Spud cried to himself as he reached Frankie. "Frankie!" Spud whispered urgently. He pulled at Frankie's arm. "Frankie!"

"Not now, man!" Frankie mumbled, jerking his arm free without looking.

The bus slowed as it neared the flashing police car lights and it pulled onto the shoulder. Spud grabbed Frankie by the hair. "Frankie, listen to me, damn it!" He hissed.

Frankie disengaged from Tricia, who rubbed her eyes in the darkness. "Are we stopping?" she asked, looking over Dreamy's seat ahead of her.

"Spud!" Frankie said with irritation. "What is—, holy shit! What in the name of God are you—?"

"Shut up and listen to me, will you! I need your shorts!"

"You whaat?"

At this moment every interior light in the bus came on brightly and Spud froze in terror.

Both the hippie Dead-heads standing in the front of the bus now spun to face the passengers, and tugged badges on strings from beneath their shirts. "Freeze!" one of them bellowed belligerently, holding his badge aloft. "Federal Narcotics Task Force! Nobody moves!"

Spud Bleaker lapsed catatonic.

"Everybody remain seated and keep your hands whe—!" The undercover state police officer cleaved his sentence and gawked with his mouth still open. In eleven years of law enforcement, he thought he'd seen it all, but for a moment he wondered if all the marijuana fumes had done a number on him. He could swear that, standing smack in the middle of this bus, staring bug-eyed, was the Pillsbury Doughboy wearing nothing but a yellow-plastic mini-skirt and white patent-leather shoes!

"Spuddy-buddy?" Dreamy Wilcox whispered, gaping in shock, just before she screamed.

Chapter Ten
The Room

Happy New Year, American soldiers, sailors and airmen! This is your hostess, Specialist Fourth-Class Barbara Stafford, and once again it's time for *Events In Review*, brought to you by *Newsweek Magazine*, which wants you, the American fighting man, to be informed!

January 1969 finds astronauts Frank Borman, James Lovell and William Anders, like the three wise men of old, following the stars to seek man's destiny and hope. Soaring through space enroute to orbit around the moon, the astronauts are laying down the groundwork, so to speak, for a near-future mission onto the lunar surface itself. God speed astronauts Borman, Lovell and Anders.

Meanwhile, back on Earth, a recent Gallup poll indicates a growing number of Americans favor the transfer of the major fighting role in the Vietnam war to the South Vietnamese. The war has lasted as long as World War II and has killed over thirty-thousand American fighting men. The public message to newly inaugurated President Richard Nixon is clear: End the war in Vietnam.

What do eight consecutive U.S. Presidents since Calvin Coolidge have in common? Not the least would have to be their appointments of head G-man J. Edgar Hoover as director of the Federal Bureau of Investigation. President Nixon's recent vote of confidence marks Mr. Hoover's forty-sixth year at the helm of the FBI. Dedicated, disciplined and absolutely incorruptible, Mr. Hoover, at age seventy-three, still rules the FBI with a widely respected iron hand. Not without his critics, Director Hoover has nonetheless served eight consecutive administrations and has, in the process, claimed beyond dispute the title of America's top cop. Even as it was recently announced that Mr. Hoover would remain at his post in the Nixon administration, Hoover's agents in Chicago were putting the cuffs on thirty-two suspected draft dodgers.

On the subject of draft dodgers, former boxing champ Cassius Clay, age 26, who now prefers to be called Muhammed Ali, is having his own problems. While his conviction of draft evasion is being appealed, Ali is serving a ten-day sentence in Miami's Dade County Jail for a traffic offense. "Maybe it will be good for me," the former Olympic great, now a Black Muslim, was quoted as saying "After all, if they get me on this army thing, I may do five years. This will be good conditioning."

One of America's greatest writers has died. John Ernst Steinbeck, author of twenty-four works of fiction succumbed to heart disease. Perhaps best known for his novel *Grapes Of Wrath* published in 1939, Steinbeck was a winner of both Nobel and Pulitzer prizes. Two years ago, on a visit to South Vietnam, he said of the war: "This is making real men, and men are pretty valuable things." John Steinbeck was sixty-six.

Some good news to end tonight's broadcast: It now appears the eighty-two surviving crewmen of the intelligence ship, USS Pueblo, captives of the North Koreans for eleven months, may soon be released. It is reported

117

that after months of tedious negotiations on the content of a so-called US 'apology', an agreement has been reached. The bone of contention was whether or not the Pueblo was in violation of North Korean territorial waters when she was attacked. The crew of the Pueblo is expected back home within the month to face an investigation which may have far-reaching effects on what is expected of a captured American serviceman.

There you have it once more, gentlemen. That's this edition of *Events In Review*, brought to you with the assistance of *Newsweek Magazine*, which wants you, the American fighting man, to be informed. This is Specialist Fourth-Class Barbara Stafford, on behalf of all of us here at Armed Forces Radio, wishing you all a safe and happy 1969. Good night!

Dear Susan,

I know, I'm neglecting you criminally, but it's almost impossible to find time to write. We work back-to-back days flying 10 to 15 hours a day, sometimes more, and that's logged flight hours, which do not include briefings, debriefings, refuelings and time spent waiting at some firebase or hospital for medevac patients. At night, we are so tired it is hard to write a decent letter, even if we can stay awake long enough to do it. It's a poor excuse my dear friend, I know, but it's all I've got. Forgive me!

It develops that those silly little rubber dog toys (like the one I sent you) I gave the guys for Christmas have come to be a sort of talisman for Hooch-44. The guys all carry theirs on them when they fly, as combination good-luck charms and tension relievers.

Last week, all the pilots of the battalion were at a briefing being chewed out by the major (who is a typically stiff 'Pointer', a West Point grad) for occasionally failing to salute senior officers on post. He ended his harangue the way he always ends everything, by demanding, "Do you officers read me loud and clear?" No one in the briefing room answered, but from somewhere in the back there came a loud EEH-EEE! EEH-EEE! The whole place erupted in laughter, except for the major, of course, who stalked off the stage. I don't know if it was Hale, Pot, Spud or Charlie—they were all there.

Come to think of it, Hatch was there too. He got angry the night I gave him his 'critter', and he threw it on the floor, but I noticed when we got back from chow that Hatchette's critter was gone. I don't know if he threw it away.

I always love to get pictures from you which I display proudly, and they are often my salvation. Still, it alternately galls and saddens me that I have to keep Ramsey's pictures hidden away on the inside of my locker door, to unlock and sneak looks at when no one else is here. All this anti-homosexual hostility is so senseless and mean, Susan, it's not right. But then I suppose I'm being awfully self-centered to complain about what isn't right here in this terrible war where everything is horribly wrong. Every day we bring in more black rubber bags containing what is left of someone's son, father or lover. Nothing is right in Vietnam.

On that upbeat note, I'll close and get this in the mail in the morning, along with a letter to Ramsey which I will write next. Don't mind me, Susan, I'm just tired and it's late.

> *I love you. Regards to Andy.*
> *Van*

119

Dear Ramsey,

I am awake, but all my roommates except Hatch are asleep, now, in the dark, early morning hours. I don't know where Hatch is, but I hope he's alright. There was some silly talk earlier of him striking the NVA base camps just over the Cambodian border, but I'm sure it's just part of the legend of The Hatchet Man. Those huge troop concentrations barely in Cambodia include training facilities, hospitals and supply depots which enable massive NVA forces to range over the border and strike us, then quickly return to sanctuary, technically out of our reach by virtue of Cambodian sovereignty. Even though the NVA roundly ignores the international law that forbids foreign military forces to be in Cambodia or Laos, U.S. politicians righteously demand that we observe it. It's still another farcical example of our being politically outfoxed in by North Vietnamese diplomats at the Paris 'peace' negotiations.

As I write you now, I can see nothing beyond the dim glow of the desk lamp, but I can hear someone snoring in the darkness. There is no other sound, save the chirping of a lone cricket. Across the runway, several hundred meters distant, a group of shirtless men scurry in the glow of floodlights about a mammoth, 175mm track-mounted field artillery piece, a 'cannon' if you will, which has a thirty-foot barrel and a bore the size of a beach ball. A 300-pound shell is fitted gingerly with a fuse and all three-feet of the shell are hydraulically inserted in the gleaming breech and shoved home. Behind it are rammed several large, tubular, fabric bags of ultra-high explosive charge. The men say nothing; they only sweat, their backs glistening in the glare of the floods. The heavy breech is swung shut and a wheel is spun to lock it.

A loud humming noise intrudes upon the quiet night, and the long barrel rises toward the moon. A pilot flying many miles away hears on his radio: "Attention aircraft, vicinity Pleiku; stand by for a heavy artillery warning..." Though in the cockpit I have monitored and heeded similar messages many times, tonight I am unaware as I stare at nothing in the dark and hear only the guys snoring and the cricket chirping.

Across the runway, final adjustments are computed into the colossal gun. Someone, twenty miles away, is about to die, although they do not know it...and still it is quiet. The floodlights go out, an arm snaps down, a long lanyard is yanked, and thunder to the tenth power shatters the still night. There are no words for that noise.

In my hooch, I am aware first of the bright flash, I feel the ground beneath me jump, then the crashing explosion sweeps over the hooch, and the death missile roars away like a departing jet. In that instant of confusion, an alarm clock clatters to the floor from the ammo crate upon which it rested. Someone says: "Jesus Christ!" Another spits viciously: "Damn!" There is much stirring of bunks as men shift and roll over. A voice in the dark cries: "Momma? I'm comin' Momma!"

My heartbeat, which leapt to twice it's normal rate at the moment of the blast, now slowly recedes. There is always that split second after an artillery detonation that even the experienced mind needs to distinguish a blast as outgoing and not the dreaded incoming rockets which have split the nights so many times before, nights when rocket after rocket crashed in and men screamed and bled and died. But for now my wire-tight muscles slowly relax, and all is again quiet...even the cricket.

Thanks for the wonderful photo of you in your

121

long-tailed tux, seated for a performance with the symphony. How I wish I could brag about you— I'm so proud! Sometimes it weighs on me that we must always—

Chapter Eleven
The Room

The alarm clock now lies on the floor of The Room, but its ticking can still be heard, even over the snoring. Van writes at the desk to your left under the weak glow of the old office lamp. Hatchette's bunk in the corner to your right is empty, still neatly made, but Spud, Pot, Charlie and Hale lie in their bunks in the pre-dawn darkness. Charlie sleeps with his rubber dog-toy by his head. Pot lies clothed on his bunk, curled-up, cradling an empty Jack bottle like a teddy bear. His rubber dog-toy, 'Arlo', is positioned beneath his bed, by his boots. You cannot be seen, of course, but you can see that, of those in bed, only Spud is awake. He holds his rubber 'critter', rolling it over and over in his hand as he stares at the dark ceiling.

"Van?" Spud says in a low voice.

"Hey Spud," Van answers softly, "I didn't know you were awake."

"Yeah man, I couldn't get to sleep."

"Feel alright?"

"I'm OK. I was thinking. You know where Hatchette is right now?"

"I thought he said after chow that he was going to visit some of his old Special Forces buddies. I didn't know he meant to stay all night. Hope he's alright."

"Oh hell, son, don't sweat for Hatchette. It's the rest of the goddamn world you gotta worry about when Hatchette's out walking the night, believe me."

"What do you mean?"

"I mean that after chow tonight, The Hatchet Man and his snake-eater pals from the Special Forces loaded

123

up a fully armed C-model hog with parachute flares, extra jerry-cans of JP-4, and two cases of iced-down beer. And right now they're flying around in the dark somewhere over Cambodia, drunk, shooting up every campfire the gooks were dumb enough to light tonight."

"What? You're kidding! We aren't even supposed to be in Cambodia."

"No shit, Sherlock. But Hatch and his Delta Team buddies ain't much on rules. Word is, division makes 'em wear unmarked fatigues and leave all their ID here, but gives 'em an unnumbered bird and all the ammo they can get off the ground with. I've heard tales, man. They will fly around over there all by themselves shooting up NVA base camps until they run low on fuel, then they'll land somewhere in a clearing, in deepest, darkest, off-limits Cambodia, refuel the hog with the jerry-cans, and take off for more machine-gun fun and games. They'll come in late tonight when they're finally out of ammo, fuel and beer. I've heard it said that they've come in before with souvenirs from the gooks they killed—not just helmets and weapons and stuff— but ears, man! And fingers—even gook dicks, man!"

"My God, Spud."

"I shit you not, brother. Sometimes they're so drunk, including Hatchette, they fall asleep out on the fucking flight line because they can't even walk to their hooches."

"That's incredible."

"Shit. The brass looks the other way 'cause they're so pissed that the fatcat politicians won't let us go over the border and wipe out those giant base camps the NVA is operating out of. And that's The Hatchet Man, Van. That's his idea of a fun night out. Man, Hatchette may be fucking crazy, but he ain't afraid of nothing."

Van considers a trembling giant, huddled in a ball, terrified of the crashing rockets. "Everybody is afraid of something, Spud."

After a pause, Spud agrees. "Yeah. I guess you're right, Van. But I'm damned if I can imagine anything that would scare Hatch. What about you, Van, what are you afraid of?"

"All the usual things, I guess."

"No I mean really, what are you really afraid of? Like man, I'm scared shitless of crash fires and getting captured, you know? What really scares you, Van?"

Van reflects on this question. "Spud, I guess what I'm really afraid of most is that I will never be able to hold the one I love on a park bench among all the other lovers in the park. I fear that I will never, ever, be able to walk the streets of America hand-in-hand with my lover."

"Yeah man, I can dig it. If I had a girl like Susan back in the world, I'd be afraid of that too. But don't worry, Van, you'll make it home alright."

"Yes." Van whispers. "That's not what I'm afraid of..."

"What's that?"

"Nothing, Spud. Better try to get some sleep."

"G'night, Van."

Spud rolls over and Van resumes his letter, but he is soon distracted by heavily clumping footsteps on the boardwalk approaching unusually slowly. The door swings back and Van turns to look.

The Hatchet Man stands stooped in the doorway, leaning on the side of the door frame and holding an AK-47 assault rifle in one hand. His is the slow and labored breathing of the extremely drunk, and he gazes malevolently in Van's direction. A western-style gun belt is about his waist outside the fatigue shirt. In its holster is Hatchette's immense, .44 magnum, Smith & Wesson revolver. Hatchette's jaw hangs slack, and his eyes are half closed. Dark stains spot the front of his fatigue shirt.

"Good evening, Hatch," Van says.

"You betcher ass it was," Hatchette replies after a pause. He steps inside and looks around as though searching for his bunk.

"Man, we flat woke up some gooks tonight!"

Hatchette snorts a burst of cruel chuckle, "And we flat put some of the little fucks to sleep, too. Yessir. We unloaded everything we had on them campfires. Campfires! Those arrogant little dicks are so smug...'cause they know we ain't sposed to...violate Cambodian soverty...they sit there one lousy klick over the border and light fuckin' campfires! Campfires! Like this is a fuckin'...boy scout jambree...or somethin'..., 'stead of a war. Well...tonight them fires got a bit too cozy. We put them gooks through some changes, I mean. We shot the shit out of 'em. They fired up at us. Tracers flying everywhere. Looked like fourth of July in Vegas, man. We were showin' no lights, of course, so they never touched us ... well no more than three or four rounds ... they couldn't hit a fuckin' dumpster if they were locked inside it. When we ran out of ordnance... we threw out two cases of empty Budweiser bottles on 'em. That's...our callin' card!" Hatchette snorts again. "We landed to take us some...trophies...found some blood trails, but no fu-, fuckin' bodies. Little shits are always draggin' off their dead. All I could find was this AK!"

Hatchette yawns and waves the short, stocky firearm with its broad, curved magazine. "See this? Folding-stock, Soviet paratroop version...new too. Only gook officers get to carry these. Or fuckin' Russian advisors. And they don't just leave 'em behind. Means we got us a gook officer or maybe even a fuckin' Ivan tonight. Ain't that some sweet shit?"

"Well, I'm glad you're safe, Hatch. Better get some sleep." Van puts away his writing items and inspects his bunk carefully for rats.

"Safe!" Hatchette laughs. He slides the captured rifle under his bunk and unhooks his pistol belt which he hangs on a wall nail. "Ha! That's a hoot." He peels his shirt back from hairy shoulders. "Fuckin' gooks have a price on my achin' soldier's ass. No shit. G-2 interrogated a prisoner last week who had a list written in them gook chicken-tracks...named certain American

126

gunship pilots they want dead, soonest, and they got a reward out for us. No shit. Me and ole Bernie Clark and Marvin Adams are on that list. And we're fuckin' proud of it too...we aim to kill enough gooks to get our names at the top of that goddamn list. Betcher ass."

Spud turns over and covers his head with his pillow. Van slides beneath the sheet and lies down. Hatchette strips to his green undershorts and drops his fatigue-pants in a heap. He stabs his size-14 feet into rubber-tire flip-flops and walks unevenly out the door. The door swings to with a bang that causes Pot to start and cry out as though he were struck. The ka-plop, ka-plop of Hatchette's flip-flops fades toward the latrine shack. Van turns out the desk lamp and pulls the sheet about him. The Room is scarcely saved from complete darkness by a few rays from distant lights which struggle through the high screens.

Van is exhausted. It is late and the pace of virtually uninterrupted eighteen-hour work days in blistering, wet, tropical heat has taken its toll on even his young and healthy body. Still, he lies awake, wondering about a man who flies forth in the night to challenge his avowed, deadly enemy in its own sanctuary, but cowers helplessly in dark corners from the impersonal horror of the flesh-eating rockets.

We are all afraid of something.

Van slides down a gentle slope into a warm pool of blessed sleep.

You hear a distant, concussive 'ploomp!' The perimeter guard is periodically firing mortar-launched parachute flares to illuminate the kill-zones outside the wire. They are checking for infiltration by sappers, extraordinarily skilled NVA soldiers who creep like deadly worms with uncanny agility through the barbed-wire and mines to penetrate the perimeter, to cut sleeping throats and plant satchel bombs in hooches. The big magnesium flare detonates a thousand feet above the ground, ignites in a brilliant, white-hot glow, and swings lazily from its parachute as it descends, trailing a plume of smoke. The Room is partially illuminated in piercing spears of bleached-white light which stab through the screens and sweep back and forth with the shadows in time with the swing of the descending flare. A dog, somewhere out beyond the wire, bays mournfully.

Hatchette returns from the latrine, holds the edge of the door to steady himself against the vertigo his equilibrium is suffering due to alcohol-overload and the swaying beams of flare-light. He gropes to his bed, lifts the sheet and slides beneath it. A sigh seeps from him.

"Yeeeeaaahhhh! Shit! A rat!" Hatchette bellows, violently startling every sleeping occupant of The Room. He kicks wildly to clear his bed. He thrashes, tangled in the sheet, falls from the bed and scrambles away from it on all fours.

Spud jumps to a standing position on his mattress, Pot sits bolt upright, clutching the empty liquor bottle, with a wide-eyed gape of terror on his face. Van, Hale and Charlie come awake and struggle to see what new catastrophe has befallen them in the bizarre, zebra-striped atmosphere of oscillating white light beams and black shadows.

Hatchette has seized his revolver; he spreads his feet, aims at the foot of his bed and lets fly. The big handgun recoils, spews yellow flame and roars. The blasts are deafening in The Room. PLOOM! PLOOM! PLOOM!

Pot can be heard screaming between rounds. Charlie rises from his bed in groggy confusion, but is promptly run over by Pot fleeing mindlessly to cower by the refrigerator. "Hatchette!" Hale yells, but he is drowned out by more painful blasts from Hatchette's flame-belching hand-cannon. Van's ears ring shrilly and his heart is pounding him senseless.

"Aaah fuuuckin' raaat!!" Hatchette spews in fury. He runs out of bullets but continues to click the empty, aimed weapon at his target. "It bit me on the fuckin' toooe!" Hatchette throws the heavy gun at the frayed foot of his bed, and then, to the added horror of The

Room, he drags out the AK-47 he left beneath it. Pot is wailing by the refrigerator, his hands over his ears. Van moves swiftly to get Pot under control.

Hale bails out of bed. "Get him!" He yells. Hale, Charlie and Spud leap for Hatchette. Hatchette has yet only a one-hand grip on the loaded automatic-rifle. Hale grabs the weapon with both hands, wrenches it from Hatchette's grip and throws it away from them. He joins Spud and Charlie in attempting to restrain Hatchette. The four of them revolve about in a tangled, struggling mass of men; given the swirling light and Hatchette's inebriation, it is inevitable that he loses his balance and falls. The three younger men pounce on him to hold him down.

By the refrigerator, Van is calming Pot who is hyperventilating viciously.

Running footsteps pound the boardwalk outside. "What's going on in there?" A voice cautiously calls.

"Nothing!" Hale shouts, "It's alright!"

"Nothing my ass," the major's voice answers. "What's all the shooting about? Anybody hurt?"

"Get the fuck off me!" Hatchette grunts, still quite drunk.

"Shut up, Hatchette!" Hale hisses. He shouts over his shoulder, "It's alright, Major! One of our guys saw a rat and he killed it, sir!" To Charlie and Spud, Hale whispers, "Get him up, quick!" They struggle to haul the shaky, massive Hatchette to his feet.

A flashlight beam appears at the screen door and probes about The Room. Spud hurries to turn on the ceiling lights. Everyone squints at their sudden brightness. The major says, "Alright, let's get your act together in there, men! No more discharging weapons in the middle of the goddamn night, or I'm going to have somebody's ass! You officers read me loud and clear?"

"Yes sir!" All but two within reply in unison.

"Fuuuuck you," Hatchette mutters.

"SSSSH!" Hale says.

Pothead Willows weeps quietly into a towel Van holds over his face.

The footsteps fade away amid mumbled curses.

"I cain't take it!" Pot is now sobbing. "I cain't take this no more, Van!"

"Sssh," Van says, "Get some sleep. You'll feel better in the morning. Come on. Back to your bunk. Let's go."

Charlie, Spud and Hale stand in their underwear, sweat-soaked and heaving for breath. Hatchette staggers to his devastated bunk. Fluffs of mattress stuffing, wood-splinters and concrete-chips pepper the entire area. Hatchette draws back the blanket and sheet to reveal a bloody mess.

"Gotcha, you little shit!" Hatchette announces.

"You crazy bastard!" Pot croaks hoarsely, groping in his seemingly bottomless footlocker for more whiskey. "You almost got all of us! I cain't take this no more."

"Me neither," Spud agrees, breathing hard, "I'm too short for this nuthouse bullshit."

"You got four months to go!" Charlie observes.

"That's too short for this crazy shit!"

"Spud, bag that thing up," says Hale. "The flight surgeon will want to test it for rabies."

"Me! Why me?"

Hatchette finally registers. "Rabies!"

"Relax, Hatch," Spud says, looking with revulsion at the mutilated rodent. "It don't look rabid to me, and besides, ain't a germ known to medical science mean enough to live in your blood. More likely you'd give the damn rat some terminal fucking disease..." Spud delicately scoops the carcass into a PX bag and takes it outside.

Pot sits trembling upon his bunk, glugging from a fresh bottle of sustenance. He wipes his mouth and scowls at The Room. "Ca-ca-can we ge-get some goddamn sleep now? I nee-need some fucking quiet!"

"Easy, Pot," Van says, patting Pot on his shoulder.

"Sleep sure sounds good to me," Charlie mumbles, making up his bed while eyeing Hatchette nervously.

"What a day."

Hatchette unceremoniously flips his mattress up-side-down and dives into bed. He is almost immediately asleep.

Spud returns from disposing of the rat and observes Hatchette. "Look at that psycho, would you! Sleeping like a baby!" Spud notes that everyone is now back in bed except Pot who still sits upon his bunk drinking morosely. He slaps the light switch off.

"Man, I hope I sleep like a baby. I'm too short for this shit." Spud settles in his bed.

Charlie decides a word to God on behalf of The Room is in order. In the quiet darkness he prays softly. "Dear Lord, we humbly thank thee for watching over us and keeping us safe from harm. We thank thee for thy gift of gentle slumber and peaceful rest, Lord, we—"

Charlie's prayer is cleaved by a loud hiss followed by an explosion several hundred yards away.

"Oh God, incoming!" Hale says, throwing back his sheet and blanket.

"Lord?" Charlie says.

"Christ, no! We're getting hit again!" Spud cries, scrambling, clutching his rubber critter. All facility lights go out and the banshee wail of the attack siren rises. It is pitch dark.

"I don't believe it!" Pot says, his voice catching, "I don't fucking believe this!"

A second round detonates very near with a flash and a crash and a shower of debris raining down on the metal roof.

"I believe it!"

"Lord? Did you hear me, Lord?" Charlie is now groping by his pillow for his critter.

"Run, goddamn it!" Hale shouts in the darkness. "They're getting the range quick this time!"

There is the shuffle and thump of men scurrying to exit The Room. The screen door bangs shut. A third rocket arrives. In the flash, Van sees Hatchette backed into his corner, eyes wide. The blast is like a stout

131

punch in Van's face. He shakes his head.

The roof sings with falling debris.

"Savatch?" A deep but very frightened voice calls in the dark. "Savatch?" A note of panic marks the tone, now. "Van?"

"I'm here, Hatch. I'm right here."

"Don't leave me, man, don't leave me!"

"I won't Hatch. Meet me at the door, now, we don't have much time. Come on, Hatch. You can do it. Just like we did all the other times. You can do it. Come on, now."

"I'm comin'. I'm comin', Savatch. Don't leave me, man!"

"I'm right here. Good. Quick, let's run. Don't stop 'til we make the bunker."

"I'm comin'! Don't leave me!"

The screen door bangs behind Van and Hatch as they stampede for the bunker. The siren wails for the dead.

Chapter Twelve

Easter 1967

Charlie

> "Praise God from whom all blessings flow,
> praise Him all creatures here below.
> Praise Him all of ye heavenly hosts,
> praise Father, Son and Hoooooo-lyyyyyyyy
> Ghooooooost."

"Aaaaahhh-mennnn..." Charlie Dermott sang with the entire congregation and the choir, all of whom could not cover the strong, bold voice of his father, The Reverend Doctor Jacob Lester Dermott, DD.

The big, roaring pipe organ that dominated the wall behind the choir ground to a halt like a stopping train. The relative silence in the sanctuary accentuated the coughing and shuffling of the parishioners, who closed hymnals and sat on crimson velvet cushions upon oaken pews.

Normally, Charlie loved church. He loved the majestic hymns, the grand old organ and the stylish, dignified sermons delivered by his father. Most of all he loved the splendid, cavernous sanctuary where the Fellowship Christian Church of Macon, the second largest protestant congregation in the state of Georgia, had gathered for Easter sunrise services.

Charlie always sat with his sister, Loreen, who was home from Auburn for the Easter break, and his mother, Charlotte, in the front left pew during services, but Charlie especially loved to come into the sanctuary when it was empty but for him. The old church was like a womb to Charlie. It was as though there prevailed an unwritten but inviolable law of the universe that whatever troubled or frightened or distressed Charlie had to wait outside until he came out; such feelings could never accompany Charlie past the towering oaken doors, through the vestibule and into that huge, holy room.

Whenever Charlie entered alone, he walked reverently over the silent carpet between the long rows of pews and down the aisle, bathed in the soft, gentle, comforting hues of light that filtered through the massive stained-glass windows dominating both sidewalls. Charlie thought of all the glowing brides he'd seen step so deliberately down this aisle, of all the proud young men in tuxedos or military dress uniforms who had met and married those brides. He thought of all the times the congregation had advanced down that aisle to take communion. Even the funerals had been appropriately dignified, majestic ceremonies.

Charlie loved Easter; even now he admired the mammoth white lilies which scented the holy room with their fragrance. He especially cherished Christmas, when the sanctuary smelled of evergreen and candle wax and bore the decorations of the greatest celebration of the Christian year. Here in the sanctuary there was peace. Always there was peace. There was relief, however brief, from whatever troubled Charlie Dermott.

Except today.

As his father rose to the pulpit, resplendent in his magnificent black robe with maroon collar, Charlie's heart thumped so loud he glanced to see if his older sister could hear it. Loreen didn't hear Charlie's heart but she did hear his labored breathing. She turned to him and frowned her disapproval.

'Dear Lord,' Charlie intoned silently, 'I pray for thy holy strength and divine guidance; see me through this most difficult hour.'

As he had for over a thousand Sunday mornings,

The Reverend Dr. Jacob Lester Dermott stood tall and imperious in the massive oaken pulpit. He surveyed his flock, looking, they were convinced, directly into the eyes of every solitary one of the hundreds of them packing the grand old church. Then the great, comforting, all-is-well smile that Dr. Dermott was famous for spread over his face, and he commenced.

'Please, Dad,' Charlie thought. 'Please, please, please, just for once, say it simple. Introduce me, and let it go at that. Please, please, please.'

Jacob Dermott's powerful, soothing baritone carried throughout the large sanctuary. "As you have no doubt noted in this morning's bulletin," The Reverend Dermott said slowly, pausing to allow those who hadn't read the bulletin to frantically page through it. "Before I begin the sermon on this grand Easter morning with which our good Lord has so blessed us, my son, Charles, will offer the morning prayer."

Charlie felt all the stares and smiles raining over him and his ears reddened. 'Please Lord, help me.'

"As most of you know," Dr. Dermott continued slowly, deliberately, with a broad smile, "Charles has provided this congregation its morning prayer each Easter Sunday since he was twelve years old."

'Oh please, Dad, just introduce me and sit down in that giant pastor's chair, and let me do what I have to do.'

"But on this, Charles's sixth consecutive year of assisting me in the Easter sunrise service, I have a special announcement to make, and I beg you and the good Lord to permit me just a tiny slice of the sin of pride." Doctor Dermott smiled and the congregation chuckled politely.

'Oh God, no, please no.'

"It is with no small pride, I must confess, and with great joy, that the Dermott family learned early this week -"

'Oh no.'

"—that Charles has been awarded the Reverend

135

Holcomb W. Jared Scholarship at my alma mater,
Whittingham College."

Charlie rubbed his eyes and sighed. 'Well, Lord,' he
thought, 'I guess you decided to bless me with a little
more challenge.'

A reverent applause sounded, subdued as the polite
laughter had been, but clearly genuine. Charlie saw
his mother beaming at him. Even grumpy Loreen
grudgingly smiled.

The Reverend Dermott now frowned and proceeded.
"As you know, my fine Christian friends, these are sad,
trying days for our beleaguered, traditional, American
values, especially among today's young people. And
so, in this time of the so-called sexual revolution,
of rampaging drug abuse among our young, and of
this great nation's regrettable military involvement
in southeast Asia, it is an immense comfort to Mrs.
Dermott and myself that the Lord has seen fit to bless
us with such a wonderful son." The Reverend Dermott
paused for effect.

'Oh Dad. Dad, Dad, Dad.'

"It is my prayer that, as Charles begins his divinity
studies this fall, he will serve as a beacon of inspiration
to a troubled generation of youth. My dear friends, it
is my great pleasure to introduce to you this morning,
the 1967 awardee of the Whittingham College Jared
Scholarship, my son, Charles Jacob Dermott."

Charlie forced his leaden legs to carry his tall,
lanky body up the carpeted steps, all the while feeling
like Judas Iscariot reincarnated. Doctor Dermott gave
Charlie an affectionate pat on the shoulder en route
to his massive, throne-like chair behind the pulpit.
The gesture only cemented Charlie's dismal feeling
of betrayal. Looking out upon the assembly, Charlie
suffered tunnel vision and had to pivot his gaze about
to maintain his balance. Charlie hated neckties, and his
was hanging him at the moment. 'Please Lord. Help
me.'

Charlie drew a deep breath. "Good morn-. Uh. Uh-hum. Uh, good morning. Uh, hap-, happy Easter to you all. Uh, be-, before I offer the prayer this beautiful Easter morning, I would like to make an announcement of my own."

The congregation merely looked on, smiling benevolently, but Doctor and Mrs. Jacob Dermott both locked eyes on Charlie. Loreen glanced first at her father, then at her mother. All three knew this wasn't in the bulletin.

"I, ah, I—" Charlie stammered.

Mrs. Dermott sat forward, her lips pursed with concern; Doctor Dermott struggled to keep the alarm from showing in his face.

"Ah...as Dad just alluded, these are difficult days for the youth of America. It's...always been hard for young people to know what to do in times of...crisis, I suppose. I, ah, there, there is a war, we are in a war in Ve-Vietnam, and it is hard, very hard to know what to do. Our country calls for many of us boys to fight in uniform, yet many of us, boys and girls, wonder if we really belong in this war. Like so many kids...young people my age, I have had to...decide how, what I should do, how this...crisis in America affects me, what I, what is expected of me. What is right. What God would want me to do."

Charlie looked out over a now rapt audience. His mother was studying him carefully, a pained expression in her eyes. Loreen was incredulous. Charlie couldn't see his father, who sat behind him, but he didn't have to to envision that face of Moses frozen in shock.

"Y'all know I, I'm into bicycle racing. I train fifty miles a day. Last -, uh uhmm. Last Wednesday, I... happened to be passing the uh, the uh, Negro cemetery down by the Ocmulgee River. There was, ah, a funeral going on. A young negro, uh, black soldier killed in Vietnam, was being buried. There was an honor guard to carry his casket and to fire a salute. They, uh, they gave his mother a flag."

For possibly the only moment in the history of the

Fellowship Christian Church of Macon, Georgia, not a
soul slept or daydreamed in the service. What on earth
was Reverun and Miz Dermott's boy, little Charlie,
talkin' about? What was all this talk of...nigras, when he
was s'posed to be givin' the prayer?

"I thought," Charlie went on, "standing there, how
sad it was that this boy was killed while he was still
a...a teenager, like me. I asked a man with a shovel
who the soldier was, and he said he was Mrs. Mattie
Johnson's only boy, Richie. He said Richie was a sole
surviving son, and so he couldn't be drafted, but he had
joined the Marines because he was an American and he
believed he owed it to his country to serve in her time
of need. To fight for ...freedom...in Vietnam...because...
because, once, his people were not free."

Nobody coughed. Nobody moved.

Charlie scanned the hundreds of faces of both sexes
and all ages now so focused on him, and he felt a warm,
tranquil peace settle over him. He was committed now;
there was no turning back. There was some comfort in
that. 'Thank you Lord.'

Charlie forged on. "I...I got to tell you folks...I
thought, standing there in that cemetery watching that
family cry, I thought, if a dirt-poor, black, Georgia boy
felt he owed it to America to put his life on the line for
her, and ultimately to die for...her ideal of freedom for
all men, then Charles Jacob Dermott, blessed as he is
with a fine family and a good life, has no right to shirk
his duty...or hide behind a student draft deferment."

Mrs. Dermott gasped and put her hand to her mouth.

"Sooner or later, I guess, all of us get old enough
that we need to accept responsibility, make our
own decisions about our lives...and then live with
the consequences. That time has come for me, and
I have made that decision. And I will live with
the consequences. I...last Friday, I resigned my
scholarship...and I have enlisted in the United States
Army."

A palpable shock wave emitted from the

congregation. Frantic whispering rose like wind in
summer trees. The congregation knew only too well Dr.
Dermott's vehement opposition to that Veet-nam thing.

"Now..." Charlie said loudly, giving the stunned
assemblage time to collect itself, "now, if you will
allow me, I wish to offer the morning prayer. I thank
you for your kind patience. Will you please bow your
heads?"

Not all heads bowed; many stared at Reverend
Dermott and the back of Mrs. Dermott's head. Mrs.
Dermott wept silently, and the good Reverend looked
like the life had been let out of him.

"Our father in Heaven," Charlie prayed, "We...I...
thank you for this beautiful, peaceful Easter morning
in America upon which we rejoice for the resurrection
of thy son, Jesus. I thank you for life in America, for
peace...and opportunity...and even for the duties that
go hand in hand with those blessings. Lord, I ask
thy blessing on this congregation for its many years
of fellowship toward me. I ask you to help my good
family to forgive me for any hurt or embarrassment I
may have caused them. I pray, dear God, that you will
guide me as I go upon the journey...I believe you would
have me make. I ask that you help all of America's
young men and women to make their own decisions, as
you have helped me, and that their decisions may be the
right ones for them and for thee. Last, Lord, I ask that
you welcome into your heavenly embrace the soul of a
young man who saw his duty and did it, even in the face
of death. Lord, please bless the soul of Lance Corporal
Richie Leroy Johnson, and help me to have his courage.
In the name of thy blessed son, our Lord Jesus Christ, I
pray. Amen."

Charles Jacob Dermott turned and briefly met the
eyes of his father, who stood, clearly still struggling
to comprehend. Then Charlie walked down from
the pulpit, strode slowly past his weeping mother
and gaping sister, and he walked up the aisle of the
Fellowship Christian Church of Macon, Georgia,

without looking back.

Outside, the rising Easter sun was warm on his face.

Charlie's night to be God came fourteen months later, after he had graduated from Army flight school and pinned on the bars and silver wings of a warrant officer aviator, exactly thirty-eight days after his arrival in a frightening, if exotic land called Vietnam.

Charlie and Hale and Arnie Wycovski were asleep in The Room when the exec burst in and turned on the lights. Spud and Pot were out on missions, and The Hatchet Man was at another hooch drinking and telling macabre, hysterical stories with his fellow gunship pilots. The three young pilots in The Room sat up on their bunks, shielding their eyes from the sudden fluorescent brilliance.

"Christ, XO," Arnie Wycovski said, squinting at his watch, "It's two-thirty in the goddamn morning."

"Let's go, you guys!" Captain Tolby said urgently. "We got a mission. The whole damn flight platoon. They're calling for every available ship. Some firebase out on the border is gettin' the livin' shit kicked out of it. They're screaming for big-time resupply and medevac. Get your gear and be in operations in ten minutes. Let's go, damn it! This thing has come down from division!" The Captain hurried out to arouse other flight crews.

Charlie felt chilled, and he found it hard to breathe as he hurriedly tugged on his pants and boots. Night flights in The Nam were terrifying. Hell, day flights were dangerous enough, but unlike in the world, where there were ground lights almost everywhere, in Vietnam the totally-featureless, black void went on forever. There was nothing, especially on overcast nights like this one, to give a pilot a clue as whether he was climbing, diving, turning or even upside-down, except his instruments.

And this was the Central Highlands; the mountains ran to eight-thousand feet above sea level! Unlike the jet jocks, helicopter drivers were always close enough to the hard earth to smell the locker-room stink of NVA troop concentrations beneath the jungle canopy. Worse, the night meant that, down there in that jungle you couldn't see, there moved thousands of pitiless little slot-eyed men with weapons and abiding hatred for the crews of the death-wielding American helicopters. Thank God I'm too new in country to be a command pilot, Charlie thought, shrugging into his shirt. Thank God a senior, experienced combat pilot who knows what he's doing will be the AC, aircraft commander. 'Lord, help me perform my duties as co-pilot with courage and skill.'

"Man, I don't believe this shit!" Arnie Wycovski whispered angrily, heaving his flack-jacket over his head, "Forty-six days and a wakeup! Man, I'm too short for this hero night shit!"

Hale, Charlie and Arnie hurried to the airfield operations building carrying their helmet bags and rifles. "It must be bad," Hale said grimly, looking at the starless, moonless, black air close above them. "If they're calling out the bean haulers for a night mission in this weather, it must be really bad out at that firebase."

Arnie Wycovski's facial muscles flexed as he looked up to confirm Hale's ominous assessment. "Christ, man. Forty-six days and a wakeup! Shit! What the fuck firebase is this again?"

"The XO didn't say, did he?" Charlie answered. Lord, it was dark.

In the operations briefing room, briefers revealed the worst. A firebase none of the pilots had ever heard of, way to the west, had come under attack by NVA forces at midnight. It had not gone well for the defenders. The cloud ceiling was too low for jet support and the base was too far west for artillery support. Radio communications were sporadic, but what there

141

were confirmed an ongoing disaster. Many were dead including the unit CO and both medics. Worse, they were running out of ammunition and had whole squads of wounded desperately in need of medevac.

"LZ what?" Arnie whispered, eyeing his map. "Out-what?"

"LZ Outstar," Hale repeated softly for the second time.

"Never fucking heard of it! How can it be 'too far west' for fucking arty? Man, I don't like this shit!"

"Alright, gentlemen," the ops officer said looking up from a clipboard and avoiding eye-contact with the men he was dispatching, "The, ah, the location is as follows."

"Good," Arnie whispered. Now we can plot the coordinates and find out where this LZ Outlaw—"

"Outstar!"

"—is."

"Gentlemen, at a constant and precise airspeed of ninety knots, you will clear IP-tango and follow course two-eight-seven degrees for thirty-four minutes."

The ops officer now stared at the group of pilots, blankly.

Everyone waited for the grid coordinates that were always used to establish destinations. None were forthcoming.

"Ah, Captain Landover," said Hale, "Could you give us that location in coordin—"

"I repeat," the ops officer interrupted bluntly, "You will clear IP-tango at a precise and constant airspeed of ninety knots, and you will proceed on course two-eight-seven degrees for exactly thirty-four minutes." Captain Landover continued to stare as though trying to say without saying that the flight crews had received all the destination information they were going to get. Captain Landover promptly moved on to routine code information and frequencies shared with the Graverobber gunships which would fly cover.

"Aw man!" Arnie Wycovski whispered with distress

as he hurriedly plotted the course on his chart, "Fuck! That's in fucking Cambodia, man!"

"No," Charlie answered, "Can't be. We don't have any troops in Cambodia. President Johnson just said so in his speech night before la—"

"Fuck Johnson, you dumbshit newby! Look where that azimuth, time and airspeed will put us, man! It's a solid klick inside fucking Cambodia!"

"He's right," Hale agreed, consulting his own chart.

"Aw Jesus, man!" Arnie almost cried. "Man, I'm too short for this shit! Cam-fucking-bodia, man, they got whole fucking divisions of NVA over there with them thirty-seven mike-mike anti-aircraft machine guns! I do not fucking believe this!"

"Alright, gentlemen," Captain Landover broke in, "Listen up for your aircraft and crew assignments."

All pilots readied pencils. 'Oh dear Lord,' Charlie prayed, 'I hope I'm assigned with a good aircraft commander tonight, because this does not look good.'

Landover read off the aircraft assignments and the pilots to fly them. The crew chiefs and gunners would not be mentioned as they were already briefed and assigned, and were at their aircraft preparing them. "Three-seven-niner, Peltier and Schuman. Oh-niner-five, Hooper and Greizhek. Five-four-four, Preston and Gibson. Two-five-five, Dermott and Bradford. Seven-niner-one, Wycovski and Perez. Eight-eight-eight, Stokley and -"

"What?" Charlie suddenly hissed at Arnie and Hale. "What did he say? Did he list me and Bradford for two-five-five? There must be some mistake. Bradford just got here last week. There must be some—"

"Alright, gentlemen!" Landover said loudly. "Let's everybody keep their heads out of their asses! Stay alert and think. And bring my toys back to me undamaged. Takeoff is in...twenty-five minutes. Let's move!" Everyone rose and shuffled hastily for the door and the dark night beyond.

"Captain Landover!" Charlie called, as the ops

officer headed for the side door. The short, portly
Captain paused and looked soberly at Charlie.

"Mr. Dermott, I know what you're going to—"

"Uh, sir, I just wanted to let you know there's been
an error. Uh, you listed me with Bradford. Uh, I, uh,
I've only been here a month, uh, five weeks, and
I'm not on AC orders, and of course Bradford...well,
Bradford just got here last week and—"

"Congratulations, Mr. Dermott, you're now an
aircraft commander," Captain Landover said so
nonchalantly that Charlie thought he was kidding.

"Seriously, sir, I've only been here—"

"Seriously, Mister Dermott, eight of my pilots are
grounded taking the rabies series from rat bites. Grimes
is on R and R, and Levine...well, we all know what
happened to Levine and that newby, Cross, yesterday.
Division is screaming at me for everything we got
that'll fly. I don't have enough qualified AC's to fly all
the ships that're up, and you're the next senior newby."

"Captain, you can't be serious!" Charlie said with
strain. "I've only got about a hundred-fifty hours in
country! I haven't even had an AC checkride! I—"

"Look Dermott, I know all that! You'll just—"

"You can't do this!" Charlie cried, "I'm not
qualified! I could get somebody killed, sir!"

"Mister Dermott," Landover said tersely, "Division
is telling me they got thirty-two confirmed KIA at
Outstar. The mountains are too high and the ceiling
too low out there for tactical air support. They're out
of range of division artillery assets; they've got no arty
but their own internal mortars. They are running out
of fireworks, they got wounded laying everywhere,
and there are gooks in the fucking wire! They need
everything we can get to them bad and now! Welcome
to the big leagues, command pilot Dermott. Lotsa luck
out there." Landover stared at an incredulous Charlie
Dermott for seconds, then he turned and walked away.

Charlie was still in shock as his big, thundering
UH-1H helicopter flew left echelon in a formation

of ten ships bound for the ill-fated LZ Outstar, Arnie
Wykovski's ship in the lead. His mind raced over the
plastic-coated level-off checklist on his kneeboard,
checking and rechecking, while Bradford operated the
controls. 'Oh God, oh God, oh God. Please help me.
Don't let me make a mistake.'

The heavy Huey swayed slightly as Bradford
tensely maintained its position in the formation. The
sole interior illumination came from the red instrument
lighting, giving the helmeted pilots the appearance of
looking through a hole into glowing hell. The machine's
thick, churning main-rotor gave off a drumming,
staccato thump and caused the aircraft to ride like a
truck on a concrete highway. The high, scream of the
overhead turbine engine soaked through the foam ear
cups in the crew helmets.

Although Charlie's Blackjack five-five was not in
the lead position, Charlie knew that a few streaking
touches of ground fire might down Arnie and then
Charlie would instantly become flight leader of a ten-
ship combat night extraction under fire. In Cambodia!
It was insane! He reviewed his chart with emphasis on
the elevation and azimuth figures for the surrounding
mountains, trying to steady the bouncing map and read
the tiny numbers faded in red light. He found it hard to
focus on one concern, so many were there clamoring
for his attention: altitude, airspeed, fuel quantity, fuel
burn-rate, compass heading, call-signs, authentication
codes, frequencies, the nearest potential safe landing
area, main-mast torque, exhaust gas temperature, and
five-five's crucial position in the formation where
counter-slashing rotor tips were separated only by feet.

Briefly, Charlie looked to his left and studied
Bradford who sat in the left seat wearing his green
flight helmet, actually flying Blackjack-five-five
while Charlie read off the checklist. Charlie was still
astonished at Bradford's having called him 'sir', when
they were preflighting the ship. 'I'm nineteen years
old!' Charlie railed silently. 'Bradford's twenty-one!

I'm not a sir!'

Normally, Huey aircraft commanders preferred to ride in the left seat as the huge instrument panel was offset slightly to the right, providing the left-seat pilot a better downward view on steep landing approaches. But Charlie had never flown a Huey from the left seat and he didn't intend to try to learn on a night combat flight. Besides, the better set of red-lighted attitude instrumentation was installed for the right-seat pilot.

Unfortunately, this evening's copilot, Warrant Officer Cliff Bradford, had also never flown from the left seat, and he was weaving and wandering in flight, trying to get accustomed to the odd position.

"Left," Charlie said on the intercom, looking to the right-front at Arnie Wycovski's aircraft, visible in the black night only by tiny red and green running lights. "Left...left...left! Wake up, Cliff! You're gonna get us in a mid-air! Keep your scan moving! Don't fixate on that attitude indicator! Watch Arnie!"

"Yes sir!" The thoroughly terrified Bradford replied on the intercom.

'I'm not a sir!' Charlie wanted to shout. Instead he keyed his intercom foot switch and said, "Just take it easy, Cliff. Keep your eyes moving around. The other ships are all lit up now. When we get near the LZ, we'll all turn out our exterior lights. We'll have to be super alert or we'll mix blades and become falling debris."

On the radio, Charlie heard the unmistakable growl of the Hatchet Man on the VHF radio net. "Blackjack-niner-one, Graverobber-two-two."

Flight leader Arnie Wycovski's nervous voice crackled over the frequency. "Uh, Graverobber-double-deuce, this is Blackjack-niner-one. Glad to see you boys."

Charlie looked way to his right and saw only the blinking red lights of four Graverobber gunships joining the mission, but he knew they looked like the 'slicks' that he flew except they were an earlier model. Charlie thought about the almost obscene ugliness of the gunships with their grenade-firing snout bulges, heavy outboard rocket tubes and their vicious pairs of six-barreled, electric machine guns. He was surprised and unsettled to find that all that lethal ugliness had suddenly taken on a certain warm, motherly beauty for him.

LZ Outstar proved not at all difficult to locate in the great eastern Cambodian void. The mortar flashes, arcing tracer streaks and the fires of burning bunkers could be seen for miles. Laser-like, red tracers streaked outbound, and Chinese-communist-manufactured, green tracers poured into the firebase.

"Shit..." Someone said on the radio.

Charlie thought his heart would blast its way out through his flack vest and chest armor. He drew a deep breath and released it slowly. He flexed his fingers and wrapped his hands around the cyclic and collective controls. "I've got it."

"You got it, sir!" Bradford answered, snatching his hands off his set of controls like they'd shocked him. He was only too happy to relinquish them.

'Stop calling me sir!' Charlie howled inside. "Cliff, you call out the altitudes on the way in. Chart says the elevation is about thirty-two hundred feet. After we go below four-thousand, give it to me in fifty foot increments. On the—"

"Yes sir!"

'Uuuh!' "On liftoff, read me the torque settings every time they change, but keep your hands near the controls in case I...get hit. Sergeant Poole, you and Private Rickman use those guns until we get short, then be looking for obstacles in the touchdown. On the way out, fire as soon as we clear the trees and keep firing until Mr. Bradford says we're above forty-seven hundred." Charlie winced as all three crew members replied "Yes sir!"

The plan was that they would land in pairs while the remainder of the flight orbited, as there was not room on the stark, bunker-studded hilltop for more than two ships. Wycovski and Perez in Blackjack-niner-one, and Charlie and his crew in Blackjack-five-five, would be the first pair in. There were pluses and minuses to this. You had the surprise element of being first, which might mean less enemy shooting at you on the way in, but who knew what was on the ground down there? Radio contact was sporadic and confused enough only to understand that most of the command structure was dead. Arnie and Charlie might land only to find the whole place overrun with NVA.

The Graverobber gunships would lay down suppression cover-fire in the bordering trees while the slicks were on final, and as they took off.

In the LZ, Charlie knew, the grunts would be organized into teams, one of which would rapidly snatch the ammunition crates off one side of the aircraft as soon as it touched down, while another team on the opposite side of the aircraft would simultaneously load wounded. Charlie thought they should not be on the ground in the hot LZ for more than twenty seconds. They would take off under gunship cover and, just as they cleared the LZ, the second pair of slicks would be on short final. It was all organized with military precision.

Charlie marveled at how well things were going. Wycovski went ahead and to the right of Charlie's aircraft. As they descended below seven-hundred feet above the ground, even with their exterior lights now out, tracer fire like supersonic, green fireflies suddenly soared up from several points in the wooded blackness surrounding the shallow hilltop.

Charlie's rectum clenched tight at the hollow PLOO-PLOONK! sound of a bullet entering then exiting the thin aluminum sheet metal somewhere on his aircraft. He was about to trigger his radio when Arnie Wycovski called, "Graverobber, Blackjack! We're takin' fire from ten and two!"

"We see 'em, we see 'em," Hatchette's bored voice replied.

Charlie had to tear his eyes from their morbid fascination with the glowing-lime tracer streaks rocketing up from the black void. All tracers seemed to Charlie to be coming straight for the bridge of his nose. Most streaked past but two hit the ship. PLOONK! PLOO-PLOONK! Charlie fought to concentrate on his position relative to Arnie's ship, and on his own airspeed, altitude and rate of descent.

"Thirty-nine hundred!" Bradford called, clearly on the edge of panic, swiveling his head at the passing tracers.

"Easy, Cliff," Charlie said, forcing all the calm he could manage. "I need you to keep your head inside now, Cliff. Read me the altitudes, now, come on. Keep your hands near the controls in case I'm hit."

"Thirty-six-fifty, sir!"

"Good," Charlie said soothingly. "Stay with me now, keep your hands near the controls."

Part way through Bradford's reply, the door gunners in the back opened up. The heavy M-60's were painfully loud, and their ragged, yellow-white muzzle flashes destroyed night vision acuity.

"Yes sir! Thirty- Hah! Jesus! Thirty-five-hundred feet!"

Just as the rising tracer volume seemed like a green-lighted geyser, Charlie and Cliff were startled by several blindingly swift rushes of white flame tearing past them for the jungle, passing almost under their own rotor. The streaks disappeared into the largest of the sources of tracer fire in the darkness below and exploded in brilliant white flashes. The enemy shooting from those sources ceased instantly.

Then the air on both sides of the landing helicopters was filled with thousands of red neon streaks that swarmed by them from behind and poured into the jungle bordering the LZ. Some ricocheted presumably from rocks and curled erratically off into the night. Charlie flinched as Hatchette's gunship dove past them, still hosing the ground with what looked like glowing

149

red water. Even over the scream of his own turbine engine and the thump of the pounding rotor, Charlie could hear the howling chainsaw roar of the electric machine guns on Hatchette's 'hog'.

Hatchette pulled off his dive just as Arnie was about to touch down, but the Graverobber wing man, still behind Charlie's aircraft somewhere, immediately resumed cover fire.

Even the best of military plans have too many variables to be secure, Warrant Officer and rookie aircraft commander, Charlie Dermott, was now to learn. The best battle plans usually all degrade to the chaotic pandemonium of combat.

As Arnie Wycovski's big machine neared the ground, the rotorwash spewed up an horrendous, mushroom-shaped cloud of dust and debris. From his following and offset vantage, to his profound horror, Charlie saw a jagged tree stump outlined in the dust beneath Arnie's ship, suddenly silhouetted by the glow of fires burning in the LZ.

Charlie had just keyed his radio transmit trigger and yelled, "Arnie, watch—" when the lead helicopter settled hard onto the tall, pointed stump which tore up through the bottom of the fuel tank and caused the ship to roll hard to its left. When the flailing main rotor hit the ground, the ship disintegrated into lethally flung parts and became engulfed in dust, debris and a deep-orange fireball gushing black oily smoke.

Men on the ground ran and dived for cover. One, on fire, whirled about like a ballerina.

Charlie maneuvered violently to dodge flying debris, but took some in the rotor blades with horrifying bangs, and he tried to decide whether to abort the approach or land. Before he had time to decide, he was settling the aircraft onto the ground twenty yards from the wreckage of Blackjack-niner-one, blowing back the roiling flames and thick smoke with his rotor wash.

Instantly, as though there had not just been a fatal aircraft crash only yards away, skulking teams of shirtless, sweating soldiers crab-walked to the aircraft and Charlie could hear the scrape of the heavy ammo crates being dragged from the cargo floor behind him.

Charlie was still trying to order his mind to cope with what he was staring at. The twisted hulk of Arnie Wycovski's helicopter would occasionally and briefly show through the giant globe of orange fire boiling up into the night. Deep within, Charlie saw something alive, just a blackened silhouette, but something moving, struggling to rise from its back, waving its arms. Charlie Dermott would wonder for the rest of his life whether that writhing figure was Arnie Wycovski or another of his crew.

A brain already stretched to the ripping point could scarcely believe what Charlie saw next. A helmeted soldier strode quickly from a bunker toward the burning wreck, cradling a machine gun, its ammo belt swinging beneath. 'No,' Charlie thought, 'No, you can't rescue the burning man. The flames are too—.' Charlie tried to cry out but he could only croak in horror. The machine gunner poured a burst of rounds into the thrashing silhouette in the flames until the burning man flopped down and moved no more. Only much later would the macabre kindness of this act soak in to Charlie Dermott.

A grunt suddenly leaped onto the skid step and thrust his face at Charlie, who jumped and recoiled. He was a young man, no older than Charlie himself, but he looked like death warmed over. His anguished face was streaked with soot, dirt and blood, and he appeared to have recently been crying. "Who you gonna take, sir?" he screamed over the howl and thunder of the aircraft.

"What?" Charlie yelled back.

"Who you gonna take, sir? Who you wan' us to load?"

"Uh, well, you mean you don't—? Why're you asking me?" Charlie was lost, He struggled to collect himself.

The bug-eyed young soldier now seemed to Charlie to be on the verge of hysteria. "You a off-sah, ain't you?" His voice squeaked. "Who...who the hell else I'm gon ask? The Captain and the Lieutenant is dead an' I ain't seen the platoon sergeant fer a hour! Who you wan us to load, sir?"

"Uh, well...uh, load the worst ones first!"

"They all fucked up, sir! All of 'em fucked up bad! Who you wan us to load, sir?"

"Where's your medic?"

"Dead!"

"Who's in command?"

"How da fuck I know, sir? Chubby's talkin' on the radio an all, but he just a private like me! We all shot to fuck and gone, sir! Ain't nobody in command! You a off-sah, ain't you? You be in charge! Who I'm gon load? Tell me!" The soldier was running hoarse.

Charlie assigned the controls to Cliff Bradford and threw off his harness. Door gunner Rickman jumped down and ran forward to open the cockpit door and slide back the heavy armor side-plate on Charlie's seat. Charlie jumped to the ground and scrambled with the private to a nearby ditch.

Away from his roaring aircraft, Charlie could hear the heavy perimeter gunfire; he looked up to see Hatchette and his wing man pouring tracers, rockets and grenade rounds into the darkness beyond. When he lowered his head and the dust cleared from his eyes he was aghast to note at least thirty wounded men squirming in the glow from the crash fire. All were wrapped in brown bandages and torn jungle fatigues, and the blood, wetly black in the eerie, swirling, orange firelight, seemed to have been heaved about from buckets. It glistened hideously. Some wounded reached out to Charlie, possibly seeing some symbol of their salvation in the tall boy in the flight helmet. Flight helmets meant pilots, pilots meant helicopters, helicopters meant hospitals, and hospitals meant life.

"Who you wan'—"

"I'm thinking, damn it!" Charlie yelled, cursing for the first time in his religious life. The hot, damp,

Cambodian mountain air was thin, Charlie knew. He could only take off with about eight wounded men safely, any more than ten and the aircraft simply wouldn't fly, or worse it would fly a short way and crash. "Who's hurt worst?" He called to the soldier.

The private surveyed the suffering men. Charlie now saw tears streaking the dust on his cheeks. "I don't know sir!" He screamed, on the edge of collapsing. "I don't know! I ain't no medic! I done the best I can, but they all fucked up! They dyin' faster than I can help 'em. You a off-sah! You—"

"Alright!" Charlie replied with anger. He walked among the butchered men and he learned why the boy had surrendered. In broad daylight, in a peaceful, secure meadow, with an hour to decide, it would have been impossible for a team of trauma physicians to accurately determine exactly who was hurt seriously enough to rank first transport, who was hurt so badly that segregation on morphine was the only option, and who was sufficiently stable to await later evacuation. For a nineteen-year-old pilot with only seconds to decide, with only basic first aid training, under fire, in the dark, with seconds-dead friends burning yards away, it was lunacy. *Lunacy.*

Some of the injured men stared blankly, but many reached to Charlie or called to him. Some thrashed in pain and shrieked.

'Please, Lord!' Charlie pleaded. 'Tell me! Who?'

Charlie got no reply that he could discern. He looked at the faces of the dying men and called out again, 'Who? Please, dear Lord, help me! Help me make the right choices! Who?'

A hand seized Charlie. He turned to see his crew chief, Sergeant Poole. "Sir!" the big black man yelled, "we got to get the fuck outta here! The gunships only got about ten minutes more on station, and they got to get them other slicks in, one at a time, now!"

Almost on cue, a painfully-loud, metallic clank exploded in a cloud of white smoke on the far edge of

153

the firebase.

"Mortars!" The crew chief yelled, crouching instinctively and leaning back toward the helicopter. "We're gettin' mortared, Mr. Dermott! We gotta get outta here! Now!"

"Who I'm gonna load, sir?" The private yelled shrilly. "You cain't just leave me here with all these hurt men! They all fucked up an—"

Charlie's nose clenched at a choking cloud of jet-fuel smoke with a nauseating smell of burned meat mixed in it. 'Please, God! Where are you? Help me!'

"Who, sir? Who I'm gon' load?"

Sgt. Poole: "We gotta go, Mr. Dermott!"

Charlie turned to see the private standing before a stone-faced, exhausted squad of soldiers awaiting leadership. There are no atheists in foxholes, Charlie had once heard it said. Now he wondered if there were any gods on battlefields.

"Him!" Charlie yelled, grabbing the private by his bloody shirt and dragging him toward the ditch. Another mortar round exploded, then another. "Him!" Able-bodied men pounced on Charlie's choices and hustled them to the aircraft. "And him!" More men moved to grab the corners of the rubber ponchos upon which the wounded lay, to hoist them to the booming helicopter. "And him! And this one...him...this one...that guy, and that one! That's all I can carry. Move!"

"Yes sir!" the private yelled, scrambling with his buddies, relieved at the order of commands.

"Listen to me, Private!" Charlie yelled.

"Yes sir?"

"Next ship lands, load him...and that one over there! This guy. This guy. Him. Him. Him. And him! Get 'em ready!"

"Yes sir! I got it!"

"Check for dead guys and get 'em out of the way! We'll pull the KIAs in the morning!"

"Yes sir!"

Charlie found a soldier whose entrails and

Charlie had no idea what organs lay splayed from an eviscerated mid-section. The injured man looked at Charlie with wide, terrified eyes, his tongue out. Charlie flashed the man a thumbs up. "Hang in there, soldier!"

Charlie grabbed the private by his neck and pulled him near. Into his ear, Charlie said, "Dope this guy big-time. Leave him there 'til he passes out so he thinks he's going to live, then put him with the dead!"

"Yes sir! Yes sir!"

As Charlie hurriedly heaved himself back into his cockpit seat and strapped in with Rickman's frantic assistance, the last of the chosen few were slid aboard. Some of the wounded screamed from the pain of movement, some stared glassy-eyed at the ceiling. The aircraft was permeated with a repulsive odor combined of feces, blood and sour sweat.

"Blackjack five-five; we're coming out!" Charlie called on the VHF. He pulled pitch and the big machine climbed forward and up.

"Yeah, five-five," Hatchette's maddeningly calm voice sounded on the radio, "Bring it on out." Charlie was startled by another roman candle sweep of rockets and red tracer fire that swept over his head into the few sources of gunfire focused on his takeoff. The crew chief and gunner opened up with the door guns. Hot brass bullet casings showered about the cabin full of writhing wounded men. Bradford called out the torque gauge readings as they climbed. "Forty...forty-four... forty sev-, forty-nine!" Fifty pounds mast torque was all the engine could deliver without overheating.

In flight to the Air Force hospital in Pleiku, Poole and Rickman scrambled awkwardly about the dimly lighted, crowded cabin floor feverishly tending to the moaning and thrashing wounded. Cliff Bradford flew. Charlie consulted his com cards for the hospital alert frequency.

Charlie and Cliff both flinched at a painfully loud shout spearing through their helmet earphones. "Whose...leg is this!?" Sergeant Poole was screaming in the cabin. "Whose leg is this?"

Charlie twisted to look back over his cockpit seat at the cabin. Poole was on his knees, wide-eyed, holding a dusty boot with ten-inches of bloody leg protruding from it. The leg's pale bone was jaggedly broken; limp white vessels hung in strings.

"Whose leg is this?" Poole railed at the tangled pile of wounded men. "Whose leg is this? Whose leg is this?" Mercifully, he now yelled without keying his microphone, but his hoarse, hysterical shouts could still be heard over the engine's howl, the rush of the wind in the open doors and the thunder of the rotor blades . "Whose...fuckin'...leg...is this!?" Poole howled, gasping, his voice cracking falsetto.

"Terry!" Charlie called over the intercom, but Poole kept maniacally yelling. "Terry!" Charlie called sharply. "Sergeant Poole!" Charlie shouted, deafening on the crew intercom.

Poole stopped shouting and turned his head toward Charlie. He still held the macabre leg, he heaved for breath and his eyes were bulged wide.

"Sir?" Poole croaked.

Still on the intercom, Charlie continued softly now. "Terry, Terry, Terry. Easy, buddy. Easy. That leg's a loss, Terry. Throw it out the door and do the best you can, buddy. Just do the best you can."

Poole still heaved for breath, but he raised a hand toward Charlie and nodded his helmeted head. He seemed to suddenly remember the destroyed leg he held. He curled his arm and viciously hurled it out the cabin door into the black void beyond. A streak of blood arced onto the interior side of the aircraft.

"Good," Charlie said. "Good. That's my man. Just do the best you can back there. ETE about twenty minutes."

Blackjack five-five landed at the 71st Medevac Hospital at Pleiku in a storm of dust. Masked, green-gowned hospital personnel swarmed the aircraft, gingerly extracting the wounded and placing them onto stretchers which were hurriedly humped away from the landing zone.

After further intercom conversation with his crew, on the flight back to Camp Enari, Charlie marveled that it no longer felt embarrassing or odd to be called...sir.

For days afterward, Charlie brooded with extremely disconcerting thoughts. They were not about the death of Arnie Wycovski or even about the horror of the burning man, nor Terry's hysteria, nor even the terrible choices he'd had to make. His concerns were much, much more deeply disturbing.

Where was God at LZ Outstar?

It was in this profoundly troubled frame of mind that Charlie was shortly to meet a sixteen-year-old Vietnamese laundry girl named Sung Tranh, who, regrettably, was neither sixteen nor a laundry girl.

Chapter Thirteen
The Room

Dear Loreen,

I guess I should say thanks for writing. Certainly I enjoyed seeing the photos of you and your new guy, what's his name? Jacques?

But I'm sorry to read that you feel you can't tell Jacques or your other Auburn classmates that your brother is fighting in Vietnam. In one breath you say you're not ashamed of me, and in the next you say you tell your friends you don't have a brother, so you don't have to explain where he is. Nice going, Tokyo Loreen.

It's pretty clear that I don't know what is going on in today's cool, college in-crowd. It astonishes me that anyone, let alone a sister of mine, would feel anything except proud to have a son or brother or boyfriend fighting for his country, or at least for his country's democratically determined interests, and another nation's freedom, but I guess that's it, isn't it? You guys don't think we are fighting for America. What is it, I read about in the papers and news magazines from home? We're fighting for LBJ and something called the defense industry establishment? It's a war of oppression and American imperialism? Right.

What's not so clear to me is this: Is communism a good thing for the people of southeast Asia? Sure doesn't seem so to me. With all their talk of 'the people's' this and 'the people's' that, all of today's communist regimes seem to do the very thing for which they complain

*about capitalism, namely the concentration of
wealth and privilege among a narrow ruling
group to the exclusion of the teeming masses of
poor. Only as near as I can tell, the communists
do it worse, leaving their populations in far
worse shape than America's relatively few poor.
As a form of government and as a tool for social
welfare, it looks to me like communism sucks,
Loreen. I'm not saying America's motives are
all freedom and justice for all and 'mom's apple
pie', but I don't think you have to hold a PhD in
political science to see democracy works better
for more of 'the people'.*

*I've prayed a lot since I got here, more than
ever before. There is so much butchery and
suffering, and it's so hard to understand how a
kind and loving God could permit it. It's one thing
for God to let adults suffer the consequences
of their sinful ways; I can understand that; but
there are so many innocent here, Loreen, so many
children and old people caught up in it.*

*Last week I flew an intelligence team up the
Kontum highway several miles to investigate
a terrible event. A little, three-wheeled, Italian
scooter truck loaded mostly with children, headed
for the Catholic pre-school in Kontum, ran
over a tank mine, a tank mine, Loreen. That's
a buried bomb about the size of the top third
of a large garbage can, designed to destroy a
sixty-ton armored tank. It blew that little truck
and everybody in it for a hundred yards in every
direction. There were kids' bodies in the trees.
Division intelligence figured there were two
adults and 'probably' eleven children under the
age of six.*

*Since the NVA don't have tanks in this area or
use these roads for their movement, presumably
it was an NVA or VC mine, but that's not much
comfort to those kids or their relatives. Or me*

*either. I ask God, why? Why, why, why? Just tell
me your greater purpose, here! Tell me any holy
justification for this! If You're the Almighty, how
can You let this happen to innocent people whose
hearts are pure and who know no sin? How?
Send me a sign! I'm listening, but I'm not hearing
anything. It scares me, Loreen.*

*One thing I guess you have to say for
communism is that it expands voraciously if
you let it. If you recognize that it's a bad thing,
that wherever communism goes, free elections
and economic prosperity don't, then it has to be
stopped where it attempts to expand, otherwise
why believe in freedom and democracy?
What good are all our lofty principles if we
aren't willing to stand for them? Many other
governments, especially those communist,
aren't going to cooperate with the principles of
democracy just because we ask them politely,
especially when it may mean the loss of the power
and wealth bases of their ruling elite. And if
we don't back up our ideals with military might
where others force us to, then why even have a
foreign policy? Why indeed even have ideals?*

*Maybe you and your crowd ought to look
beyond your comfy campus at a little reality,
Loreen. If you or your friends think there are
any nice, clean ideological answers to this mess,
you're dreaming.*

*Oh well. I read recently that Marlene Dietrich
is supposed to have said that there are two things
which people who haven't experienced them can't
possibly understand: making love and making
war. I'm making war and I still don't understand
it.*

*One thing I do understand though is I'm going
to be in even hotter water with Mom and Dad.
When I told everybody about my decision last
year I thought Mom would cry herself to death,*

*and if Dad was a pope he'd have excom'ed me
on the spot. You know how Dad feels about this
war, any war, and of course Mom lost both her
brothers in World War Two.*

*But now I'm about to muddy up the water. I
think I'm in love, Loreen. I really do. The sticky
part is, she's a Vietnamese and you know how
Dad is about interracial marriages, and Mom
has always pushed me at Katie Cantrell because
Katie's dad is the manager at the shoe plant and
all.*

*Her name is Sung. She's what we call a 'hooch
maid'. She comes on the base every morning to
clean the officer's rooms and polish boots and
do laundry and all. But she's not just a maid.
Her father was an educated man, and Sung was
supposed to go to college in Saigon except her
father got killed and his restaurant business
failed, and making a living over here is even
tougher than in America. So Sung has to work to
help her mother support her two little brothers.
Sung's older sister is a teacher in France, and she
sends money for them too. I'll tell you more about
Sung later but right now I got to write Mom and
Dad and try to explain her to them.*

*You may as well pretend to your college
friends that I don't exist, Loreen. After today,
Mom and Dad are probably going to do the same
thing.*

> *Your loving brother,*
> *Charlie*

Dear Mom and Dad—

Dear Mother and Father—

My dear parents—

No, no, no; keep it simple, just like always.

> *Dear Mom and Dad,*
>
> *I have met the most wonderful girl and—*

No, you can't just throw it in their faces like a cold fish, you gotta lead in to it. Gotta set 'em up in the right frame of mind...

> *Dear Mom and Dad,*
> *How's the weather there? Awfully hot here.*
> *Listen, I met this—*

"How's the weather?" Get serious!
Wrinkle it up again. In the trash can again.

> *Dear Mom and Dad,*
> *I guess you're wondering why I'm writing this*
> *letter. It's to—*

Aaah, no, too serious, like you're trying to tell them you're a homo or something crazy like that. This is ridiculous. Mom and Dad have always listened when you talked to them; they didn't always agree but they always listened. You're going to have to trust them on this. Just lay it out honestly like they always said to do, and trust them to listen fairly. Go for it.

> *Dear Mom and Dad,*
> *I want to share some great news with you. I*
> *have met the most wonderful girl in the world!*
> *She is beautiful and sweet and very smart, and*
> *she is crazy about me too. Her name is Sung*
> *Tranh, and she is a Vietnamese.*
> *Now before you get all upset, let me tell you*
> *more about her. Remember how you always said*
> *that you were so happy that I always seemed to*
> *pick good kids from good families to be friends*

with? You said I had a good instinct for nice
people, remember? Well, try to trust me on this;
I'm a grown man now, and I know what I'm
doing. OK?

Sung is only five feet tall, which causes lots of
jokes from the guys because I'm six-foot-four, but
I don't care because I know they are just jealous.

Sung is sixteen-years-old, going on seventeen;
she has short, shining black hair and the prettiest
smile you ever saw. She speaks very good
English, well, not like an American, but good
enough that we can have long, deep discussions
about everything.

Sung's father was the owner of a very nice
supper club in Saigon from the time that the
French were here up until about two years ago
when he was killed. It is awful how he was killed:
the Viet Cong were fighting in Saigon one night
when Mr. Tranh was riding his bicycle home from
the restaurant, and American MP's thought he
was a VC and they shot him. This happened right
in front of the apartment the Tranhs lived in, and
Sung saw it happen. (Sung has an older sister
also, but she was in Paris where she is a teacher.)
It was awful! Sung was very close to her father, so
this was even more terrible for her.

When Sung's father was alive, he sent her to
a private school in Saigon where she learned
both English and French. She was supposed to
go to the University of Saigon, except when her
father was killed, the Tranhs had no way to make
any money and so she couldn't go. Her mother
is some sort of clerk with the South Vietnamese
government in Nha Trang now, but she does not
make enough to pay her rent because the war and
the relatively rich Americans have caused the
price of everything to go out of sight. That's also
why Sung is a sort of house cleaner now. She has
to work to help her family, and there are almost

no jobs like in an office and so forth.

I know you think kids—men—my age are too young to know what love is, but I know that Sung and I are in love. I can see it in her eyes when she smiles at me, and she is always holding my hand. Besides, she says she loves me and I, well, I know I love her.

I have told Sung all about America and what a great place it is, and I told her about you all and Loreen and how she would really like you.

Everybody here says you have to be careful about Vietnamese girls because they all want to marry an American because they think we are all rich and will take them to America, but that just proves how different Sung is. She has said many times she loves her country and does not want to leave it. She says that even though Vietnam is a poor country, and they don't have McDonalds and football and their education system isn't as big as in America, that Vietnam was still a culture hundreds of years before America. Sung is proud she is a Vietnamese.

Sung will not let me take any pictures of her so I can't show you how cute she is, yet. She says it has something to do with Buddhism or something, but I think it's just because she's so shy. I think when she feels more comfortable with me, and she knows I really love her, she'll let me take her picture.

You may as well know that, although I haven't asked Sung to marry me yet, I am thinking about it. I am talking to the chaplain about it now. It is an awful lot of red tape and hassle to marry a Vietnamese, but Chaplain Perry says I can do it if I am really sure that's what I want to do. I am sure, Mom and Dad, but I think I should wait until Sung feels more comfortable about leaving Vietnam before I ask her, because of course we couldn't stay in this awful country. I'm going to be here seven more months, so there's plenty of time.

Don't try to talk me out of it, please. I know what I am doing and I know that Sung and I love each other. I think that in time Sung will become a good Christian too, and if you just get to know Sung I know you will love her also.

> *Your loving son,*
> *Charles*

Chapter Fourteen

1968

Sung

Nguyen Van Tranh had been a survivor. When the Japanese came in the forties, he endured their arrogance and labored with his father at the bread ovens eighteen hours a day to feed the Nipponese legions come for his country's rice and rubber riches. Nguyen was only seventeen then, and for a while he had almost admired the Japanese Army with its rigid discipline, impressive uniforms and ceremony. It was when his mother was raped by a quartet of Japanese officers that Nguyen Van Tranh began to understand that war was not entirely an adventure waged by noble warriors for the beloved motherland.

When the 'invincible' Japanese fled in panic, Nguyen assumed the British and American forces which had vanquished the Samurai must truly be supermen, but here too Nguyen Van Tranh would grow and learn.

Though the French military had in varying degrees been in Vietnam since 1858, their post-war colonial force seemed to Nguyen Van Tranh even more arrogant and racist than the Japanese had been, if such an extreme were possible. It became clear to Nguyen and other struggling young Vietnamese family men that, if the French were not so openly brutal as the Japanese, they were nonetheless in Indochina not for the Vietnamese but for the rubber plantations and the immense rice production. Further, under the French, the opium traffic previously banned by Vietnamese emperors had flourished, and Nguyen saw more and more of his countrymen succumb to the addiction that enriched French opium merchants.

Following the French defeat at Dien Bien Phu in 1954, six years after his second daughter, Sung, was born, the land of Nguyen Van Tranh's birth was named The Republic of South Vietnam, by treaty. For a while, there had been hope for his people, but Nguyen had watched that hope crumble as a long train of despotic South Vietnamese leaders shot, or otherwise overthrew, their predecessors, only to become ousted themselves after milking the people for personal gain.

Then, in the sixties, the Americans, who had always hovered in the background of Indochinese affairs while leaving the role of enforcer to the French, sent their tall, smelly, loud, multi-racial troops to South Vietnam. At first there had only been a few 'advisors' and several of what the Americans called their 'Special Forces', who wore green berets and bore the war-hungry look that Nguyen had seen in the eyes of Legionnaires. These men, at least, had for the most part been respectful of the Vietnamese people and culture in ways that succeeding regiments of regulars would never be.

Nguyen Van Tranh hated all foreign armies beginning sharply with the assault on his mother by four drunken Japanese officers who had not been content to degrade and invade her, but felt a need to beat her and eject her naked from their quarters. More, foreign armies were odious symbols of his country's weakness and the greed of alien peoples who sent their henchmen to exploit it. Nguyen was young, enraged, and full of passionate nationalism. Thus he was ripe for recruitment in 1946 by the successor to the Indochina Communist Party, the Vietminh, which by the mid-sixties would become known as the Viet Cong. The VC.

It was the Vietminh who silently provided the capital for Nguyen Van Tranh's restaurant venture. Vietminh intelligence sought to establish a superior restaurant in Saigon to which high-level French officers and government officials would be drawn for excellent

French cuisine. It was hoped they would of natural course indulge in fine drink, and ultimately would speak of things secret and private which might be garnered by attentive Vietminh agents and call girls among restaurant personnel.

There was a young local man who ran a popular if tiny cafe in the Cholon section, near Minh Mang University. He was by all accounts a talented restauranteur but, more importantly, his zeal for the communist cause was well established. Cafe Lorraine opened in 1951 under the youthful but skilled management of Nguyen Van Tranh. In a respectable time it would grow into one of Saigon's social meccas.

Sung Tranh wasn't sixteen as she'd told Charlie Dermott. She was twenty, but she could easily pass for fifteen, especially if she dressed and wore her hair in certain ways. She knew a younger girl's innocence attracted American soldiers more effectively. It also lowered their guards.

When Sung really had been sixteen, she, of all Nguyen Van Tranh's children, evinced unusual maturity for her age. Sung and her father were exceptionally close and as with all his children he endeavored to isolate her from the dangers of his secret life. Yet Sung was observant and insightful, and in time she began to probe him about his mysterious, if subtle, activities. Nguyen saw in his lovely, tiny, second daughter the look of the revolutionary, of the Vietnamese patriot. He knew it well. It was a look he had seen in the mirror every day since his own adolescence.

By age seventeen, Sung had become her father's confidant, aware of activities about which even her mother was not told. She knew, for example, that her father had a document drop to make on his way home from Cafe Lorraine. She didn't know that the two American MP's who stopped Van Tranh on his bicycle that terrible night were actually operatives of the Central Intelligence Agency who had at long last discovered that the most celebrated club owner in

Saigon was a ranking officer of the Viet Cong.

Nguyen Van Tranh was one of the few Saigon citizens who rated a car, and he could have been driven on the rainy night, but Nguyen believed that the bicycle cemented his image among his subordinates as one of them. If his countrymen in the North could push a bicycle laden with two-hundred pounds of mortar shells through the jungle over five-hundred miles of muddy, mountainous Ho Chi Minh Trail, then he could certainly ride one home, as opposed to being driven like some corrupt puppet-politician.

Pedaling wearily, he was waving to Sung through a gentle night rain shower when the green American army jeep pulled into view from the alley. From her vantage in the small park across from their apartment, Sung initially thought it would simply be another nuisance harassment by the American police-soldiers who patrolled her city. Her eyes widened and her hand flew to her mouth when, instead of merely asking her father for his papers, the two uniformed soldiers with MP bands on their arms calmly emptied two twenty-round, M-16 magazines into Nguyen Van Tranh. Then they searched his body, removed papers and drove away, leaving Sung's father flayed in the street among a litter of gleaming brass hulls. A lone dog barked in the night. Sung Tranh would always remember the dog.

The province Viet Cong mourned Nguyen Van Tranh, and held a secret ceremony in his honor. In less than a week, agents moved to recruit the daughter Comrade Tranh had spoken so highly of. Three years later, Sung Tranh was a dedicated, NVA-trained, experienced and respected Viet Cong operative posing as a 'hooch maid' on the massive American Camp Enari army base in Pleiku.

Only an agent of Sung's proven skill and zeal would have been given her assignment. She was to become close to a certain American army helicopter pilot who in and of himself was insignificant, being but a lowly warrant officer, but whose task was to fly

Fourth Infantry Division intelligence personnel. Merely
knowing where such men went and when they went
there was highly useful. Anything else Sung could learn
would be even more valuable. This particular pilot
was carefully selected. He was known to be unmarried
and only nineteen, young by American standards, and
he was thought to be naive in spite of his sensitive
position. He was a perfect target for Sung Tranh. His
name was Warrant Officer Charles Dermott. 'Charlie,'
in American vernacular.

It was arranged for Sung Tranh to replace the maid
for Hooch-44, and at first she involuntarily caused quite
a stir. Sung was quite unlike the former hooch-maid,
who had been thirty-three and had looked fifty, and
whose few remaining teeth were disgustingly blackened
by years of chewing betel nuts. Sung's bright, clean
smile, shapely, diminutive stature and extraordinary
cuteness evoked delight in the occupants of The Room
and envy in the officers of other hooches.

Predictably, Sung immediately became the subject
of feverish speculation by the woefully celibate young
men of the Fourth Aviation Battalion. All the self-
declared Don Juans and a few of the merely desperate
tried everything from cash to proposals of marriage to
seduce Sung Tranh, but none succeeded. A few pilots
bragged that they'd had her but they weren't taken
seriously. Too many had tried too hard and gotten
nowhere with the sexy little hoochie in 44 to believe
some dickhound's boasts. No matter how fucking cool
you were, no matter what you said or did, Sung simply
and quietly ignored you.

Except, the goddamn little witch had threatened
Pothead Willows with a knife when the dumb fuck
grabbed her one day after exhausting his limited charms
without success. Everybody agreed. The little bitch was
cute as a kitten but she was definitely either a carpet
muncher or retarded, not to mention dangerous. Shit.
This was The Nam, wasn't it? What else could you
expect? Everything was fucked up so far God couldn't

reach it with a ladder.

Consequently it was all the more astonishing when the sexy little hoochie seemed to take an interest in that tall, skinny, geek-assed preacher's kid from Georgia who looked at his toes and called her 'ma'am,' for Christ's sake!

At first, Sung Tranh acidly resented Charlie Dermott's height. She had memorized his photograph with the rest of Charlie's file, of course, and she knew his face with it's hideous beak nose and ugly round eyes, but his surprising height only seemed to symbolize the great American bully for her. One of the 'MP's who'd coldly stitched her father full of bullets had been tall and slender.

Sung had presumed Charlie Dermott would be as easy to hate as all the other American bullies, and thus she was unprepared for what evolved. Charlie treated her with quiet respect and courtesy. That it was merely a deference to all women unique to most well-bred southern American males was not something Sung could understand, but she understood that it made Charlie Dermott different in ways that were difficult for her to adjust to.

Unlike his comrades, the big American boy never attempted to touch her. Though Sung could see the male interest in his eyes, he somehow bore it with grace and without making a single suggestive remark, never even snickering about her to his comrades when they did not know she was listening outside the screens.

On the contrary, Charlie Dermott treated Sung almost as a cultured Vietnamese would treat an honored mother. It was unheard of. It was also confusing and ironic, since Charlie was the only of the Fourth Aviation Battalion's men Sung was actually prepared to go to bed with, if it became necessary, to obtain information from him. Indeed, Sung doubted that she could effectively fulfill her mission unless she could become intimate with Charlie Dermott, but he was the first American bully she'd met who didn't make advances toward her!

The situation degraded from ironic to frustrating. Sung had never needed to be seductive; her natural beauty and the desperate, forced celibacy of soldiers had always ensured she could easily attract anyone whom her mission might have dictated. Yet despite Sung's attempts to turn on the charm for Charlie Dermott, he continued to treat her only with irksome courtesy and respect. The other hooch-maids giggled and offered lewd remarks in Vietnamese when they observed Charlie insist on holding doors open for Sung and carrying her laundry basket for her. And despite her initial suspicions, his respect proved to be without ulterior motive, for never once did he so much as leer at her.

Sung was grievously aggravated. She'd never known an American man for whom there was any reason for a woman other than sex and cooking, yet this big, smiling, gentle young man seemed quite content to enjoy a friendship with her, exacting no price other than an apparent joy at her company.

Some disturbing changes began to occur in Sung, and by the time she discovered them she was alarmed to note they'd been happening to her for longer than she realized.

Somehow, Charlie Dermott's height no longer seemed threatening; it now seemed very...masculine. When Sung's compatriot hooch-maids teased her with the theory that Charlie's immense height necessarily translated into commensurate penis length, Sung was at first irritated at such a frivolous peasant mentality, but now she was embarrassed to admit to herself that she had begun to wonder. Moreover, Charlie's nose was no longer gross; it seemed...noble. In a sheerly western way, of course. At some undetermined recent time his blue eyes had ceased to be bug-eyed-ugly; they were now intense, yet...soft and gentle. Charlie's smile no longer seemed lascivious to Sung; it seemed...beautiful.

Sung Tranh was falling in love, though she didn't

see it coming at first, and then denied it furiously. Driven with the hate evoked by her father's murder, and filled with the fervent zeal of a young intellectual revolutionary enduring the rape of her nation, Sung had had no time and little interest for romance. Vietnamese boys, like all boys, seemed obsessed with sex in a manner that had long since become boring to Sung.

There had been that brief if passionate involvement with a young NVA Lieutenant of the 9th Regiment during her training, but of course he'd been killed while she was on assignment. One second he'd been teaching American colonial history at the training base hidden in Cambodian jungle so thick the bamboo classrooms were oil-lighted even by day; and the next second, without so much as a neural impulse of warning, hundreds of two-thousand-pound bombs detonated.

Contrary to western movies, modern bombs didn't whistle when they fell, Sung had learned from the few survivors. They simply rained silently from the dreaded B-52 formations seven miles up, out of sight even in a clear sky, but their impacts were the horrific opposite of silence. With a sustained, concussive thunder that made the earth quiver for miles around, ancient, 200-foot-deep rain forest was reduced to a denuded moonscape pocked with acrid craters sixty-feet deep and wide. Along with virtually his entire battalion, Lt. Ho Ba Dan, Sung's only lover before or since, had been converted from flesh and bone to vapor. Sung did not see love as a many splendored thing.

When her feelings for Charlie became so strong she could no longer pretend them away, Sung went to her cadre command and complained falsely that she was unable accomplish her mission, was thus ashamed, and hence humbly requested reassignment. Perhaps in Ban Me Thuot, where the Americans were setting up a small air force base, she would not fail so contemptibly.

Cadre command would have none of it. Nonsense, they told Sung. On the contrary, you have provided us priceless data on the movement of Fourth Division intelligence personnel, for where they go, so follow the troops in time.

A senior woman operative was assigned to counsel Sung. It is odious and difficult labor, she told Sung, this pretending affection for the filthy, barbaric American imperialists. Yet it is vital to the cause of Vietnamese independence.

And too, the old woman said, with her arm about Sung's slumped shoulders, over a year later now, still you grieve at the tragic loss of your Lt. Ho Ba Dan. Do I not know? I who have lost a fine daughter like you, and a husband to the barbarians and their terrible killing machines? You are tired, my child, you suffer the draining weariness of war, but you must not relent. The gallant struggle for the freedom of our people demands that we subjugate our personal woes. You are performing splendidly. Regimental headquarters is immensely pleased. Reassignment is out of the question. Indeed, you must now capitalize on your successful penetration. You must now develop your contact, grow ever closer to him, secure even more of his trust. You must not only track his movements, now you must extract all he knows, even learn to manipulate him to bring you specifics. Remember your father the great patriot, young flower, I knew him well. Consider what he would have you do.

Sung only briefly contemplated trying to tell her superiors that she was in love with her target, but she quickly dismissed the notion. For a dedicated revolutionary, such political heresy was both socially reprehensible and professionally disastrous. It could even threaten her life. Worse, it would shame the memory of Nguyen Van Tranh.

Besides, it was moot, for the Old Mother had been wise.

Sung knew her beloved father would've wished her to persevere, whatever the cost.

Chapter Fifteen
The Room

A soaking rain has ended, and the morning sun
heats the wet earth, raising a clinging steam from the
mud. Sung Tranh sits alone in The Room on Charlie's
bunk folding his freshly laundered fatigues, socks and
underwear carefully. She pauses to fan herself with her
conical straw hat. Sung wears loose, black silk pants
and a bright red, patterned, cotton blouse which hugs
tightly about her small, pointed breasts and narrow
waist, before flaring over her full hips. On her tiny feet
are the indestructible sort of molded, translucent-red-
plastic sandals imported by the thousands from Taiwan.
Her hair is jet black and gleams in the intense sunlight
now spearing through the screens; it falls rich, thick
and straight to just above her shoulders where it sways
gracefully when she moves.

Sung has tuned the radio atop battered Old Faithful
to a Vietnamese station; a strident voice harangues a
political message in a shrill, twanging dialect.

Sung lifts a jungle-fatigue shirt from a nail on
Charlie's portion of the wall. It is yesterday's shirt
which she overlooked for the morning laundry. The
long, green, multipocketed shirt is dusty and musky
with the dried sweat of Charlie Dermott mixed with
a slight scent of Old Spice deodorant. Sewn above
the slanting upper pockets are green cloth tapes with
black embroidery, one with the name DERMOTT, and
another with U.S. ARMY and the wings of an army
aviator. On the collar tips are sewn the insignia of the
warrant officer.

Sung holds the big garment to her face and inhales

175

slowly. She likes the smell of Charlie, masculine, arousing, but clean. She dons the shirt, which dwarfs her, and she rolls the sleeves up several curls. She hugs herself in the shirt and smiles.

Footsteps clump on the damp boardwalk outside but Sung pays them no attention; the big, loud, American soldiers are through their billeting areas constantly during the day, moving to or from their varied missions. Now that the storm has passed and the low gray clouds have lifted, Sung is also not surprised to hear the rising whine of dozens of helicopter turbines being started on the nearby flight line. Soon The Room quivers with the beat of scores of heavy, churning rotors, several hundred yards distant.

The rank, oily odor of burned jet-fuel stings your nose and throat as well.

The screen door suddenly twangs open and Sung, startled, whirls about. "Chah-ree!" she exclaims with a bright smile of pretty red lips and straight white teeth.

Charlie beams broadly, amused at the diminutive girl enveloped in his big green shirt. "Sung! Uh, hi!"

Sung stands, flushed with embarrassment; she hurriedly shrugs out of the fatigue shirt. She smoothes her hair and tugs the tail of her blouse downward, tightly about her breasts and hips. "I—I not think you come back so soon. Why you not fry today?"

"Well I was supposed to," Charlie replies, awed by Sung's simple, perfect beauty, "I was supposed to fly the division intelligence people on a reconnaissance again, but our ship's grounded."

"Groun-dead?"

"Yeah, grounded, uh, broken! Helicopter broken."

"Ah! Hericoptra broke! You no fry?"

"No, they have to be just right mechanically, uh, means the helicopters must fly very good or we do not fly them. At least that's the way it's supposed to be. So they're working on the hydraulic fluid leak right now; they'll have it ready in a couple of hours and we'll go out then."

"You be here two our-rahs?" Sung asks, holding up two fingers, smiling, looking at Charlie from the tops of her eyes.

"Yes!" Charlie says, melted by the obvious delight Sung displays. He holds up his own two fingers. "Two hours, maybe a little more. The maintenance guys will have to test-fly it a couple of times to make sure the fix is right."

"Fits?"

"No," Charlie laughs. "Never mind, I'm just glad to see you are still here!"

Sung blushes and stares at her toes. "You happy see me?"

Charlie walks toward Sung. "You bet," he says, now studying the floor himself. "I was hoping you'd still be here, Sung, you...you are so beautiful."

"No, no! I not bootifur, Chah-ree."

"Oh yes. Yes you are." Charlie whispers.

"Ah...you want beer, Chah-ree?" Sung spins and trots to Old Faithful.

"Uh...no Sung, I can't drink when I'm flying."

"Not can drink?"

"Not alcohol. Give...get us both a coke!"

"Coka-co-ra?"

"Yes," Charlie holds up two fingers again. "Two. And I'll get the cookies my mom just sent me. Which reminds me, aren't you glad they finally built the new blast walls?"

"Brass-wawz?"

"No," Charlie says, smiling, "Blast-walls, the walls of sandbags around the hooches to protect us from shelling. They've just finished building the new blast-walls using plastic sandbags."

"Oh," Sung says, taking two colas from the old refrigerator, "Those brass-wawz. Yes. New brass-wawz ver good!"

Charlie punctures the can-tops with the opener he carries on the dog-tag chain about his neck, and they drink. Sung sips delicately at hers, and Charlie drags on

177

his like a starved calf.

"You bet. I'll tell you another good thing too: They finally got the Chemical Corps guys in here and, I don't know what they did, but I haven't seen a rat in a whole week. Come to think of it, I haven't seen a dog, or a bird or a bug or anything else alive but us. Wonder what they used on those rats. On second thought, I probably don't want to know."

"Where you fry today, Chah-ree?" Sung asks, plopping down in the chair by the desk between Hale's and Van's bunks.

Charlie sits on his footlocker, unlaces his boots and kicks them from his feet. "Whew. Feels good to get those boots off."

"Go Ban Me Thuot again?"

"Hmm? No, not today. That's a long flight for a helicopter, and G-2 - uh, that's division intelligence— It's, well, never mind, you wouldn't understand it and it's boring anyway, but I almost always fly for division intelligence, and they don't usually go to Ban Me Thuot because it's out of the division operating area. They only go there when they're discussing some big joint activity. That's why we flew down there last week. But today we're just supposed to go inspect landing zones up near Dak To."

"Dak To?"

"Yeah," Charlie drinks long and wipes his mouth on his sleeve. "They never tell me much, but I think they're planning to move a bunch of artillery people up there soon for some new offensive. I think they're planning to hit the Ho Chi Minh Trail over in Laos 'cause ever since President Johnson stopped the bombing of the North, the NVA have been hauling in supplies like crazy."

Sung smiles and cocks her head like a spaniel. "You so brave, Chah-ree!"

Charlie laughs. "Not me. You get brave in my business and you get dead."

Sung frowns and pouts her mouth. To Charlie, she is

impossibly cute. "Oh no, Chah-ree! I not want you die!"

"Yeah, well, I not want me die either. That's why I don't do brave."

"I think you ver brave, aww same!" Sung insists.

Charlie decides to settle for this assessment. "Thanks."

"Hatch-ette also brave?" Sung asks, indicating Hatchette's corner of The Room, with it's now slightly charred, diving-gunship cartoon, proclaiming: Happiness Is A Dead Gook! And the cracked-glass, framed portrait of the special forces soldiers and their NVA kills.

Charlie winces, looking at Hatchette's corner. "Oh Lord, yes. Hatchette's not afraid of anything. He's crazy. Flies around over Cambodia at night, drinking beer and blasting away at NVA base camps. You know the goo-, uh, the local Viet Cong have a list of American gunship pilots they want to kill, and Hatch is one of them? He's proud of it! Says he and his buddies, Marvin and Bernie, want to kill enough NVA and Viet Cong to get their names at the top of the list! Hatch is nuttier than a Georgia pecan patch, but he is brave."

"Oh, Hatch-ette ver brave rike you!"

"No, he's a lot braver than me, believe me."

"Mah-vin and Ber-nee, they riv here too?"

"No, thank heaven," Charlie answers, looking at the radio. The political diatribe in Vietnamese has ended and music has begun. "Marvin and Bernie are old Special Forces sergeants that Hatch served a previous Vietnam tour with before they all went to flight school and became pilots."

"Mah-vin and Ber-nee, they not riv here?"

"Oh. No, I think they live up in the Graverobber area."

"Greyrobba?"

Charlie laughs again. "No it's, well, it's an American name the gunship guys call their unit, that's all. The Graverobber guys live up around Hooch 46 or 47, I think. I don't know. The gunship pilots are a pretty private bunch, and Hatch never invites any company when he goes up there."

On the radio, a Vietnamese woman begins to sing a mournfully slow, high-pitched song. "What're you listening to?" Charlie asks, nodding toward the radio.

"Risten to Radio Saigon. Too much tawk. Tawk arra time. But sometime make pretty music. You rike this music, Chah-ree?"

"Yeah, Sung, it's very, well, sort of lonesome. What's she saying?"

Sung sits on the chair at the desk, holding her soft drink in both hands like a little girl. Her sandals dangle from her toes just above the floor. Charlie sits on his bunk. "She sing...she sing song of much unhappy. She... her hup-band...you know hup-band?"

"Husband, the man she is married to, yes, I understand." Charlie smiles.

"Yes! Her hup-band, he go away to army and he die...get ver kirred. You know kirred?"

"Killed, yes. Yeah, I know killed, believe me. I worry about getting 'very killed' myself."

"Yes, he ver kirred. Now she have just her and her rittre babies. Ver sad song, Chah-ree. Much unhappy. She not have hup-band, so no mon-nee. Not can buy foods for babies. Ver bad."

"Yeah," Charlie nods soberly, "I can imagine. I remember hearing that the South Vietnamese Army has no funding for pensions, so, when ARVN soldiers die, their widows receive no benefits at all."

A frown crinkles the brow of Sung's doll-like face. "This terr-bur, Chah-ree! Much unhappy! Happen to many Vietnamese girrs; happen in aw provinces of South and happen ver bad in North, too! Thousands many South Vietnamese men be kirred; in North, mirrions many! Many babies hungry. Many Vietnamese girrs, they must be prossatutes to get money, buy foods to eat and have prace to riv with babies. This ver terr-bur, Chah-ree."

"Yes, Sung, I know it is. Ah...you know, if a woman

180

is married to an American soldier...and he gets killed, she gets his pay for the rest of her life, and she gets free medical care for her and her children in military hospitals."

"This ver good, Chah-ree, but never happen in Vietnam."

Charlie pulls his hat from his crewcut and sets the hat and his drink on the ammo-crate by his bed. He crosses The Room and kneels before Sung. Even on his knee, he looks down slightly at the little woman seated in the chair. Charlie gently pulls Sung's drink from her hand, places it on the desk, and he holds her tiny hand between his. She looks deep into his eyes, her lips slightly parted.

"Sung...you're right. That'll never happen in Vietnam. There are a lot...many, many things which are so good about America that will never, ever happen in Vietnam. You could know and enjoy all these things, Sung...if you, ah, if you...were...married to an American soldier. You could live...comfortably, where there is no war, where there's plenty of food, where our...uh... where kids can go to great schools and grow up to be doctors and lawyers."

"Chah-ree," Sung whispers, tears welling in her eyes. She touches his cheek with her free hand. "Oh, Chah-ree."

"Sung...you don't have to say anything right now. In fact, don't! Don't say anything! Just think about—"

"Oh, Chah-ree," Sung repeats, now crying. "I not can—"

"Just think about it for now! That's all, just think about it! I want you to marry me, Sung! I want you to be my wife! We can be so happy in America together, Sung, I know we can!"

Tears trickle down ivory cheeks and collect in tiny pools at the corners of Sung's mouth.

Charlie is distressed by Sung's tears. He holds her head to his chest and kisses the top of her head. "Don't cry, Sung! We can figure out some way to get your mother and your brothers over. We can make it work, I know! I love you, Sung!"

"I rov you, Chah-ree," Sung weeps, holding tightly to Charlie. "I rov you ver many, but I not can marry—"

"Don't answer right now!" Charlie holds Sung by her shoulders and looks into her face; he puts a single finger to her lips. "Don't try to decide right now, Sung. Just think about it. I've got seven months to go on my tour, so there's plenty of time."

"Chah-ree..." Sung cries quietly, agony etched in her face. "You not can unnerstan..."

"Sssshh! Don't answer now. Just think about it, for months if you need to! Don't say no, just think about it. Please?"

Sung rests her head on Charlie's chest and cries still. "Oh Chah-ree, I rov you Chah-ree," the girl weeps miserably, "I rov you."

Charlie lifts her face to his.

"I love you too, Sung. I love you so much."

They kiss lightly, tentatively at first, then with more force. Sung slides her arms about Charlie's neck and clutches him tightly. Charlie is electrified by her slippery wet lips and the incredibly arousing scent of her heat and perfume combined. He slips his hand beneath her blouse and cups a small breast peaked with its erect, brown nipple. Charlie has never touched anything that felt so good. Sung suddenly pulls back.

Charlie retracts his hand, his heart thundering. "I'm sorry, Sung, I guess I got a little carried—"

"Sssh," Sung whispers. She frees herself and walks quickly to the door.

"Aw, don't leave, Sung! I'm sorry. I won't—"

To Charlie's profound astonishment, Sung swings the heavy wooden inner door shut and she drops the latch-bar lock into place. Slowly, with her head down but her eyes up, she walks to Charlie's bunk. There, she extends her hand to him and looks him full in the eyes. "I want you rov me, Chah-ree," Sung says softly. "Prease...do rov to me."

Charlie is struggling to breathe. "Sung...ah...I guess I ought to tell you, I've never, well...I haven't ever—"

Sung takes Charlie by the hand and she leads him to his bunk. She unbuttons his shirt, slides it down his arms and rubs her face softly in the hair of his chest.

"Sung," Charlie gasps.

He lifts her face to him and kisses her again, gently at first, then fiercely. Not knowing how to proceed, Charlie opts to follow Sung's lead. He drops to his knees, unbuttons her blouse and tongues her nipples as she holds his head cradled to her. Sung kicks off her sandals and sits on the bunk; she rolls onto her back and slides her black silk pants and lacy yellow panties down her thighs and off her ankles. Charlie hurriedly tears at his belt, unable to take his eyes off the first nude woman he has been in the same room with since he was too young to remember.

Finesse is not uppermost in Charlie's mind. He rips his feet from his trousers, dislodging from his pocket his rubber dog toy which emits a sharp squeak when it bounces on the floor.

"What that?" Sung asks with mild alarm.

"Nothing! Just my critter! Nothing!" Charlie kicks his underwear across The Room and hops about trying to extract a foot from a sock.

"You what?"

"Nothing! Don't worry about it!" Charlie flings his last sock and lies down gently upon Sung. She smiles and wraps her legs about him and he feels he will explode with the pleasure of her smooth, warm skin, the smell of her perfume, and an entrancingly female scent he has not experienced before. He kisses her, but briefly, as both are fighting for their breath. He instinctively thrusts at her but his penis slides over her belly, then beneath her. Sung guides him with her hand; he finds the wet softness and slides into her, knowing a hot ecstasy he had not thought could exist.

The lone, plaintive, feminine voice on the radio sings sadly in a strange tongue Charlie doesn't understand but will never, ever, forget. Charlie becomes lost to primal genetics, and Sung moves against him frantically, gripping him with her calves. Soon she cries out in Vietnamese, and Charlie learns that there is yet one greater ecstasy in store for him.

Still, the high, sad voice on the radio sings. Charlie will never forget that song.

When they can breathe again, Charlie holds her to him and turns over on the bunk. Sung lies on him, gently wiping the sweat from his face with a corner of the sheet. Charlie gazes into Sung's dark eyes, his own watering. He smiles at her, full of himself. "Wow," Charlie says over and over, between breaths. "Wow. Wow."

Sung lays her head on Charlie's chest. "I rov you, Chah-ree," she whispers.

Charlie cannot see the tears of Sung Tranh.

But you can.

Chapter Sixteen
1967

Pot

From the day of his birth, on the date the atomic
bomb rendered Nagasaki a radioactive ash pile, Edward
'Pothead' Willows had lived what in a more romantic
era would have been called a star-crossed destiny.
When he became old enough to understand some of it,
Pot, never much the poet, called it 'fucked up'. Nothing
occurred afterward to alter his assessment.

Pot was born the illegitimate 'love child' of a
terminally naive New York Catholic missionary
to the Filipinos deep in the island jungle outback,
the massively unintended result of a sporadic if
tempestuous love affair with an American submarine
officer who went to a watery tomb while Pot was still
in a watery womb. Theresa Salvatore went into labor
three weeks early while doing the Lord's work among
the heathen in the village of Bongabong on the island
of Mindoro. It would later seem ironically fitting to Pot
that he should be born in a place called Bongabong.

After bouncing cruelly for forty minutes in the back
of a jeep driven by a panic-stricken Filipino houseboy,
Theresa Salvatore was carted sweating into the tiny
midwifery clinic that was Mindoro's closest answer to
a hospital. It proved to be enough for Pot who survived,
but inadequate for his mother who suffered fatal post-
partum hemorrhaging. Theresa had intended to name
her baby, Hampton, for his father, or Maria, for her
mother, depending.

No sooner had baby Hampton arrived squawling at a

Catholic orphanage in Manila when the north of Luzon Island began to shake with volcanic rumbles. The seismic activity subsided days later, never becoming an eruption, and was later written off as 'minor.' However, when you live in the South Pacific, one of the things you learn from childhood is that on the first day the earth trembles you never assume it is minor. Hence, the infant Hampton came to be loaded into an early-thirties-vintage school bus enroute to evacuation by ship from Subic Bay.

The driver of the bus was a middle-aged practicing Catholic priest which was probably good, but he was also a life-long practicing alcoholic which was not. The priest was not overly concerned with the twelve babies (one of whom was his), the sixteen older orphans (two of whom were his), or the three nuns (none of whom he had yet succeeded in making his), who were crammed onto the creaking old vehicle. He was, nonetheless, utterly consumed with the notion of getting his own ass aboard ship before it got buried in lava. Thus he was busy establishing the world land speed record for antique buses when the fabric cords which had been showing through the front tire treads for a year finally gave out. The old bus was precarious enough to control on its best day; with a blown steering tire at fifty-two miles an hour, it became an unguided missile.

The priest left this world through the windshield, ostensibly for heaven. The senior of the nuns was also killed, but all others aboard survived with varying degrees of injury. Baby Hampton suffered a painful broken leg, but it was to heal satisfactorily. Fatefully, however, no one who survived could say with any certainty which infant went with which birth record with regard to some of the babies. Footprinting babies was not a standard procedure in outback Philippine midwifery clinics in 1945. The nuns did the best they could but, in the process, the theretofore officially nameless son of the late Lieutenant Hampton Greeves and the even later Miss Theresa Salvatore accidentally

became known as Edouardo Vejos. Pot's new, if
misplaced, surname was pronounced "way-hoose."

The ground stopped shaking while authorities were
still cleaning up the bus wreck, the evacuation was
called off, and the children were trucked back to the
St. Thomas Aquinas orphanage where a confused little
Eddie Vejos lived for five years.

In 1951, an arrangement was struck to transport
those children who were clearly of at least half-
American parentage to a Catholic orphanage in Los
Angeles, California, in the hope of enhancing their
adoption potential. Two days out, northeast of the
Yap Islands, the American liner Fortunata ran into an
aimlessly drifting Japanese mine which had not been
notified that the war was over. Eddie Vejos was born in
Bongabong to get sunk near Yap above the Marianas
Trench, the deepest part of ocean in the world.

Fortunately for the orphans aboard, one of whom
was certainly due some fortune at this point, an
American naval task force en route to Subic Bay was
almost in view. All but a hapless few stokers in the
Fortunato's forward engine room were rescued before
the ship descended seven miles vertically to the bottom
of the Pacific. Six-year-old Eddie Vejos went back to
Manila with little more physical injury than bruises
from being yanked about lifeboats by harried seamen.
He had, however, been quite old enough to know fear,
not so much from the sinking as from his child's ability
to tell when adults were afraid. Eddie beheld many
very frightened grownups when the explosion gored the
Fortunato, and their fear made him sick with his own.

Within a year, however, the transfer to the Los
Angeles orphanage was brought off successfully. On
arrival, a confused clerk listened to Eddie struggling to
pronounce his name with a Filipino accent and wrote it
down as Edward Willows. Hampton Edouard Salvatore-
Greeves Vejos Willows had acquired his third surname
in six years.

In his eighth year, the LA orphanage burned and

Eddie barely made it out the door clinging to the hot
coat tail of a fire fighter carrying two smaller children.
Just as they cleared the building, the propane gas tank
behind the orphanage exploded, demolishing what was
left of the building and hospitalizing Eddie with burns.

When he was ten, Eddie was adopted by an Irish
Catholic brick mason and his barren wife, both in their
thirties and desperate for a son.

Adopted father Sean Hannagh was a good soul,
but he was fond of his ale and was never averse to a
good brawl, as his lumpy nose and scarred knuckles
testified. Hampton Edouard Salvatore-Greeves Vejos
Willows Hannagh, on the other not-so-beefy hand,
was positively not a fighter. He'd been jeep-rattled,
bus-wrecked, sunk, burned out and blown up all before
the age of nine, and bravery was not what he did best.
Bullies at his school homed on Eddie's vulnerability,
and he was trounced at least once a week, only to be
roundly berated for cowardice by Sean Hannagh and
sent back to find his attackers to "show 'em nobody
bests a Hannagh in a tiff!" Inevitably, Eddie would get
trounced a second time, and get still another lecture
about "puttin' up the old dukes!" by Sean.

Convinced that life "on the job" would "put some
spine in the lad!" Sean, now a construction foreman,
arranged for Eddie to work construction beginning in
the summer of his sixteenth year.

Eddie's job was to operate a pulley-lift designed
to raise brick to the floor being worked on. A cable
extended from the ground to a small derrick at the edge
of the third floor where it passed over a big pulley and
ended in a hook. On the ground, workers would load
brick into a wooden cradle with a metal superstructure
and they would call the weight up to Eddie. Eddie
would then select a concrete counterweight equal to the
weight called up, and he would roll it over and hook
it to his end of the cable. Then he would wind a crank
while the concrete weight descended and raised the
brick to the third floor, whereupon he would swivel-

boom the load inboard. When all the concrete weights were spent, a crane would be dispatched from more critical tasks to lift them back to the third floor. This was low-bid construction work in 1961.

One cold Tuesday, the ground crew loaded several cans of paint onto the cradle. Both workers were Mexican illegals for whom English was a daunting challenge and addition may as well have been quantum physics. They only knew the correct weight of the brick loads because brick came in one of three premeasured batches easily distinguishable by view. The two workers studied the numbers on the sides of the paint cans, scratched their heads. They came to a consensus with each other in Spanish and hailed up to Eddie: "Two-hundray paoons, man!"

Eddie frowned and sighed and rolled the 200-pound counterweight to the derrick. He connected the hook and tripped the release, expecting the usual leisurely lift operation.

Investigators would later determine that there was only 110-pounds of paint in the load. Eddie made a similar determination a whole lot sooner. The instant he released the counterweight, it plummeted and the cradle full of paint took off like a shuttle launch vehicle. Eddie panicked, mostly out of the fear of having to answer to Sean Hannagh for a screw-up. The pulley was a simple—read cheap—jury-rigged apparatus which worked well enough if kept to the task of raising predictable loads of brick, and thus it had no braking mechanism.

To his credit, Eddie knew better than to try to slow the skyrocketing cradle full of paint cans by grabbing the cable, which would certainly have fed his hands through the pulley like hamburger through a meat grinder. All he could think to do as he stared at the rapidly rising load was to put out his foot to cushion its arrival at the top of the lift.

Physics, however, was not Eddie's strong subject either. When the 110-pounds of paint whizzed up

189

the pulley and reached Eddie's foot, the descending
200-pound counterweight kept right on plunging until
it hit the ground like an artillery shell, sending the two
Mexicans scrambling. The rising paint load hit Eddie's
stiffly held foot and launched him about three feet
straight up, and over the edge of the building. The paint
cans sprang up from the cradle as it slammed against
the derrick, but they settled instantly back into it,
followed shortly by a now really panic-stricken Eddie
who grabbed onto the cradle to avoid falling three floors
to the ground.

The cradle now held 110-pounds of canned paint
and another 150-pounds of Eddie, for a grand total of
260-pounds, offsetting the concrete counterweight on
the ground considerably. The cable twanged and the
pulley whirred as Eddie and the paint headed for the
ground and the concrete weight took off for the third
floor.

Half way down, Eddie was struck by the rising
concrete counterweight which broke his left arm and
dislocated his left shoulder as it streaked upward. He
clung to the cable with his remaining arm and hand.

Eddie and the paint crashed into the earth, and
Eddie became entangled in the metal frame from which
the wooden cradle was suspended. On impact with
the ground, the woefully overstressed wooden cradle
disintegrated, spilling the paint cans through its bottom,
leaving only 150-pounds of equally overstressed Eddie
attached to what remained of the cradle.

Meanwhile, back at the third floor, the 200-pound
counterweight smashed into the derrick, nearly
dislocating it from the building. Now once again vastly
outweighing the load on the other end of the cable,
the counterweight again descended with a vengeance,
snatching the terrified Eddie off the ground like a
miniature poodle on a leash. Still again, half way back
up, Eddie was hit by the now dropping counterweight
which this time broke his right arm.

When the concrete counterweight thudded to still

another undesigned-for impact with the ground, it cracked and split and the metal loop that was imbedded in it pulled loose with only a pound or so of concrete stuck to its root.

Aloft, Eddie collided with the bottom of the derrick, shaking it in its mounts again and bashing his head. He escaped death only by virtue of his aluminum hardhat which got jammed down over his ears and eyes. His legs were still tangled in the cradle framework. The Fates Of Physics had contrived that Eddie now outweighed the opposite end of the cable by about 145-pounds, and the miracle of gravity once more arrived to collect. The slight drag of the cable whipping through the pulley was all that enabled Eddie to survive the fall in the destroyed cradle frame three floors to the ground. If he'd still been conscious after he again hit the earth in a cloud of dust, he might have considered it salt in the wound that when the ascending hook-end of the cable whipped around the derrick, the derrick separated from the building and fell three stories to land on Eddie and the cradle frame, followed, of course, by the cable itself.

The OSHA investigators agreed it was absolutely the damndest thing they'd ever seen. They stared at the destroyed cradle in amazement and shook their heads slowly while listening to excited accounts rendered by the animated Mexicans, complete with graphic gestures and sound effects. The investigators awarded Eddie a full ten points each for originality and for technical merit. They could only give him a nine-point-five for execution, however, since he didn't kill anybody.

Eddie was three weeks in the hospital and seven months back to full use of his arms. He would forever embrace an abiding empathy for the hapless coyote in Roadrunner cartoons. Mbeep, mbeep!

Some young men run away from an unhappy home life to join the military. Eddie Hannagh wanted out of his crazy Irish household pretty badly, but not near enough to join the United States Army at a time when

it was engaged in a hideous southeast Asian war.
Eddie was no dummy—he'd seen all those grim-faced
newscasters on the TV every night going on and on
about death tolls and body counts. It was just his luck,
Eddie reflected, that now there was this fucking draft-
law thing that threatened to put him right back on the
other side of the Pacific in another war!

Eddie wanted away from Sean Hannagh, his ditsy
wife and their dismal little row house in LA's Irish
neighborhood, all three of which were making him
crazy. The Shamrock Shithead was forever going on
with his dumb, cornball paddy philosophies and his
stupid belief that "a good man's hard honest work could
make a commoner a king in America!". Eddie wanted
out of all this silly mick bullshit bad, but becoming a
player in a major-league overseas machine-gunning
contest wasn't what he had in mind. This conviction,
coupled with Sean Hannagh's dream that he become
the first in his family to put a child through college, got
Eddie into Bellflower Community College in spite of
his marginal grade-point-average.

Bellflower wasn't exactly an ivy league pillar, but
Eddie didn't care; it had a dorm which allowed him to
live away from that stupid paddy adopted father of his.
Eddie even registered in his orphanage name, Willows,
so much did he desire to disassociate himself from
that dumb bonehead who was always rattling on about
"doin' the family proud!"

More importantly, enrollment at Bellflower
constituted a student draft deferment, which meant
the goddamned government couldn't send him off to
get blasted by little yellow dudes with funny hats and
machine-guns. For Eddie's academic goals, Bellflower
was every bit on a plane with Harvard.

Another thing Bellflower offered, Eddie learned to
his delight, was a student counter-culture that was the
equal of any university, if not in size, certainly in its
fervent pretension that somewhere in the use of mind-
altering, illegal drugs lay the meaning of life. Eddie was

far more concerned with the simple extension of his life than with its obscure meaning which, he suspected, was probably fucked-up anyway, but he did like to get high and giggle. Thus, '60s campus life was a gold mine of opportunity.

Unknowingly, Eddie had an allergy that caused him to vomit for days after using heroin or any derivative thereof, and LSD simply scared the living shit out of him. He was into drugs for fun, not to puke his guts out or wake up screaming while being clawed and fanged by slavering gargoyle-groundhogs from hell, thank you very much. For this shit, he could have stayed at home with his Irish nutcake adopted father.

Marijuana, however, was another matter. Mary Jane, weed, hemp, grass, dope ... pot! Whatever you called it, Eddie Willows loved it. It sent you off to la-la land but it never sent giant demon woodchucks to fetch you back. Use it together with enough alcohol, and a guy could, at least for a little while, forget entirely about explosions and fires and terrified, running adults on sinking ships, and lunatic brick-lifts and potato-head fathers and malevolent little yellow dudes with machine-guns. Hell, with enough Mexican miracle weed and stone mellow Tennessee sippin' whiskey, even hordes of ten-foot, drooling, LSD-generated groundhogs could be brought marginally under control.

So much did Eddie Willows enjoy Puff the Magic Dragon that he went about ole BCC in a nearly perpetual cloud of pungent gray smoke, drug enforcement having been rather out of vogue on campus in the late '60s. The nickname, 'Pothead,' was inevitable.

Bellflower Community College did have other annoying qualities in common with Harvard; it had academic standards and an alarming propensity for expelling students who consistently failed to meet them. For many draft-age males of no means in the late '60s, expulsion was tantamount to a death sentence as it meant the revocation of one's student draft deferment, which meant the army, which meant confrontation with aggravated little squinty-eyed yellow dudes with machine-guns on the other side of the world. It meant 'We regret to inform you...' letters. Long aluminum boxes with ex-people in them. Credits rolling on the screen. The end. Dark...ness.

When Pothead Willows got the notice of academic expulsion from BCC he would gladly have exchanged it for the acid groundhogs if he could have. His two closest friends, Mary Jane and Jack Daniels, could drive it away for brief spans of time, but the letter from hell, or, more appropriately, the letter to hell, was always there on his desk when he sobered up.

It was unavoidable that Sean Hannagh should learn of Pot's dilemma, of course, and when he did he had a solution to offer that put Pot into apoplexy. "Aye, lad, it's the National Guard ya should be a joinin' noo!" Sean was now a senior shift manager at a brick foundry, and it was his job to solve such problems.

"The National Guard!?" Pot had screamed in his rather unique Filipino/Irish-American accent. "The National fucking Guard!? I'm trying to stay out of the goddamn army, Pa!"

Sean Hannagh clucked, lowered his eyelids to half-mast and vaguely lifted a freckled and scarred fist the size of a ham hock. "Noo, ya be keepin' a civil tongue in yer head, lad, er Ay be movin' yer nose to the other side o' yer bleedin' head."

Pot was alert to this sort of reasoning. "Yes sir. Sorry Pa. I just don't see how—"

"Wul, zip yer bleedin' lip whilst Ay tell ya. Ya be expelled from school noo far at least a year and that be long enough far the draft ta git ya. But. If ya be joinin' the National Guard, all ya be havin' ta do is go ta basic trainin' in the ormy fer eight weeks, which, by the by, would do ya good. Then ya be assigned ta a local guard unit where ya only have ta be drillin' one weekend a month and two weeks in the soomers. Otherwise ya be a civilian," Sean Hannagh leaned forward and looked hard into Pothead Willow's eyes, "And ya no longer be eligible far the draft, lad. Then, in a year or so, when yer academic suspension is up, ya kin reenroll in college and become the very first Hannagh ta git a college dagree!"

The prospect of any kind of a uniform was as scary as rabid mutant groundhogs to Pot, and he knew he'd have to forsake sweet Mary Jane long enough to get her out of his blood for a physical. Still, he had to admit the idea beat the hell out of humorless little yellow guys with pith helmets and machine-guns, let alone an aluminum box with six handles on the sides and a flag on top.

It wasn't easy to get Pot a coveted, political and expensive acceptance into the Army National Guard in that day, but Sean Hannagh, secretly in the Order of Masons, called in a few markers. On the day before the draft board meeting that would certainly have inducted Pot, an appointment to the Guard was secured. The nick-of-time suspense made Pot a nervous wreck.

Yet the Bongabong Curse persisted. Six days after Private Edward "Pothead" Hannagh raised his right hand and swore to protect the United States of America from all enemies foreign and domestic, the 179th Mechanized Infantry Regiment, of the California Army National Guard, became one of only two National Guard units in America for the whole duration of the war to be nationalized for active duty in Vietnam.

Pot didn't even approach sobriety for nearly four days. He'd have gleefully strangled Sean Hannagh in his sleep had he not been concerned that Pa would awake and reduce him to a bloody puddle for his troubles. When the cops deposited Pot's limp, pickled and stoned remains on Sean's doorstep, however, Sean had yet another bright idea.

"Helicopters!?" Pot sputtered. "Helicop-, you mean those things that buzz around in the air? Above the ground? You crazy mick son-of-a, aah! Look Pa, I couldn't fly a hot-air balloon! I can't—"

"When ya be finished prattlin' on, boy, Ay be explaining some hard facts o' life ta ya."

"What? I'm shipping out to the Republic of South fucking Vietnam in two months, Pa! How much harder can the facts get?"

"Do ya know anythin' aboot the infantry, lad?"

"I know they get shot at!"

"All soldiers get shot at, me boy. But infantry has ta hump heavy gear up steep mountains, sleep in mud holes, eat cold garbage, stay up all night on guard, an' when the shootin' starts there be no one closer ta it than the bleedin' infantry. An' all this they must do fer precious little pay, lad."

"Oh, well that's wonderful, Pa! That's truly just fucking wonderful! I'm so delighted we had this conversation!"

"But," Sean continued patiently, "One o' me brothers at the lodge just retired from the ormy, an' he tells me the ormy needs lots o' helicopter pilots."

"So?"

"So, pilots be officers. They make lots more money. Pilots dun't hump eighty-pound packs in hundred-degree jungle. They sleep in nice dry barracks near officer's pubs, an' somebody's bleedin' infantry stays up on guard all night whilst pilots sleep."

"Pa, you still get shot at in a helicopter! At least as a ground soldier you can dig a hole or hide behind a tree!"

"Aye lad, until the enemy comes ta yer hole or yer tree. Then ye be havin' a face-to-face discussion o' a ballistic nature with 'im. On t'other hand, that pilot has long since relieved himself of the battlefield at over a hundred miles an hour. He be gone back ta his base, ta his pub an' his hot food an' his safe dry bed. An' ta his bleedin' bigger paycheck."

Oh how Pot hated it when Sean Hannagh made sense.

He still had an army lawyer change his name back to Willows.

Pot's acceptance into the Warrant Officer Rotary Wing Aviator Course was testimony to the U.S. Army's ravishing thirst for pilots to help establish the revolutionary new Airmobile Doctrine of land warfare. At first Pot was ecstatic at being accepted to flight school, until he focused on the fact that it meant he would actually have to fly. Himself. By himself, on occasion. With no...real...pilot there.

Pot distinguished himself in flight training, though not in any way that inspired him or his superiors. On a solo, night-cross-country training flight out of the Fort Wolters, Texas, primary flight training base, Pot became so lost even God couldn't find him. Seeing with relief at last the lights of an airport in the rough vicinity of his destination, Pot set off an alert when he landed at Carswell Air Force Base while talking on the radio with, and presuming he was at, Fort Worth's nearby Meacham Field civilian airport.

At night, Carswell Air Force Base had looked like any other big airport to Pot, who was so lost he considered himself lucky to still be in the state of Texas. But, as Carswell was a B-52 installation under sabotage threat, the Air Force reacted crossly to any unidentified aircraft that blundered into their restricted airspace without radio contact, let alone approval. Fortunately the pilots of the two fighters sent up to shoot Pot down suspected he might be another goofy Army kid out of the helicopter base to the west, so all they did was scare him utterly witless with a close, blistering and deafening fly-by in their F-4 Phantoms. With his aircraft's fuel-gauge needle motionless against the "E" peg, Pot landed anyway. The Air Force refueled Pot's little Hiller OH-23 Raven, pointed to the west and told him not to come back.

Months later, when he was transferred to Fort Rucker, Alabama, for advanced flight training, Pot and his fellow students were introduced to the much larger, new-generation, turbine-powered, UH-1 helicopter.

It was in one of the big thundering 'Hueys' that

Pot was on another night training flight with a second
student, who wasn't handling the controls but was just
as lost. Both were staring bug-eyed at the 'low fuel'
warning light glowing ominously on the instrument
panel. With a night flame-out followed by a nearly
certain crash as the only alternative, Pot and his co-pilot
approached the only lights they could see in the black
Alabama countryside.

Pot then landed his 1600-horsepower man-made
hurricane in the middle of an outdoor Episcopal church
social, blowing tables and chairs akimbo, sending
scores of screaming parishioners diving for cover,
and calling out every fire truck and police car within a
twenty-mile radius.

When Pot's army instructor pilot and the training-
company commander showed up two hours later in a
fuel tank truck, Pot and his co-pilot told their story and
assumed, almost with relief, that they'd be driven back
to Fort Rucker for court martial and be washed-out
from the flight program. They were flabbergasted when,
after refueling the big helicopter, the two officers said:
"Catch you later, gentlemen," then got back in the truck
and drove away into the darkness without so much as
telling the two students where they were.

No one could have been more astonished than Pot
when the U. S. Army finally pinned on his warrant
officer bars and silver aviator's wings, two months later.

Mary Jane and Jack Daniels were in Vietnam to
meet Pot. He was overjoyed to see them and to find
their access both cheaper and less encumbered by
irksome local laws. His initial assignment was to a
'slick' company of Hueys flying a general resupply and
transport mission. Three months later, as a co-pilot,
Pot became involved in the first aerial dogfight in the
history of helicopter aviation.

Pot, his aircraft commander, crew-chief and gunner
made the grievous error of loading five German
Shepherd tracking dogs and their handlers into the
crowded cargo bay just behind the cockpit seats and

ahead of the gunner stations of their Huey. Marginally
restrained on chains tightly gripped by their sweating
handlers, the fang-bearing, drooling, trembling dogs
were as nervous as Pot stayed. Nonetheless, the
decision was made to cart them all to the firebase in
one flight. Less than a mile after takeoff, the gunner
asked for and received permission to test the guns, as
was standard procedure on the first flight of the day.
Aviation history was about to be made.

The first deafening machine-gun rounds had barely
emitted, peppering the interior of the helicopter with
hot brass shell casings, when the dogs went berserk.
Pandemonium is too gentle a word for what ensued.
Pot whirled about in his cockpit seat to behold a scene
Dante couldn't have envisioned on his best day.

The five raging dogs were a whirling hellish dervish
something like the tigers in Little Black Sambo. The
air was filled with shreds of green fatigue cloth, tufts
of dog hair, unidentified bits of bloody flesh and, most
alarmingly, little pieces of quilted-fabric insulation that
was supposed to be protecting vital wiring in the ceiling
of the aircraft. The snarling of the thrashing dogs, the
screams of the hysterical dog handlers, and the shouts
of the gunner and crew chief could be heard over
the roaring engine and the rather emphatic intercom
conversations filling helmet earphones.

The aircraft commander was flying at the time and
he instantly turned back for the airfield. Pot beat off a
homicidal, loose dog with his revolver and considered
the lesser evil of getting his face chewed off or loosing
a gunshot round in the crowded confines of an aircraft
in flight, containing nine men and five dogs. The crew
chief and the gunner were leaning into the cargo bay
from the aft gunner stations flailing dogs and handlers
indiscriminately with a folded fox-hole shovel and a
spare M-60 machine-gun barrel.

It was on a fore-stroke with the shovel that the
gunner snagged a smoke grenade hung on the gunner-
station seat post, ripping it from it's detonation pin

and sending it spinning into the maelstrom of enraged dogs and terrified men. The grenade popped loudly and spun about spewing copious clouds of thick red smoke while it reached a temperature of about 180 degrees. The world's first helicopter aerial dogfight went into hyperdrive.

All Pot could remember of his emergency procedures at the moment was that incapacitating smoke from an on-board fire should be vented by jettisoning the cockpit doors. Pot seized the emergency-jettison t-handle connected to his door and yanked it. The door flew away. Regrettably, Pot had overlooked the part of the emergency procedure that said to slow the aircraft to a hover before jettisoning any cockpit doors. As the ship was still doing nearly a hundred knots, Pot's cockpit door blew aft in the slip stream and cut the tail-rotor drive shaft, leaving the big helicopter without the anti-torque control that was essential for a normal landing.

The aircraft commander followed his only option and skated the machine onto the pierced-steel runway at fifty knots, like a landing airplane. When the ship finally slid to a smoking, spark-trailing halt and the dogs were ejected, Pot allowed himself to think all was well.

Then the airfield crash crew screamed up in their silver moon suits, on their huge yellow crash truck, and they flushed the still smoking aircraft and everyone aboard with torrents of stinking, slimy crash foam.

The lift-company commander arrived on the airfield in a jeep staring at what he saw like OSHA investigators had gaped at the scene of Pot's construction accident.

Soaked in crash foam and blowing red phlegm onto the runway, Pot watched crash-crewmen beating a die-hard dog back from its comatose handler. He now knew for certain that his career as a pilot was ended in a court martial. They would surely strip him of his wings and banish him to the infantry and hand-to-hand combat with legions of little yellow karate maniacs with bayonets on their machine-guns.

"Awright!" the major finally barked. "You men go preflight another aircraft, and then get these damned dogs out to the firebase!" He turned and stalked toward his jeep as the astonished flight crew gaped. "And this time, men," the major growled over his shoulder, "No fucking around!"

Five months after Pot arrived in-country, he was quite involuntarily transferred to a gunship company, owing to an attrition-accelerated shortage of immediately available gunship pilots. The overloaded gunship helicopters flew right into the face of the enemy at low altitudes to deliver rockets and streams of machine-gun fire in close support of friendly troops, and more than a few of them either crashed for the mechanical strain on the aircraft, or were shot out of the sky. One could say Pot had managed to go from the frying pan into the fire.

Pot's nerves deteriorated steadily from none-too-high a point of origin. After a while, even the soothing ministrations of sweet Mary Jane and good old J.D. weren't quite enough to help Pot hold onto himself. He took downers by the handful so he could sleep, then he took uppers to wake up enough to find his aircraft. He took aspirin to kill the headaches of hangovers until the stomach pain drove him to buying stolen prescription pain-relief medicines for his head and his stomach. The more he took, the more he needed. Local marijuana suppliers had an eight-by-ten color photo of him on their wall, and if the pharmaceutical and whiskey industries had known of Pot's contribution to their corporate welfare they'd have taken out a key-man insurance policy on him.

This was Pot's state when, in his seventh month in green hell, he took off as copilot to The Hatchet Man for a gunship mission into the new free-fire zone.

Chapter Seventeen
The Room

Charlie Dermott lies shirtless on his bunk in the late afternoon. Sung is gone but Charlie can still smell her on him; he can still feel her slippery heat. He hears over and over and over the magical, mysterious, erotic words she moaned in Vietnamese when she came. When he rises he is embarrassed to find a telltale wet spot on the sheet. He draws the blanket over it. Charlie's body and soul cry out for Sung Tranh. Again and again he whispers her name, the most beautiful sound in any language for Charlie.

Each time he hears footsteps pounding the boardwalk outside The Room he springs up again to peer out the high, screened window to see who approaches. Finally, he is rewarded.

"Van!" Charlie almost shrieks, and he seizes Van by the arm as he enters carrying his rifle and flight bag. "Van! Man, am I glad to see you!"

"Well...hi Charlie," Van says, bemused at being towed bodily into The Room. "It's nice to see you again, too. What's it been now, about eight or ten whole hours?"

"No man, you don't understand! Come in! I gotta talk to somebody so bad I could split, and you're the only guy I can trust, and I've been waiting all afternoon for you to get back!"

"Didn't you go up today?"

"No, no, no, we grounded the ship for a hydraulic leak and maintenance is having a hard time locating it. I've been here all day. That's why I gotta tell you what I gotta tell you!"

"Okay, well let me put my stuff away and get a beer, and—"

Charlie snatches Van's rifle and flight bag from him and dumps them on his bunk. He charges to Old Faithful, whips out a beer, spears it with his opener, and jams it at Van.

Van accepts the beer, which is foaming over his hand onto the floor from the violence with which Charlie has delivered it.

"Good grief, Charlie! What in the world—wait a minute—has this got something to do with Sung Tranh?"

"Yes!" Charlie spurts, a grin about to tear open his face.

"She said she'd marry you!"

"Ahhhh...no!"

"No? I thought you were going to—"

"I did! I did! She didn't say yes, but she didn't say no either!"

"Oh. Well I guess—"

"She said she loves me!"

"Wonderful, Charlie, but I thought you already thought—"

"Yeah I did, Van, but today she, she, well...she sort of proved it."

"She proved it?"

"Yeah, you know, she...really...proved it."

"What do you...uh-oh...are you trying to tell me you two—"

"Yes!"

"You...made love to Sung?"

"Yes! It was...great!"

"I'd never have guessed. You mean, right here in—"

"Yes! Right there! It was...fabulous! It was... amazing! It was —"

"I get the picture, Charlie. Well I don't know what to say; congratulations, I guess!"

Charlie strides about The Room waving his arms in the air. "Aw Van, she is so...wonderful! I love her so

203

much it's making me crazy!"

"Charlie, why wouldn't she agree to marry you?"

"Well, she didn't disagree, either. She just, well, she needs to think about it. She's not just marrying me, Van, she's marrying a whole nation! She'd have to move to The World, and there's her mother and brothers, and her sister in Paris, and besides, she's got like seven months to make up her mind."

"I see."

"It's a big decision, Van. I didn't even really ask her for an answer, I just said think about it. But, shoot, given what we did, and it was...like, her idea, man, believe me, I mean that sort of makes it a sure thing, doesn't it?"

Van smiles gently. "No."

"No? Aw come on, Van, I thought you were with me on this!"

"Charlie, I am very much with you in terms of your being happy with Sung, if that's what you want. And yes, I'd agree that if she took you to bed that's a good sign she cares for you."

"Okay! Then what's the—"

"I just wouldn't call it a sure thing until it's a sure thing, that's all, Charlie. I'd hate to see you get all your emotional eggs in a fragile basket. Like you said, marriage is a big decision; it's even bigger given the cultural factors that bear on you and Sung. Things don't always work out the way we want, that's all I'm saying."

"This is going to work out, Van! I'll make it work out! I love her and she loves me!"

"Okay!" Van says, smiling again. "I am with you Charlie, I really am! I would just like to see you maintain an option in case it doesn't go exactly the way you'd like. Nothing to be lost in doing that, right? Remember what they told us in flight school meteorology? Always leave yourself an out; you can be surrounded by evil weather on three sides, but you never get into a position where that fourth side closes, too. Never."

"Oh man, that's different! This is...this is...love, man! I'm in love!"

Van smiles as he studies Charlie. "I can see that, Charlie, and I'm thrilled for you. And I still say that you should follow your heart. Just do it with some caution, Charlie. This is a big decision, especially for Sung."

"You just don't know what she's like, Van! She's the most...the most..."

"Let me see if I can guess...the most wonderful girl in the world?"

"Yes! She's so pretty and sweet and smart and—"

"And was it good with her in bed?"

"Aw Van, it was fantastic! You can't imagine what this girl is like!"

"Mmm. Truer words were never spoken."

"She was...it was...like...the greatest experience in my life!"

"Too bad your first time only happens once."

"I didn't say it was my first time!" Charlie retorts, indignantly. "I'm almost twenty-two years old, man!"

"Charlie, it's no shame. I'll be perfectly honest with you: I am twenty-two years old and I've yet to make love to a girl."

Charlie is dumbstruck. "No kidding? You mean you and Susan have never...?"

"Nary a time."

"Lord, and I thought I was the only guy on earth our age who'd never...you know...never...um...done it."

"Well it's a moot point now, isn't it?"

"Yeah! Yeah, it is!"

A voice outside approaches, singing, "Rollin'...Unh! Rollin' on the riv-ver! Rollin'..."

"Here comes Spud!" Charlie says in a hushed tone. "Not a word to anybody about all this, Van, I don't want the guys kidding me about it, and if Hatchette ever finds out about Sung...well, you know how he feels about, ah, orientals."

"Your secrets are safe, Charlie. Thanks for sharing

them with me. And hey, congratulations!"

"Thanks man! It was great! It was fan—"

"I know, already!"

Spud pulls back the screen door and swaggers into The Room. "At ease, men; as you were! I'll be in the area all evening!"

"Well, thank you, General Spud," Charlie says.

"Hi Spud."

"Evening guys! Well, I cheated death again today. Wait 'til Hollywood finds out about me. I am the hottest rotorpig in The Nam. Speaking of rotorpigs, where's the rest of our happy little family tonight?" Spud piles his equipment by his locker. He eyes Charlie suspiciously. "Charlie, what the hell is the matter with you? You look like you...just got laid or something."

Charlie blanches. "What?" he croaks.

"Ah, Spud's just kidding, Charlie," Van says quickly. "Charlie's been off all day, Spud, he just woke up."

"Fuck, of course I'm kidding, Charlie. How the hell could a guy get laid around here? Jesus. Where are Hale and Pot and The Hatchet Man?"

"Hale and his crew are up directing an artillery strike over near the Cambodian border," Charlie answers, vastly relieved.

"Oh hey, that's right!" Spud replies, yanking open Old Faithful's door. "Saigon declared that whole border area to be a free-fire zone last week. I remember now."

"Yeah," Van joins in, "The Civic Action Teams have supposedly notified the Vietnamese and Montagnyard populations to remain clear of that whole greater border area. Now anything seen moving in the free-fire zone, anything, can be attacked on sight without clearance from operations."

"That's where Pot and Hatchette are now," Charlie adds. "All the Graverobber gunships are up patrolling the new free-fire zone looking for targets of opportunity."

Spud laughs, pulling a beer from the refrigerator. "Oh shit. It's gonna be hell on all the monkeys, elephants, wild hogs and cattle out there, I can see that now. All the gunship boys will be flying around out in the free-fire zone, blasting anything that moves or even rustles a tree limb."

Van shakes his head. "I just hope those Civic Action guys did their jobs and warned off all the population. I don't know how you can get word to every isolated peasant in those mountains where there has never been a phone or a radio or a TV or a mail system in -"

"Fuck the gooks, man!" Spud exclaims. He spears his beer. "That stupid bastard Johnson was crazy to stop the bombing north of the seventeenth parallel! The very next day, from the air, you could see dust clouds rising over the Ho Chi Minh Trail from all the gook supply convoys moving south! Hell, I ain't no general, but even I can figure out we ain't gonna beat Uncle Ho in his own sandbox if we have to play by his rules! How do you think all those goddamn rockets they been blowing our asses off with got down here, Van?"

"I know Spud," Van says patiently, "But those rockets were brought down the Trail by the NVA, not by the South Vietnamese border farmers or Montagnyard tribesmen that have been farming, hunting or living out in the border zone for centuries."

"Ah, bullshit," Spud responds, sitting on his bunk. "A gook's a gook, man. They're all in it somehow."

"No they're not!" Charlie retorts with heat, surprising Spud.

"What the fuck's the matter with you, Charlie? I hear the grunts captured a chi-com, 37mm, anti-aircraft machine-gun in that firefight near Polie Djarang last week. The gooks are bringing some industrial-grade toys down the Trail this time! Maybe the new free-fire zone will slow 'em down some. I say kill 'em all and let God sort 'em out."

Charlie flares, "Well, how would you like it if—"

"It's getting dark," Van interrupts, firmly. "The guys should be getting back soon. Hope the chow's decent tonight."

"Hoo-haaah!" Comes a deep, satisfied voice from outside.

"Even as we speak," Spud remarks dryly, "Sounds like The Hatchet Man had good hunting today."

The door swings back, and Hatchette and Pot enter, Hatchette highly animated and Pot notably less enthused. Still wearing his flak jacket, Pot hurries to his stash and retrieves his bottle of Jack Daniels Black Label and a small plastic snap-container of pink capsules. He uncaps the pills with shaking hands, pours forth an undetermined number of them, gulps them, and flushes them with the Jack until his eyes water and he gasps.

Hatchette flings his equipment onto his bunk and turns to The Room. "Hot damn!" He roars. "We did it! We finally fuckin' did it!"

"Did what?" Van asks, anxious to share Hatchette's enthusiasm.

"What every hog pilot fuckin' dreams of, troop! We finally caught gooks in the open! I haven't had so much fun since we zapped those gooks that shot you down that time!"

"Oh," Van says, sadly.

Pothead Willows glares at Hatchette, then sucks again at his bottle. The brown liquid spills down the sides of his mouth but he seems not to care.

"It was goddamn beautiful, man!" Hatchette continues. "For weeks all we've been able to do is fire on tree-lines, rice-paddies, gook hooches, cave entrances—everything you can think of—but we never get to see if we hit anybody! But this time, man, this time we caught the little fucks in the open! God, it was great!"

There is a loud clink as Pot's bottle is set on the floor. Pot now buries his head in his hands as he sits on his bunk. Van eyes him with concern.

"Where?" Spud asks. "Over in the new free-fire zone?"

"You bet your ass! We were low and fast, under a

low cloud deck; in fact, we almost missed 'em. But
the crew chief spotted some movement in the bushes."
Hatchette illustrates with his hands in the time-honored
fashion of all combat flyers since the Red Baron.
"Marvin Adams was flying my wing in Graverobber-
one-niner. We both pulled around in a tight turn and
there they were, runnin' through the scrub brush!"

"Cong or NVA?"

"Couldn't tell. The sun was low and they were in
shadows runnin' fast as hell through tall brush; could've
been either one! We let fly with all the fleshette rockets
at once, and then we hosed 'em with the chain guns!
As soon as we rolled off the target line, ole Marvin and
his crew gave 'em a dose of forty-mike-mike grenade
rounds just for good measure. Man, we fucked those
gooks up!"

"How do you know you hit 'em?" Spud asks with
excitement.

"That's the best part, man! We could actually see
pieces of 'em flying through the air!"

Pot springs to his feet and fixes Hatchette with a
look of fury for a moment, then he sits hard and drinks
harder. Hatchette is oblivious of Pot.

"Good God, Hatch..." Van whispers, eyeing Pot with
caution.

"God ain't got shit to do with it, flower baby, it was
superior American fire power, all the way!"

"How many?" Van asks, looking at the floor.

"At least four! Maybe more! We went over so fast
it was hard to tell. Marvin and his boys never did see
'em; they just fired where all the leaves and dirt was
churned up. We'll know the body count soon, though;
the colonel sent Preston and his crew out to put a patrol
on the ground to search for bodies. Man! I hope we got
at least one gook officer!"

Pot now sits, sobbing quietly, his head hung low,
the bottle dangling from an arm propped on his knee.
Unnoticed, Hale Preston appears at the screen door, his
feet spread, still wearing his flak vest and carrying his

209

flight helmet. He is not happy.

"What's the matter, Pot?" Van inquires, concerned.

"Aw, fuck him!" Hatchette spits with contempt, towering over Pot. "We finally get a confirmed kill and all this gutless, hippie dope-head wants to do is blubber about it. Jesus! What the fuck is this man's army coming to?"

Hale jerks the door back and pushes roughly past Hatchette, surprising him, he stalks to a spot near Van, and turns. He is breathing hard through his nose, and sweating profusely.

"Hale...What is it?" Van says.

"Preston!" Hatchette echoes. "That was some kill we made, wasn't it? How many did we get? Any officers? Did you get any trophies?"

Hale eyes Hatchette coldly, then he throws his flight helmet to the floor with a bang.

Pot jerks his head up, looking with clear fear at Hale. Hale steps to Pot, who draws back as if he expects Hale to strike him.

Hale snatches the bottle from Pot's grip and drinks long on it. Pot cannot pull his eyes from Hale. Hale finally lowers the bottle, savoring the relief the rich hot whiskey burns into him. He regards Pot with scorn, and then he flings the bottle at him. Pot cries out and shields his head with his arms. The bottle clatters to the floor. Pot collapses in sobs.

"Hey, troop!" Hatchette snarls, confused and angry. "I asked you a goddamn question! Answer up!"

"Hale, what's wrong?" Van asks, alarmed.

Hale covers his eyes with his hand, as though shutting something out.

"What about it, Preston?" Hatchette demands.

"Ask him," Hale answers, tightly restrained, pointing to Pot. "He knows. Don't you, Pot?"

"Noooo!" Pot moans, frantically shaking his head. "No, no, no, no!"

"Damn you, Preston!" Hatchette says. "Answer my fuckin' question! Any officers? Any trophies?"

210

Hale answers with rigidly forced restraint, "You
want...trophies, Hatchette? Hmmm?" He removes
from his flak jacket pocket a fistful of colorful fabric
which he holds forth at Hatchette. "You want a trophy,
you...sorry...son of a bitch?" Hale seems to be having
difficulty breathing. "Here's your fucking trophy!" Hale
sidearms the cloth at Hatchette.

"Hey!" Hatchette barks angrily, catching the cloth
in self defense; he unfolds and examines it. It is torn
and heavily spotted with dry, brown stains. "Preston,
what the hell are you talking about? This is...this is just
some dink kid's shirt! What the fuck does...hey...wait a
goddamn minute ..."

"Oh Hale, no." Van says softly.

Hale spreads his feet and stabs an arm and accusing
finger at Hatchette. "YOU MURDERED FOUR
MONTAGNYARD CHILDREN PICKING BERRIES
IN THE FREE-FIRE ZOOOOOOOOOOOOONE!"
Hale bellows, holding the last syllable.

Pot jams his hands over his ears and wails. Charlie,
Spud and Van look on in horror.

"You're fuckin' crazy!" Hatchette snarls.

Hale is out of control. "THE OLDEST ONE
WAS ELEVEN! ELEVEN, YOU MURDERING
MOTHERFUCKERRRRR!"

Pothead stands with his hands still clapped over his
ears. He yells, "Nooooo!" And runs stumbling from The
Room. "Nooooo!"

Van rises, stunned. "I'd better go with him; he may
try to hurt himself."

"I'll go with you!" Spud says, and the two of them
rush out in pursuit of Pot.

Hatchette and Hale are locked in a bitter stare-down.
Charlie looks rapidly back and forth from one man to
the other.

Hatchette suddenly drops the child's shirt as though
it has just burned him. "You're fuckin' nuts, Preston!
I've got over a thousand combat flying hours! I know a
gook soldier when I see one!"

211

Hale is regaining his control. He turns away and
runs his fingers through his matted, sweaty hair. "It's
been confirmed by division intelligence, Hatchette!
They've got Polaroid pictures!" Hale almost whispers
now. "God. Pictures I'll remember to my grave..."
Still breathing deeply, Hale walks slowly to Pot's
bunk and retrieves the Jack bottle from the floor. "You
slaughtered four kids...four...children." Hale pants
and squints with undiluted contempt at Hatchette.
"You motherfucker." Hale drinks what remains in the
bottle, grimaces, and shakes his head. "You rotten
motherfucker..."

Hatchette is momentarily stunned, as the truth sinks
in. He speaks as much to himself as to Hale. "It...all
happened so fast. They were in shadow, and running in
deep brush. I—"

Hale rails savagely, "Why didn't you take a second
to confirm your target? God damn you, Hatchette!"

"Take a second! Take a second? This is a war, not
a goddamned rabbit hunt! You shoot first or die! You
'take a second' when you overfly the gooks and they'll
use that second to blow you right out of the fuckin' sky!
You know that! And that was a declared free-fire zone
out there! You know that too!"

Hale stands and scoops the bloody shirt from the
floor. He holds it toward Hatchette. "I know you
greased four kids!"

"I DIDN'T KNOW THEY WERE KIDS!" Hatchette
shouts, breathing hard, a tinge of panic in his deep
voice.

"Fuck you! Pot knew! He was half stoned and he
knew! You were so goddamn kill-crazy you didn't want
to know! You bastard!"

"I'll tell you what I know, Preston! I know that's
four little gooks who'll never grow up to be big gooks
who shoot at me! I know that what I kill now I don't
have to kill later! That's what I know!"

"Oh Lord, Hatch," Charlie says. "You can't mean
that! These were Yard kids, anyway, not goo—uh—

Vietnamese!"

Hatchette glowers at Charlie. "A gook is a gook, flower-baby, and the only good one is a dead one!"

Hale is cold, low and intense. "You get out of my sight, Hatchette," he seethes. "You get the fuck of my sight."

Hatchette strides to his bunk and snatches up his cap. He jams it onto his massive skull, pauses to glare at Hale, and then he stalks out, kicking the screen door hard against the outer wall. It swings slowly back.

Hale stares at the closing door, still breathing hard. Charlie looks sick; he sits and places his face against bowed hands.

"Our kind and merciful Father," Charlie whispers reverently, "We pray you will receive into your heavenly kingdom the souls of these poor children and—"

"AWWSSHUT-UP, CHARLIE!" Hale yells, teetering on the edge of his control, his eyes moist. Charlie looks up, stricken, lowering his hands. "Don't lay that pious bullshit on me right now! I can't handle it! Where was your 'kind and merciful father' when Hatchette rolled in on those kids? Hanh? And don't hand me any of those inane pulpit platitudes like, 'it's God's will', or 'the Lord moves in mysterious ways'! That blather is an insult to any intelligent person, and I don't want to hear it!"

Charlie rises, pained. He spreads his open hands. "Hale, I—"

"Bullshit! Your 'god' is a...pathetic fantasy...conjured up by weak minds to give them solace in times of fear, and to cover up questions they can't find logical answers to! Like why did four helpless children get their entrails hung in the trees this afternoon? Why, damn it? Whyyyy?" Hale aims his finger at a stunned Charlie. "You believe in this 'god', Charlie? Well you call him in here, right now! Because he's got some tall explaining to do to Hale Preston!"

Hale and Charlie stare at each other: Hale sucking

air fiercely through his nose, Charlie lost. Hale breaks the trance, sits upon the chair, and rests his head in his hands. In a moment, he continues, but more gently now.

"I'm sorry, Charlie. I have no right...to take all this out on you, and you have every right to believe what you will...without my ridicule." Hale pauses, and frustration creeps back into his voice. "I just can't bring myself to believe in...gods...anymore, Charlie! I've listened to all the arguments and they just don't hold water. That 'faith' you Christians keep talking about won't cut it anymore. There is too much that goes on in this world that a god, if there was one, should do something about, but doesn't."

Charlie can only look back at Hale in distress, his own eyes watering.

Hale draws a deep breath and releases it slowly. He stares at the floor. "You know...Charlie...when I'm informed by operations that some artillery or air strike I directed killed twenty or thirty men by actual body count, I think...oh man...if there is a god...I'm in a lot of trouble, but..." Hale looks at Charlie with agony, "if there is no god...then we're all in a lot of trouble."

Chapter Eighteen
Spring 1968

Hale

"Haaaaaale! Hale Prestonnnnnn!"

No sooner had he stepped down from the elevated
marble foyer to the floor of the grand ballroom did
Hale hear the familiar sing-song call of Mrs. Galway.
Of the delectable if august body of women Hale looked
forward to meeting at the Trevanthe Country Club
Spring Ball, Mrs. Travis Galway was way down on the
list. Nonetheless, officer and gentleman and all that;
he straightened, tugged the blouse of his dress blues
taught, and turned with a dignified smile.

With her weary husband in tow, Mrs. Galway
charged through a ballroom crowded with elegantly
attired dancing couples. The husband frowned with
irritation. With his free hand he shielded an ear from the
music of the band and singer blaring a rousing Age Of
Aquarius.

"Hale, honey, what a surprise to see you!" Mrs.
Galway gushed over the din. "We heard about you
going in the army, and now just look at you!" Mrs.
Galway smothered Hale in a heavily perfumed embrace
of voluminous breasts and belly. "Hale, darling, you
remember my husband, the captain? Travis, you
remember little Hale Preston? Went to public school
with Perry until you sent our boy off to that...place."

As the 'the captain' had been retired from the navy
for over ten years, he was attired in the requisite tuxedo,
but he still bore the close silver hair and crisply cut
moustache of his days commanding a heavy cruiser off

215

Okinawa. He also walked with a slight limp awarded
him by a Japanese shell. "'Little Hale Preston' looks to
stand about six-two and tip the bar at about one-eighty,"
the captain observed. "Good evening, Mr. Preston."

"Mrs. Galway," Hale said, bowing slightly. He took
her husband's extended hand firmly. "Captain Galway, a
pleasure to see you, sir."

"Why Hale," Mrs. Galway forged on, "you look so
cute in your dress blues! Why all the young ladies will
be a-twitter I'm sure. But what is..." Joyce Galway
squinted at the gold-trimmed shoulder boards on Hale's
dark formal uniform, "I declare I don't recall this rank
insignia. Are you a lieutenant or—?"

Captain Galway sighed and eyed the chandelier.
"Mr. Preston is a warrant officer, Janell."

Mrs. Galway struggled to conceal a sudden distaste.
"Oh. Well, God knows the enlisted men have their
place. Why the captain has always said the enlisted are
the backbone of—"

"And indeed they are," Captain Galway interrupted
with irritation, "But Mr. Preston is not an enlisted man,
Janell. You were a navy wife for the last eleven years
of my career. I should think you'd know the warrant
ranks are officer technician grades equal in pay to the
four commissioned ranks from ensign to lieutenant
commander, or lieutenant to major outside the navy.
Further, warrant officers are accorded all the privileges
and courtesies due commissioned officers."

Mrs. Galway appeared slightly irked at the rebuke
from her husband. "Well, Travis, I never did understand
army dress—"

"We see damned few enough young men these days
voluntarily don the uniform of their nation's armed
services, let alone have the fortitude to wear it proudly
to an occasion like this. I'd expect such confusion from
one of those silver-spoon, 'flower-children' Perry loafs
around with, but not from a navy wife."

"Travis! Just because our son prefers to—"

"Perry prefers to be a sloppy, long-haired,

216

philosophy graduate student instead of serving his country in its time of war as have—"

"'Generations of Galways before him.' Really, Travis, I do wish you'd alter your speeches once in a rare—"

"If you'll excuse me," Hale elected to interject, "I see my parents by the bar. Mrs. Galway, Captain Galway, so good to see you again." Making his escape, Hale was glad to hear the Galway's bickering become absorbed by the audio overlay of the band and the swiftly dancing couples. Thousands of swirling spots of colored light reflected from a rotating glitter dome and flew about the ballroom. More interestingly, Hale noted, they gleamed in the sequined fringe of the sexy singer's dress.

Hale grimly reflected that it was altogether fitting if not proper that he should locate his parents, Drs. Garrett and Diane Preston, by one of the ornate bars, full glasses in hand.

He supposed he should do his duty, and there would be no better time in the evening to do it.

On Hale's approach, a beefy and droopy-eyed Dr. Garrett Preston, internal medicine, clumsily clicked his heels and straightened his arm toward Hale. "Heil, mein General...or whatever you are," Dr. Preston remarked sourly. He held his drink back to avoid spilling it on his expensive tux.

The other Dr. Preston, Diane, an OB/GYN with a body and a gown that drew male eyes from seventeen to seventy, was slightly less under the influence, Hale saw. She glared at her husband's tactless salute. "Oh Garrett, for God's sake." Diane Preston frowned at Hale and examined him as though he were a hemorrhoidal tumor. "Hale, dear, I must say I wish you'd worn your tux. You're the only young gentleman in the entire place in a...uniform. Must you display—?"

"I'm an officer in the United States Army, mother. You'll forgive me for not sporting the crown of thorns... effete, contemporary American academia would proffer upon me."

"Effete, indeed!" Garrett hissed.

"You pretend to erudition, dear," Diane Preston said to her son. "It doesn't become you."

"I do not, at least, pretend to sobriety," Hale replied softly, waving for the bartender. He ordered rum and coke. "You may write off my appalling taste to my squalid public school upbringing, Mother. You both tried hard enough to send me off to Danforth with that insufferable Perry Galway, but—"

"You stubbornly refused to attend a decent school!" Diane retorted. She paused to compose herself. They'd not seen Hale in ten months. Why did she let her son get to her this way?

"There you have it!" Hale said, accepting his drink. "Proof of retardation. Surely you must have taken thalidomide or, oh, I know! You almost certainly drank like a hockey goalie while pregnant with me. That's it. Now we can nurse the illusion we all so cherish that nothing about my behavior is genetically derived of either of you." Hale held up his Cuba libre. "Here's to that great American institution, family!"

"Damn your glibness, Hale," Garrett Preston growled. "You wear that...preposterous costume to the most important social affair of the year just to embarrass me!" He took another angry draw on his unmalted scotch, gulping it down. "Unbelievable. In this era of moral crisis in America, my son, my son, not only enlists in the goddamned army, but he comes home on leave to flaunt this...uniform...before everyone of any substance in the whole goddamned community!"

"Garrett, keep your voice down!" Diane whispered tightly.

"Why?" Garrett replied, sweeping his drink in an arc, indicating the huge ballroom. "Why, I ask you? What's to reserve to dignity? We're embroiled in this illegal, immoral war, and my...son...who hasn't deigned to visit us since before he went to that...helicopter school...nearly a year ago, suddenly shows up at the

Trevanthe Country Club Spring Ball in his, his...field marshal's costume!"

"I'd have waited for a legal, moral war, Dad, but they're all illegal and immoral. You see, war doesn't begin until law and morality have failed. In fact war is the clinical definition of the failure of law and moral—"

"You will spare me your pseudo-Machiavellian rationales! You know I'm president of Physicians Against the War at the university! You parade in here tonight just to—"

"Physicians Against the War." Hale mused. He sipped his rum. "P-A-W. PAW. I swear, Dad, couldn't the most brilliant professorial minds in a leading medical university have come up with something more catchy? Like...Physicians Obviating War...POW! Or Physicians Advocating Peace...PAP. Now there's—"

"I have endured enough of this!" Garrett Preston replied with force. "I see Bass Haley, the club tennis pro over there. I think that for a refreshing change I'll go talk to an interesting person with some knowledge of the subject matter upon which he discourses, like my backhand. Excuse me."

"Oh I think you could teach him a thing or two about backhandedness, Dad," Hale said to his father's back.

"Stop it, Hale." Diane insisted. "He's just upset."

"He's drunk."

"And you know he takes the Physicians Against the War effort very seriously."

"He sure does. For enough of a 'contribution', the right young draftee can get a doctor's statement from that bunch of quacks that'll get him a 4-F exemption while he's fully capable of winning a triathlon."

"That's nonsense! Your father believes in saving lives, and if it saves them to keep them out of an army that sends them off to be killed, then—"

"Now who's engaging in pseudo-Machiavellian rationales, Mother? We both know it takes thousands of bucks 'for the cause' to get your magic letter from Doctor Do-good and coven."

219

"Oh, stop it. Hale, I love you but as usual you go too far. Your father and your sister—"

"You mean the peace-princess who eternally wears eau-de-cannabis, and who—"

"—are disgusted with you—"

"—think's Bob Dylan is a prophet, and Mao Tse Tung is a populist visionary? That sister?"

"—and I'm very close to agreeing with them! I trust you have some warm little delight's bed to sleep in tonight, because until you grow up, you aren't welcome at home!"

Hale watched his mother stalk away through the throng, and he drew yet again on his drink. She's right, he thought. I always go too far.

He was surprised by a feminine voice from behind. "Do you?"

Hale turned to see the top entry on his list of the august and delectable he looked forward to seeing tonight. She had short hair, blonde by nature he suspected and deeply longed to ascertain for certain. She was beautiful and she possessed the bearing of a young woman who knows she is beautiful but bears it with grace. The red gown she wore had been carefully selected and dearly custom-ordered, but as far as Hale was concerned, at least, it was worth all the care and every cent of the expense. It discretely draped, yet left no question of, long dancer's legs, a waist Hale imagined he could encircle with his thumbs and fingers, and breasts that absolutely ensured the strapless bodice would not descend accidentally, alas.

"Dawes," Hale whispered.

"Hello Hale," Dawes Shannon Glade said with a model's smile of perfect white teeth that had entranced Hale Preston since the sixth grade. Dawes was petite but powerful of spirit and mind, Hale knew. She walked gracefully to him on tall, red-leather heels and he bent to receive her. She wrapped both arms about his neck, he wrapped both his about her waist, and he lifted her from the floor to the happy laughter of them both.

People stared, and neither Hale nor Dawes cared.

"Dawes, am I glad to see you! I was hoping you'd be here!"

"And the chance that you might be here was all that could have brought me to such a pretentious affair! How are you, pretty boy?"

"I feel as good as you smell, Dawes, and that is pretty goddamned fine."

"Then next week in Paris I'll buy out the entire inventory of the fragrance. Um...I think we've been sufficiently scandalous. Perhaps you should put me down?"

"Oh, sorry. Felt so good I forgot myself. Damn it's good to see you, Dawes! What's it been? Four years?"

"Since our high-school graduation dance in this same ballroom; just over four years."

"Can I get you a drink?"

"No, I have one here on the ledge. I didn't want to spill it when you ravished me. But you can answer my question."

"I'm sorry; what question?"

"Do you?"

"I see you're still fond of speaking in riddles. Do I what?"

"Have some 'warm little delight's bed to sleep in tonight?' Seeing as you won't be sleeping in the one at Casa Del Preston."

"Are you offering?"

"A statement in reply, not an interrogatory, if you please sir."

"No, regrettably. If I can't break my life-long record of failing to seduce you, then I guess it's my solitary cell at the Holiday Inn."

Dawes took Hale's arm and towed him to the window where her drink trickled condensation. "Bosh. I don't seem to remember you trying all that hard."

"You were the homecoming queen and the goddamned valedictorian, for Christ's sake. You dated Porsche-driving college guys from your sophomore

221

year in high-school. I could've gotten an audience with His Holiness sooner than a date with the famous Dawes Glade."

"Maybe you underestimated your appeal to the infamous Dawes Glade."

"Perhaps. But I preferred the dream to the possibility of being laughed off by her, thank you very much."

Dawes smiled warmly up at Hale. "So. In ten words or less, tell me your last four years, Hale."

Hale sipped his drink and mulled. "Went college. Dropped out. Joined army. Became pilot." Hale looked at Dawes. "Vietnam Thursday."

"Oh Hale," Dawes said, stopping suddenly and studying Hale's face. "Vietnam, really? So soon?"

"Later than for some of our classmates, Dawes. Henry Agee is already under a white stone at Arlington."

"I heard."

"And your time since our graduation, Dawes? Women always need more time to talk, so you can have twenty-five words."

"Chauvinist pig."

"Now you only have twenty-three."

Dawes grinned wryly. She'd so missed bantering with Hale Preston. Why had they not corresponded? Why had anything happened these last four years?

"Went Vassar. Graduated with honors. Off to Paris Wednesday to begin my masters program at the Sorbonne."

"French poetry, no doubt."

"Aerodynamic engineering."

Hale laughed without derision. "You always defied prediction."

Dawes punched Hale's arm. "I lied, you pig. It is French poetry. You were always the only guy who could figure me out." Dawes examined Hale's face over her drink, then she asked, "Hale, why did you never write me?"

Hale looked back at lovely soft-green eyes. "I could

ask you the same -"

A mixture of voices called their names from several yards away, barely audible over the music. Both looked to see a crowd of young men and women dressed to the nines, clustered near the opposite bar and waving come-hither gestures. "Uh oh," Dawes said, squeezing Hale's hand, "We've been discovered by Spanky and the gang. I suppose we have to—"

"Uh, look Dawes, military men are a little out of fashion in our crowd these days, as you must've gleaned from that touching Preston family vignette a moment ago. I'm sure it's you our old classmates are calling, and they'd prefer—"

"Poo. I spent most of my youth in dutch with my peers for not giving a lace-edged damn about what people 'prefer'. If boys hadn't salivated over my boobs and girls hadn't hated me for it no one would have paid me a whit of attention. Except you, maybe. Anyway, I'm not about to become conventional now. If you won't go with me, I'll throw them all the bird from right here; I swear I will." Dawes paused, looking at Hale. "Okay, here it—"

Hale seized Dawes's free hand as she raised it. "Alright, alright, you win."

Dawes took Hale's arm and they boldly marched around the dance floor to the elegantly gowned and tuxed young crowd by the opposite wall. Hale caught many glances aimed their way, some discrete, some lascivious, some contemptuous, all interested. A beautiful woman who behaves as though she is proud to be in the company of her man is a very nice thing, Hale reflected.

On arrival the introductions, ceremonial hugs, cheek-kisses and handshakes went round. Predictably, all the what've-you-been-up-to questions from their former classmates were directed at Dawes, but Hale was relieved instead of offended. It didn't last.

"So. Preston." Tall, slightly stooped Perry Galway had ten-inch brown hair carefully cultivated to lie over

one eye from which he peered disdainfully after a toss
of the hair. He wore a red plaid cummerbund and bow
tie with his tuxedo.

Battle stations, Hale thought.

Perry Galway smiled like a snake and studied Hale
from head to toe. "I see you're protecting truth and
justice and baseball and Mom's apple pie from the
godless communist menace." Perry smirked and several
of his collegiate entourage tittered. Notable among
the latter was a young woman with ironed black hair
extending halfway down her back who wore a madras
gown and polished brass jewelry that was supposed to
make her look like she just came off a caravan from the
Rajasthan. She'd been introduced as Elspeth Demaine.
Hale suspected the Ghandi's-mistress outfit was
designed in Paris, made in Japan and sold in New York.

"No, Perry," Hale replied topically, "Actually I'm
a doorman at the Ritz. I'm working my way up to
bellhop."

More titters went round, irking Perry this time.

"No, no," Perry continued, tossing his hair still again
and reaching to finger the silver wings pinned to Hale's
left breast. "I would have thought just that, except, I
know this trinket signifies you're a...oh God, deliver me
sufficient reverence to say it...a...pilot?" Galway looked
quite pleased with himself.

"Damn. Nothing gets by you does it, Perry? Guess
my cover is blown."

Elspeth Demaine gave Hale a frosty squint. "I
presume that means you're one of those brave lads who
drop napalm on agrarian, southeast Asian children."

Like a locomotive jerking suddenly at a track switch,
the tenor of the banter changed. Polite smiles faded.
Dawes eyed Elspeth with curiosity.

"Actually no," Hale answered, pleasantly locking
eyes with Elspeth. "I'm a helicopter pilot. If we
dropped napalm from typical helicopter altitudes we'd
get fried along with the ASACs —uh that's military
technical talk for agrarian, southeast Asian children, of

course. No, we rotary sky warriors prefer to make a low pass over the village and throw out candy. Then when the starving ASACs run out to pick it up, see, we—"

"Hale," Dawes said.

"—blast the little heathen crumb-snatchers with machine guns."

The entire group flinched.

"Ever seen what a seven-point-six-two millimeter, full-copper-jacket slug does to a three-year-old agrarian, southeast Asian child Elspeth? Me neither, but I'm sure looking forward to it. They say they're hell to hit, especially when they're wounded and you can't predict where the little rascals are going to run. Hard to lead 'em, see, they—"

"Hale," Dawes repeated.

Elspeth Demaine was trembling with fury. Her jaw muscles rippled and her lips pursed. She glanced at her drink and then back at Hale.

"If you're contemplating throwing that drink on me, Elspeth," Hale said, leaning closer to the furious woman's face, "In some dramatic, Bette-bitch-Davis gesture of contempt, then consider that I will very shortly thereafter slap you flat on your condescending, patronizing, arrogant—albeit tasty—ass. I'm a believer in equal treatment for women, trust me."

"Listen, Preston!" Perry Galway interjected angrily.

"Shut up, Perry; nobody's talking to you."

"You can't—"

"Shut up, Perry!" Elspeth said this time, viciously. "I can fight my own battles! You think you're real cute, don't you soldier boy? Well you don't impress me. I'll tell you to your face you're a perfect example of what's wrong with this country. You're fed a dish of Eisenhower-era patriotic bullshit about communist aggression and you eat it right up! Like a wind-up monkey, you put on your soldier suit and babble about defending freedom! All the while you're nothing but a dim-witted lackey given an expensive toy and told to go slaughter peaceful Vietnamese farmers for imperialist

American political and commercial interests!"

Elspeth's voice had risen enough to attract the attention of several people on the fringes of the group.

"Well said, Elspeth," Hale replied with respect. "You're right about the lackey part; I'm going for the trial and adventure unique to war. Damn the politics and the morality." Hale sipped his drink. "And there's certainly no doubt in my mind that a sheltered, elitist debutante like you considers patriotism to be bullshit, but I'm a little cloudy on the peaceful communist bit. Let me see if I have this straight. Those were peaceful Soviet tanks in Budapest? The Berlin wall was erected to keep the peace in? The North Koreans swarmed over the 38th parallel for a peace rally? The red Chinese threaten Taiwan for peace? The NVA is violating the UN 17th Parallel Accord and invading Laos, Cambodia and South Vietnam to restore peace? And the fucking VC are peacefully disemboweling South Vietnamese village officials before their families and neighbors?"

"Hale, please," Dawes appealed. A crowd was drawing near to hear over the band.

"Are we talking about the same communists here, Els-peth? Or are all those events just figments of Eisenhower-era propaganda?"

Elspeth Demaine's composure seemed undisturbed but that she was sharply exhaling, and sweat beaded on her upper lip. "My God. You sound like Barry Goldwater. 'Extremism in the defense of liberty is no vice!' So you're a Dominoeist. You want to charge forth and 'stem the red tide, over there, before we must repel them from the beaches of California', no matter how many foreign children you have to kill to do it. How noble."

"Oh hell no. The commies can have California. I told you, I'm a paid lackey going for sheerly personal reasons; I seek what Hemingway found in Spain, what Remarque found in France, what other writers found in later conflicts, the insight into the mind and heart of man that cannot be distilled outside the crucible of war. But since you bring it up, Elspeth, tell me, which is better for more of the common man, communism or democracy? Which system feeds more and frees more? And if the answer is democracy, then what good is it as a credo if we are not willing to defend it against its enemies? And if defending it is worthy then where do we do it? Whose freedom is so unimportant we should not trouble ourselves to defend it? Where do we draw a line in the sand?"

And the band played on, but for several feet around the group no one spoke. Elspeth stared hard at Hale and her cheeks hollowed, but she declined to respond.

Perry Galway didn't. "What maudlin balderdash," he sneered testily. "Vietnam is not about freedom, Preston, it's about enriching the defense establishment, it's about genocide against black Americans by drafting them for slaughter, it's about extending and securing American political—read commercial—interests. You're a hypocrite, Preston. By your own admission you aren't going to Vietnam for freedom or democracy or the Vietnamese people, you're going for...literary research, for God's sake."

"Stunningly insightful, Perry. But at least I admit my hypocrisy. And I'm laying my ass on the line as payment. I won't be contriving ludicrous economic plots from the safety of Trevanthe Country Club. I won't be hiding out in comfy American academic circles with the other intelligentsia striving to ignore their cowardice, desperately attempting to dignify it with genocide fantasies and pseudo-noble protestations of peace at any cost in liberty."

"Now just a minute!" Dawes Glade said. Hale was surprised and turned to face her. "There are many of us who can't or won't go to war, Hale. There are those of us in and out of academia who deeply believe that killing is wrong, that it's too easy to rush off to war when most of the dying, suffering and property damage will be inflicted upon others. There are many of us who simply believe war is wrong! Are you saying we are to

227

be branded cowards?"

Hale felt attacked from within and he was momentarily taken back. "Dawes, I don't argue that war is morally reprehensible. It is, without qualification. Of course it should be avoided where any reasonable alternative exists, but the surrender of liberty to unchecked aggression is not a reasonable alternative. What I'm saying is that there comes a time in the course of all nations when war is unavoidable because all else in law and morality has failed. And when that time comes there are those eligible who fight, placing their lives behind their convictions, and there are those who, though eligible, choose to hide or run and then try to perfume their cowardice with flowery benevolent themes and lame conspiracy myths." Hale glanced at Perry Galway, who got the message.

Dawes was riled. "Well, well. Intellectually, it must be just peachy warm and cozy to see everything in such conveniently categorical terms. Nothing is gray for you is it, Hale? Everything is so neatly black and white. Maybe some of us think things through a little farther, Hale. Maybe we analyze complex issues a bit more in depth and we find that there are no pat black and white answers, only grave, gray, difficult considerations! Maybe we—"

"Maybe you are the ultimate hypocrite, Dawes. Maybe I've actually thought the issues through farther than you have. Maybe I've realized that any grandiose cocktail wizard can roll the options around in the mind indefinitely while mewling about how dreadfully 'gray' everything is. That's an incomplete process. The gray is what you're supposed to pass through en route to a conclusion. Maybe I've discovered that if one is to claim any integrity for one's intellectuality one must eventually choose a conviction, however gray, and say: 'This is what I believe! And here is where I stand!'"

Dawes sipped her drink and eyed Hale hotly. "Oh. And so now we're all weak minds without conviction? Is that it?"

"May they whom the shoe fits wear it, Dawes."

"Yeah?" Dawes seethed. "Well wear this!" Dawes heaved two thirds of a cocktail glass full of Bloody Mary and ice at Hale's face, spun on her heel and strode away, her head high, breasts bouncing.

Hale had read the message in Dawes's fiery eyes just in time—he knew it well—and he took immediate care not to hold his own head high. Consequently, the vehemently propelled libation sailed completely over him and splashed full into Perry Galway's face, eye-draped hair and plaid bow-tie. Galway reflexed involuntarily, and tossed most of his own drink down the appealing front of Elspeth Demaine's gown.

As Hale slammed the door and started the engine on his long-suffering '59 Chevy with the cat's-eye taillights, he had a second occasion that evening to reflect on his mother's words. A heavy spring rain began to fall as though nature confirmed the admonition in his mother's words and indeed in Dawes Glade's lovely, angry eyes. 'You go too far, Hale.' He sighed and put the car in gear. 'You always go too far.'

Two hours later, in room 114 at the local Holiday Inn, Hale lay in the dark, still in his blues less his shoes, blouse and bow-tie, his shirt collar open. He was morosely studying the ceiling and listening to the steady hiss of the rain when there came a knock at the door so soft he was at first unsure he'd heard it.

Hale opened the door and was astonished to find Dawes Glade standing there looking up at him with a sort of sad dignity in her eyes. Her hair was wet. The soaked gown clung to her every curve.

They stared at each other for a moment while the soft rain fell. "I..." Dawes began, "I'm cold, Hale."

He lay on his back in the tub as the warm shower streamed upon them and steamed the bath. She sat astride him, her hands on his chest, he deep inside her, she rocking and gasping, her wet hair dangling. Deep water sloshed over the edge of the tub as Dawes and Hale washed over a different edge.

At dawn he woke to find her crying quietly, her head on his chest. "Please," Dawes whispered, choking. "Please, Hale...don't get killed in Vietnam."

Chapter Nineteen
The Room

And good evening again, American soldiers, sailors and airmen; I'm Specialist Fourth-Class Barbara Stafford, and this is *Events In Review*, brought to you with the best wishes of *Newsweek Magazine*, which wants you, the American fighting man, to be informed!

The top story on the stateside scene is the continuing trial of Sirhan Bishara Sirhan for the assassination of Senator Robert Kennedy last June. No one, including Sirhan himself, denies that Sirhan did in fact shoot and kill Senator Kennedy. The issue of the trial is premeditation. Did Sirhan stalk Senator Kennedy in cold malice for days before the shooting, as the prosecution maintains? Or was he, as his defense attorneys contend, so possessed by demons that he was unable to control himself? Sirhan's own life may hang on the outcome.

On the opposite side of the US, in Lewisburg Federal Penitentiary, Teamster boss Jimmy Hoffa is celebrating his 56th birthday. Loyal fans arranged for a plane to overfly the prison towing a banner bearing birthday greetings.

The Ford Motor Company previewed its much-heralded new car this week, the revolutionary new, small Maverick. Developed as part of Ford's plan to combat the rising tide of foreign small cars, the Maverick will boast a price tag under $2,000. The Maverick will debut in April, followed in the fall by additional new small cars from GM and American Motors.

Here in Vietnam, it is now safe to say that this year's Tet holiday will not mark a massive communist offensive on the scale of last year's Tet. With the bloody spectacle of Tet-1968 fresh in mind, US and South Vietnamese forces went on one-hundred-percent alert in anticipation of a large-scale assault by communist units. No such assault materialized, but the enemy presence was made known in scattered but intense attacks: At the 'Rockpile', just south of the DMZ, scores of North Vietnamese suicide troops laden with explosives stormed Marine positions and were beaten back only by point-blank artillery fire. At Cu Chi, sappers penetrated the perimeter and blew up several Army helicopters. Saigon was hit by rockets, killing more than two dozen civilians. At Da Nang, rockets sank Navy Riverine patrol boats. The attacks constituted the first test of the nerve of the Nixon administration. On a European tour, President Nixon responded cautiously, maintaining that moving toward peace is more important than over-reacting to scattered small-scale incidents.

In Coronado, California, a Navy board of inquiry is investigating alleged violations of the US Code of Military Justice by members of the crew of the USS Pueblo while captives of the North Koreans. As the investigations bore on, it seemed that the crew of the Pueblo was not on trial as much as the Code itself. Having signed a confession that the Pueblo was indeed a spy ship, Lt. (JG) Fred Schumacher

pleaded that he was merely admitting to what
the North Koreans already knew as a result
of captured Pueblo documents. What point
was there, Schumacher asked, in denying the
obvious at risk of torture? And torture was
the case. Upon discovering that all the Pueblo
crewmen in a North Korean propaganda
photograph distributed worldwide were
displaying a classic American hand-gesture
of defiance known as 'The Bird', North
Koreans beat ringleader Charles Law for nine
hours. Repeatedly breaking 2" X 2" boards,
the Koreans resorted to 4" X 4" lumber.
Law suffered a partial loss of his eyesight.
Law testified before the board of inquiry:
"We waited for the United States to come
in and annihilate this bunch of barbarians."
Lt. (JG) Tim Harris, also a victim of savage
beatings, said, "I was hoping to hear bombers
overhead." Apparently, when the crew of the
Pueblo realized there would be no rescue, not
even retribution, the signing of "confessions"
became merely a matter of survival. Can an
American prisoner of war be fairly expected
to forego survival for allegiance to a possibly
outdated code of conduct? That seems to be
the real question to be answered by the board.

The oldest ruling communist leader in the
world, North Vietnamese President Ho Chi
Minh, 78, made a rare appearance this week.
Apparently belying speculation that he is ill
or senile, Ho danced in the streets and helped
plant trees.

Tonight's last news item will come as
perhaps back-handed good news to American
fighting men. It seems that researchers at
Philadelphia's Temple University School of
Medicine have recently achieved advances
in the development of artificial limbs for

amputees. Conventional artificial arms are cable and pulley devices operated by physical movement of the surviving anatomy of the amputee. Temple researchers have pioneered an electrode-activated device which can sense signals from the brain. It is reported that even handwriting will be possible with the new Temple arm.

And that's it for tonight's edition of *Events In Review*, servicemen. This is Specialist Fourth-Class Barbara Stafford reminding you that *Newsweek Magazine* wants you, the American fighting man, to be informed. Good night, guys!

Chapter Twenty
The Room

At 01:41, The Room is relatively quiet and dark, lighted only very dimly by the glow from porch lights on distant administration buildings. All within are asleep, except for Hatchette who is absent due to a late flight. He has volunteered to fly gunship escort for the dangerous night extraction of a long-range patrol team discovered and pursued by NVA elements in Cambodia.

Slumbering young men lie under olive-drab sheets which rise and sink with their slow respirations. The dominating sound is Spud snoring, a disgusting racket not unlike a walrus dying of a gunshot wound to the lungs. A piercing EEH-EEE! breaks the stillness as someone rolls over on his toy rubber critter. This disturbs no one, for all are lost in the deep sleep of the chronically exhausted.

At first it is almost imperceptible, but soon its chilling wail builds and drills into the consciousness of The Room. Van sits up rubbing his eyes. Hale snaps awake. Spud stirs. The siren howl peaks, but then, unlike previous nights, it begins to recede.

"Hey!" Hale yells, kicking back his sheet. "Wake up everybody! We're getting hit! Get to the bunker!"

"Hit by what?" Spud shouts over the siren now rising again. "I don't hear any incoming!"

"Hale!" Van cries as he struggles into his pants and boots, "Spud's right! Listen! There are no incoming rounds!"

The siren begins to wail once more, rising, shrieking, and then it fades again.

"Oh, sweet Jesus!" Hale says with pronounced

dread.

"What?" Pot calls in the dark, panic at the edge of his tone. "What is it?"

"A broken tuh-tone!" Charlie says, almost choking, clawing his fatigue pants on.

Hale buttons his pants frantically, and jams his feet into his boots. "Charlie's right, it's a broken tone, not a solid tone! It's—"

"What does a broken—"

"—gooks in the wire!" Hale says sharply. "It means the perimeter's been penetrated by sappers! There are gooks inside the goddamned compound! Get your flak jackets and steel-pot helmets on, quick! Everybody see how much ammo you've got! But hey! Don't turn any lights on!"

Charlie shrugs into his flak jacket whispering, "Oh God, oh —What was that?"

There come many hollow, concussive 'ploomp!' sounds; mortar flares being fired in rapid succession on the distant perimeter. The first of them ignite high in the air, swinging from their parachutes, and then The Room is pierced through the screens by dozens of stark, eerie, bleach-white light beams which sway back and forth in concert with coal-black shadows. You see everything in freeze-flashes as the beams and shadows swing to and fro and elevate as the parachute-flares descend.

"Mortar flares!" Spud says soberly, looking through the screened window, the flare light beams slashing across his face. "Damn, man! The goddamn weather's come down! The visibility's too low for helicopters to fly. Aw man, they're puttin' up dozens of flares! It must be a major infiltration, maybe even a full-scale attack! Oh shit, we are in big trouble!"

The siren rises and falls, screams and ebbs.

The Room shuffles and clatters with the frantic donning of combat equipment and searching for ammunition magazines for the M-16s. Trunk lids thump and locker doors clang at either side of you.

"It's not an assault," Hale grunts, hurriedly tying

his boots. "No way they could have gotten a force big enough to take this base this far in without being detected days ago. It's a sapper attack. They must be after the aircraft!"

"Aircraft, my ass!" Spud whispers hotly, clacking a magazine into his M-16 rifle and racking the bolt. "They could mortar the goddamn ships without the risk of breaking the wire! They're coming for people, man!"

Pot tugs on his pants. "Wha-what are we going to do, man?" His voice is high and strained, "We're fucking pilots, man! We're not infantry! We're not trained or equipped for this shit!" Pot is clearly on the edge.

"Take it easy, Pot," Charlie says, resting a hand on Pot's shoulder. He coughs, then with forced calm he asks, "Uh, what are we going to do, Hale?"

"Me? Who the hell promoted me to general? I don't know!"

"Let's get to the bunkers!" Pot says, nearing his frayed edges.

"God no!" Spud says. "A sapper would wipe us all out just chucking a satchel charge down the bunker entry!"

Hales wipes his face. "I guess we put on our grunt helmets and our flak jackets, grab our rifles ... find some cover, and lie low while the real grunts clean the sappers out! Spud! Get your fucking head out of that window!"

Spud jerks his head down like a startled tortoise. "Are you shittin' me?" He huffs, struggling into his boots. "This could be the sapper probe for a full-scale assault! The perimeter guards will have to stay in their bunkers. The only 'real' infantry that ain't out in the field or on R&R is clean on the other side of the camp—that's a mile away! And half of them will be drunk or high!"

"A mile! Oh, Jesus! Where're we gonna hide man?" Pot is losing it. "Oh Jesus, man, we got to get to the bunker—aah!"

Pot is startled by a loud bump at the door, followed

by the crack of the screen door being hurled back.
Everyone recoils and whirls to face the door. Hale
whips his rifle to his shoulder and sights on the door.

The Hatchet Man's huge bulk fills the doorway,
silhouetted by the stark, white flare light which glistens
from the sweat on his scalp. Around his neck and
shoulders are draped several long, gleaming bandoliers
of machine-gun ammunition. He carries an M-60
machine-gun by its breech-top handle.

"Wake up, girls! It's party time!" Hatchette
says, breathing hard, as though he has been running.
Hatchette hurries into The Room and sets the bulky
black machine-gun on its stock and bi-pod muzzle legs.
He throws open his locker and flails about within.

"Hatchette!" Spud says. "What's going on, man?"

Hatchette's deep voice echoes in his locker, broken
by his heaves for breath. "They did a radio roll call...
and three bunkers down on the other side of the flight
line...didn't answer up. They sent the sergeant of the
guard...to check up on 'em and he didn't come back.
They sent a patrol down there...and found everybody in
all three bunkers with...their throats slit, or they were
shot through with crossbows!"

"Shot what?" Pothead squeaks. "Slit what, man?"

"Dead, dope head!" Hatchette gouges in the contents
of his locker. "Deader than Bobby Kennedy's country
club card! And it was all done quiet as a tomb! These
guys are 9th NVA Regiment sappers, man. They are
Uncle Ho's best and they have come to kill pilots.
Count on it."

"What?" Pot repeats, heaving. "Oh my God."

A distant yellow orange flash briefly illuminates The
Room, followed shortly by a dull PLOOM! Van jumps
to the window and peers out toward the flight line. "It's
a Huey on fire," he says. "They're not after us, guys;
they're blowing up aircraft instead."

Hatchette slams his locker door viciously, getting
everyone's attention. "Listen to me, goddamn it!
Blowing up the ships is just a diversion! Watch my lips,

flower children, they are coming! After me!"

"Oh bullshit, Hatchette," Hale says. "You're just paranoid because your name is supposedly on the gook's hit list. You're exagger—"

Hatchette stands tall in The Room, visible only in slashing sweeps of eerie, white light cast through the screens by the mortar flares swinging on their parachutes. He laughs in a low, haunting way that hushes all other sound. The Hatchet Man never laughs.

"You pussies just don't get the message do you? Yeah, I'm on the hit list! So were Marvin Adams and Bernie Clark!" In a passing sweep of flare light, Hatchette's eyes spear outward like lasers. "I landed just ahead of this shitty weather. I was coming off the flight line when I got word of the sapper penetration, before the alert sounded. I got this M-60 and ammo off a helicopter. On the way here, I ran to the Graverobber hooches to warn them and...every...fuckin'...one of 'em...is dead. Throats cut in their sleep!"

"What?" Pot's vocabulary has become focused. Still another fiber within him snaps and furiously unravels.

"Oh, dear Lord," Charlie whispers.

"Shit!" Spud spits.

"But Hatch," Van says urgently, "If they killed every...all the...guys up there, what makes you think they're after the gun pilots on the list?"

Hatchette laughs for only the second time anyone can remember, shivering the spines of every other man in The Room. "Because...you might say...they cut Marvin's and Bernie's throats a little deeper than the rest—"

"What?" Hale exclaims, angrily. "Hatchette, you're full of—"

"They cut their heads clean off, you fuckin' smartass college boy!" Hatchette snarls. "Just Marvin's and Bernie's! I slipped and busted my ass from all the blood in the floor! The heads were gone! Zip! Nowhere! What does that tell you, troop? Hanh?"

"AAAH! AH! AH! AH! AH!" Pot is hyperventilating

239

ferociously.

Hale gapes at Hatchette, stunned.

"I'll tell you what it tells me, flower babies! It tells me they're after the hit list and anybody else they find enroute! It tells me the yellow bastards somehow know where we're billeted! And it tells me they're coming here after me! Trust me!"

"Oooooh, shit!" Pot says, grabbing his steel helmet and his rifle. "That's it, motherfucker. You're on your own, Hatchette, I'm outa here!"

"Yeah," Spud says, "Me too!"

Hatchette sweeps up the heavy machine-gun as though it were a feather duster and cradles the thick, black weapon in one arm. He opens the breech, inserts an end of an ammunition chain-link, snaps the breech shut, and racks the bolt to chamber the first round. The expended chain-link pings across the concrete. "Yeah, dope head, that's a good idea. Best all you flower babies haul your pink asses outa here, most ricky-ticky. 'Cause the best stone-pro killers in the NVA are coming after The Hatchet Man, and they'll waste anybody that gets in their way."

Van steps forward. "Hatch, it's you they're after! You've got to come with us!"

Hatchette strides to the front window and cautiously peers out. "Not a fuckin' chance, troop. These gooks know they'll never get off this post alive. They volunteered for a suicide mission to come after me and the other guys on the list. It'd be downright rude to stand 'em up."

"What?" Pot croaks with an incredulous expression on his face.

"Hatchette, you are fucking crazy!" Spud says.

Van continues. "You can't stay here, Hatch! They must know how to find you if they found Marvin and Bernie. If they took out three bunkers on the way in, there must be dozens of them. Too many, Hatch, even for you! They'll kill you! You've got to come with us!"

Hatchette's low laugh is nerve chilling. "Nope.

No way. Those are some bad little fucks, and when they find hooch-44, I intend to be here to greet 'em. Besides," Hatchette spits on the floor and wipes his mouth on his sleeve. "They got some serious dues to pay for Marvin Adams and Bernie Clark."

"Come on, Hatchette!" Hale says. "You can't—"

Hatchette swivels his heavy skull to face Hale. "You're wasting your breath, Preston. I'm not leaving and that's the final word! If you girls want out, hit the road. You know where the door is."

"Fuck you, Hatchette!" Hale snaps. "If you have some lunatic death wish, that's your problem! But I'll be goddamned if I'm going to stay here and die with you!"

"Me neither!" Pot announces righteously. "I'm with you, Hale! All the way, buddy!" Pot moves toward the door.

"I'm going with you, too, Hale," Spud says, snatching his rifle and helmet. "I'm a lover, not a fighter."

"Alright, everybody." Hale says, "Grab your shit and let's get out of here." There is hurried shuffling of gear.

"I'm not going," Van says. Everyone freezes.

"Whaat!" Four voices exclaim in unison.

"I'm staying. It's alright, it's my choice. You guys go on."

"Van, are you fucking nuts?" Spud says, exasperated. "Come on, man, we ain't got all night!"

"Van!" Hale whispers. "Goddamn it, the nastiest jungle warriors in the whole world are on their way here! You can't save Hatchette! You'll just get your head cut off along with him! Come on!"

A flare beam passes over Van's taught, sweat-wet face. "Take the guys and go while you can, Hale. I'm staying. The subject is closed. Go on, Hale. Go while you can, please."

Hatchette looks on with a tiny hint of amusement.

The siren wails and ebbs, wails and ebbs.

"Fuck these assholes, man," Pot cries. "Let's get

241

outta here!"

"Yeah, Hale, come on, man!" Spud says.

"Shut up, goddamn it!" Hale is staring hard at Van and breathing heavily through his nose. The spears of flare light swing back and forth across their sweating faces. Hale suddenly slams his steel helmet onto the floor. It rolls under his bunk. "Damn it! I cannot believe we're doing this!"

"Doing what? Doing what?" Pot wails.

"We?" Spud cries, "Who's we?"

"I'm staying too," Hale says, grimly. "Damn it!"

"Aw no!" Spud whines. "Charlie, what're you gonna do?"

The Room looks at Charlie, who stands in the corner by Old Faithful. Charlie Dermott is breathing in gasps; he is so scared he must try twice to speak. "If...ah, ah, ah...Van and Hale are staying...I'm...ah, ah, ah...I'm staying, too."

The siren wails high and low, high and low.

Spud holds both fists up by his head. "Aw man, I don't fucking believe this!" He puts his hands over his face. "We're all gonna get killed!"

"The hell we are!" Pot howls. "You stupid shits can stay here and get your heads cut off, but I'm getting to the bunker!" Pot kicks the screen open. "Fuck you guys!"

"Hey, dope head," Hatchette growls, without looking at Pot.

"Hey, fuck you, Hatchette! I ain't stayin' here and—"

"Be my guest," Hatchette says with a maniacal grin. "I'm not stopping you. But you might want to consider that when I was up in the Graverobber area just now, there were bodies laying all over the place. The way I figure it, the sapper detail assigned to get Marvin and Bernie and me is probably pretty close, now. My guess is, you might make it thirty yards before you take a crossbow bolt in the back. 'Course, if they're closer than I think, they'll probably fight over who gets to cut your heart out with a knife, so they can save the bolt."

"Bullshit, man!" Pot says, almost crying now. "You're just trying to scare me, man! I'm leavin', man!"

Pot flinches at a sudden eruption of gunfire that penetrates the cyclical wails of the siren. Several automatic weapons chatter in a chaotic sound storm that seems to originate from several hooches away.

Hatchette cocks his head. "Oops. Somebody found 'em. Those are our M-16s and their AK-47s and... sounds like some kind of nine-millimeter...a Swedish-K maybe; some gook officers carry them." The gunfire rages for a full minute, then tapers off to one or two weapons, then stops.

A man's scream slices the moist night air. It is shrill but it ends abruptly.

"Oh God!" Charlie whispers.

"Christ, man, what was that!?" Spud cries, knowing full well.

"AAAAH. AH. AH. AH. AH." Tears stream down Pot's face.

"Awright, listen up, goddamn it!" Hatchette snaps. "If you pussies are gonna to pretend like you're soldiers, you're gonna to do it right! All of you, zip those flak jackets and fasten the chin straps on your helmets. Collect all your ammo and keep it on you. Savatch, move the rug and bunks out of the way. Dermott, you and Preston and Spud slide that refrigerator over here and barricade the door with it. Move, damn it! The festivities are going to get underway any second now."

Hatchette slams the wooden inner door shut and latches it.

Charlie vividly remembers the last time he heard that latch drop.

Old Faithful screeches in protest as it is shoved over the gritty concrete floor, it's power cord trailing behind. It slams against the closed door.

"Ooooooh nooooo!" Pot wails wandering about in a

circle, crying, "We're all gonna die! We're all gonna—acch!"

Hatchette has taken two quick steps and seized Pot by the throat with one giant hand. "Listen up, troop!" He seethes. "You're already dead! You only got two choices: I can crack your neck with a squeeze of my hand right this second, or you can try to kill as many gooks as you can before they kill you! Either way, you're a dead motherfucker! What's it going to be, troop? Hanh?"

Pot gurgles and his eyes bulge.

Van's hand slaps onto Hatchette's hard, hairy arm. "Let him go, Hatch. He's afraid. You know what that's like. I'll take care of Pot. He'll fight. Turn him loose, Hatch."

Hatchette glares quickly at Van and releases Pot, who drops to his knees heaving. Hatchette pivots his gaze to Pot. "You're either part of the solution or you're part of the problem, dope head! You better decide which, and fast!" Hatchette kicks a bunk aside and returns to the high, wrap-around, screened window. With a slash of his bayonet, he slices a slot in the screen and jams the muzzle of the big machine-gun through it.

Van helps the weeping Pot to his feet.

"Listen to me, girls!" Hatchette snaps. "Nobody fires a round until I say! Anybody shoots before my order gets shot by me. When I say cease fire, stop shooting instantly. Anybody who doesn't gets shot by me. When you shoot, aim! If you can't see a hard target, don't shoot. If you see muzzle flashes, aim at the flash and fire - there's a gook behind that flash. Shoot aimed bursts of four rounds at a time - don't hold those triggers down! We got to make every round count. Listen, goddamn it! When the shooting starts, don't come apart on me! Keep your heads, and shoot controlled, accurate fire. Listen up for my commands, and when I give you orders, move on them without hesitation. There's good news and bad news here, children! If we fight well and we are goddamned lucky, some of us might make it."

"What, pray tell, is the good news here?" Hale asks sarcastically, peering over the blastwall. New light beams lance about in The Room as fresh flares are fired.

Hatchette wipes his mouth with his arm. "The good news is we got decent small-arms cover with these thick new blast walls that come all the way up to the window. We're surrounded on three sides by buildings with concertina razor wire in the narrow gaps between the buildings. That means the only way they can come at us is across the open ground between here and the Graverobber area. It's only a few dozen yards, but it's completely without cover. More good news is they probably won't be carrying a lot of ammo. It's tough to infiltrate through a heavily mined perimeter choked with razor-wire while carrying a lot of gear on you, and what they came to do they didn't plan on doing with bullets. Furthermore, they've been seen and they've spent a lot of ammo shooting at whoever found them. Already, I'm sure our grunts have infantry patrols out looking for these assholes, but finding gook sappers in the dark is a cast-iron bitch. The grunts will be here eventually, but they'll come slow and careful. If we can hold the gooks off long enough, we may have a chance."

"That's the fucking good news?" Spud says incredulously from the darkness by the old refrigerator blocking the door. "What's the bad news?"

"I don't want to know!" Charlie yells from the corner where Old Faithful once stood.

Even Hatchette has a sober tone now. "The bad news is these guys are veteran pros, and worse, they know damn well they ain't gettin' out of here alive, and they don't expect to. They got nothing to lose and the most dangerous thing in the world is a man with nothing to lose."

"Oh!" Pot says bitterly. "That's...wonderful! That's just fucking wonderful!"

"Hatchette," Hale calls, "Shouldn't we knock out the

screens so we can shoot?"

"No! Those screens are the only protection we've got against them throwing in grenades. Just take your knives and cut small vertical slots in the screen. Just enough to get the muzzles through. Everybody get up to the front wall now and take a firing position. Keep your heads high enough to see but no higher, and then keep still. The eye seizes movement." There is a clatter of scurrying men and sliding bunks.

Van cuts a slot in the screen before him with his bayonet, and he sheaths the knife. "What do we look for, Hatch, what are they going to look like?"

"Sssh! Keep your voice down when the siren is low! They'll be little gooks dressed in all-black outfits. They'll have black bandannas tied around their faces and black kerchiefs around their heads. The only thing showing will be their darked-out hands and their eyes."

"Fucking Ninjas!" Spud hisses.

"Shit. These guys make Ninjas look like choir boys. They move like cats and it's hard to see them even when you're looking right at them. Sssssh! Listen!"

"I don't hear anything!" Charlie says.

"Listen to me, troops! When the shooting starts, if somebody gets hit, I don't want to see anybody stop firing to be a Florence Nightingale. Stay on line and keep shooting controlled fire 'til I tell you to stop. There'll be time later to tend the wounded, and if they die in the meantime, it's tough shit. We'll need every gun on line when they charge or we're all gonna die."

"Oh, wonderful! That's just—"

"Shut up, dope head! And keep your eyes open."

"There!" Hale whispers. Everyone but Hatchette tenses visibly. "By the supply hut! "Over th—"

"I see 'em," Hatchette says calmly. "Keep your fuckin' voice down. That's their point element and we don't want to let 'em know how many we are. We want 'em thinkin' it's just little ole me." The Room jumps as Hatchette suddenly roars, "OVER HERE, YOU LITTLE GOOK SHITS! THE HATCHET MAN IS

WAITIN' FOR YOU!"

"What the fuck are you doin', Hatchette?" Spud howls low, clutching his M-16 and peeping over the window sill. "You lunatic!"

"Fuck it," Hatchette says in a low voice. "They know where I am. We know where they are. Let's get this tea party served. Let's rock and roll. It's time to kill folks."

"Holy...shit!" Hale swears, looking out on the bleak landscape of swinging shadows and piercing shafts of bleached flare light. "There're dozens of 'em, man! Look at 'em moving up by the supply building and the headquarters shack! Let's get 'em!"

"Steady, girls; I'll shoot the first fuck who fires without command. They're too far out to hit in the dark; all you'll do is mark your position and define our number. Just hold your dicks and wait for my word."

Now a strange, heavily accented, Asian male voice calls from many yards out in the writhing moonscape of indigo shadows dancing with swaying beams of blue-white flare light. "Hatch-ette! Hatch-ette!"

"Oh dear God!" Charlie croaks. "Man, it's them! It's the sapper hit team!"

"WHAT DO YOU WANT, TURTLE-DICK?" Hatchette bellows.

There is a pause, the silence of which is broken by the siren and distant gunfire from somewhere on the flight line. The Room wheezes with heavy breathing. The far gunfire ends.

"You die, Hatch-ette!" The voice calls from the shadows, bitterly, soaked in hate.

"I DON'T THINK SO, NOO-YEN! I KILLED ALL YOUR BROTHERS AND I FUCKED ALL YOUR SISTERS, BUT I AIN'T HAD TIME TO HIT THAT UGLY WIFE OF YOURS, YET. I THINK I'LL STICK AROUND!"

"Oh my Lord," Charlie whispers.

"JEEEE-sus Harley Davidson Christ! Hatchette, do you have to piss 'em off?"

"Relax, troop, they been pissed off since they were three-years-old. He's just trying to scare us into shootin' at him so they can pin down where we're positioned, how many of us there are, and what kind of toys we're holding. Ole Nguyen C. Gook only knows three words of English; hell, you just heard his whole vocabulary."

"Hatch-ette!" The accented Voice In The Dark shouts. "We cut you eyes out, Hatch-ette; piss on you brain!"

"Three words, huh? Three fucking words, huh? Jesus!"

"NOT BEFORE I SHOW YOUR OLD LADY SOME REAL DICK, YOU COCK SUCKIN' GOOK FAGGOT!"

"We're all gonna die; it's that simple," Pot says, matter-of-factly.

"Sssh!" Van hisses tightly, staring bug-eyed over the wall. "Pay attention, Pot. Pay attention and do what Hatch tells us."

"I can't see 'em anymore!" Charlie whispers.

"Well, I doubt they just packed up and went home!" Spud says.

"They're out there," Hatchette growls. "They're behind cover. Listen up, troops. Most everybody around here has didimaued, so I'm bettin' ole Luke the Gook thinks I'm alone in here. I look for 'em to mass a charge any second now. The gooks are big on banzai-style charges, and besides, right now they're all comin' in their pants to be the first one to get to me. I think they'll try to blitzkrieg us before we know what hit us. They'll rush a wave of about half their people at us who will be shooting on the run. They'll be backed up by supporting fire from their reserve element out by the supply hut and the headquarters shacks."

"Oh, wonder—"

"Listen to me, goddamn it! The attack element will fire as they run at us, but it's dark in here and their night vision will be fucked up by the flares. They won't be able to see specific targets, so just keep your heads low

and aim. Don't waste ammo! We ain't bullet-rich here!
Fire controlled, short bursts...and let's kill these fucks!
They're pros but they ain't bulletproof. You hit 'em and
they'll bleed, trust me."

"I don't believe this," Spuds whispers, scanning
out the window. "I do not fucking believe this. I'm too
short for this shit!"

From a dark corner, Pot suddenly begins to sing,
softly and slowly. "Yer in the army nowwwww, you
ain't behind the plowwwww." Everyone, including
Hatchette, gawks at him. "You'll never get rich...you
son of a bitch...yer in the army nowwwwwwwwww."

"You better shut that dribblin' idiot up, Savatch!"
Hatchette snarls. "Or I will!"

"Pot!" Van calls, alarmed. "Are you alright?"

"Wonderful, man. Just fucking—"

"Listen up!" Hatchette rumbles. "I don't think they'll
chuck any grenades at us until they can be sure they'll
get 'em inside the hooch. Otherwise they know it'll
likely just roll off the roof or bounce off the blastwall
back at them. But if a grenade gets in the hooch with
us, forget that hero shit about throwing yourself on it!
All that'll do is gut you and kill us anyway. Try to grab
the damn thing and throw it back out before it goes off.
You usually got a couple of seconds. Don't panic—you
got nothing to lose at that point—throw it carefully
outside."

"Oh sure," Spuds says, highly agitated. "Let me ask
you a question, Hatchette, what do I look like to you?
JOHN-FUCKING-WAYNE!?"

"Sssssh!"

"Shut-up, Spud!"

"I barely got out of basic infantry training, goddamn
it!"

"Here they come!" Hale says, two octaves higher
than normal.

All conversation now doubles in speed.

"I see 'em!" Hatchette says, "Hold your fire!"

"Hold it? Are you nuts? There's at least twenty of

'em! They're running right at us, man!"

"Hold your fire 'til I say, girls.

"Why aren't they shooting, Hatch?"

"They're pros, flower baby. They're waiting for clear targets. That's good news!"

"Oh yeah!" Pot says, struggling to sight his rifle. "That's just fucking wonderful!"

"It means they're short on ammo too, children!"

"Now? Jesus, they're almost on us! Goddamn it!"

"Not yet!"

"Now!?"

"No!"

"Oh god, we're gonna die. We're all gonna—"

"NOW!" Hatchette roars. "Kill 'em! Kill 'em! Kill 'em!"

The big M-60 machine-gun roars, painfully ringing all ears. Brass shell casings arc out from the side of the weapon. Its muzzle spews flame which lights in yellow, micro-second flashes the sweating, scarred face and slick skull of a consummate killing machine at work. Hatchette sights down the thrashing, thundering weapon and sweeps it methodically from target to target. The ammunition belt jerks and twists, consumed like a dangling snake being gulped by a voracious hawk.

Van has not come to kill, but neither has he come to be killed. This is not a faceless 'struggling people' imagined through marijuana smoke in a coffee shop; it is not a theoretical entity bantered about a political science classroom; this is The Enemy. It doesn't care about your moral distinctions or the absence thereof. It only knows you are here and It has come to kill you for that alone.

The Room goes to war.

Fast, high-pitched, ratcheting sounds of five M-16's join with the rapid but slower, deeper thump of the machine-gun. The Room glitters and sparks like water in a fuse box. Spent brass hulls shower the concrete. The crescendo is physically hammering. The acrid odor of gun powder fumes and light smoke fill the air. All motion is in snapping, flash-lit freeze-frames, like an old black-and-white movie. Clear, white holes begin to dot the screens.

Except that the sound is excruciatingly vivid. The shouting voices are gold brocade woven in a fabric of continuous, audibly painful gunfire.

"There! There!"

"I got one! I got one!"

"AAAAAAAAAAAHH!!"

"Reload! Reload!"

"—close! They're coming—"

"Shut up and shoot!"

"Where is? There! There!"

"Look out!"

"Get him!"

"—is WONDERFUL, man! Just fucking WON—"

"—out! Somebody throw me a magazine!"

"Here!"

"Watch it! Over there!"

"Ow! Shit!"

"He's running!"

"—go!"

The heavy slam of the machine gun stops but the high, chattering rifles do not.

"Cease fire! Cease fire!" Hatchette bellows hoarsely.

"I got him! I got the little motherfu—"

"Cease fire!"

"There! By the headquarters—"

"CEASE FIRE! Knock it off, goddamn it!"

The gunfire ends in a deafening silence. Ejected shell casings ping over the concrete making a brass snow upon the floor. Over the shrill ring in your ears you can hear five men struggling for oxygen and one with too much.

"AH! AH! AH! AH! AH!"

"Pot!" Van calls. "Try to hold your breath. Try to hold your breath."

Pot retches, trying to limit his runaway breathing.

"Listen up, troops! Reload. Keep watchin' the head-shed. They'll be back as soon as they can organize. Who's hurt? Dermott?"

"I'm okay!"

"Me too, Hatch," Van says, "Pot, are you—"

"I...am...wonderful, man! Just—"

"Yeah, yeah," Hatchette grumbles, loading a fresh ammunition belt in the scalding, smoking machine-gun.

"Preston?"

"I'm hit, Hatch, but near as I can tell it's just a flesh wound."

"What other kind is there?" Spud whines. "Will somebody please tell me that? What other fucking kind of wound is—"

"The fatal kind, flower baby."

"Fuck you, Hatchette!" Spud hisses, heaving. "Just tell me what they're going to do next, man, just tell me what they're gonna do!"

"Well," The Hatchet Man muses with satisfaction, as more mortar flares ignite over the perimeter. "Whatever it is, they're gonna do it with about twenty or so less of their little gook buddies. Man, you little hippies can shoot when your pink asses are on the line."

"Christ, look at the fucking bodies!"

"He probably is."

"They're all over the goddamn place out there!"

"I see. I...see." Van says, softly.

A pitiful cry of agony is heard from beyond the blastwall.

Hale says, "Hey! One of 'em's still alive!"

The wounded man cries out again in Vietnamese; the shrill, dignity-void plea is universal in its meaning. This is a man in agony.

"He's hurt bad," Van observes, distressed.

"Tough shit," Hatchette says.

The man screams again.

"There he is!" Spud whispers. "Over there by—"

"I see the little cocksucker," Hatchette says, sounding bored. "Fuck him."

The cries become even more intense.

"Aw man!" Spud says. "Look at that guy's face! He is fuuucked up, man!"

"Get your head down, Spud!"

The wounded man screams and holds it for an eternity. He follows it with a pathetic yelping not unlike Pot's hyperventilations, just louder. He pauses, then screams out something in Vietnamese which is clearly a graceless, desperate plea radiating with fear and glowing with pain. It is repulsive. No living thing should suffer so.

"Goddamn it!" Hale says, "Jesus, Hatchette, shouldn't we, shouldn't you...well...you know...put him...out of his misery?"

"Not me," Hatchette says casually. "I like his fuckin' misery just fine."

"Fuck you, Hatchette, you're crazy! Alright, I'll do it!" Hale sights his rifle.

"Hey, troop!" Hatchette growls. "You shoot that gook and I'll shoot you! This ain't a goddamn Tupperware party! That fucked-up gook ain't going anywhere; we can kill him later. Right now he's good bait. He blubbers long enough and maybe some of his buddies will be heroes and try to rescue him, and we can cap their asses, too. Besides, we ain't got the ammo to spare to shoot wounded."

The Room ponders a stark, hard, combat truth while the far-off siren wails up and down, up and down. The wounded sapper cries out again, weaker this time.

Hale turns his back to the wall. "Damn it! Goddamn it!

"Okay, listen up, troops!" Hatchette says. "How're we fixed for ammo?"

"Not much, man."

"Me neither!"

"I only got two magazines!"

"I ain't got—"

"Okay, okay, I get the picture. I'm down to about a belt and a half, myself. Pay attention. They didn't know there were six of us and they paid the dumb-tax, big-time. There ain't many of the little fucks left now, and they spent a whale of a lot of ammo, but they won't make that mistake again. I look for 'em to select a couple of die-hard volunteers to rush us with satchel charges while the rest of 'em lay down a covering fire at the top edge of the blast wall where our heads are gonna be. They'll try to get close enough to lob a charge in here or at least blow a hole in the blast wall. Listen! Whoever rushes, concentrate on them first! We got to take out the bomber before he gets close, you hear me, children? We got to—oh shit."

"Oh shit?" Spud squeals. "What the fuck does that—"

"They got an anti-tank rocket! Get down! Get down! Get back from the wall!"

There is a loud hiss like a very big roman candle; a white-hot light streaks out of the swaying shadows toward hooch-44 and impacts upon the blastwall near the door. There is a bright flash and a devastating blast concussion that collides like a train. The metal roofing over the doorway is blown back like a banana peel. Old Faithful dives on its face and slides across the floor, screeching loudly. Chunks of sod, green plastic sandbags and screen-wire soar about The Room. Jagged shards of lumber rain down. The air smells of dank earth yet dry dust. It is filled with splintered hardwood and explosives fumes. Smoke clouds swirl in the oscillating streaks of flare light.

Hatchette throws a bunk bed off his chest and clambers to his feet, dragging the machine gun. "Watch the wall!" he yells. "They'll try to come over the wall! I'll cover the door!"

Hale spits dirt. Van is shaking his head. Charlie is plainly dazed and is holding his rubber dog toy. Spud is staring vacantly.

Pothead Willows is lying on his back, bleeding from the head. He sings gently. "Yer in the army noooow, yer not behind—"

There come many rapidly closing footsteps, fast and

hard on the earth outside. They are followed by several
simultaneous thumps upon the blast wall. Dark shapes
of hands and arms appear in the window space, outlined
against the flare glow, grappling to climb the wall. At
the same time a figure carrying an AK-47 rifle emerges
from the smoke cloud where the door used to be. The
machine-gun booms and the rifles chatter. There are
screams of pain and drowned shouts. Small pieces of
wood and concrete and people careen about The Room.

Spud feels something hit his foot. He looks down
to see what appears to be a green soup can with a
wooden handle on its lid spinning slowly on the littered
concrete. Spud Bleaker barely graduated basic infantry
training, but he knows a chi-com grenade when he sees
one. And he knows The Room is dead.

Van slams into Spud, who goes down like a clipped
defensive end. Van scoops the grenade and sidearms
it over the wall. It instantly explodes, showering
The Room only with dirt, its razor-edged, white-hot
shrapnel absorbed by the wall and the sappers outside.

"Oh Jesus!" Spud gasps, propping on his elbows.
"I'm too short for this shit!"

"I'm out! I'm empty!" someone cries.

"Me too! Shit, man!"

"That's it. That's it, man. We're fucked."

"Hale, are you—"

"I'm dry, Van. Not a round left."

"Aw man," Spud croaks, panting, "Aw man, what are
we gonna—"

There is the startling clatter of the heavy machine
gun being dropped to the floor. All heads snap toward
Hatchette.

"COME ON, YOU MOTHERFUCKERS!" The
Hatchet Man shouts, his voice a ragged croak. He
staggers, slipping on the hundreds of brass hulls
littering the floor.

The Room looks in the dust and smoke to see
Hatchette standing among the bodies and debris, feet
apart, arms spread, facing the smoke-shrouded hole in

the wall. He clutches a bayonet in his right hand and a short, stubby foxhole shovel in the other. Veins stand out like worms upon his gleaming scalp. "COME ON, YOU LITTLE YELLOW SHITS!" The Hatchet Man roars hoarsely, "I'LL...KILL ALLA YOU BASTARDS! COME ONNN!"

Hale rips his bayonet from its sheath and moves to stand at Hatchette's left. "COME ON!" Hale screams.

Spud pulls his own entrenching tool from his locker, folds out and locks its spade in the ninety-degree position, and he stands in the smoke to Hatchette's right. He raises the small shovel like a batter at the plate. "COME ON!" He yells.

Then there comes the sound: EEH-EEE! EEH-EEE!

Charlie stands weaving behind the Gang Of Three, a bayonet in one hand and his rubber dog toy in the other.

EEH-EEE! EEH-EEE!

Now there is a chorus of squeaking dog toys from Charlie, Spud, Van, Hale and even Pot. The Room is alive with cacophonous squeaking which goes on and on and on.

Fast running footfalls approach.

"COME ON, MOTHERFUCKERS!"

"COME ON!"

"COME ON!"

EEH-EEE! EEH-EEE! EEH-EEE!

With high, savage war cries, three sappers burst out of the smoke and dust. They are covered in black linen but for their eyes and hands, and are armed only with knives. More crowd into The Room behind them.

The Hatchet Man splits the skull of the leader with a vicious blow of the short, steel fox-hole shovel and slashes a second across the face with his bayonet. Sappers pour screaming into Spud, Charlie, Hale and Hatchette. Hale takes a stab in the chest which is blunted by his flak vest. The sapper draws the knife back for a second thrust, but Hale pushes his bayonet hard into his attacker's throat. The little man in black thrashes and clutches the blade with bloody hands.

Charlie slashes at an enemy, misses and axes the sapper
across the shoulder on the backswing. Spud bashes
a sapper with his shovel before being knocked to the
floor. Hatchette is flailing in all directions. Van stands to
defend Pot, knife in hand.

A short sapper squeezes through the melee and slams
into Charlie, driving him backward. They tumble over
a bunk and crash to the floor between the beds. The
sapper is on top of Charlie and has Charlie's knife arm
seized in both hands. Charlie thrashes frantically to free
his knife and to get the sapper off him.

Spud is on his knees, but he sees a black fabric
leg and he swings the shovel. There is a yowl of pain
and the sapper falls before him. The sapper flails
with his knife but the blade cuts only the green outer
fabric covering Spud's flak vest. The knife comes at
him again, but he intercepts it with a blow from the
shovel and chops a bloody trough in his attacker's face
with a second slash of the sharp shovel. Spud now
feels himself grappled and choked from behind. His
attacker is smaller than he, but has a grip like wire.
Spud's ears begin to ring and he feels the beginning of
unconsciousness. He smells sour sweat and he hears
a gagging sound near his right ear. Abruptly, he is
released and he turns to see Hatchette savagely kick his
attacker's body from his bayonet. Spud gains his feet,
dizzily. He feels a object impact with a clank upon the
back of his steel helmet. He spins and arcs the shovel at
his next attacker.

Charlie struggles on his back between the bunks, the
sapper atop him wrestling to hold his knife arm.

Hale is clumsily trying to get his knife into a skilled
opponent, swinging and missing repeatedly.

Van is rushed by a small, screaming, black-draped
sapper who effortlessly deflects Van's knife thrust. The
sapper's stab is absorbed by Van's vest, but the charge
bowls him over with its ferocity. Van lands on his back
against a bunk, losing his knife, and he slips to the floor.
The sapper is upon him instantly and Van grapples with

him, clinging desperately to his attacker's knife arm. Sitting near Van, blood streaming down the side of his head, Pot sings merrily now, "You'll never get rich, you son of a bitch! You're in—"

The sapper is in superb condition. He wrenches his knife arm from Van's grip and whips it high for a final strike. Van crosses his arms in front of his face in hope of deflecting the killing blow.

Then, looming behind is The Hatchet Man. His deadly shovel smashes into the sapper's head and the dark figure collapses to Van's right. To Van's morbid fascination, Hatchette kneels, smiling, and whips the shovel into the fallen sapper's neck, nearly severing his head. Hatchette raises the shovel; a stream of blood, black in the eerie, shifting light, slings from the rising shovel blade.

Spud feels as though his heart will pound through his chest. He is on the last reserves of his strength as he battles weaponless with still another sapper who is attempting to choke him.

Charlie still thrashes madly between the bunks trying to free his knife hand and dislodge the sapper from atop him. The sapper has a two-handed grip on his wrist. The eyes are but inches from his, peering intently from between the folds of black cloth. The eyes. The beautiful eyes. Then Charlie hears a sound, an urgently whispered voice he will never forget, though he will try hard to do so for the rest of his life. "Chah-ree! Chah-ree! Chah-ree, you must be stirr! Be stirr, Chah-ree! Pretend dead!"

"Sung?" Charlie cannot believe his ears. He seizes the fabric across the sapper's face and yanks it down. "Sung! My God! What are you...oh no...oh no!"

Sung Tranh whispers intensely, "Chah-ree! You must pretend dead! Not move or you be ver kirred! Prease, Chah-ree!"

Charlie's world is caving in. "Oh no, Sung! Oh no! Not you! Not you!"

Charlie's horror has only begun, for in the furor

above them both appears The Hatchet Man, who looks down with the fierce, pitiless eyes of a Huron war chief.

"NOOOOOO!!" Charlie screams.

Sung somehow knows. "I rov you, Chah-ree," she whispers.

The shovel hits in the small of her back with the wet crunch of heavy metal carving through bone and meat. Sung's eyes widen, and then they close.

"NOOOOOOOOOOOOOOO!" Charlie Dermott shrieks, his stiffened hands quivering, reaching for Sung.

Hatchette's mammoth hand crashes down onto Sung's head, closes on a fistful of her hair, then it snaps her head back, far beyond the vertebrae-stops. He whips her lifeless body off of Charlie and flings her away like a killer whale tosses a shredded seal carcass.

Charlie is lost in agony. He wails the cry of misery come home to stay.

Hatchette looks on in disgust. "You can stop your blubberin', flower baby!" he shouts over the siren and the clatter, checking over his shoulder. "I killed the son of a bitch about three times! He ain't gonna hurt you, trust me." Hatchette turns back to the battle.

Charlie rolls onto his side, curls into a fetal ball, and he sobs as only the heart-wrecked can.

Hatchette wades to Hale who spins, grappling with a sapper. Hatchette clubs the attacker and then stabs him through. He calmly walks to Spud's struggling opponent and crams the bayonet blade upward into the back, beneath the ribs and through the heart. He wrenches the knife in a circular stirring movement, then he kicks the man from his knife. He kneels before another fallen sapper who is still alive. He draws the bloody bayonet across his own tongue before the man's eyes, laughing cruelly at the terror those eyes reflect. Spud watches, mesmerized with horror, as Hatchette plunges the long knife into the sapper's eye socket, spearing his skull to the floor. The body convulses wildly and then is still. When Hatchette raises the blade,

the impaled head comes up with it. Hatchette puts his
foot upon his victim's throat and pulls the bayonet free.
The head drops with a dull clunk.

The Room is swept by swinging shadows and light
beams. Dust and smoke choke the air. There is an odd,
warm odor. Blood. The siren wails. High, low. Up,
down.

Hale stands, bent, heaving for breath, bleeding from
an eye, his hands on his knees.

Spud sits on the overturned refrigerator, glassy-eyed,
gasping.

Van kneels by a bloody Pothead Willows who
continues to sing with a silly grin on his face.

Charlie lies between the bunks, weeping wretchedly.

Bodies litter the floor in grotesque, undignified
heaps. Blood flows over the concrete in black rivulets.
A nauseating smell of feces and sour sweat stains the
air.

Now even Pot stops singing and stares when
Hatchette, blood streaming down his face, staggers over
the bodies and wreckage to the hole in the wall, slipping
on hundreds of tinkling shell casings. There, before the
smoking gap in the wall, silhouetted by the orange glow
of distant flight-line fires, The Hatchet Man raises his
bloody weapons over his head and howls with the siren.

"HAAAAAAAAAAAAAAAAHH!"

Charlie covers his ears tightly with his hands as he
sobs on the floor between the bunks, his face and his
life hideously contorted.

The war cry of The Hatchet Man is primal, a
sustained cry of victory together with something else...
the joy of life dearly earned. It is a hoarse cry of
victory and joy.

"HAAAAAAAAAAAAAAAAAAAAAAAAAAAA
AAAAAAAAAAAAHH!"

Chapter Twenty-One
The Room

Susan,
This will not be a very uplifting letter, I'm
afraid. Thank God I have you to talk to. You are
so much stronger than Ramsey in ways; there is
so much I feel I must withhold from him.

If I don't sound very coherent it's because we
have all undergone a terrible experience here,
just a few days ago. It's hard to know where to
begin. There was an atrocious fight, a small-scale
battle no less. North Vietnamese Army 'sappers',
soldiers specially trained to infiltrate and
attack from within, penetrated the Camp Enari
perimeter at night and blew up several aircraft,
but worse, they killed eleven of our pilots, six
in their sleep and five in isolated gunfights.
Hooch-44 was one of those attacked.

First, I guess I should say that all of us in
hooch-44 are okay, physically at least. I have
some cuts and scuffs and a stiff neck but I feel
much better than yesterday. Spud has a twelve-
stitch gash in his left arm, which he is proud of
because it will earn him the Purple Heart. Hale
had some fragments of some kind in his eye,
but the flight surgeon was able to extract them.
He also took a bullet through the outer part of
his right shoulder which is sore and makes his
arm stiff, but is healing well. Pot got a wound
from a bullet which went completely through
his steel grunt helmet. It glanced off his skull
somehow and he bled like crazy, but it wasn't all

261

*that bad, considering. Charlie was only scuffed
and bruised, but he...well, I'll get into that in
a minute. And Hatch got two new scars for the
collection on his face and bald skull. Given
what we went through, it's a genuine miracle
we weren't all killed, let alone that no one was
seriously hurt.*

*Emotionally, it's a different ball game. I doubt
any of us will ever be the same again. Hatch is
another story altogether, but I'm most worried
about Pot and Charlie.*

*I'm convinced Pot is mentally unstable. The
pressure has been too much for him. He seems to
have recovered somewhat since the battle, but he
still isn't right. I talked him into consulting the
flight surgeon about his mental state, but he said
they just told him that they were under orders not
to ground pilots except for 'the most legitimate
causes', because of the sudden severe shortage
of pilots. The flight surgeon said he thought Pot
was just trying to evade duty. Maybe Pot is more
mentally stable than the flight surgeon. I wish that
doctor had been in hooch-44 that night.*

*Charlie has suffered a tragedy of staggering
scope. You remember the Vietnamese maid I
told you he was in love with? Her name is, was,
Sung Tranh. It seems Sung was actually some
kind of spy all along, and was part of the sapper
team that attacked us. Charlie may even have
unwittingly given her information that assisted
the sappers in their mission. Along with all forty-
seven other sappers on the flight line and in the
pilot's quarters area, Sung was killed in the raid.*

*Charlie babbled a little to me in shock right
after the battle, though now he won't talk about
it, even to me, but it looks like she was trying to
kill him during the attack when Hatch intervened
and killed her. Fortunately, I seem to be the only
person other than Charlie who knows about his*

*indiscretions with Sung, and I don't see anything
to be gained by telling anyone.*

*Poor Charlie is devastated. As I said, I can't
get him to talk to me any more, but it's obvious
that aside from the terrible heartbreak he must
certainly feel because of Sung, he also feels
immense guilt at having given her information
that possibly helped lead to the deaths of so many
of our men that night. The former is a horrible
betrayal and loss to endure; the latter a crushing
burden for anyone to bear. I feel so sorry for him,
but I can't get him to open up to me about it. He's
gone inside himself, and I can't get him to come
out. Charlie's hurt bad.*

*All of our bodily injuries will disappear. The
emotional wounds, however, have permanently
scarred Pot and Charlie; maybe the rest of us as
well.*

*Me? I think I'm coping. You better than
anyone, save perhaps Ramsey, know much how
I hate the thought of harming another human
being. Yet I have killed, Susie. As hard as I tried
to avoid being assigned to where I would have to
kill, I could no longer avoid it. Someday, when
we can sit quietly for a few hours, I'll tell you the
details —it will do me good, I suspect—but for
now I will only say that we fought a bitter fight
which, in the end, came down to hand-to-hand
combat in hooch-44.*

*In the whole process, I was forced to shoot at
least four sappers—enemy attackers, but no less
living men—or I would certainly have been killed
by them. I hope I did the right thing. At least I
hope I did a forgivable thing. It weighs on me. Oh
God, it weighs on me. Enough of this.*

*Old Faithful, our old refrigerator, was the only
non-enemy fatality from the Battle of Hooch-44.
It was blown up by an anti-tank rocket which hit
the outer blast wall. It probably helped save our*

lives, may it rust in peace. We chipped in and
bought one of those little Japanese refrigerators
from the combat engineers who came in to repair
the extensive battle damage to the hooch. It's not
as big as Old Faithful was, but it'll chill beer
nearly to ice and that's what matters. And we got
a new roof in the bargain.

We are shelled almost nightly now. One of
former President Johnson's brilliant last acts
was to stop the bombing north of the seventeenth
parallel. He said he was assured by his
commanders that it wouldn't harm Americans in
the south but, if the increased shelling attacks
on us are any indication, they're getting a lot
more of those big anti-personnel rockets down
the Trail since then. The things have phenomenal
concussion which can be as damaging as the
shrapnel they produce. A close detonation will
rupture the metal-wrapped hydraulic, fuel and oil
lines on a helicopter, sheerly from the concussion.
It has a similar, if magnified, effect on people.

One good thing to report out of all this is
Hatch is almost able to cope with the incoming
rockets now. He still needs some encouragement
before he'll run to the bunker, but about half-way
there, he runs ahead on his own. I sense that soon
he will be able to go by himself. It's so strange.
The rockets seem to be the only things the man
ever feared, but they absolutely paralyzed him.

We used to repeat Truman's credo that war
is too important to leave to the generals. I'm
afraid it's also too complex, and the mistakes are
too costly, to leave to politicians. And as there
is no one else qualified to run our wars, maybe
we should consider not having any. Generals,
politicians or wars.

Susie, enclosed you will find a sealed letter
addressed to Ramsey. I would like you to hold
that letter and give it back to me when I come

*home, but if I should not come home—and only
then—please give the letter to Ramsey. I also
have written Ramsey a 'normal' letter which I am
mailing at the same time I mail this to you, but I
feel a need to convey some special thoughts which
I would want Ramsey to have if something should
happen to me. I know I can depend on you.*

*I don't mean to sound morbid or dreary with
any of this, but Spud said something to me the
other day, in his blackly humorous way, which is
at the root of my mood right now, I think. He said,
"Death has a way of taking the fun out of war."
I never thought war was fun, of course. But I
think I did come here with the sort of immortality
complex that is common to youth, which is
probably the reason politicians and generals send
young men, rather than older, wiser men, to do
most of the fighting and dying.*

*But the Battle of Hooch-44 forever removed
from me that sense of being bulletproof, that
conviction that ultimately it will only happen
to the other guy, or, at worst, only when I get a
lot older. I now appreciate, perhaps more than
I would like to, the frailty and capriciousness
of life, and by extension, its preciousness. It is a
proverbial cloud with a silver lining. I know now
how easily I could die, yet that somehow makes
life more vivid.*

*One of the wounded we medevac'd yesterday
left his helmet in the ship. On it he had written in
magic-marker: "For the warrior, life bears a fruit
of unparalleled sweetness, which the protected
never taste."*

*Not to worry. All this is just the ranting of a
mind under strain for too long without a break.
I'll write more later, Susie. I'm so tired.*

> *Love,*
> *Van*

My Dearest Ramsey,

*As the months drag by, I miss you more
acutely. It is natural enough to need to be near
one's love in a time of stress, yet I'm glad you are
not here, for it is a colorless, warmth-void, hostile
place where life is far too cheap. It is not a fitting
place for so gentle and loving a soul as you.*

*Thank you for the wonderful photographs.
It looks like you really enjoyed yourself on the
New York concert trip. It's funny; I find myself
literally examining the pictures you sent me with
a magnifying glass I bought at the PX. First, I
enjoy your beautiful face and your lithe, fit body
of course, but then I study all the objects in the
background of each photo, objects I have not seen
for what seems like forever. Stark too, are the
objects missing from the photographs.*

*My love. It's incredible what we Americans
take for granted. When I can tear my eyes from
you, I see things in these pictures I would not
have noticed before Vietnam, things which now
seem to hold a beauty that defies description.
Ordinary things: Road signs; green, neatly cut
grass; big, shiny American cars; mailboxes;
school buses; people wearing colorful, varied
attire instead of everyone wearing the same color
and style of muddy green. I don't know how to
help you appreciate what the American way of life
is really worth to you, but I know I must try.*

*Look around you, Ramsey! Treasure the fact
that nowhere do you see sandbags, barbed wire,
bomb craters, armored tanks or artillery. Listen!
No cannons thunder. No attack sirens wail in your
nights, no screams pierce your soul, no gunshots
sound. That is peace you behold, Ramsey,
something no living resident Vietnamese has ever
known for more than a moment.*

*Forgive me for ending this letter so soon,
but I am terribly tired and it is late. We get so*

*little sleep for so long that we are continuously
exhausted. How I look forward to leaving this
brutal experience and coming home to you, my
kind and caring love. Sometimes, that vision is all
that sustains me.*

> *I love you,*
> *Van*

Mom and Dad,

*Forget Sung. Don't ever ask me about her.
Never talk to me about God again.
Ever.*

> *Charles*

Chapter Twenty-Two
The Room

Crickets emit a shrill chorus in the dark, and the monotonous, pounding rotor beat of a Huey swells and fades periodically as the flare patrol helicopter circles enormous Camp Enari. An occasional flare pops way out on the perimeter and drifts slowly to earth in its parachute. While the flares are descending, ghostly, pale arrows of bleached light wander about The Room but, between flares, the battered old office desk-lamp is the only light. Hale, Charlie and Pot are asleep; Hatchette and Spud are out. Van writes at the desk.

The Room smells pungently of fresh-cut lumber from the extensive repairs it has undergone after the Battle Of Hooch-44. It is a welcome fragrance after the rank stench of decay that dwelled in The Room for days, especially when the midday sun beat down on the new metal roof. Except for Hatchette, who said he liked the smell. The Room forced stiff, sore muscles to flush and scrub the concrete. Still, dry, brownish-red stains remain on the floor, visible around the edges of the old Montagnyard rug. Bullet holes are still evident in some of the lockers and in the bulletin board where you dwell.

Van hears footsteps slowly approaching on the boardwalk, and he smiles when he hears a weary voice singing, soft and tired: "Rollin'...unh...rollin' on the riv-verrr..."

Spud pulls the door back and stumbles in with his flight bag and rifle. "Whew!" he says, quietly. "Hey, Van."

"Hi, Spud," Van says in a subdued voice. "Been

flying the night-light mission?"

"Yeah. We musta dropped twenty parachute flares. The grunts on the perimeter are spooked now on account of the sapper attack. Every time they see a leaf drop, they're on that radio callin' for flares. Had to land twice to reload."

Spud deposits his equipment near his bunk. He struggles to pull his boots off.

"Is Hatch on gunship stand-by, tonight, Spud?"

"Oh yeah," Spud says in a low voice. "Christ, yeah. Every time we'd pop a flare, Hatchette and his crew would come soaring over in that big ugly gunship with the graverobber painted on the nose. They'd flop around low, trying to draw ground fire."

"Did they draw any?"

"Hell, no. Them gooks' mommas didn't raise no fools. If they were out there, they wadn't about to give up their location to Hatchette and his wing man, and get their asses blown all the way back to Hanoi. It's a court-martial offense in the NVA to shoot at an American gunship without specific orders, man."

Van contemplates for a moment. He stands and looks out the window toward the distant lights of the flight line, obviously worried. "Spud?"

"Hmm?"

"Hatch went off duty when you did, didn't he? I mean, your crew and his were relieved at the same time, right?"

"Yeah. Why?"

"Just wondering where he is, that's all. He's still on that gun-pilot hit list, you know. In fact, by now he's probably gotten his wish to have his name at the top of it."

"Fuck, nothing can kill Hatchette. He'll be along in a minute." Spud hangs his flight bag on a wall nail. He eyes Van curiously. "Hey. You know what I think, Van? I think you're actually concerned about that psycho! You're, like, worried for him! How could you be so worried about such a...a...fucking Frankenstein, man?

Jesus Harley Davidson Christ."

"Doctor Frankenstein was the creator, not the monster," Van remarks, smiling.

"Aw, Van, you know what I mean!"

"Hatch isn't so bad, Spud. Not really. Not inside."

"What?" Spud says, exasperated. Van shushes him with a finger to the lips, glancing at the sleeping Charlie, Hale and Pot. Spud waddles over and sits on Van's bunk. "You saw him during the fight, Van, he was like, like what's that thing people say, the... apocalypse! That's it! He was like the fourth Horseman of the Apocalypse with a fucking fox-hole shovel! Fire, famine, peskylence—"

"Pestilence, Spud."

"—and the fucking Hatchette Man!" Spud pauses, then sighs. "Thank Christ he was, or we'd all be dead... but I can't believe you're defending him after he's always been so...nasty to you with all that 'queer' bullshit!"

"I'm not defending what he's done, Spud. I'm just saying we're probably throwing stones from a glass house. We haven't been where he's been, seen what he's seen. How do we know we'd be any different?"

"Shit! I'd be different! Nothin' on this earth could make me be like The Hatchet Man."

Van looks at Spud and speaks slowly, soberly. "Torture...by North Korean interrogators...might."

Spud stares back in surprise. "What? Hatchette? How do you know that?"

Van smiles again. "You forget my father, the general, I'm pleased to see. I managed to get one of Dad's staff to look up and copy Hatch's record."

"No shit! What'd it say, man?"

"In October of 1950, Hatch, who was an eighteen-year-old paratrooper at the time, jumped into North Korea with the 187th Regimental Combat Team. He was captured near a village called Sunchon."

"Man, that is amazing!"

Van whispers. "Spud, Hatch was subjected to

barbarous interrogations, which he resisted beyond all
the creativeness of North Korean torture experts. That's
where many of his scars came from." Van stares out
the window grimly. "Worse, Hatch was tied down and
raped by a certain homosexual North Korean officer."

"WHAT!?"

"Ssssh!"

"What? Raped! The Hatchet Man? Get serious!"

"I am serious, Spud. It's in the record. He was young
and, probably because of his tremendous size, he was a
target for the sadists among the Koreans."

"A gook fag stuck it to—? Man, I don't believe it!"

"Homosexuals, like all other kinds of human beings,
Spud, come in all minds and moods. Some of them—
not many, but a few—are dangerous people. Such
things happen. It's sad, but it's a fact."

"Holy shit, man," Spud whispers, stunned.

"Ever wonder why he's so vocal about homosexuals?
Why he's so obsessed with killing orientals?"

"Jeeeesus Harley—, I didn't know!"

"We never know, Spud. That's my point. We should
be a little slower to condemn, a little quicker to try to
understand. We never really know about anybody."

Spud stares at Van. "You're right, Van. You're
dead right, man. Thanks for the lesson, I'll try hard to
remember it."

"I'm sorry, Spud. I didn't mean to preach."

"No man! I mean it! You know, you're alright, Van.
If everybody was as big-hearted and decent as you, we
wouldn't be havin' no wars!"

Van smiles nervously. "Thank you, Spud, but you
flatter me."

"Aw, Van, you're just—"

Van holds up a hand and cocks his head to hear.
"Here comes Hatch now. I trust you know he'll
pound us both to oatmeal if he finds out we know his
background."

"Fuckin'- A! I ain't sayin' nothin' to nobody. Depend
on it. Hatch'd pull my goddamn head off."

271

Heavy footsteps pound the boardwalk. A deep voice rumbles, "Fuckin', chicken-shit gooks!"

"So much for decent guys," Spud says, wryly, returning to his own bunk.

Hatchette enters and tosses his gear on his bunk. "Shit!"

"Hi Hatch," Van says, "what's wrong?"

"Hell, nothin' you'd understand, flower baby!" Hatchette turns in tight circles, his massive hands on his hips. "We scrambled six times tonight, man! Six times! And not one time did we get a target. Those goddamn gook cock suckers are too chicken-shit to shoot at us!" Hatchette whips his fatigue shirt from his bulky shoulders. As he does, his orange rubber dog toy slips from a pocket and hits the floor.

EEH-EEE!

"Hey!" Spud says, excited. He sprints to the fallen dog toy and picks it up with a grin on his face.

EEE-EEH!

"Hey Hatchette! I thought this was just for 'morons'! How long you been carryin' this 'stupid toy' into battle with you?" Spud turns to Van and laughs. He doesn't laugh long.

A bear paw seizes a clutch of Spud's shirt, and another snatches away the rubber dog toy, which squeaks in protest.

EEE-EEH!

The Hatchet Man glares down at Spud who is now reconsidering the cleverness of his wit.

"By God, if I like my little rubber dog, what the fuck's it to you, you fat hippie fart?"

Spud imagines he smells the breath of Death.

"Nothin', Hatch! Jeez man, I like my critter, too!"

To Spud's enormous relief, Hatchette releases him and returns to his bunk where he places his critter on the floor under his bunk by his other most valuable possession, his .44 magnum revolver.

Unseen by Hatchette or Spud, Van smiles once more.

"What's going on?" Pothead Willows asks, propping

on one elbow, cradling an empty Jack bottle in the other arm. He rubs his bleary, bloodshot eyes.

"Hey, goddamn it!" Hale says, squinting in irritation. "If you guys can just be a little louder you can wake up the whole damn camp!"

Charlie Dermott looks up. In the dim light, only you can see Charlie's expression. It is the not-present look of a man whose pain threshold has collapsed, who no longer cares about anything. Charlie has The No-care Stare.

"Fuck off, flower babies." Hatchette growls.

No rats have been seen since the visit from the chemical corps, but Hatchette checks his bunk very carefully anyway. In his green, boxer underwear, he slides into bed.

"Good night, Hatch," Spud says sweetly, getting into his own bunk. "Me and Petunia and Begonia and Tulip and Rosy, we love you too, sweetums!"

"Kiss my ass."

"Hey! Now there's a lovely thought to keep one snug in tranquil slumber. Night, Van, thanks again."

"Good night, Spud. See you in the morning."

The Room is soon only crickets, the rising and fading rotor beat of the circling flare-patrol ship, and the snores of exhausted men.

Van addresses an envelope, rereads his letter to Ramsey and seals it in the envelope. He stands, works the combination on his locker, and swings open the door. He lifts a card, hinged at the top with tape, on which are pictures of Susan and beneath which are pictures of Ramsey. Van swings the door back farther to let the desk-lamp light play on the photos. The pictures portray a bright-eyed, handsome young man in a swim suit, standing by a surf-board impaled in the sand, the blue Pacific in the background. They show a distinguished young musician, regal in his long-tailed tuxedo, cradling a violin, sitting erect upon a chair in the string section of the National Symphony Orchestra. One photo displays the warmly-dressed young man glowing with happiness, clutching upright skis in one hand and, with the other, holding the hand of an equally content and smiling Van Savatch. Love shows in their faces.

Van lightly touches one of the pictures. "Ramsey," he whispers. "I love you. I miss your—"

He hears it, and he freezes, tense, knowing that if this rocket is the one, it is already too late to seek cover from it. There is a brilliant white flash from a short distance away, followed immediately by a slamming blast and the clatter of falling objects. Shortly, there is the thunderous cascade of falling dirt upon the metal roof. The desk lamp goes out, and the siren wail fills the air. It is a solid tone.

"Incoming!" Hale shouts, kicking his way out of his bed and jamming his feet into his boots. "We're gettin' hit!"

"Incoming!" Spud yells, clapping his grunt helmet over his head and seizing his rifle. "Rise and shine, guys, let's get to the bunker!" Spud races out.

In the pitch-dark confusion, only you see that The Hatchet Man has already donned his flak jacket and boots and has blown through the door on a dead run for the bunker, rifle in hand.

The siren howls high and steady. Another rocket detonates nearby.

Pot springs up, his scream muffled by a blanket over his head.

Charlie merely sits up in bed and stares at the wall from which you observe. He stares, the bags beneath his eyes rendering him ghostly in appearance, but he does not see you.

Van slams his locker door, inserts the padlock and spins its combination dial. He pulls on his gear, scrambles to an hysterical Pot, and yanks the blanket from his head. Hale grabs Pot on his way to the door, and drags him whimpering from The Room. "Let's go, Van!" Hale says urgently. "They're hitting close!"

Charlie stands calmly by his bed. A flare ignites near

the perimeter and illuminates his vacant, uncaring stare.

Van seizes the taller Charlie by his shoulders and shakes him hard. "Charlie! Charlie, listen to me! You've got to go, Charlie! Now! Run!"

Charlie looks Van in the face, blankly. He puts out a hand and pats Van twice on the shoulder. "Fuck it," says Charlie Dermott, son of the Reverend Doctor and Mrs. Jacob Lester Dermott of Macon, Georgia. He pats Van once more on his shoulder and walks, barefooted in his underwear, out into the deadly night.

A third round crashes in close. Through the window, Van can see in the flash that Charlie is standing still on the boardwalk outside, motionless, his face lifted toward the black sky despite the dirt that showers down upon him.

"Charlie!" Van shouts. "Run!" Van shrugs into his flak jacket and pauses briefly on his way out to check Hatchette's dark but unoccupied corner. He allows himself a brief smile, and then he rushes outside. "Run, Charlie, for God's sake run!" Van is heard to say, grunting with the strain of pushing Charlie along the boardwalk.

The siren wails its mournful sonnet. Rockets explode. The Room takes on a dim, flickering, orange glow from the towering flames of helicopters burning on the flight line. More rounds impact, nearer now.

Lone footsteps on the boardwalk hurry near. Panting, Van charges into the unlighted room in his green boxer shorts, flak jacket and boots, the long, untied bootlaces trailing. "Hatch!" Van cries in the darkness. "Hatch, where are you?" Van scurries to Hatchette's corner and upturns the bunk. In the dim light from the distant fires, Van can barely see that Hatchette's revolver lies upon the concrete, but his rubber critter is gone. "Hatch," Van whispers. "Where are you?" Another rocket crashes in, only yards away. Van runs to the door.

The moment his hand shoves back the screen there comes yet another blinding flash and jarring explosion, very close this time.

275

Too close.

Van is blown backward, his head snapping down upon his chest then pitching back as he flies. Ruptured sandbags spew dirt as they spin through the air. Van lands sliding upon his back, his skull bouncing on the old rug, his eyes open. Smoke rises in the pale flare light from sizzling black holes in Van's flak jacket; there is a bubbling hiss and a wisp of steam as blood oozes from the holes and trickles in shining black streams down the green nylon sides. Earth rains down on the roof of hooch-44.

The siren tolls.

Van pushes himself to a sitting position, his head back. Blood trickles from his ears and nose. More rockets split the night, now well beyond The Room. With great effort, Van rolls onto his hands and knees, his arms trembling. Now he rises, staggering backward, then forward, like a drunk. He stabilizes, his feet apart, hands out, head down, blood dripping from his nose, staining his teeth. He stumbles forward to the old ammo-crate desk where the sealed letters to Susan and Ramsey are littered with dirt and wood splinters. Van lifts the letters with one hand and, methodically if clumsily, he brushes the debris from them with the other.

The death siren dies in a slow, declining wail.

All is quiet.

"Got...got to mail..." Van mutters as he exhales deep breaths. "Got to...mail." He turns, grabbing the desk for support, then he walks slowly, erratically toward the door, his eyes half-closed. In the center of The Room, Van Savatch's legs buckle and he collapses to his knees upon the Montagnyard rug, still clutching the wrinkled envelopes tightly. "Ramsey," Van whispers. He topples forward, crying out on impact with the debris-littered floor.

The desk lamp suddenly comes on as power is restored to the billeting area. The slick, black blood now turns vividly red.

"Jeeesus Harley Davidson Christ!" Spud's voice says from the darkness outside. "Watch out for this hole, you guys! Man! This motherfucker hit close!"

"Damn," Hale's voice says, also from outside. "Looks like we have another mess to clean up before we can get any sleep."

Spud again: "Yeah, looks like we got another call to make to the post engineers, too. Man, that blastwall is fuuuuucked up."

"Where's Pot?"

"Fuck, I don't know. He was still blubberin' in the bunker when I left," Spud replies. "Charlie! Hey Charlie, watch that hole! Char-, Jeez, Hale, what the fuck is the matter with him? He's like a fucking zombie or somethin'!"

"I don't know, Spud," Hale answers, worried. "He's been real weird ever since the big fight."

Charlie enters The Room, still bearing a vacant stare. He flips on the ceiling light fixtures, only one of which now works. He squints at the florescent brightness. His eyes pass over Van who lies face down on the rug, two wrinkled letters in one hand. Charlie stares, uncomprehending at first. Then he yells. "Hale! Spud! Get in here, quick!"

Charlie rushes to Van and kneels. He reaches to Van then withdraws his hands, unsure what to do. "HAAALE!" Charlie screams.

"Here I am, Charlie. Man, look at this mess! What - holy shit. Van!" Hale hurries to Van, rolls him onto his back, and opens the bloody flak jacket.

"Jeeesus Harley—" Spud says, hurrying into The Room, distress reflected in his round face.

Unnoticed, Hatchette enters behind Spud, and stands near his bunk, peering with disdain at the scene on the floor of hooch-44. He hangs his flak jacket on a nail.

"Aw man, Van's hurt big-time," Hale says. "Spud! Get down to the enlisted guys' hooches and see if you can find one of the medics. Bring a stretcher! Charlie, haul your ass up to the flight surgeons' compound

277

and get one down here, quick. Move! Move! Move, goddamn it! He's hurt bad!"

"Okay, Hale!" Charlie says and he rushes from The Room.

"Hatchette!" Spud cries on his way to the door. "It's Van, man! He's hurt!"

"Go Spud! Hurry up!" Hale yells.

"Yeah man, I'm gone!" Spud's footsteps fade down the boardwalk.

"Van!" Hale says. "Aw come on, man!" Hale lays a green towel over Van's chest. Dark stains spread quickly on the fabric.

"Shit," Hatchette says, disconcerted, his eyes moving, looking everywhere, anywhere, except at Van bleeding in the floor. "Man, when the rockets come in, you...you cain't lay around on your pink ass...writing love letters. You got to...you got to haul balls to the bunkers." With a hint of pride, he continues, "Man! I was the first one outta here! I didimaued all the way to the Graverobber's bunker instead of ours." Hatchette seems to be talking too fast, as though distracted. "I got there before the third round hit. Savatch shoulda shagged it to the fuckin' bunker instead of—"

Hatchette cleaves his remark in mid-sentence as he sees Hale rise, looking at him with cold contempt.

"He was in the bunker."

"What?"

"Van was in the bunker, you heartless bastard. He couldn't find you! So he came back here in the middle of the attack! For you, you miserable son-of-a-bitch! He came back for you!"

Hatchette's suspicions are confirmed. His mouth opens and closes, opens and closes. "I—wha—"

"FUCK YOU, you bastard! He came back here for your sorry ass! Where the hell are those guys with some medical help? Goddamn it! I'm going down to the flight line and get a first aid kit from one of the aircraft. Help him, damn your soul! Do something for him!" Hale stumbles over the debris in the doorway and is gone.

Hatchette casually looks around to assure himself
that Hale is out of sight, then, as though stuck with a
cattle prod, he scrambles frantically to Van's side and
drops heavily to his knees.

"Savatch!" Hatchette whispers urgently. "Savatch!"
Hatchette lifts the bloody towel, unzips and opens
the penetrated flak-jacket and examines Van's chest
with the eyes of a veteran combat soldier who
knows wounds. His jaw muscles become taught as
he examines Van. "Aw...shit," he whispers through
clenched teeth.

"Hatch," Van whispers, straining.

"Savatch! Hey man, hang in there! We got people
comin'—"

"Hatch."

"Yeah man, I'm right here!"

"Hatch...you're okay."

"Yeah, I was the first one out, man! I went all the
way to the Graverobber bunker instead of ours. I didn't
think you'd—"

"Good...good, Hatch," Van says, as though very,
very tired. Van pushes Susan's and Ramsey's letters
clumsily at Hatchette, with the wobbly arm of an infant
handing its mother a rattle. "Mail my letters...Hatch.
Mail my letters...please."

Hatchette takes the crumpled letters. "Sure...uh...
Van. Sure, I'll mail 'em."

"Hatch." Van Savatch says. "Ramsey."

Van emits two slight choking sounds, then his head
rolls very slightly to one side. His eyes are still open,
but Hatchette has seen many dead eyes.

Hatchette's own black eyes are set deep in his heavy,
bald, scarred head, at either side of a broad, lumpy nose
broken many times. The eyes look down on the lifeless
gaze of Van Savatch. At first, there is but a barely
discernible gleam at the inner corners, then the hard
agate eyes fill and tears flow, running down the tanned,
pitted, stitched face of a Huron war chief.

"Aw, naw...aw, naw...aw, naw." The deep baritone

quavers.

Hatchette gently slips his thick arms beneath Van
and he lifts the limp corpse to his chest, cradling the
head with an arm.

Though he makes no sound, tears stream down the
warrior's face. His lips are tightly pursed.

Hatchette carries Van to the oft rebuilt corner of
The Room at the foot of his bunk. There he sits with
his back to the walls, holding the limp body of the boy,
the man, the soldier. He holds it to him, rocking side to
side.

The Hatchet Man weeps.

The surviving boys of The Room, together with
a flight surgeon and a chaplain, will spend nearly an
hour gently trying to talk Hatchette into ceasing his
now silent rocking, and giving over to them the tightly
clutched body of Van Savatch.

The major will arrive in a huff. Pushing others
aside, he will stalk to the catatonically rocking giant
in the corner and announce: "Mister, you will release
that body right now, do you read me loud and clear?"
Ignored and exasperated, the major will sigh, bend
and reach forth to pull at the one of Hatchette's arms
which cradles Van's head. The instant he makes
contact, Hatchette's right boot will impact the major
square over his flak-vest, eliciting a concussive grunt,
dislodging his helmet and propelling the major, reeling,
four steps backward to fall over Spud's bunk. When
Spud and Hale help the major to his feet, and he can
breathe again, he will declare that he has pressing duties
elsewhere and he will weave unsteadily out the door.

Hatchette, left alone in The Room, will go on
rocking until the gray, rainy dawn, when he will rise,
carry Van outside and silently hand him to the shocked,
soaked, drained compatriots of The Room.

Hatch, in his underwear, boots and flak-jacket, will
slog through the heavy rain to the Camp Enari post
office with two wrinkled, blood-spotted letters held
sheltered beneath the thick flak-jacket. He will carry an

odd, orange-rubber dog toy in his free hand. Every few steps he will squeeze the toy, and it will squeak. EEH-EEE! EEH-EEE! Other soldiers and officers, wearing ponchos against the downpour, will glance nervously at The Hatchette Man from the corners of their averted eyes as he passes.

Chapter Twenty-Three
The Room

...And in other news tonight, an item
is reported by the *Associated Press* which
illustrates that the sorrow of a loved one lost
to the seemingly endless Vietnam war extends
even to the highest ranks of the military. A
U.S. Army helicopter pilot stationed in the
Central Highlands area of II Corps was among
those killed yesterday in a rocket attack on the
Fourth Infantry Division base at Camp Enari,
near the city of Pleiku. He was Warrant Officer
Robert Savatch, Jr., son of Fourth Infantry
Division commanding officer, Major General
Robert Savatch, Sr.

Elsewhere in Vietnam, fighting claimed an
additional twelve American lives in scattered
firefights throughout the theater...

Miss Dawes Glade
88 Rue De Pauline
Paris, France

*...now Van is gone. It seemed so impossible
that Van, the strongest guy in The Room, could be
killed.*

*It's making us all crazy. Pot was already nuts;
he shorted out weeks ago. Now he just drinks and
sings to himself. Spud's omnipresent good humor
died with Van; he mopes around and lies on his*

*bunk staring at the roof. Charlie has lost his god,
and I suspect that for a guy like him that's as lost
as a man can get.*

*We were all dumbfounded at The Hatchet
Man's reaction. He sat in a corner in the dark
that night, clutching Van's body to himself like
a little girl with a rag doll. The docs and I tried
to talk to him, but it was like trying to converse
with Klatu the implacable space robot in The Day
The Earth Stood Still. At one point Major Fisher
reached out to pull Hatchette's arm away from
the body; Hatch suddenly snarled and kicked
the major flat on his ass, scaring the crap out of
everybody in The Room. Then he just went back
to rocking slowly to and fro, holding Van. We left
him alone with the body, and waited outside in the
rain. I've never been so depressed. Hatch finally
gave Van up at daybreak. Now he broods about
like Charlie and Spud.*

*I just know I hurt like hell. I didn't have any
god to lose but I'm really fucked up anyway. Or
maybe that's why I'm fucked up. I came here to
find for myself, in my own time, what Hemingway
wrote about. Now I know. I know for whom the
bell tolls.*

*I have to go. It's all too heavy for me right
now. I'll be okay. I'll write again when I feel
better.*

I love you, my beautiful

Dawes.

Hale

Miss Susan Echevera
P.O. Box 8771
University of California, School of Medicine
Los Angeles, California

Dear Susie,

I hope that you do not mind that I call you Susie because that is how I think of you and that is what Van always called you.

My name is Paul Bleaker but everybody calls me Spud. Van was my friend and I miss him like I know you do too. Me and him used to talk all the time, and I just wanted you to know how much we all thought of him.

I don't know what you been told, but Van was killed by a rocket that exploded on him while he was trying to rescue one of our guys. He died pretty quick and he didn't have no pain. I want you to know that so you won't fret.

I hope you don't mind that we kept his pictures of you for our wall because they kind of remind us of him sort of, since we don't got any pictures of him.

All the guys here wanted me to tell you Van was a good old boy, and I got to quit writing now on account of I am crying.

Yours truly,
Spud Bleaker

TO: Mr. Ramsey L. Willamere
3491 Santa Maria Circle, Apt. 203
Los Angeles, California

FROM: Lt. Colonel Purvis Matlock
Commanding Officer
4th AVIATION BN, 4th AVN BGD, 4th INF DIV,
US ARMY
Pleiku
Republic of South Vietnam

DATE: 20 Mar 69

SUBJ: As follows:

Dear Mr. Willamere,

It is with deep regret that I must inform you of the death of Warrant Officer Robert Savatch, Jr., from injuries received in combat on the night of Tuesday, 18 March, 1969.

It was Mr. Savatch's written request that you be notified in the event of his death.

Warrant Officer Savatch was a fine young officer whom I was proud to have in my command. At mortal risk to his life, Mr. Savatch braved intense enemy shelling to rescue a fallen fellow officer. His actions were in the highest tradition of the United States Army and reflect great credit upon himself and the service. For his actions above and beyond the call of duty, Warrant Officer Savatch will be posthumously awarded the Silver Star Medal.

In addition to Mr. Savatch's fellow officers, including myself, your grief is shared by Major General and Mrs. Robert Savatch, Sr.

Yours in sympathy,
Purvis Matlock, Lt. Col., USA

Ramsey, my dear love,

If Susie has given you this letter, you will already know that I am gone.

There are two themes I would ask you to keep closest to your heart when the grief of losing me has done as it will surely do in enough time, when it has taken its course and has faded to a place of history in your gentle heart.

The first is this: Force yourself to bear ever in mind, through your grief and beyond, that it is I who have died, Ramsey. You have not died, though doubtless it will feel that way for a time.

*You are still alive, my love, you still have a life
to lead, and life is much too precious to waste.
Hence you owe it to yourself, and if I ever meant
anything to you, you owe it to me, to live that life
in the fullest pursuit of happiness. I would not
have you make of yourself a monument unto me.
You serve neither of us so. Weep for me, Ramsey,
then dry your tears and go in earnest search of
a new love. Do not expect to find him soon, for
few are they like us and fewer still worthy of you,
but seek him no less. When you find him, rejoice.
Treasure the memory of me, please, but do not let
it hinder in any way the richness of the new life
you deserve.*

*And the second theme is this: When you draw
your resined bow over the strings and the note
is absolutely correct, it is I who will thrill to that
perfect tone. When the audience demands still
another encore, I will be there amidst the cheers
and applause. When you laugh, as in time you
should and shall, the echoes you hear will be my
laughter. And when you find him, the brilliant
color with which joy shall then paint your life will
in part be the hues of gladness I feel.*

*In the time I was blessed to share with you, my
Ramsey, you enriched my life beyond measure.
I will say of you only the very best that could be
said of anyone: that you know how to laugh, you
know how to live, and you know how to love.*

*Good bye, dear Ramsey. Heal, and live again
soon, please.*

My love always,
Van

Chapter Twenty-Four
The Room

A small, white refrigerator stands humming in the corner of The Room where Old Faithful once served so stoically.

Van's locker is empty. The door hangs open, pieces of tape stick where once hung pictures. Daylight gleams through a ragged bullet hole in the steel door.

All the bunks in The Room are neatly made except for Pot's, which typically looks as though it has hosted a cat fight, and the late Van Savatch's, on which the GI-issue, striped mattress is folded in half, exposing the springs. The wall over Charlie's bunk no longer displays the God-Is-My-Copilot crucifix. The wall over Pot's unkempt bed is only bare, fresh, raw wood and screen. The wall above Spud's bunk has a new, nude, foldout magazine centerfold, but his precious taco analogy is missing only by virtue of having been obliterated in one of the rocket attacks. Over The Hatchet Man's bunk in the corner hangs the macabre photo memento from his Special Forces buddies, its frame glass shattered. Missing is the Happiness Is A Dead Gook! gunship cartoon.

Slow, listless footsteps upon the boardwalk come closer. The screen door swings back and in walk Hale, Spud, Charlie and Hatchette, all in clean, pressed jungle fatigues and polished, if dusty, boots.

Hatchette shuffles to his bunk and sits. He props his elbows on his knees and wearily cradles his face in his huge hands.

Hale goes to the little refrigerator, yanks open the door, and retrieves several cold cans of beer. He tosses

one to Spud, who spears it and sucks hard on it, his
eyes squinted tightly. Hale raises a beer to Charlie, but
Charlie just shakes his head and waves it off. Hale is
about to offer Hatchette a beer, but he sees Hatchette,
face in hands, and decides better. Hale opens one for
himself and drinks.

Spud wipes his mouth and belches. When he speaks,
he is uncharacteristically bitter. "Shit. What a fucking
award ceremony! Did you ever hear such bullshit in all
your life?"

Hale sits on his bunk and stares at the floor. "Yeah. It
was disgusting, that's for sure."

"Right after Van's death last month," Spud continues
in exasperation, "Pothead Willows, stoned out of his
mind as usual, negligently overshoots on a gunship
attack dive, and he accidentally wipes out a gook
sniper who, unknown to him, had just taken a shot at
Colonel Matlock. So the Colonel puts Pot in for the
Distinguished Flying Cross! Un-fucking-believable!"

"Of course," Charlie mutters acidly, "Pot had to
put the Colonel in for the Air Medal to round out the
Colonel's ribbon portfolio, and naturally Pot was drunk
when he received his DFC at the ceremony, just now.
What a farce. What a pompous, meaningless farce.
Symbolic of this whole damn war."

"So, what else is new?" Hale asks. "Officers have
been putting each other in for medals to improve their
promotability for this whole war, maybe even in earlier
wars; I don't know. What really nauseated me was all
that preposterous exaggeration of Van's death, when
they posthumously awarded him the Silver Star."

"Oh yeah!" Spud says. He continues with an air
of mock pomp. "'Warrant Officer Robert Savatch, Jr.,
without regard for mortal risk to his life, did brave
intense enemy shelling to render aid and rescue to a
fallen fellow officer...'"

Hatchette looks up slightly, and stares at the floor
over his hands. He blinks several times before looking
at the corner at the end of his bunk.

Charlie leans on the window sill and stares out at the bleak, colorless, military landscape. "It's all true, even though the...'fallen officer'...wasn't fallen." Charlie glances coldly at Hatchette.

"God damn it, Charlie," Spud says. "I thought we agreed—"

"Charlie..." Hale says with a note of warning.

"Yeah...okay," Charlie says, his eyes watering as he gazes out through the new screen wire windows. "But it's all bullshit. What Van did last month was certainly brave, but it was much more than an act of battlefield heroism. It was a simple act of...love, a higher form of... achievement."

"You're right, Charlie," Hale says. "What Van did needed no glorification, let alone all that flowery, hokey rhetoric. What galled me was, the more they tried to fluff up how Van died, the more they cheapened it."

The Room contemplates this theme in silence for a moment before Spud makes an effort to change the morose subject matter.

"Hatch! The first-sergeant says you requested transfer back to the world. You're going home, man! You gonna retire?"

The Hatchet Man slides his hands from his face slowly, stares grimly at the floor, drops his hands and sighs. "Yeah."

"Hey," Charlie observes from his position at the window. "Here comes our hero, now. He's so plastered he can barely stay on the boardwalk. What a sick farce this...existence...is."

Pothead Willows weaves unsteadily through the door, a red-white-and-blue-ribboned medal pinned crookedly to his fatigue shirt pocket. "Hey, you motherfuckers," he slurs with a silly grin. "Guess what? The general's comin'."

"What?" Hale says, standing. "General Savatch is coming here?"

"What for?" Spud adds with alarm, looking out the window.

289

"Beatsa fuck outa me, man. All I know is his aide,
Captain whatsisname, told me to scare you guys up
and stand sharp 'cause the general's comin' by to say...
somethin'...to say to us. Or somethin' like that."

"Oh, marvy," Charlie says with disgust.

Spud glances out the window. "Jeeeesus Harley Dav-
, here they come! General Savatch and some captain!"

The men of The Room stand. Spud gulps down the
remainder of his beer and stashes the can under his
pillow. Hale sets his on the desk.

The screen door is snatched back by an
arrogant-looking young captain in gleaming boots
and immaculately starched jungle fatigues with a
camouflage-colored silk ascot at the neck. A tall, silver-
haired man with an aquiline face held high strides past
him into The Room. Two black stars are embroidered
upon his collar, and his fatigue blouse is sewn with a
Combat Infantryman's Badge and the wings of a Master
Parachutist. He wears a polished black leather gun belt
around his waist, held by an white porcelain buckle
bearing the green cloverleaf crest of the Fourth Infantry
Division. His flawless fatigues fit like a tailored suit,
his boots are like glass and he too wears a camouflage
silk ascot. Major General Robert Savatch, Sr., carries
himself like a man who commands a multi-million
dollar infantry division, who holds not only the power
of life and death over thousands of his men, but who
with a softly whispered phrase can order the utter
destruction of entire cities. He stands ramrod erect on
the faded old Montagnyard rug.

Hale jumps to. "At-tench-HUN!" he calls. The Room
snaps straight, except for Pot, who calmly announces,
"Heeeeeeeere's...the gen-rul!" As Spud rolls his eyes
with horrified astonishment, Pot mimics a Johnny
Carsonish golf swing and assumes a shaky position of
attention, evidently very pleased with his introduction.

The captain eyes Pot with suspicion as he swaggers
forward to join the general. "Gentlemen!" he says
pompously, "I'm...Captain Mellwick. I'm sure you

all know General Savatch." Captain Mellwick bows slightly at the general. "Sir?"

"As you were, gentlemen," General Savatch says cordially, yet with a bearing no soldier takes lightly. The Room assumes an uncomfortable stance of parade rest; feet spread, hands clasped behind the back. Pot remains at attention until elbowed by Spud. He then registers surprise and assumes parade rest with false nonchalance.

The general sounds as though he is addressing an assembled parade, with long pauses between slowly delivered sentences. "Gentlemen...I know you were all at the awards ceremony, but I did want to speak to you five officers in particular. Young Robert spoke very highly of all of you in the few occasions I had to converse with him while he was in my command. He was quite emphatic that you all comported yourselves proudly in repelling the recent cowardly sapper assault on this facility. I want to personally convey to you gentlemen that your patriotism, bravery and determination to defend freedom are in the highest traditions of The United States Army, and that, gentlemen, is the highest there is."

Hatchette stares straight ahead, his face rigid. Hale reflects ill-concealed disgust. Charlie stares sadly at the floor. Pot assumes a stance of exaggerated nobility. Spud glances nervously at Pot.

General Savatch continues. "As you know, there has been a lot of unfounded accusation from the press and the Congress lately that this man's army is not what it used to be. Well, gentlemen, I tell you that one has only to have the honor of decorating a such fine, brave young officer as Mr. Willows here, to see beyond a doubt how silly and uninformed these preposterous allegations are!"

At the mention of his name, Pot suddenly snaps to a shaky attention and salutes, poking himself painfully in the eye and flinching. Surprised, General Savatch uneasily returns Pot's salute, but Pot remains frozen until Spud can bear it no longer and he jams Pot's arm down forcibly. Pot resumes parade rest with a pout.

General Savatch eyes Pot curiously. "I...uh...I'm quite confident that you men share all America's united determination to rid the freedom-loving South Vietnamese people of the communist aggressor."

At this, Hale fires a heated glance at the general, and the beginnings of tears form in the corners of Charlie's sad eyes. Spud rolls his eyes, and Hatchette continues to stare grimly straight ahead.

"You men are splendid assets to the Fighting Fourth Infantry Division, and I am proud to have you in my command." General Savatch pauses briefly as he looks at the folded mattress on the bunk bearing the nameplate: WO Savatch, Robert, Jr. His composure seems to arrest, but only fleetingly. "I...am also very... very proud of young Robert. I am all the more gratified that he chose to give up a promising medical career to pursue the military service traditions of his family. And while certainly I deeply regret his untimely passing, it is nonetheless a great source of comfort to know...that young Robert...died a good soldier...in the service of his beloved country, and in the cause of defending freedom wherever—"

"BULL...SHIT!" Hatchette suddenly roars, startling the entire assemblage. He slams his green ballcap onto the floor, spreads his feet, and props his hands on his hips.

The Room gapes in horror. Captain Mellwick is clearly aghast.

"Uh ooooh," Pot says.

General Savatch turns to face The Hatchet Man. "I, uh...I beg your pardon?"

Hatchette is angry and loud. "I have sucked up all this cockamamie bullshit I can stand!"

"Easy, Hatch!" Hale hisses, alarmed.

Hatchette takes a stride closer to the General and stabs a finger at him. "You save that phoney hogwash for the widows, General!" Hatchette slashes his accusing arm to point at the pictures of Susie still tacked to the wall over Van's empty bunk. "Tell that shit to Susan, if you even know who she is, but don't tell it to me! I been there! I am a soldier, sir! Don't talk to me like I'm some pussy visiting congresswoman!"

Captain Mellwick steps aggressively before Hatchette and shakes a finger at him. "Now just one minute, Mister! You'd better remember who you're talking to!"

Still excited and angry, Hatchette ignores Mellwick and addresses the general with a flourish of his arm. "That boy was a good soldier, sir! Damn fine! But he didn't have no business over here! He only done it on account of you! He wadn't here for freedom or America! He only came here because he didn't wanta shame you!"

Captain Mellwick rapidly repositions himself in front of Hatchette. "At ease, Mister!" He commands, belligerently. "Right now!"

Hatchette places his scarred brow one inch above Captain Mellwick's upturned, indignant face. He snarls low, fast and intense: "Captain, if you expect to live long enough to see that oak leaf you're suckin' butt for, you better stand your pink ass outa my way!"

Mellwick is sycophantic, not suicidal. He wilts, swallows, and steps discretely aside.

Spud grabs Hatchette by the arm. "Back off, Hatch! You can retire in a year; don't blow it!" Hatchette shakes off Spud's grip.

"Come on, Hatch," Hale pleads. "You're asking for a court martial!"

"Let him speak," General Savatch commands, some of the ceremony missing from his tone. "You can speak plainly, Mr....Hatchette."

Hatchette is distraught. "Van didn't 'give up' his medical career, General, and you know it! He'd a made a fine doctor. He didn't want no part of this war. He came over here to keep from disappointin' and embarrassin' you, and now he's dead! And you talk about him like he was just a number on a casualty list. He was your son, General!" Hatchette pauses, his agony showing. He continues, somewhat subdued. "Or...or has that daily...parade of dead American soldiers got so long your own son goes by without notice? How many, General Savatch? Forty thousand? Hell, I killed some of them myself! Weapons and tactics have become so deadly and complex you don't know who you're killin' any more! Their grunts, our grunts, elephants, old men, women...and...ch...children." Hatchette shades his eyes with his hand, then recovers. More softly, he asks, "Is that it, General? So many dead guys...you can't find your own kid in the crowd?"

General Savatch holds Hatchette's hard gaze for several seconds. "I am...well aware my son is dead, Mr. Hatchette. However, it would hardly be fitting for me to commiserate his death to any greater extent...than I would the deaths of the other men in my command. And yes, there are many."

Hatchette turns away, still highly agitated.

The general's superior manner returns. "I think you need a rest, Mr. Hatchette. No one ever said war was going to be fun."

Hatchette whirls in anger, but before he can speak, Hale Preston springs before the general, incensed.

"Fun? You...arrogant martinet! Nobody was expecting any fun, and I can promise you there hasn't been any! But is it asking too much for a little purpose?" Hale throws up both arms and his voice rises. "What's this crazy ring-around-the-real-estate game all about, sir? After six years, forty thousand dead Americans, and untold billions of dollars, we are right where the French were in 1954! I ask you, General Savatch, aren't we entitled to a sense of accomplishment? What are we achieving besides death and destruction?" Hale's expression is now pained, pleading. "Can you tell me that, General? I want to know." Hale is now almost whispering. "I really want to know."

"Mr. Preston, we are soldiers," the general
replies, tersely. "We do not concern ourselves with
philosophical or diplomatic matters. We follow our
orders."

Hatchette growls, "Well. Jawohl, mein fuhrer!"

Pot interprets all this as another reason to snap to
and salute. The highly strung Spud slaps his arm down,
and Pot resumes a vacant, Stan Laurel look.

"That's not good enough any more, General
Savatch," Hale says, shaking his head, his voice
cracking. "We came here following orders. We hung
our asses out following orders. Some of us got killed
following orders! We have earned the right to know...
what the fuck it is we are supposed to be fighting for!"

The general's voice rises, taking on a threatening
timbre. "I've had just about enough of this!" He says,
glaring at The Room. "Are you people quite finished,
now?"

"No, sir," The Hatchet Man says, and he steps before
the general. "Not yet. There's one more thing that has
to be said here, General." Hatchette withdraws from his
fatigue shirt pocket an orange rubber dog toy. He places
it before the face of Major General Robert Savatch, Sr.,
and squeezes it briskly.

EEH-EEE! EEH-EEE! EEH-EEE! EEH-EEE!

Nothing in thirty years in the United States Army,
including West Point and three wars, has prepared the
general for this. He draws a breath and his mouth opens
to reply, but it just hangs that way. For the life of him,
he can't think of anything quite...adequate...in the way
of rebuttal.

"You think about that, General," Hatchette says
softly, then he salutes crisply, turns about-face and
walks out of The Room. The battered screen door
swings slowly to, it's rusty spring twanging.

Without hesitation, Hale produces his rubber critter
and solemnly squeaks it at the general, looking him
squarely in the eyes. Then he too salutes, spins on
his heel and marches out. Charlie now stares down at

295

General Savatch. He raises his own critter before the commanding officer and gives it three sharp squeaks before himself saluting and leaving a frozen Spud and a blissfully unconcerned Pot to their own devices.

General Savatch looks with complete bewilderment at Captain Mellwick. Mellwick is glassy-eyed, utterly without a clue. The general looks at Spud and Pot.

Spud thaws slightly. He gestures helplessly. "Aaaaaah, uh. Weh, I, uh..."

Pothead Willows, recent recipient of the Distinguished Flying Cross, is suddenly seized with a fervor, and he breaks loudly into a familiar theme song: "You're in the army nowwwww! You ain't behind the plowwwww! You'll never get rich, you son—"

Doubly horrified at a time he did not think anything could horrify him more, Spud glances panic-stricken at the astounded General Savatch and Captain Mellwick. Then he grabs Pot by the shoulders, spins him toward the door, and propels him out, Pot singing all the way. "—of a bitch, you're in the army nowwww!"

A long, long silence ensues in The Room. Captain Mellwick occasionally glances anxiously at the general, who is trying very hard to wake up from the nightmare of his dead son. General Savatch walks slowly to the grey metal office chair by the ammo-crate desk and he sinks into it wearily. He removes his green ballcap with its two black stars, closes his eyes, and runs his fingers over his graying, crew-cut hair. He draws a long, deep breath, lets it out gradually, and opens his eyes, staring at the blood-stained old Montagnyard rug.

In the long silence which follows, Captain Mellwick hears only the slow breathing of the general, who now gazes sadly at the stripped bunk of still another young, dead, soldier of heart and courage. Then Mellwick and the general raise their heads. Their glances turn.

You hear it too, way in the distance, rapid and high-pitched.

Eeh-eee! Eeh-eee! Eeh-eee...

Chapter Twenty-Five

Memorial Day, 1993

The Vietnam War Memorial

Washington DC

"...and as you can see, Barbara, the President is making his way back to the presidential limousine, having completed his remarks before this huge and diverse crowd at 'The Wall', The Vietnam Veteran's Memorial. Everywhere before and behind the imposing, somber, black-granite, sunken wall bearing the names of the fifty-eight-thousand-plus American veterans killed in Vietnam, there are thousands more Vietnam-era veterans, many wearing all or part of their old uniforms. Some, as you can see, are in blue-jeans and jungle-fatigue shirts with medals pinned to them and patches on the right shoulder signifying the combat military units in which they served while in Vietnam. Some are in the complete and correct dress uniform of senior officers and non-commissioned officers still on active duty. Some are in three-piece suits and dark glasses, difficult to distinguish from Secret Service agents. Many have what are obviously their families with them. Present also, Barbara, is an unknown but sizable number of friends, wives, sisters, mothers, fathers, brothers and children of veterans named in the shining black stone. But all of them, Barbara, all of them, are here to honor comrades and loved ones fallen in Vietnam."

"That's right, Roland. We are informed that President Clinton will not be staying to hear the remarks of the other speakers. Instead, he will proceed to Arlington Cemetery where he is scheduled to lay a wreath at The Tomb Of The Unknown Soldier. He will speak briefly there and we will carry live coverage of that speech as well in approximately one hour."

"Well, Barbara, I think the best that could be said in summary about President Clinton's appearance this cloudy Memorial Day at The Wall, before this mammoth crowd of veterans, is that his reception was one of mixed sentiment. The military bands and honor guards were present as usual for a Commander in Chief, but there was also a very large contingent of veterans who turned their backs on the President en masse, and who interrupted his speech with frequent boos and catcalls. In fact, we can see several of them now shouting past grim-faced Secret Service personnel at the President as he moves to the motorcade."

"Roland, if the heated feelings evident here today are a fair indication, and I would say they are, then it seems that many of the wounds inflicted upon America by the terrible Vietnam conflict are yet to heal even after more than twenty years. Many, indeed most, of the veterans here at The Wall, on this sacred day upon which the nation honors its war dead, are extremely bitter about the President's appearance. One veteran put it this way: 'I'd rather see Benedict Arnold show up to speak. At least he served in the American military.' Quite a few of the remarks shouted at the President don't bear repeating on national television, but even the more civil comments left little to doubt about how many Vietnam veterans feel about the President. Roland?"

"Yes, Barbara, clearly most veterans
here today deeply resent the appearance of
President Clinton whom they feel dishonors
the Americans who died in Vietnam by coming
here on Memorial Day, given his background
during the Vietnam era. The information
on President Clinton's actions during the
Vietnam War is conflicting, and evidence is
scarce, but what does not seem subject to
question is that Mr. Clinton avoided the draft
by fleeing to England during the war, where
he helped orchestrate, if indeed he did not
actively participate in, public demonstrations
against his country in a time of war. Perhaps
of even more concern, Mr. Clinton is alleged
to have traveled to Moscow at a time when
Soviet money, weaponry and advisors were
contributing to thousands of American deaths
on the Vietnam battlefield. Further, Mr. Clinton
has admitted to limited marijuana use during
the period, making the claim that haunted him
during his campaign, that he 'didn't inhale'.
The President's admitted use of marijuana
would seem to be the one thing he has in
common with some Vietnam veterans. In fact,
it's a safe guess that some marijuana, as well
as other illegal substances, are being used
within view of our cameras even as we speak.
Nonetheless, Mr. Clinton's inescapable image
as a draft dodger and anti-war demonstrator
has evoked charges among this crowd ranging
from treason to cowardice, and it does not
seem that forgiveness, or even tolerance, is
what many Vietnam veterans have in mind."

"Thank you, Roland. The Vietnam War;
still dividing Americans two decades after
its official conclusion. We return you now
to our anchor desk in New York; we're glad

you could be with us for our Memorial Day
1993 coverage at...The Wall. For Roland
Edmondson, this is Barbara Stafford, *News
Now*."

"Momma!" whines a girl of twelve. "Every year we
have to dress up and drive all the way here and stand
here while Daddy goes down to that old black wall and
just stands there looking at it! It's so boring!"

"I know you feel that way, Celia," the girl's mother
says patiently, watching her husband standing among
the crowd with his head bowed. He stands before the
tallest panels, those accounting for 1968 and 1969, the
panels with the most names engraved upon them. "But
we'll come again next year, and the year after that."

"Well, what for? Daddy always cries and it's so
bor—"

"It's not about your entertainment, squirt!" Snaps
a slightly older boy standing on the opposite side of
his mother. "Dad was in the war and one of his good
buddies was killed! You don't know what you're talking
about, so just shut up!"

"Paul!" The boy's mother scolds, "I will not have
you talking that way to your sister. And Celia, you
will stop thinking about yourself. This is an important
place and an important time for these people. They,
or someone they loved, followed the call of duty in a
terrible and confusing time, and they fought in Vietnam.
Most of them endured a frightening, difficult experience
that will affect them for the rest of their lives; thousands
of them were killed."

"Well, it's still boring!"

"Hey, squirt! I told you—"

The boy cleaves his words instantly upon a look
from his mother he has not seen her make before. "Be
quiet, Paul," the woman says, kneeling. She takes her
daughter by her shoulders and looks hard into her eyes.
"You listen to me and you listen good, young lady," the

mother says. The girl listens, for she too has never seen this expression from her mother. "You love your father, don't you?"

"Sure, Momma," the girl says soberly. "Of course I love my daddy!"

"Well when you get so 'bored', I want you to think about this: If your daddy's name was on that wall, you or your brother wouldn't even exist. It's only by the blessing of the good Lord almighty that you aren't like so many of those young people down there by The Wall, wondering what their own daddy was like. Kids who grew up without a loving daddy to hold them, and take them to soccer, and fix their bikes, and walk them past the mean dogs to school. And if your daddy wants to bring us up here once a year so he can commemorate his friends and so we can appreciate how lucky we are, then you will come, Celia Bleaker, and you will stand tall, and you will thank God you have a daddy to bring you!"

"Yes ma'am, Momma," the wide-eyed child replies.

"And if I hear any more 'bored' complaints, I am going to drive you up here from Richmond on a Saturday and you will personally count every single name on that wall. They were all people, Celia, people with lives! Many of them had children just like Dad."

"I'm sorry, Momma," the girl whispers.

The mother stares at her child briefly, then she smiles, kisses the child on the forehead and stands. "It's alright baby. You aren't the only one who forgets." Her husband has returned, wiping his pudgy cheek on his sportcoat sleeve.

"Need a tissue, Spud?" The woman asks.

"No, thanks hon, I guess I'm done."

"Are we going to Arlington Cemetery this year too, Dad?" The boy asks.

Spud Bleaker puts his arm on his son's shoulder. "Yeah, son, but we'll go tomorrow when there won't be such a crowd. Just once a year I want you kids to see all these names on The Wall, and all those acres and acres of gravestones in Arlington. I want you to understand, son, war is a terrible thing. It's not an adventure like in the movies; it's not exciting, it's not fun. War is horrible. Sometimes it seems we can't avoid war, but I want you to see why we should always try to, within the bounds of our honor and our national security."

Suddenly, Celia runs around her mother and clutches her dad, crying. "I love you, Daddy!" she weeps, "I love you, Daddy! I'm so glad you didn't die in the war!"

Spud holds his child tightly. "Here, here, Munchkin, now what's come over my baby?"

The wind blows. Costanza Bleaker reaches to smooth the hair that fluffs at the sides of her husband's otherwise bald head. "I think Celia has begun to take a more mature view of history, hon."

"Oh," Spud says, confused. "Okay. Well, everybody ready to —Hey!" Spud Bleaker exclaims.

"What is it, Dad?" Paul Jr. says as he scans in the direction his father seems to be looking with such excitement.

"Over there! Talking to that news guy! I know that guy!"

"You know the news guy, Daddy?" Celia asks.

"No! That tall guy he's talking to! I know him! That's Hale Preston! Man, I haven't seen him since we left The Nam. Come on!"

Hale Preston swears he hears someone call his name. He waves to the departing newsman and cranes his head to hear. Now he's sure.

"Hale! Hale!"

"Spud? Spud!"

The two men hit together like long-lost brothers to the astonished amusement of those looking on. They clap each other on the back and shake hands, Spud effusive in his joy, Hale more reserved but no less pleased.

"Jeee-sus Harley Dav—"

"Spud!"

302

"Yes, honey. Hon, this is—"

Costanza waves her husband off and steps forward to hug Hale. "My silly husband thinks that after sixteen years of listening to him tell me about hooch-44, that I wouldn't know who you are! Hello Hale. Costanza Bleaker. It's lovely to meet you."

"Damn!" Spud cries, still excited. "Soon as this is over, Hale, we're takin' you to dinner. We got a lot to talk about, man! How about *Hogates* for lobster, you know, down by the river?"

Hale is struck by how the impact of passing time is illustrated by the bald, vastly overweight personage of his former comrade in arms. He realizes that time has not ignored him either. Though he is trim, his own hairline has moved back and become silvered at the edges. "I'd like nothing better, Spud. *Hogates* it is; I know it well. I have a concert to attend tonight, but afterward, I'll join you there. But tell me, what are you doing now?"

"Shi—"

"Spud!"

"Yes, honey. Shoot, I'm a medevac pilot for the big hospital group in Richmond, man, I got over ten-thousand hours now! Man! I can't believe this! I've read about you in the papers over the years, Hale! I've read your books! You married?"

"I married the girl I used to talk about in—"

"That gorgeous fox with the funny name! Dawes!"

"Yes. We—"

"Where is she, man?" Spuds looks around.

"Spud..." Costanza says with a tone of warning.

"Divorced," Hale says with a sad smile.

"Spud, you big-mouthed—"

"Oh, uh..."

"Actually it's not as dismal as it sounds," Hale continues pleasantly. "We got married too young. She was temperamental and...Vietnam had...sort of spun my head, and I...Anyway, I went my way and Dawes taught French at Harvard. I never remarried; she did but it only

303

lasted two years. Then, at our class reunion last year,
we ran into each other again. The truth is, I think we
both went in hope of doing so. We're seeing each other
again. We're different people now. Who knows what'll
happen?"

"Awwww," Costanza coos.

"Hale!" Spud suddenly says. "Do you know what
happened to Charlie Dermott? I know about Pot, but—"

"Charlie's dead, Spud."

"Oh. Damn, I'm oh for two on cheery subjects ain't
I?"

"Maybe Charlie got hurt worse than any of us, Spud.
He went to the Israeli embassy after he got out of the
army, and volunteered as an instructor pilot. He wrote
me a letter when they shipped him over. Said maybe he
could find in the holy land what he lost in the unholy
land. What he found was a Syrian rocket. I'm pretty
sure he was doing a lot more for the Israeli Air Force
than instructing. I'd like to think he found his god
afterward, if not before."

"How'd you find out?"

"I have...some contacts. Spud, you mentioned Pot."

"Ah...he's a zombie in a hospital now, Hale. Won't
talk to nobody. Pot and me went to work for PHI, the
offshore helicopter operator in the Gulf of Mexico, in
'70 when we got rifted from the army. But they fired
Pot inside of a year for drinking on the job. He grew a
beard and long hair. He picked vegetables in Louisiana
for a while, but the bottle ate out what was left of him.
A lotta guys were driven to alcohol or other drugs over
there, and wasted themselves over here. But you'll not
see their names up on The Wall, I reckon. Anyway,
he's wrote me a lot of letters over the years. I always
write him back 'cause I feel I ought to, but I ain't sure
it's good for him. All of his letters are full of questions
about the war and my life before and after. Always
asking for copies of letters I wrote back then, and all.
I called him once but the hospital people say he won't
talk on the phone either. Drove up to see him a few

years ago, but he wouldn't say a word. Just sat there and stared like I wadn't even in The Room."

"What hospital?"

"That big VA place up in Martinsburg, West Virginia. But ain't no use in going to see him. He won't talk to you. He's a coupla balls short of a full rack. Calls himself Edward Hannagh, now, for some reason."

Hale suddenly stares intently at Spud. "Well, I'll be damned!" he says.

"What?"

For years I've been getting letters from a guy named Ed Hannagh in the VA hospital in Martinsburg, West Virginia! And he also asks about The Room and my life before and after. He asked me for letters. He even asked me about...Pot...himself!"

"Damn. Ole Pot's crazier than I thought. You write him back?"

"Yes. I thought he was some lonely old World War II military buff who got off on war stories. It seemed to please him, and it was cathartic for me to talk about it to someone who seemed to understand, but was unconnected to me."

"Yeah. I guess, truth be known, that's why I write him. He's someone who understands what we went through, and it does me good to get it outa my system from time to time. Kinda like talking to a free shrink. Kinda...healing, you know? Guess I'll write him about today, too. It's...like he deserves to know."

"Amazing. Spud, he asks me about...himself...Pot... as though this Ed Hannagh is some entirely different person."

"He is, I guess. Poor Pot."

Spud Bleaker and Hale Preston stand silently watching the crowd milling slowly along the cobbled walk before The Wall.

"And Hatchette?" Hale asks.

"I don't know, Hale. After I got back to the world, I checked on him through the army, but all they knew was he retired. I ain't got no idea what happened to The

Hatchet Man. Hell. He must be sixty by now. If he's still alive."

To Spud's surprise, a young man in a suit appears at Hale's side and whispers in his ear. "Very well. I'm on the way," Hale replies. To Spud and Costanza he says, "If you and your beautiful family will excuse me, Spud, I've a duty to attend to. I look forward to dinner. Nine?"

"You bet! Damn, it's good to see you, buddy!"

"You too, Spud," Hale says, smiling and shaking hands. He turns and strides briskly for The Wall.

"And now, Ladies and Gentlemen," a heavily amplified voice carries over the crowd, "I have the distinct honor of introducing our next speaker. A distinguished expert in the field of military intelligence who holds a Ph.D in American History from Yale, our next speaker is also a combat veteran of the Vietnam war as well as Grenada, Panama, Desert Storm and I imagine a few more that he can't tell us about." A laughter-colored cheer rises from the crowd and fades. "He is also the author of the best-seller, *Myths Of The Vietnam War*, and six other works of military history. Ladies and gentlemen, veterans and loved ones, who better to help us all understand the Vietnam experience today, than...Brigadier General, retired...Dr. Hale Scott Preston!"

The applause is substantial and it lasts while the handsome man in the gray suit takes the podium before The Wall.

"My fellow veterans," Hale's voice is strong and clear, echoing over the crowd to the Reflecting Pool beyond. "Ladies and gentlemen, children. I have been asked to come before you today and attempt to explain what the Vietnam war was about, given a twenty-year retrospective. I suspect that, for a gracious many of us, that question has long been a haunting one."

A bird flying overhead peeps in passing. The bird alights in a tree near the podium. Otherwise there is but silence at The Wall.

"A difficult task, this," Hale continues, solemnly.

"Perhaps we should begin by clearing up what the Vietnam war was not.

"The so-called Vietnam conflict was not a 'conflict'. It was a war. Fifty-eight-thousand-one-hundred-eighty-three American military men, and eight American military women, died in the longest war in the history of America."

Hale pauses, then speaks slowly. "Five...eight... comma...one...nine...one."

The numbers echo back from distant buildings.

"And that figure does not begin to trace the deaths that were incurred subsequently, indeed are still occurring, as a result of the war. That the death figure was no higher was due only to the advent of the medevac helicopter and to extraordinary advances in military medicine. Even that long, terrible number does not convey the scope of the suffering. There remains no accurate way to determine how many American men and women drank, or drugged, or crashed, or shot, or simply worried themselves to death because of their exposure to the phenomenal...trauma...that was the Vietnam war. War. Let us always be suspicious of those who for reasons of political spin define any event in which our military men and women go in harm's way as a 'conflict', a 'police action', a 'containment operation', a 'peace-keeping mission' or any other pseudonym for war.

"The Vietnam war was not genocide against the African-American race. It has been popular, especially in black political and academic circles, to suggest that the Vietnam war was a plot to draft, and kill by assignment to the infantry, greater numbers of blacks than whites. In fact, blacks comprised thirteen percent of the deaths of American servicemen in Vietnam, exactly equivalent to the percentage of blacks in the military in that era. Fine soldiers of all races served in Vietnam. Death played no favorites.

"The Vietnam war was not a 'criminal' endeavor. It is absurd to refer to any war as 'illegal', since war is by

307

definition a breakdown of and a departure from law, the
ultimate manifestation of the failure of law to prevail.
The Vietnam war was as legal as any war can be. From
President Kennedy's original placement of 'advisors' in
the early sixties, right on through to the constitutionally
questionable enactment of the War Powers Act during
the Nixon administration, the Vietnam war was
conducted according to law, insofar as law can address
war. Throughout America's future, let us never send
our military men and women to fight unless our clearly
defined national interests are threatened in ways which
all peaceful means have not resolved. And if we must
do so, may we subscribe to only one law: Win.

"The Vietnam war was not, I say...not...significantly
more traumatic for those who endured it than were
the Korean or World Wars or indeed the Civil War, for
those veterans who endured them. To be sure, there are
those of us who are drastically and indelibly affected by
Vietnam. Still, the notion that we as Vietnam veterans
are any more entitled to sympathy or privilege than
veterans of previous or subsequent wars is a dangerous
one for us to entertain. Such a notion invites self-pity.
Self-pity corrodes one's sense of responsibility for
one's self, and therein is the ruin of recovery. Let us be
very careful how we blame agent orange, or delayed
stress syndrome, or flashbacks, or anything else for
what may simply be our own shortcomings. May be.
Let us always look first to ourselves for the cause of
our woes or failures. And only when it is clear that
we have exhausted that examination, let us explore
the possibility that 'our' war is at the root. Then let us
reach out to help the unduly affected veterans of all of
America's wars.

"The Vietnam war was not a reason for military
shame. I'm not referring here to the terrible and
unforgivable My Lai massacre or the few similar
such occurrences. They were atrocities which have no
excuse, though they occur on some scale on each side
in every war. I refer instead to the notion, promulgated

largely by the post-Vietnam American academic
community, perhaps to dilute its own sense of shame
in the affair, that the American military performed
shamefully and lost the Vietnam war. No assertion
could be more ridiculous. Despite the undeniable truth
that drug use was relatively widespread in the Vietnam-
era American military; despite the clear deterioration
of the officer corps, owing to generational changes
in education and in social values then occurring
throughout the nation; despite all this, the American
military never lost a single significant engagement
against the enemy in Vietnam in the entire ten-year
war. The American military did what it was sent by its
nation's leaders to do with unprecedented efficiency. It
killed the enemy in ratios over which historians dicker,
but which vary between ten-to-one and sixty-to-one.

"The American military did not lose the Vietnam
war. North Vietnam brilliantly exploited the American
public of the era through the most effective propaganda
endeavor in the history of warfare. Regrettably, North
Vietnam's most effective tool was America's own news
media whose gullibility and self-orientation defied
measure. Woefully underrated and misunderstood,
except perhaps by North Vietnamese strategists, was the
immense power of a modern American news industry
bent on feeding the public its private political or profit-
making agenda.

"Throughout the war, the American people were
never given the objective truths nor were they allowed
to decide for themselves what the war was about.
Instead, they were constantly fed a contrived selection
of film and reports, usually according to its ratings
potential but always followed with a media-spun
political interpretation of the depicted events. This
media-censored package was presented night-in and
night-out for years as the whole truth.

"Walter Cronkite, for but one example, could not
simply do his job and report the battles of the '68 Tet
offensive; he presumed instead to tell all America that

the war was lost, a personal opinion wholly inaccurate
at that time and one which he was neither qualified nor
mandated to deliver from that powerful forum.

"Only three of forty engagements of the '68
Tet offensive lasted longer than a few hours before
communist attackers were annihilated or driven off.
None lasted as long as three days and even they
were also put down soundly by American and South
Vietnamese forces. Further, the vaunted uprising of the
South Vietnamese people against their 'oppressors',
which the offensive was designed to ignite, never
materialized in any fashion.

"Even General Vo Nguyen Giap, the master North
Vietnamese commander, initially believed he would
be court-martialed for the dismal military failure of
Tet '68. Were it not for the propaganda coup delivered
by the American news media, he probably would have
been, if unfairly, for he too was a splendid soldier. But
the talking heads said the war was lost, and America
believed them. Subjected for years to similar defeatist
media propaganda, an unfortunately high percentage
of the American public folded, lost its resolve and
whined at leaders to quit and run. And then the
American government ordered home its military, which
to that point had taken and held all the land it was
instructed to, and had killed the enemy in chillingly
disproportionate ratios. The Vietnam war was not a
military defeat.

"So. I contend that this is what the Vietnam war was
not. What, then, was it?

"The Vietnam war was a noble endeavor gone awry.
Noble? Yes. In 1961, when the Kennedy administration
sent American advisors to South Vietnam, the goals
were laudable. We went because we felt it was our duty
to the ideal of human freedom to combat communist
aggression, which was rampant in Asia, not to mention
Europe, at the time. But somewhere between then
and the panic-driven evacuation from the roof of the
American Embassy in Saigon in 1975, a noble effort

went awry. Where? This is a question with as many answers as those asked, but here is my answer which you may take or leave. In a word, the American failure illustrated by the Vietnam defeat was...selfishness.

"At some hard-to-define point between World War II and perhaps 1963, we as Americans began to put our private interests ahead of the common good. We became, and we continue to be, not a nation but an auto-consuming pack of self-interest groups living on the same real estate. Somewhere, we stopped being Americans and became hyphenated Americans at best: African-Americans, Native-Americans, Hispanic-Americans, Italian-Americans, German-Americans, Asian-Americans, and so on, ad nauseam. At worst we became, and I fear we remain, a noisy cat box of squabbling special-interest groups. We are Republican or Democrat, male or female, gay or straight, bloods or crips, pro- or anti-abortion, union or non-union; we're any of a plethora of convenient religions; we're black or white or red or whatever the latest politically correct label we decide to call ourselves...in our obsession... with personal aggrandizement. We're anything, it seems, but we are no longer Americans. It began between 1945 and 1963, but it is with us still.

"We lost our national character—our own personal, special-interest group came to mean more to us than America—that is what went awry.

"Nowhere is there a more graphic manifestation of this loss of American character than in those who avoided the legally mandated military service of their country in its time of war. Many who chose to declare themselves above this law were among the loudest voices extolling the so-called illegality of the Vietnam war. How convenient, the ability to pick and choose the duly enacted laws one will elect to respect. How useful to contort the meanings of laws to serve a personal interest. How trivial the whole notion of the rule of law for a civilized society then becomes.

"Mr. Clinton was only one of the corroded strands

311

in the cable of our national resolve in those crucible years; there were so many. All of the responsibility-dodgers and pretenders of the Vietnam era have tried desperately, as I regret the President has done, to alibi their shameful behavior with all the most creative, faux-logic excuses, but in the end it all boils down to no better than that so succinctly defined by still another Vietnam war veteran, General William Westmoreland. I read now from the general's book, *A Soldier Reports*.

"Quote: 'As in all wars in all democracies, the Vietnam war produced deserters and others who fled the country to avoid service. I lament the fate of those young men, the disrupted lives, the separation from family, the loss of native land, and I lament the twisted emotion and logic that prompted them to leave. Yet how to condone or pardon their conscious flight from responsibility? When a man deserts, another man has to take his place; and there are legitimate ways in which a man who is a genuine conscientious objector can serve his country. Just because he might object to this or that war has no legitimacy, for if a man is allowed to pick and choose his war, the entire democratic system, whereby all men share in a nation's responsibilities as well as its benefits, breaks down.' End quote.

"My fellow Vietnam war veterans, go from this sacred place secure in the knowledge that you went in harm's way to do what your country asked of you through its duly elected government. Even you who were drafted elected to comply with your nation's constitutionally enacted law rather than shirk, or hide in a foreign country. The original goal of American involvement in Vietnam was a honorable one, and the fault for its corruption, as well as for the failure of national resolve, lies elsewhere than in this august group here today, which warmly embraces in its number the souls named on the black granite before you. Vietnam war veterans...regardless of your gender, race, creed or any other standard...think of yourselves first and always as undiluted, undivided, unhyphenated...

Americans...for you...more than most...have earned that right."

Brigadier General, retired, Hale Scott Preston looks out over the huge crowd for many seconds, then he steps back and bows his head.

They who sit, stand. The long, strong applause is more reverent than enthusiastic. More than merely for the man who has spoken, it is for the souls named in gold on The Wall.

When at last the applause fades, the bird takes flight from the tree by the podium.

Eeh-eeeee! Eeh-eeeee! it cries.

Chapter Twenty-Six

Memorial Day, 1993

The Vietnam War Memorial

Washington DC

The speakers have spoken, the bands have played, the honor guards have marched. Spud Bleaker, Hale Preston and their entourages have left, agreeing to meet for dinner at *Hogates* later in the evening. Hale has a concert to attend, and Spud's family must visit Costanza's mother in Alexandria. Programs, guides to Washington, paper food wrappers, and other trash items blow lazily on the trampled grass in the late afternoon breeze. Park Service personnel circulate with small trucks, collecting stacks of folding chairs. A widely spread few dozen people remain, moving about The Wall.

Behind the black granite edifice, on Constitution Avenue, a yellow cab draws to the curb. Out of it steps a man, expensively and meticulously attired in a business suit and Gucci shoes. He appears to be an educated, refined gentlemen of average height in his forties. He wears rimless glasses.

The man walks to the west end of the Vietnam Memorial grounds to one of several book stands which contain logs of the names upon The Wall. There he searches the pages, locates what he seeks, and he moves east down the cobbled walkway before The Wall, looking for a numbered panel.

The walkway descends, as it parallels The Wall, before rising again from the center, and near the center The Wall extends several feet higher than the man.

He stops, eyes the identifying number and letter in the corner of a panel, and he traces his finger down the marching tableau of engraved names on the panel until he finds the one he knows. He sighs deeply and bows his head.

After a time, he withdraws a sheet of paper from his coat pocket, unfolds it and places it against The Wall, over the name. He then draws a pencil back and forth over the page, causing the engraving to imprint clearly upon the paper. When he is done, he folds and puts away the page and his pencil, and then his shoulders shake as he begins to cry quietly.

The man has his view toward The Wall, and he notices reflected in the polished black granite that something now stands behind him. He turns away from the wall, jerks, and gasps. "Oh, my Lord!" He says, and involuntarily he steps back.

Barely three feet from him stands a huge, older man, way over six feet tall and pushing three hundred pounds. He wears worn but shined western boots, faded blue-jeans and a denim shirt with a tie beneath a brown leather sportcoat. He is massive, but nowhere fat. He has a bushy, gray mustache, his face is wrinkled, pitted and scarred, and his tanned, scarred scalp is completely bald.

"Relax, troop," the giant says with a deep voice and a warm smile of enormous white teeth, "I ain't killed nobody on this side of the ocean."

Recalling all too vividly Washington's reputation for violent crime, the shorter man glances nervously about for a policeman, but none is in sight. In his frantic scanning he notes only a few feet away another man, seated in a wheelchair. This man has a full, wiry beard and long, graying hair tied back in a bushy ponytail. He wears an old and ill-fitting suit and tie and he stares vacantly from the chair, his head tilted slightly to one side.

"I...ah..." the small man stammers, dabbing his eyes, "I beg your pardon?" His English is flawless.

"I said don't have yourself a heart attack, troop, I'm big and I'm ugly, but I ain't a cannibal. Roller-buddy there, he's with me. I just happened to see the name you were tracing. Did you know him? Savatch? Van Savatch?"

The smaller man adjusts his glasses and regains his grace. He studies the big man's face. "Why, yes. Yes I did. And you, sir, did you know him also?"

"Yes sir, I'm proud to say I did." The big man squints toward the setting sun, as though seeing something very far away. "Truth is, I hated him for what I thought he was...until he risked his life to save mine on several occasions. The night he died he was doing the same thing."

The man in the suit steps back and studies the big man.

"My God. You're...him," the small man in glasses whispers, his eyes narrowing. "Of course. You're... The Hatchet Man. Van called you Hatch in his letters. I still have them." He extends his hand, smiling. "Sir, I am Ramsey Willamere, and as I am a concert violinist performing solo at the Kennedy Center tonight, I would be very grateful if you would not crush my hand."

The Hatchet Man smiles more often these days. "I recognize your face now, sir. I have two of your CDs," he says, carefully shaking the hand offered him. "I'm pleased to know you. I'm Jerome Hatchette, and you're right, most folks just call me Hatch. I got me a big-game guide business up in north Idaho. Elk, mostly. Folks want to photograph more than they want to shoot these days, but that just as good. Ain't so many left to shoot, anyway. It keeps me sane. The local cops send me a problem kid once in a while. I stick 'em on a horse, work 'em to death, try to teach 'em a little respect for themselves and the rest of us. Works most of the time." Hatchette swivels his huge head and indicates the man in the wheelchair. "Him, he's—"

"Pot," Ramsey Willamere says, smiling. "He would be Pothead Willows."

316

Hatchette grins. "Damn. Ole Van must have gived us all up. You're right, only now he calls himself Ed Hannagh and he lives up in the—"

"The VA hospital in Martinsburg, West Virginia! He's the one!"

"Don't tell me he's been writing you too?'

"Yes! He's told me so much about Van and the terrible events you all endured!" Ramsey steps past Hatchette to Pot and extends his hand. "Mr. Hannagh, a pleasure to meet you at last, sir. I'm so grateful—"

Pot is oblivious.

"Pot, he don't talk much, Mr. Willamere. He—"

"Hatch," Ramsey says, smiling, "I've known you for twenty-four years. Please, call me Ramsey."

"You got it, sir. Pot here, he's a letter writing fool, Ramsey, but he don't say nothing to nobody. I flew down here to bring him to today's ceremonies, and even though him and me been writing me for years he ain't said one word out loud even to me."

Ramsey kneels before the wheelchair. "It's quite alright, sir," he says to Pot, patting a limp hand that rests on a knee. "You need say nothing. I know you well, and I am exceedingly grateful to you for the invaluable information you have given me over the years, for the priceless revelations about Van and yourself and the other men of The Room. I keep every letter you write me, just as I kept those of Van's that I sent you copies of. It's been my pleasure to correspond with you. It was so vital to me to be able to talk to someone who knew Van in that troubled time. You have helped me to adjust, sir, more than I can ever tell you."

Pot does not so much as blink.

Hatch speaks. "You'd think he was dumber than a fire plug, but up at the VA they say he has the best personal library in the institution. Some of the docs and the local teachers come to borrow his rare volumes. His room's covered in them and the orderly says he's got his own room full of shelves in the basement for all the books there ain't room for. More coming in the mail all the time. Every subject you can think of, they say. And...well, you know, he writes letters just fine. He just don't talk."

Ramsey stands and faces Hatchette. "Sir, it sounds to me like you can provide a great deal of information I should also like very much to learn. I wonder if I could persuade you to endure a fiddle concert and then be my guest for dinner? Front center tickets?"

"Sir, I saw you on public TV last year with the London Philharmonic. I would be honored to see you perform. 'Specially free. And if ole Pot could talk he'd say hell yes, but only if you let us buy you dinner. There's this great seafood place down by the waterfront, *Hogates*?"

"Wonderful, Mr....excuse me...Hatch! Just give your name at the Kennedy Center box office. They'll have your tickets!"

"Out-goddamn-standing. Pot's thrilled too; I can tell."

Ramsey Willamere is obviously delighted.

They turn again to The Wall and the name chiseled in gilded letters: Robert V. Savatch, Jr.

The evening wind blows peacefully.

Epilogue
My Room

Some say I'm crazy, but I'm not anymore. I used to be, though. Back when they regarded me as sane, I was as crazy as a March hare.

When I stopped talking, some called me a fool, but the truth is, the day I shut my mouth was the day I finally ceased to be a fool.

I'm a retired drunk, of course. Not many people can be a retired drunk but I did it. Wandered out in front of a cabbage truck in Louisiana so smashed I didn't even see the end of the row I was picking. Got smashed twice that day. Put me in this wheelchair, but it had the proverbial silver lining. Seems the head injury I got in the Battle of Hooch-44 was what they call the 'root cause', and the truck just aggravated it about forty feet, so I got VA disability. That's how I come by this elegant suite on the sixth floor of the Palace of War-wrecked Souls, but it's not how I afford my books. You got any idea how much a first-edition *Grapes* signed by Steinbeck himself costs? Damn sight more than you can hack on a crippled rotorjockey's pension, you can bet your ass. Even a contemporary edition of Homer's works bought used at a book fair on field trips is steep, I'm telling you.

No, I owe my books to the man I owe the rest of my life to: That lunatic mick, Sean Hannagh. Who'd a thought that big, dumb, brick-laying paddy would survive his wife, let alone retire from his own little foundry a comfortable man? Stranger still was that he'd die and will it all to a miserable, wretched, self-pitying, drunk punk in a wheelchair, who'd always thought he

319

was too good to use the old man's name. Me, the same guy who was too obsessed with his own squalor to even attend Sean's big Irish wake, in spite of free booze.

I hit bottom that year, the ninth following the year of The Room, and, I tell you true, it's a long way to the bottom and a long way back up. But here I am, and I know now that I'm never going back.

When that lawyer came down the hall at the VA that year, I was one sorry sight. I stank, I looked like Rumpelstiltskin would have if he'd joined the Hell's Angels in a wheelchair. Worse, much worse, I had cancer of the attitude. Malignant. If I'd had any pride I'd have done the world a courtesy and committed suicide.

I jabbered obscenities at the lawyer just like I did every day to the poor orderlies and my fellow Souls. Everybody hated me and they had good reason. I hated me.

So when the lawyer looked down his nose at me and tossed the papers in my lap before stalking away, I was unprepared for what the papers documented. I guess what it came down to was that if a simple, albeit successful, old Irish immigrant brick mason could be that kind to some other man's kid, a kid who ignored his adopted father while making a world-class asshole of himself, then I was flat out of excuses for being a world-class asshole.

It didn't happen overnight, but every time I'd whip up a good batch of self-pity to wallow in, there that face would be. Sean Hannagh's puffy, scarred lips would be smiling, yet his wrinkle-framed eyes would be sadly knowing what a weak, sorry man I'd come down to. I got to where I saw that man's face everywhere: In the mirror, in everybody who looked at me, and on the insides of my eyelids at night. Within a few weeks that old potato-head's guileless kindness just took all the fun out of being an asshole.

One night, while I was rolling my chair in the fifth floor hall, drunk as usual and trying hard to feel

sorry for myself, a harried orderly had neglected to
fasten the safety chain across the entrance to the steep
gurney ramp leading down to the fourth floor. I tell
you, my palms were smoking on the hand-rims and
that wheelchair was doing about mach 1.7 when it
hit the bottom of that ramp. I rocketed across the hall
and crashed into the Coke machine, exploding it into
a sparking shower of red and white plastic panels,
aluminum trim and fluorescent light tubing. On my
back in the floor beside the wrecked chair, I looked up
just in time to see the big drink machine, which had
rocked back against the wall on impact, now slowly
rock forward, topple over and smash my goofy ass right
into the floor tiles. Ahhh. The pause that refreshes.

Mbeep, mbeep!

When I woke up in the recovery room, there was that
face again, the face of an old man who'd given all he
had to a worthless adopted son who'd never provided
him a single reason to be glad or proud, just so he
could have a son to love and to carry forth his name.
The moment had finally arrived when I knew I had to
somehow make old Sean Hannagh's eyes smile along
with the rest of his face.

It isn't easy to reclaim a tenured asshole but, after
more weeks of searching for a way, I decided on a three
part plan: Shut my stupid mouth forever, learn a thing
or two, and try to do some kind of good for somebody I
could help.

Shutting up was easier than I thought it would
be. Most everybody was so relieved not to hear me
cackling whiny, profane drivel that nobody remarked
on it for a while. By the time they figured out I wasn't
talking to anybody about anything, ever, I had it down
pat. Besides, it was fun driving the shrinks nuts.

I couldn't go to school but I could, and I did, bring
school to me. At first the hospital royalty got righteous
about all the books piling up in my room, but the
headshrinkers figured out that I was actually reading
them and was thereby improving on the old me, which

everybody agreed was a good thing. I managed to make them understand that I'd share the books and eventually I sort of became the unofficial library patron for the institution. As VA facilities are classically short of money, this seemed like a good trade to the office geeks, being as they got a quiet, clean, industrious patient in the process. My statement agreeing not to sue them over the Coke machine crash didn't hurt any, either.

Then there was the do-good part. It was a frightening experience, thinking about somebody besides myself. Initially, I worried about who was going to think about me, but each time I got there I found old Sean, and his eyes weren't smiling yet. Then I reached a stage where I realized the whole goddamn world needs help, big-time, including those who think they don't, and that's even more frightening! I mean the scope of the problem is awesome, dude.

So I settled on two channels of do-gooder effort, one grand and one personal.

First, to paraphrase Groucho Marx, I wouldn't have any woman who'd settle for a jerk like me; and not even a Chinese baby dump would've released a kid for adoption to a man with my history; thus there was little chance of Sean Hannagh's name advancing as he'd have wished. So I put a huge piece of Sean's money into the founding of the Sean Hannagh Institute for Adoption, in L.A. We invested and established a foundation which hires what I hope are the best minds to address the adoption problem. The Sean Hannagh Institute seeks suitable parents for adoptions and we do so with an eye focused strictly on whether the prospective parent can and will support, lead and love the child. We try not to get too concerned with the prospect's race, gender, marital status or sexual preference beyond how it will relate to the child's healthy, happy upbringing. It's a struggle, but we're making progress. We can get plenty of kids, of course. There is no such thing as an illegitimate child, but there damn sure are plenty of illegitimate mothers and fathers.

You might think all this would be tough to do without talking, but then you'd be surprised at how much higher the level of forthrightness in business gets when everything is put into writing. Besides, my proxy at the board meetings is a grim-looking monster nicknamed The Hatchet Man. He gets more attention and less bullshit than The Godfather, believe me.

On the personal level, I tried to locate all the survivors from The Room. I wasn't sure what I could do for them but I was certain that, like me, they could all use some release from the horrors of Vietnam.

It wasn't hard to find Van Savatch, of course. He was interred in Arlington cemetery alongside the general. I tracked down and wrote that Susan whom Van was so fond of. After she came to trust me, she gave me copies of Van's letters and Ramsey Willamere's address. She became a doctor, of course; married one too. We still write.

Took me a while to get Ramsey to open up and start writing, but I guess he finally figured neither he nor Van's memory would suffer from the truth at that point. He became a famous fiddler. We became pen pals.

Charlie was harder to find than Van, but just as dead. I don't know if he found God before he found a smoking hole in the Golan Heights or not. I just wish I'd found Charlie first. I had a tough time with Charlie. I had to deal with the possibility that I might have been able to help him if I'd gotten my selfish act together sooner. Rest in peace, Charlie. You're remembered fondly, buddy.

It took a while, but I finally located Sung Tranh's sister in Paris, too. Even she seemed so in need of telling someone about how the war had affected her and her family. She still had all of Sung's letters to her. She still cries when she thinks about Sung's body heaped in some unmarked trench-grave with all the other sappers that night. So do I.

Spud, Hale and Hatch you know about.

By the year in which I turned over my new leaf, the name Pothead had sort of lost its charm, and besides, there was old Sean. So I had my name legally changed back to Edward Hannagh. At first I was surprised that guys from The Room didn't make the connection and they thought I was some unrelated old coot in a vet's home whom they'd never met. By the time I figured it out, though, I had also figured out that they'd open up to a perceived harmless old warrior a lot more usefully for us all than they ever would have to Pothead Willows, so I let the illusion stand. Hatchette figured it out first, because he's the most suspicious of the survivors of The Room. Now Hatch helps me with the Sean Hannagh Institute. Me and The Hatchet Man, a team; now who'd a thunk that?

Now you know the story of The Room. And here I am in my room at the Palace, pecking away on the old word processor, but weep not for Eddie Hannagh, for I am happy. I have my books, and I have my letters, and I have the view on warm spring days. And at last I have a little character—just a little—but Sean Hannagh's eyes are shining, and that feels so good.

I consider daytime TV shows, I think about what I see on the evening news when I watch it, and I remember some of the movies they show us in the cafeteria.

I think: Damn! And that world thinks *I'm* crazy?

William Slusher is the author of *Shepherd Of The Wolves*, and its sequel, *Butcher of the Noble*. He has also written *Talon Force - Meltdown*, as 'Cliff Garnett.' He is currently writing an irreverent and hilarious fictional send-up of both sides of the American political circus, to be entitled *Cascade Chaos, Or How Not To Put Your Grizzly In The Statehouse*, scheduled to be on bookshelves in late 2009.

A Vietnam veteran and retired police/medevac pilot, Mr. Slusher now enjoys 5 horses, 3 dogs and 2 cats with his beloved wife, Dr. Linda Shields, on a ranch along the Okanogan River in North Central Washington.

Mr. Slusher deeply appreciates the investment of your hard-earned money and priceless time in his novel. He hopes it earns both.

Don't Miss These Other Great Titles from...
CMP Publishing, LLC
(Available from your local bookseller.)

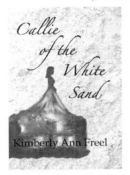

From her humble beginnings in rural Washington State, a young woman explores the pristine white sand beaches of Belize and the thriving culture of urban San Francisco, seeking courage, finding redemption...

ISBN: 978-0-9801554-2-6

Callie of the White Sand
By Kimberly Ann Freel

Set in breathtaking Angel Valley, Nevada, Calling Down the Wind offers the ultimate coming-of-age story with a heroine both as unpredictable as the zephyr she calls and as real as her extraordinarily gifts.

Calling Down the Wind
By Janine M. Donoho

ISBN: 978-0-9801554-1-9

Tensions flare as arson fires rage in Potshot, Nevada, a high desert community slated for a devastating hundred-year blaze. As both internal and external wildfires rip through the high desert, can anyone expect to remain unscathed?

ISBN: 978-0-9801554-0-2

Wildfire
By Jessie Jayne Smith

327

CPSIA information can be obtained at www.ICGtesting.com
Printed in the USA
BVOW031311051112

304702BV00001B/1/P

9 780980 155433